DUMPED

A NOVEL

JOHN W. REAVES

BROWN MULE

PUBLISHING

Brown Mule Publishing LLC
5541 Turkeyfoot Road
Zionsville, IN 46077

ISBN-10: 0-9841071-0-X
ISBN-13: 978-0-9841071-0-0
Library of Congress Control Number: 2010905807
Copyright information available upon request.
Cover Design: Cathi Stevenson
Interior Design: J. L. Saloff
Typography: Minion Pro, Bookman Oldstyle

v. 1.0
First Edition, 2010
Printed on acid-free paper.

This book is dedicated to my wife, Linda, and to my daughters, Melinda and Monica – all of whom convinced me to write it and continually encouraged me to complete it.

Acknowledgments

IT WOULD BE REMISS OF ME TO GO FORWARD WITHOUT acknowledging the team of folks who supported me throughout the creation of this novel. Thanks to Tom Bird for convincing me that I could actually write a book, and for encouraging me to get it published. Much appreciation goes to Jamie Saloff who created a great interior design while also giving me gentle and not so gentle nudges to make sure I was paying attention to detail. Many thanks also to Cathi Stevenson who, with her experienced eye, kept me on the straight and narrow and created a fantastic cover that goes far beyond my expectations.

To those who read the manuscript and provided valuable input, Carol Harrison, Monica Hecker, Linda Myers and Bob Ross, I'm forever indebted. M.Hill, thank you for sharing your knowledge on the publishing process to make my life easier. Finally, I want to thank my wife, Linda, for the many hours she put in editing, checking grammar and correcting my spelling. Without her loving touch, this book would never have come to life.

One

IN FEBRUARY, 1944, I WAS FOUR YEARS OLD. I CAN remember some things that happened before then, but they're fuzzy. They're like snapshots in time with no real connection to anything. But I clearly remember Crystal, and her telling me I was four when I asked her how old I was. Crystal was my grandmother's maid. She rode the trolley car out to Gulfport from St. Petersburg two days a week to do the laundry and the ironing and to take care of us kids when my grandmother had to go somewhere. She was tall, slender, blacker than midnight, and strikingly attractive – at least, I thought so. There were rumors that she had shot a man once for accusing her of cheating in a game of Smell the Cork.

Smell the Cork was played like five-card draw poker, but instead of playing with money, the players would chip in and buy a fifth of Wild Turkey whiskey. The one with the winning hand got to drink a shot out of the bottle; the losers got to smell the cork.

The story went that after Crystal won several hands in a row one evening, a man by the name of Lester began accusing her of cheating and pulled out a razor. He was going to carve up her face to teach her a lesson, he said. But before he even got the razor open, Crystal had reached into her purse, pulled out a pistol and shot him in the arm. I don't know if the story is true or not, but she did carry a small, silver .22 caliber pistol in her purse. I know, because she showed it to me once.

Crystal liked to smoke, and my grandmother hated that about her. She was always leaving her lit cigarette on the dresser in the bedroom where we kids slept, or on the bathroom sink. There were burn marks on the edges of the dresser in our bedroom that Crystal covered up with a scarf, hoping that my grandmother wouldn't see them. The sink in the bathroom had two brown stains on it where Crystal had left a cigarette burning at one time or another. I think my grandmother put up with Crystal's smoking because she was so good with us children. My cousin Tim and I were a few months apart in age, with me being the older. My brother Bobby James, who also lived with us, was eight years older than I and usually hung out with boys that were around his own age or older; so Crystal's attention was focused primarily on Tim and me. I think it is safe to say that she truly loved us. I know we loved her. She would play with us and take us for walks, mostly over to a restaurant on the Waterfront called the Porpoise Inn. Her boyfriend, R.C. Kitchen, worked there as a cook. It was great fun, because Crystal never checked on us very much while we were playing. She would say, "I hears ya. I don't needs to be lookin' at ya all da time."

Often times, she would let Tim and me take our fishing poles so we could fish off the pier while she visited with R.C. He was a tall, muscular man and as black as Crystal. He always wore khaki pants, a white T-shirt, a white apron and a tall white hat. Whatever fish we caught, R.C. would cook up for lunch, and all four of us would sit at a little table behind the restaurant and eat. One day Tim and I hooked a big blue crab and managed to pull it all the way up to the top of the pier without it dropping off our fishing line. We had also caught a dozen little fish called shiners.

They were tiny – about four inches long – and mostly bones, but they fought like barracudas when they were hooked. R.C. boiled the crab and fried up all the fish for us. Each of us got three shiners and part of the crab for lunch. R.C. always managed to throw in some French fries for us, too. Afterwards, with our lips smacking, we would walk with Crystal back home to my grandmother's house.

It seemed rather funny to me that Crystal called her boyfriend R.C., so one day I asked, "Why do you always call him R. C.? Doesn't he have a real name?"

"Das his real name," she said. "R.C. Kitchen, das his name."

"What does R.C. stand for?" I asked.

"Well, you know dem Royal Crown Cola drinks you and Tim likes to buy over at the Casino? Sometimes you just calls 'em R.C. Cola, right?"

"Yeah."

"Well, when R.C. was just a little baby boy, maybe a few days after he been born, someone left him all wrapped up in a blanket, inside an R.C. Cola crate on the steps of the kitchen behind the restaurant where my mama worked in colored town."

"Who left him there?" I asked.

"Don't nobody rightly knows," Crystal said. "A friend of my mama's done found him crying out dare in dat crate. She tried to find out who he belonged to, but nobody knowed. So she done raised him up like he's her own. Don't nobody knows his name, so she say she gonna call him R.C. Kitchen 'cause she done found him in dat R.C. Cola crate behind the kitchen of the restaurant where she worked. Das how he got his name."

Tim and I never seemed to get in trouble when we were with Crystal. She was like a mother to us.

"I love you, Crystal," I said throwing my arm around one of her legs and nearly tripping her.

"I loves you too, child. Now we better get on home before your grandma wonders what happened to us. I gots to be on dat 4:45 trolley before somebody lynches me."

"What does 'lynches' mean?"

"I'll tell you some other time, but now we needs to get on home to your grandma's house before she skins us all alive. She say she gots to go to da Gulfport City Council meetin' tonight and she wants you boys washed and in bed before she goes."

Two

IN THE 1940s, GULFPORT WAS A QUIET LITTLE TOWN on the southern tip of Pinellas County, just south of St. Petersburg, Florida. There was a large building on the beach called the Casino, where the trolley car from St. Petersburg used to stop and turn around for its trip back. There was only a single track between St. Pete and Gulfport. To turn the trolley car around, the conductor merely pulled the trolley pole down from the overhead wire, tied it to a cleat at that end of the trolley, walked to the other end of the car, untied the trolley pole from the cleat on that end, and then guided the pole onto the overhead wire. The trolley was then ready to head back to St. Pete.

To the right of the Casino was the swimming beach and to the left was a stretch of sidewalk known as the waterfront. It ran along the water's edge for about fifty yards between the Casino and the Gulfport pier. The waterfront had green benches where Gulfport's citizens could sit and gaze out over Tampa Bay. The walkway was covered with palm-thatched cabanas to keep the sun off the benches and the people sitting on them. Huge Australian pines, twenty to thirty feet high, lined the waterfront between the road and the cabanas. Walking there in your bare feet could be a painful ordeal if you stepped on the tiny pine cones that continually fell from the trees. They were each about the size of a small marble and covered with sharp spines. To the left of the waterfront was the Gulfport pier. It extended out into the bay about one hundred yards and had a wide area at the end with more green benches, so the old men fishing from the pier could sit while they talked and watched their lines. Sometimes dolphins came into the bay. A chorus of oohs and ahhs greeted them each time they broke the surface.

On the left side of the pier, Sonny's Bait House was about midway out. The fishermen bought their bait and also sold their catch there. Sometimes children would catch shiners and sell them to Sonny for a half-cent a piece. That's how we often earned the nine cents it cost to get into the movies in St. Pete. (There was no movie theater in Gulfport.) Sonny only bought live shiners. He would throw them in a big tank that floated in the water under the bait house.

Whenever one of the fishermen wanted to buy one or two for bait, Sonny would dip them out of the tank and sell them to the person for a penny.

At the time, the Casino was the center of entertainment in Gulfport. It sold hot dogs, hamburgers and soda pop to people on the beach, and had a large dance floor where young and old alike came to dance every Friday and Saturday night. The screened porch along the right side ran from front to back and had a plank floor made of two-by-sixes spaced about a quarter of an inch apart. The entire building was raised about three feet off the ground in case the beach ever flooded. We loved crawling under that porch to look for money that people had accidentally dropped through the spaces in the floor. Sometimes we would get really lucky and find a quarter, but mostly we found only nickels and pennies.

On the front of the Casino was the Honor Roll that listed all the young men who had been killed so far in WWII. It was surprisingly long. Though there were a number of young people living in Gulfport, it was not considered a young person's town. It was more of a place where people from "up north" came to retire. Those that didn't like St. Petersburg or couldn't afford to live in other parts of Florida like Miami came to Gulfport. It had a town council, a police force, and a city manager. Palm trees lined Beach

Boulevard, and the main streets were paved with cobblestones. All the side streets were either just sand or a mixture of sand and oyster shells, which was used to fill in the ruts.

My grandmother was very active in the town. She was a policewoman on the tiny Gulfport police force and was elected to the Town Council, and she was an active member of the Home Demonstration Club and the Garden and Bird Club. I never knew how she became a policewoman. I'm not even sure it was a paying job; perhaps she was a volunteer. Whatever it was, she took her job as a policewoman seriously and wore her badge with pride.

Gulfport had a curfew for the coloreds, who had to be out of town each day by five o'clock in the afternoon. Many of the people living there had colored maids, and there were several colored people who worked in the two restaurants on the waterfront, either as cooks or dishwashers – or both. Anyone who hired a colored had to provide them with car fare to ensure that they were out of town by curfew. The last trolley left Gulfport at four forty-five each afternoon, and the only people I ever saw on it were colored. That was the Gulfport where I spent the first twelve years of my life.

Three

MY GRANDPARENTS PICKED GULFPORT AS A PLACE to retire in 1938 because my grandmother's health was bad and she couldn't withstand another winter in Knoxville. They found a piece of property with a house on three acres, which they bought for back taxes. Although my grandfather could not afford to retire at the time, they decided to go ahead and buy it while they had the chance. My grandmother would go ahead and move down to Gulfport while my grandfather would continue to work at the coal company in Tennessee, where he was the head bookkeeper. He would then vacation in Florida until he retired.

The house sat amidst huge oak trees, orange trees, grapefruit trees, tangerine trees and guava trees. It even had a papaya tree, which was strictly off limits to us kids. My grandmother said that was her special tree. We could eat the fruit off any of the other trees that we wanted to, but if we got caught taking papayas, the punishment would be severe. There was plenty of other fruit to eat anyway, and we ate our fill.

With the exception of Tim, the only fruit we didn't eat much of were the guavas. Tim loved them. For the rest of us, guavas were best suited for throwing at each other. It was especially good if you could find one on the ground that was half rotten. Laying there in the grass, it would look like a whole guava, but when you picked it up you would find it was rotten on the side that had been lying on the ground, and usually covered with maggots, gnats, tumblebugs and worms. This was the best kind to hit someone with; because when it hit, it exploded, covering them in a stink of rotten fruit and bugs. Usually we threw them at Tim.

"Hey, Tim, you want a guava?"

"Yeah," he would say.

"Okay, here it comes."

Splat!

Since Tim was the youngest, he was not as quick as most of the kids in the neighborhood, and I think he got hit with more guavas than he ever ate. He would run in the house, covered in the rotten, stinking mess, and go crying to my grandmother to tattle on us.

"Billy, come in here," she would shout. "Did you hit Tim with a rotten guava?"

"No, ma'am," I would say.

"Well then, how did he get this mess all over him?"

"I don't know," I would reply as I stood there, shifting from one foot to the other.

"Get outside, both of you, and wait for me."

We would both run outside, and I would growl a quiet warning to Tim, swearing that next time he told on me I would hit him right in the face, so the worms would crawl up his nose.

Our grandmother would follow us outside and make us take our clothes off, and then she would turn the hose on both of us. She would aim the nozzle with pinpoint accuracy and use the stinging water to remove the rotten fruit and the rest of the dirt and grime we had collected on our bodies from playing outside. During the summer, this was our usual way of bathing. My grandmother always watered her plants just before going inside to make supper, and often the last thing she did before going in was turn the hose on Tim and me to clean us off. If we had gotten an early bath because of a guava throwing incident, then the hosing off was followed by some form of punishment.

"Now get back in the house, put some clean underwear on and get yourselves in bed."

Grandma had several forms of punishment. Sometimes we had to sit on a chair for some specific period of time, and each time we asked "Can I get up now," she would say no and extend the time. We were expected to sit there silently and think about why we were being punished until she told us to get up. Sometimes, after we had been sitting there a while, I couldn't even remember why I was being punished. I just wanted to get up and go back outside and play.

If she didn't think sitting on the chair was strong enough punishment, she would send us to bed and tell us to stay there until she told us we could get up. God help us if we got out of bed to ask her for her permission. That would guarantee us a beating with the stick that she kept on top of the icebox in the kitchen, as well as an extension of the time we had to remain in bed, usually for the rest of the day which meant we would go without any supper.

I'm convinced she *liked* sending us to bed without our supper. It had a two-fold advantage for her. First, it got us out of her hair; second, it meant she didn't have to feed us that night. With the exception of the fruit in our backyard and any homegrown items, food was scarce. World War II was still going on and nearly everything was rationed, so she skimped on our portions and we seldom had any meat. Her favorite meal was breakfast, and when she could she would serve bacon, eggs and toast with orange marmalade. It was a fairly cheap meal because she raised chickens and therefore we usually had enough eggs, and she made marmalade from the orange trees on the property. If one of the chickens died, we ate it regardless of what killed it. She also knew a man who raised hogs, and she could get bacon from him. For the most part, in the summer we had cereal for breakfast with powdered milk, and in the wintertime we had oatmeal, which looked and tasted like what I imagined wallpaper paste tasted like. I hated it.

About three times a week during the war years, we had pancakes for supper. They were the most filling and the cheapest to make. We never had syrup, and the pancakes were so dry I could barely get them down, but we had to eat them. Butter was rationed so we had something called Oleo Margarine, known as Oleo for short. I think it was pure lard.

My grandmother bought the Oleo in bricks from the store. It came with a little capsule of red dye. She would put the bricks of Oleo in a huge mixing bowl, drop in the red capsule of dye, and use a potato masher to crush the capsule and mix the dye through. She added salt to give it some flavor. The dye gave it a yellowish color and made it look like butter. I liked watching my grandmother mashing up the bricks of Oleo to make it look like butter. This was what my grandparents ate on their bread and pancakes. For us kids, we got a sprinkling of brown sugar. I never really knew where the Oleo came from, but I knew my grandmother used to save the fat from the bacon grease and put it in a tin can, and then at some point she would take it to the butcher shop and turn it in. I always thought she got the Oleo in return for her can of fat. The going joke at the butcher shop was, "Keep your fat cans off the counter, ladies."

My grandmother was a strict disciplinarian and meted out punishment for any infraction, no matter how minor. The stick she kept on top of the icebox was used liberally, but she had to be careful when our dog was in the house. Butchie would go right for her arms and throat if he saw her hit us. He was a huge black dog, part Great Dane and part Labrador retriever, who had just shown up at our house one day. My grandparents tried to run him off, but he wouldn't leave. He loved us kids, and if anyone tried to hurt us, he was on top of them before they knew what happened. It was strange how he knew when we were just playing. If Tim and I were wrestling around on the ground, Butchie would bark, jump all around us and try to lick our faces. But he never tried to bite either of us. It was sort of a happy bark, as if he was enjoying playing with us too. Sometimes we would grab him and wrestle him to the ground, and he would get all excited and lick our faces until we let him go.

For her own protection, my grandmother would put him outside before she used the stick on us. While we were getting a beating, he would bark and howl and tear at the screen door on the back of the house with his claws, trying to get in to help us. You could tell that he knew we were being hurt, and he was frustrated that he couldn't save us. I think it hurt him, too.

Butchie had a problem though, and one day it would also become a problem for my grandmother: he hated colored people. Whenever he saw a colored person, he would growl, bare his teeth and try to bite them. When Crystal came to the house, my grandmother locked Butchie in one end of the chicken coop so he couldn't attack her. But Crystal told me she wasn't worried about him. I always wondered if the reason she wasn't afraid of him was because of that gun she carried in her purse. I'm sure that she would've been happy to shoot him if need be.

Four

I'M NOT EXACTLY SURE WHEN I FIRST CAME TO LIVE with my grandmother, nor do I know how old she was. I only remember her as old. Her hair was grey, and she wore it short in tight little curls all over her head. Crystal used to give her a perm, and when she did the whole house smelled like ammonia. I never thought her hair looked very good afterwards, but she always seemed happy after Crystal had finished. She wore glasses with wire frames that seemed to bother her. She was always taking them off and rubbing the area where they sat on her nose. She was a heavy-set woman, and as a result she wore loose fitting dresses around the house. But when she went to a town council meeting or to one of the clubs she belonged to, she always put on a nice dress. She wore sturdy shoes with wide stacked heels. Lacing up her shoes seemed to be a chore for her. Her face always turned red, and you could hear her heavy breathing as she tied them.

My brother, Bobby James, also lived with us and told me once that I had been there ever since I was born. He said he thought Mom had left me just before Pearl Harbor was bombed by the Japanese. He remembered because my grandparents were listening to the news, leaning in close to the radio as if they would not have been able to hear it had they sat in their chairs normally. Bobby James said that after Pearl Harbor, they always got into some kind of an argument every time they listened to the news. My grandfather might say, "This means we're going to be at war with the Japs, now!" and then my grandmother would say something like

"I could have told you that before they bombed us. The President's pleas to that Jap Emperor were asinine. He's nothing but a figurehead and he has no influence. Tojo runs the damn country over there. Look at all that steel we've been selling 'em. Well, they'll be throwing that back at us in bombs and bullets, I can tell you."

Whenever Bobby James told me these stories, he would mimic my grandparents and he sounded just like them. He always made me laugh, and I would ask him to tell me the stories over and over.

One day he said, "It looks like the Russians are going to keep the Germans from reaching Moscow," in my grandfather's voice; and then he acted out my grandmother's reply: "It's about time. We've been shipping 'em all that equipment through the damned Lend Lease program. It's about time we got something to show for it besides Russian soldiers shining their boots with the butter we've been sending 'em."

I tried to picture someone called a Russian shining his boots with butter, which I imagined to be like Oleo since we didn't have any butter. "Why didn't we just keep the butter and send the Russians the Oleo?" I asked. "And why did the Russians shine their boots with butter?"

"Don't ask me," he said.

"How did Grandma know they did? Could she see them? How come I couldn't see them? What is a Russian anyway?"

"I don't know. Quit asking me all these questions. I'm just trying to tell you what it was like back during the war, when you arrived. Everyone was talking about us being in a world war."

I had no idea what a world war was, but I figured it must have been important. Bobby James told me that on one of the rare occasions when my grandfather visited from Knoxville, my grandmother told him she had volunteered to be a spotter for the Homeland Defense.

"Edward," Bobby James mimicked my grandmother's voice.

"I don't believe we should be in this war but, we're in it. And I'm going to be a spotter"

"Alright, Henrietta, if that's what you want to do."

According to Bobby James, my grandfather wasn't very impressed. He said my grandfather answered without looking at her and just busied himself folding his newspaper into a long column so he could read the editorial page. "And what will you be doing?"

"I'll be going over to the tower at the Florida Military Academy once a week. Now that we are at war, they're asking for volunteers to be on the lookout for enemy aircraft."

"I see. Well, I'm sure you will make a good spotter," he would say, continuing to read his paper.

According to Bobby James, my grandmother gave my grandfather a look of disgust that he did not see. I knew the look Bobby James was talking about.

"You sound about as interested as the dog would be if I told him," Bobby James would go on and on; and the more I laughed, the more stories he would act out. I'm sure he embellished them, but I didn't mind.

According to Bobby James, my grandfather half-heartedly insisted he was interested, and at that point my grandmother stomped out of the room to go look for her binoculars.

"Was Grandma mad at Grandpa?" I asked.

"Hell yes. She was always mad."

Bobby James was right. Grandma did always seem mad about something. I wasn't sure why, but I thought it had something to do with us kids. She never seemed to want us around. Every night after we finished helping dry the supper dishes, she made us go to bed. She said the evenings were for her and she didn't need us kids underfoot.

If truth be told, I think my grandmother hated all of us. Retirement was not turning out the way she had hoped. World War II turned their world, and everyone else's, upside down. She and my grandfather had bought the house in Gulfport because they hoped

to spend a quiet life together in their old age, perhaps with oc-
casional visits from their daughters and their families. Now there
was a war on, and their two daughters had dumped their kids on
them while they were out God-knows-where doing God-knows-
what.

Five

BY THE TIME I WAS FIVE, MY GRANDMOTHER HAD become a bitter woman who seemed to be mad at everyone about everything all the time. When she punished us, her methods were harsh. For example, if we accidentally stepped on the cat's tail or the dog's paw and made one of them yelp, she would make us stick out our foot while she ground the wide heel of her shoe into our instep until we cried out with pain. We all had scars on our insteps where the heel of her shoe had broken the skin and made us bleed. We would have to be careful taking our socks off to make sure we didn't tear the scab away and get the bleeding started again. "That's to teach you what it feels like," she would tell us. "Now watch where you step from now on."

If one of us bit or pinched the other, she would bite or pinch us a magnitude harder to teach us how it felt. Sometimes she would bite us on our upper arms so hard that it would break the skin and leave teeth marks. One time after I bit Tim on the arm he yelled so loudly that my grandmother came running.

"What's the matter?" she yelled.

"Billy bit me!" he cried.

"Where? Let me see it."

Tim showed her the mark on his wrist where I had bitten him.

"Why did you bite Tim like that?" she demanded.

"Because he bit me first," I said, in the whiney voice of a victimized person.

"Where did he bite you? Show me."

He really hadn't bitten me at all. He just pissed me off and I bit him to make him leave me alone.

"Where did he bite you?" she demanded again.

I had no mark to show her, so I bit myself on the upper arm, just below my left shoulder, right in front of her. "Right here," I said and showed her the bite marks I had just made.

"Get up," she shouted and jerked me out of the chair. "Tim didn't bite you. Why did you bite him?"

"I don't know," I said.

By now she had my arm in both of her hands and she bit me on my upper arm so hard that it bled.

"Now *stop* biting each other. Billy, you go sit on a chair in the kitchen until I say you can get up. And stop that crying, or I'll give you something to cry about."

Sometimes the punishment was far worse than the crime. One Sunday, when I was five years old, the weather outside was particularly awful. A steady rain had been falling all morning and the clouds hung so low and black that it was as dark as night. Occasionally a crack of thunder would send lightning streaks skidding across the sky, lighting up the outside just enough for us to see where lakes of water were forming in the yard. Crystal was ironing in the kitchen, and every now and then I heard a sizzle coming from the iron as she touched it with a wet finger to make sure it was hot enough. Butchie was asleep on the floor, and Tim was lying beside him examining his ears and paws. Every now and then Tim would say something to the dog, who would pound his tail on the floor without even opening his eyes.

"Grandma, can I go outside and play?" I knew the answer before I asked. She was sitting in her favorite chair working a crossword puzzle, and I only asked because I was bored and wanted to annoy her.

"Don't ask foolish questions," she said, erasing something on her crossword.

"I think I'll go in the kitchen and talk to Crystal," I said.

"No, you won't," she said. "You just stay right here where you belong and leave Crystal alone. She's got work to do."

"But Grandma, there's nothing to do," I whined.

Suddenly she slammed the crossword puzzle book down and hefted herself out of her chair. She was a heavy set woman, and it was an effort for her to get in and out of her chair. Her sudden decision to get up startled me, and I was sure she was headed for the icebox to get the stick to give me a beating. It startled Butchie too. He raised his head and was looking all around the room as if to say, "What's wrong? Why'd you wake me up?"

But instead of going to the kitchen, she walked over to the credenza at the end of the room where there was a stack of old newspapers. Taking a few from the stack, she opened them and began spreading them on the floor. One landed on Butchie's head, and Tim began laughing and stuck his head under the paper to look at Butchie. Then she opened one of the drawers in the credenza and took out two pairs of scissors, the kind used by kindergarteners.

"Why don't you boys cut pictures out of these newspapers and I'll show you how to paste them in a scrapbook," she said.

Since we both liked to use scissors, we thought this would be great fun.

"Oh boy, thanks Grandma," we both said as we flopped down on our stomachs and began cutting pictures out of the paper. We had been cutting for awhile when Tim decided to cut the same picture out of the paper that I had already begun cutting.

"Don't," I said. "That's the one I'm trying to cut out."

But he paid no attention and kept trying to cut it out at the same time as I was. To make him stop I decided to nick him a little bit with my scissors. It was just a quick nick. My scissors really couldn't do any harm. They had rounded tips and were completely dull. There was no blood. It didn't break the skin or even leave a mark. In fact, you could not tell where I had nicked him. But he let out a blood curdling scream that brought my grandmother out of her chair and Crystal running from the kitchen. Butchie jumped up and shook himself, looking dazed and wondering what the commotion was all about.

"What's the matter, now?" my grandmother shouted.

"He cut me with his scissors," Tim screamed.

"Where? Let me see," she demanded.

"Right here," he screamed, pointing to a place on one of his fingers.

"Where? I don't see anything," she said.

"Right here," he screamed again with huge tears rolling down his cheeks.

"Billy, did you cut Tim with the scissors?"

I could have lied and said no. There was no evidence, and she would have believed me. As it turned out, I should have lied.

"Yes," I said.

"Why would you do something like that?"

"I don't know."

She turned to a box she kept beside her chair. She kept many things in that box. I think it was an old candy box of some sort. There were pencils, rubber bands, paper clips and a very sharp pair of scissors that she kept for her own use in cutting articles out of the newspaper. She took the scissors out of the box.

"Crystal, put the dog outside," she ordered and then grabbed me by the arm. "Come with me."

She dragged me into the bathroom and turned the cold water on in the washbasin. "Give me your hand," she calmly told me.

I began to shake because I knew what was coming. She was going to cut my finger with the scissors she took out of the candy box.

"No," I screamed. "Please don't cut me, Grandma. I'm sorry. I didn't mean to do it. I promise I won't do it again. Please don't cut me. I promise I'll be good. Please don't cut me."

"I'm going to teach you a lesson. Give me your hand, damn

it!" she shouted loudly, and spittle flew out of her mouth. Her face had turned red.

"I'll teach you not to cut people with scissors," she screamed as she forced my hand down under the running water. Her grip was so tight that I couldn't get it free. She managed to extend my index finger on my left hand and got the scissors around my finger. She began to cut and slice.

"Please grandma, please," I screamed.

"Shut up!" she screamed back.

Blood was everywhere, in the basin, on the wall, on the floor and all over the both of us. I kept screaming as loudly as I could while I squirmed, struggling to get away. Suddenly Crystal appeared and tried to get the scissors away from her.

"Stop it, Miss Christian. What's da matter with you? What are you trying to do, cut da boy's finger clean off? Stop it! Give me dem scissors, now, before you ruin dis boy."

As quickly as it had begun, it was over. My grandmother let go of me along with the scissors and stomped out of the bathroom.

Crystal put a towel around my finger and applied pressure to stop the bleeding. My grandparents used iodine for everything, so she covered it with iodine and wrapped the towel around it again.

"Did she cut my finger off?" I asked her.

"No, child, you just got a real bad cut. I'm gonna put a bandage on it for you."

Crystal's hands were shaking and tears were streaming down her face. She tore a strip of material from the bottom of her dress to use as a bandage. She wrapped it around my finger and then she picked up the scissors my grandmother had dropped and trimmed it back a little bit so she could tie it.

"There now, I think you gonna be okay. Go on and lie down on your bed, and I'll come check on you in a few minutes."

When I came out of the bathroom with Crystal, my grandmother glared at me and I began to shake.

"Go get yourself in bed and don't come out until I tell you," Crystal said.

As I turned to go to my bedroom, I heard her ask my grandmother, "Miss Christian, what was you thinkin' 'bout? You could have injured dat child for life. What if you had done cut his finger clean off? I know dat things are bad, Miss Christian, but you can't take it out on dem boys. They is young. They don't know no better."

The weather was so bad that day that Crystal did not go back to St. Petersburg on the 4:45 trolley. Instead she spent the night at our house and slept in Bobby James' bed with me. When Bobby James came home later that night, Crystal told him to sleep in the upper bunk where I usually slept, above Tim. Several times during the night, she checked my finger to make sure it hadn't started bleeding again. Each time she re-painted it with iodine and changed the bandage. My grandmother had given her some clean pieces of cloth to use as bandages so she wouldn't have to tear anymore material off her dress. It was not often that Crystal stayed overnight with us, but every now and then – usually if the weather was bad – she would stay the night. My grandmother didn't like to make Crystal walk to the trolley stop in the rain, and she didn't like to drive if the weather was particularly bad. I was always happy whenever Crystal did stay, and on this particular night I was especially happy. I usually talked with her in the dark until I fell asleep, but on this night Crystal didn't feel like talking and told me to try to sleep so my finger would feel better in the morning.

The next morning Bobby James had a million questions about my finger. When I told him what happened, he said "If it were me, I'd have cut it off."

"Hush, boy," Crystal snapped at him. "You wouldn't do no such thing. Now you just go on 'bout your business."

Six

I'M NOT SURE HOW OLD BOBBY JAMES WAS WHEN HE first came to live with my grandmother. He was eight years older than I and as far as I could remember he had always been there. What I remember most about him was that he was tough, he was mean, and he was belligerent; and my grandmother could not control him. I think the hatred between the two of them was mutual.

The property on which my grandmother lived had several other structures besides the main house. To the right of the house and slightly behind it was the garage. My brother liked to climb up the grapefruit tree on the side of the house and then jump to the roof. Sometimes he would spend all night up there, running back and forth, occasionally jumping across to the garage and then back again. This would go on for hours. I'm really not sure what he was doing up there, unless he was just trying to annoy my grandmother. She would shout at him to come down, but he would only laugh at her and keep running up and down the length of the house and jumping over to the garage and back. Sometimes my grandmother would spray him with the hose to try and make him come down, but it never had any effect on him. Finally she would just give up and go back inside the house.

Sometimes he would try to get me to go up on the roof and jump around with him, but I knew better than to do that. My grandmother may not have been able to stop him from getting up there, but I knew she would gladly have killed me if I ever tried it.

Bobby James also liked to jump from the roof of the house

to the roof of my grandfather's tool shed, which was about ten feet behind the house. The shed had an entrance to the henhouse where my grandmother kept a dozen chickens. She treated them like pets. At night she would go out to say goodnight to them, and she was always talking to them when she gathered eggs from their nests or when she was in the chicken-yard feeding them. She fed them grain of some sort and something that looked like un-popped popcorn. The chicken feed was kept in the shed in galvanized trash cans with lids. Sometimes, if we didn't get the lid put back on tight enough, someone would find a rat or two in the can the next day.

We had a lot of problems with rats. They were just a fact of life at our house. I remember lying in bed at night and hearing the scratching of their tiny feet as they ran across the boards in the attic. They were always up there. This would go on until my grandfather came down to Gulfport for his vacation. As soon as he arrived, my grandmother would insist he put some traps and rat poison up in the attic. This, of course, was a messy job because once the poison and traps did their job, then my grandfather had to go up in the attic and collect the dead rats. This chore was usually accomplished a couple of days after the sound of the scratchy little feet had stopped. Not only did the dead rats have to be collected, but my grandfather also had to look for any nests they had built, kill any baby rats he found in them, and then destroy the nests as well.

My grandfather mixed the poison with peanut butter to make it more attractive to the rats. To me, it just looked like peanut butter with steam coming off it. Once, while I was watching him mix the poison and peanut butter together, I said, "I love peanut butter sandwiches." After that he made a big production of warning us kids how dangerous the rat poison was and how we had to stay away from the attic and the other areas where he had put out the poison. Thinking back, I'm surprised we didn't try it anyway.

I am not sure why we had such a rat problem, but there were

always plenty of them. It might have been because there were so many fruit trees around the house. The rats liked the grapefruits. You could always tell when they had been eating at one because the fruit was still hanging on the tree and looked beautiful on one side, while the other half was all eaten out. It might also have been because of the henhouse and the eggs, or even the trash cans full of feed and grain… or it might have been because of our next door neighbors: the Muncies.

Seven

THE MUNCIES WERE ROUGH, LOUD, HARD-DRINKING, fist-fighting people who made their living by fishing. They weren't really a big fishing outfit, like commercial fishermen. They had a couple of small boats with outboard motors and some nets. They used to catch a lot of mullet and sell them to the smoke houses around St. Petersburg and Gulfport, including Sonny's Bait House. I also heard they poached alligators in the marshy areas nearby, but I never saw them with an alligator. I guess if they were poaching alligators, they probably wouldn't have shown it openly, even though they were pretty open about every other law they broke.

They were always drinking and fighting out in the street in front of our house. The police were constantly being called, and sometimes they would get into a fist-fight with the police officer who was trying to arrest them and then more police would be called. A couple of times I saw two police cars in front of the Muncie's along with another car that my grandmother told me belonged to the Chief of Police.

Two things in particular made a lasting memory of the Muncies for me. They always cleaned their fish out behind their house and threw the heads and guts over the fence into my grandmother's yard, between our garage and the fence that separated our two properties. My grandmother hated them for that and was forever calling the police about it. Of course, when the police arrived, the Muncies denied that they had thrown any fish parts into my grandmother's yard. The more she called the police, the more fish

25

guts we found in the yard. The police always said they believed her, but unless someone actually saw them in the act, there was nothing they could do about it.

"Look at those fish heads and guts," my grandmother would say to them. "How do *you* think they got in my yard?"

"Mrs. Christian," the police officer would say, patiently, "they could have been thrown there by anyone. Unless someone actually sees one of the Muncies do it, there is nothing we can do."

I had actually seen one of the older Muncie boys throw the fish heads and guts over the fence several times, but he had warned me never to tell anyone or he would cut my dick off, and he had shown me a very long, sharp knife. Then he had grinned at me with a mouth-full of rotten teeth and grabbed his crotch, making cutting motions with the knife. I believed he would do it too, so I never told my grandmother that I had seen them; I certainly didn't want to get my dick cut off.

There was another reason I never told. My grandmother believed that children were to be seen and not heard, and I knew she probably would not have listened anyway. There were many times she had hit me square in the mouth, hard enough to knock me down, because I had interjected myself into an adult conversation.

The other thing imprinted on my memory about the Muncies was their toilet. It sat right in the middle of their living room floor. They had no front door on the house, so everyone passing by could look in and clearly see them using the toilet. I heard my grandmother say that they had done it out of spite. Before they had an inside toilet, they had an outhouse, as did many people at the time. At some point, the city of Gulfport had passed a law that all outhouses had to be replaced by indoor plumbing. The Muncies resisted changing for as long as they could, and there is no doubt in my mind that they would have been the very last people in Gulfport to convert to inside plumbing.

The Muncie's outhouse and its offensive smell were clearly observable from our property. Since my grandmother was on the town council, she knew about the law requiring everyone to convert to inside plumbing. And every day, she would call the police. Since this was something she could clearly point out to the responding police officer, proving that the Muncies were breaking the law, she could – and did – continually make complaints until the Muncies finally complied with the law and installed indoor plumbing.

I'm not sure how the city finally made them move the toilet inside, but I think several of them spent a lot of time in jail until the inside-plumbing law was conformed to. However, they had the last word. By placing the toilet in the middle of the living room, they could still offend anyone who wished to be offended.

My grandmother continued to complain about the location of the toilet, but to no avail. They had complied with the law by installing indoor plumbing, and quite probably the police were becoming tired of her complaints. Soon they quit responding, and my grandmother quit complaining.

The neighbors on the other side, the Hudson's, were also a royal pain in the ass. First, they had a nasty black dog, a chow named Skipper, that was just plain mean and sneaky. Every time I walked past their house, Skipper would come running out and corner me. I would stand as still as I could while he would crouch menacingly and slowly creep closer and closer, baring his teeth and snarling while saliva dripped out of his mouth into the sand on the road. I would shake with fear, knowing that if I ran he would pull me down from behind and maul me. Then someone from the Hudsons' house would laugh and shout, "Don't be afraid of him, boy. He won't bite. Go on about your business."

But if I made the slightest attempt to move away, Skipper would advance a step closer to me and his snarling would intensify as if to say, "I'm warning you. If you move any further I'm going to bite your balls off."

"Please come get your dog," I would beg. But the only response was always more laughter, until finally Sylvia Hudson, their teenage daughter, would come out and take the dog back in the house. As soon as she had her hand around his collar, I would take off running with the sound of laughter trailing after me.

One day I took Butchie with me as I walked past their house. I heard Skipper barking just behind their screen door, and I prayed he would come out so I could let Butchie kill him. No sooner had I wished it than the door flew open and Skipper came charging across the yard. Just as he reached the road, Butchie leaped forward and grabbed him by the neck and began shaking him violently.

"Kill him, Butchie. Kill him," I shouted.

One of the Hudson men came running out of the house with a rifle.

"Get your dog off or I'll shoot him," he shouted at me.

"Come here, Butchie," I shouted and took him by the collar.

Butchie let go of Skipper, but he kept growling, a low hateful sound from somewhere deep in his throat. I knew that if I gave the word, he would have leaped at the man with the rifle too.

Sylvia and her mother came out of the house and together they picked up the bloody, whimpering mess that Butchie had made of Skipper. "If your dog ever attacks my dog again, I'll shoot 'em," the man with the rifle said.

"If your dog ever tries to bite me again, I'll have my dog kill 'em," I shouted back. Then Butchie and I ran for home, where I hugged him and petted him and told him over and over how much I loved him and what a great dog he was. He just licked my face and jumped around with me.

After that, Skipper stayed in his own yard most of the time. But I still didn't take any chances and I stayed away from him as much as I could. If I saw him outside and needed to pass by the Hudsons' house, I made sure to take Butchie with me.

My grandmother's property wrapped around behind the back of the Hudsons', and they continually drove across our property so they could park in their side yard. My grandmother tried everything to keep them from doing it. She even had my grandfather build a wooden fence across the path they made by driving through with their cars. But that didn't stop them; they drove around it for a while and then one day we found it had been torn down. When that happened, my grandfather took his tools from the shed and some lumber that he kept behind the chicken coop, and he went across the field to repair the fence. The Hudsons came out to watch as he repaired it. He was always civil to them, and he asked them nicely not to cut across our property.

"What difference does it make? We ain't hurtin' nothin'. You're blocking our property with that fence."

"This is private property," my grandfather replied, "and I would appreciate it if you would respect that."

They paid no attention to him. The fence was either driven around or torn down again and again. Each time my grandfather went back out and repaired it, he politely asked them not to do it again. I suspect he never really cared whether or not the Hudsons drove across the property. I think, in his eyes, it didn't hurt anything either. He was probably just going through the motions to keep peace with my grandmother, who otherwise would have made his life miserable.

Eight

BEHIND MY GRANDMOTHER'S HOUSE WAS A CLUMP OF huge oak trees that were draped in Spanish moss and were great fun to climb and play in. Remarkably, my grandmother never minded us climbing in any of the trees. "Just don't break any limbs off," she would warn us.

In the middle of the clump of oaks was a large dirt area where grass never grew. I'm not sure why it didn't grow there, but I suspect it was because the trees were so large and had so much Spanish moss in them that the sun never really shone through enough for grass to grow. In any case, it made a great place to picnic. My grandfather built a long picnic table that could seat at least fourteen people. He also built a fire pit. After the war, we had great picnics back there. Friends of my grandparents would come over and we would have clam chowder, fried rabbit, hush puppies, potato salad, roasted hot dogs and toasted marshmallows. There were gallons of iced tea, apple pies and homemade ice cream. Bobby James always volunteered to turn the crank on the ice cream churn, and in return he was rewarded with the dasher. He'd lick the dasher until there wasn't a speck of ice cream left on it.

Behind the oaks was a field that extended all the way to the next street. All the neighborhood kids used to play in that field and climb in our trees. The twins, Ronnie and Donny, lived on the other side of the street. The field and trees were a perfect place to play hide and seek. The field was covered with high weeds so you could hide and no one could see you until they got right up on you.

We also played in Ronnie and Donny's yard. They had a mulberry tree in their front yard that we would climb in and eat mulberries until we were completely covered with blue and purple stains.

Although my grandmother would allow us to play at Ronnie and Donny's from time to time, she usually made them come to our yard, which included the field behind the oaks. Ronnie and Donny's parents let them come over to play anytime they wanted. So no one really cared if we couldn't always go to their house. "You don't need to be over in someone else's yard playing. You stay in your own yard and play where I can keep an eye on you," was her usual reply whenever we asked to go to someone else's house.

We also liked to play with the kids who lived at the far corner of our field, behind the Hudsons. They were the Wilsons: two boys, Jack and Johnny, and their sister, Sally Ann. Jack and Johnny were older than I but Sally Ann was in my grade. Their yard was really neat. Once, I told my grandmother how neat I thought the Wilson kid's yard was, and she snapped, "Don't use the word 'neat'. You don't know what it means. If I hear you use it again, I'll wash your mouth out with soap."

I could never figure out why it bothered her so much, but I didn't use the word around her anymore. Once my grandmother told you not to do something, it wasn't a good idea to do it again.

Nevertheless, I still thought their yard was neat. It had lots of palmettos that grew close to the ground in clumps and provided great cover for hiding. There were lots of oak trees, bushes, black-eyed Susans and kudzu vines, too. It had lots of places that you could hide, because it was so overgrown with vegetation. No one could ever find you, not even if they walked right up to your hiding spot.

Because the Wilsons' property actually joined ours behind the Hudsons', we could get away with playing over there without getting into too much trouble with my grandmother. From where she sat in her chair in the backroom of the house working cross word puzzles, I think she could look out the window and see us – or at least hear us – well enough to know where we were and that we were not getting into any trouble. So we spent a lot of time playing with the Wilsons. Ronnie and Donnie also would come over, and we all played together, hiding from each other, climbing in the trees and jumping in the kudzu vines, which acted like nets to catch us. Whether my grandmother liked the word or not, it was a pretty neat place to play.

Nine

IT'S FUNNY HOW WHEN YOU 'RE A KID AND YOU really don't have a conception of what time is or what directions are, you simply make up images in your mind to give you some idea. To me, "out west" was on my left side somewhere and "up north" was straight ahead. I envisioned an hour of time as something like a long hedge and a half hour as half of a long hedge. It also took me a long time to finally figure out what my grandfather meant when he would tell my grandmother, "I want to go uptown today" or "I need to go downtown, tomorrow." Downtown meant the town of Gulfport, and uptown meant he wanted to go into St. Petersburg. St. Petersburg was north of Gulfport, hence it was uptown and Gulfport was downtown.

My grandfather didn't know how to drive, so he depended on my grandmother to take him wherever he needed to go. During the war, everything was rationed; and you had better have a damn good reason for taking the car out anywhere. If you blew a tire, you could forget getting a new one. Gasoline was rationed too, and my grandmother wasn't about to waste it. When she did go out, she did everything she needed to do in the same trip.

A trip to the grocery store in Gulfport was always a fun day. My grandmother would load all of us – me, Tim, Butchie, and my grandfather when he was home on vacation – into the car for the short drive to the store. My brother Bobby James never went to the store with us. He was usually out playing with his friends somewhere and wouldn't come home just to go to the store, even if my grandmother wanted him to – which she didn't. Bobby James was only thirteen, but he was a problem she wished would just go away. She wanted to put him in a boarding school, but she didn't have the money to do that and my mother wasn't sending any money for her to do it either. So Bobby James spent most of his time running around Gulfport, sleeping in trees or under the house at night. My grandmother locked the doors when she went to bed and refused to get up and let him in if he came home late, which was nearly all the time. Bobby James had his own things to do, and going to the grocery store with us wasn't one of them.

Tim and I always had to wait in the car with Butchie while my grandmother shopped. Once my grandmother was finished shopping for groceries, the boy from the store would carry her bags to the car. I loved the brown bags full of food. There was usually a stalk of celery poking out of the top of one of the bags, which always had a great smell. We would wait with the groceries while she went next door to the drugstore to buy her crossword puzzle books and whatever else she needed from there. She always got some sort of rinse to soak her false teeth in and a tube of Ipana toothpaste. But most importantly – if we had been good – she would get us each a chocolate ice cream cone. She always got one for Butchie too.

It was my job to hold the cone for the dog while he licked it until it was gone. God help me if I ever took a lick of the dog's ice cream cone. I had my own, but if I ever succumbed to temptation, she had a stick in the car that she would use on my behind right then and there. I felt the sting of the stick a few times for that very transgression; but even worse was that then she would not let me hold the cone for the dog anymore.

Sometimes she would give it to Tim instead of me anyway – out of a sense of fair play, I suppose. But when she did it was always easy to get it back from him.

"Go on, Tim," I would whisper, "take a lick. Grandma won't know. I promise not to tell her."

It would usually take a few minutes of coaxing, but he would eventually give in and take a lick of the dog's ice cream cone.

"Grandma, Tim just took a lick off the dog's ice cream cone," I would immediately inform her, like the good and honest person I was.

"Can I hold the cone for the dog now? I won't lick it," I would promise.

"Tim, give it to Billy," my grandmother would say.

"No," Tim would shout, "He told me to lick it."

"I did not."

"You did too."

"Did not."

"Did too."

Whenever this happened, my grandmother would pull the car over, yank us both out of the car, throw our remaining ice cream cones away, and then beat our behinds. Afterwards, she would hold the dog's cone until he was finished, but often Tim and I would be crying and Butchie would be so upset that we had gotten beaten while he was shut up in the car, unable to help us, that sometimes he wouldn't even finish his cone. He would just whine and lick the tears from our faces until we quit crying. I loved that dog!

Ten

LOSING AN ICE CREAM CONE, GETTING SPANKED OR receiving some other form of punishment became a daily routine. In fact, it's rare when I can ever remember a day that we were not punished for something. My grandmother had very strict rules, and you had to obey them or you paid the price. If she told you to be home by a certain time, by God she meant it. If she said you better be home by four o'clock, you better be there at four o'clock and not a minute later.

My grandmother put supper on the table every day at five o'clock. Summer, winter, spring or fall, it was served at five o'clock. If you weren't there in time, part of your punishment was that you would not get any supper. My grandmother didn't save anyone's supper: she didn't warm it up, and she didn't set it out a second time. She said the reason she served supper early was, "I want you kids in bed and out of the way. The evening is my time, and I don't want you under my feet."

Another of her rules was that you had to eat everything on your plate. "I don't have enough money for you to be wasting food. There's a war going on. You can just sit there until you've eaten everything. If you think you can wait me out, just try it. You'll see it again for breakfast, or lunch or dinner until it's gone. Do I make myself clear?"

"Yes, ma'am," we would answer.

But this rule was hard to follow, especially when she served things like rutabaga, spinach and eggplant. No matter how much we hated what she served, and we hated these three things with a passion, we still had to eat all that she put on our plates. It didn't matter how long you sat there and stared at it, you were not getting up from the table until you had finished every last bite. Sometimes, when it seemed we were getting a reprieve because we were really gagging and were about to throw up, she would let us up from the table and send us directly to bed. But we always found whatever we had failed to eat that night on our plates for the next meal. If you failed to eat your rutabaga at suppertime, you not only went to bed but you could count on it being on your plate for breakfast the next morning. And, if you left it on your plate for breakfast, you would find it on your plate for lunch, unless you had to go to school and then you would find it on your plate for supper again. You *were* going to eat it, whatever it was.

I don't know how he did it, but Bobby James had a knack for not showing up for supper on the days that we had rutabaga, spinach or eggplant. Many a night, I sat there wishing the food would go away or that I could be like Bobby James and just not come home for supper. But, it wasn't going away, no matter how hard I wished. Occasionally you could get Butchie to eat your food for you, if you were careful and clever. If you could slip it under the table in your hand and get him to come over, he might eat it. For some reason, he loved fried eggplant; and since I hated it, he always got mine. However, there were occasions when Butchie fooled us. He did not like rutabaga, and when we slipped it under the table to him he might take it out of our hands but drop it somewhere onto the floor instead of eating it. When this happened, it was a disaster, because Grandma always checked the floor around our chairs after supper to see if we had spilled anything that needed to be cleaned up.

One time, she found a substantial amount of rutabaga on the floor by my chair. The next morning, I found it on my plate again for breakfast, with some dog and cat hair stuck in it. Surely she didn't expect me to eat that, I thought. Oh yes, she did. And I was going to sit there until I had finished it.

There were other ways of disposing of the hated food, but they were a little dangerous because if I got caught I would get a beating. One was to manage slipping it onto Tim's plate, which would shift the whole problem to him. Of course, it meant accomplishing the transfer while neither he nor Grandma was watching. It was not an easy accomplishment, but it was well worth the risk if I didn't get caught. Or, if I had managed somehow to choke most of the hated food down, I might get away with spitting the small remaining amount into my napkin and throwing it out when I cleared the table. Usually though, I just managed to choke it down, be done with it and move on.

On the days that my grandmother had enough ration stamps to buy meat, she used to cook it all on the same day and bring it to the table at supper time. We would see it piled on the plate, and the smell of it sitting there on the table in front of us made us even hungrier. But I was always hungry, and Tim was too. There was no such thing as second helpings of meat. You were lucky to get one serving. You could have all the rutabaga you wanted, but no seconds on meat. We only got one small piece from the plate, and the rest was to be saved for another meal. It was hard to see the meat sitting on the table and not be able to eat what we wanted. You could see it. You could smell it. But you couldn't have more than one small piece at any meal.

When he was home one evening, my grandfather asked her irritably, "Henrietta, why do you cook all the meat at one time?"

"What's the matter with you?" she shouted. "Are you stupid or something? You know very well that the icebox is not reliable enough to keep uncooked meat. I've tried it before, and it has spoiled on me. I can't afford to have the meat SPOIL!"

"I see," he said. "Well, do you think you could leave the extra meat in the kitchen instead of bringing it to the table?"

"What the hell is the matter with you tonight? Are you trying to needle me, or are you just stupid? I've told you a hundred times that I can't leave the meat cooling in the kitchen where I can't see it. The cat or dog might get into it."

"I'm not trying to needle you, Henrietta, and I'm pretty sure I'm not stupid. But couldn't we put the cat and dog outside while we eat? That way they won't get into it while it's cooling, and the boys wouldn't have to see something they can't have."

I listened to the exchange between my grandparents with interest. I knew we were never going to get seconds on meat, but I was more interested in my grandfather suggesting that we put the dog outside while we ate. I didn't want that to happen. I needed Butchie to help me eat stuff off my plate. But somehow I knew my grandmother would not put Butchie out, if for no other reason than that my grandfather had suggested it. *She* made the decisions in her house, not him.

It didn't matter much anyway, because we didn't have meat that often. Instead, my grandmother counted on meals like pancakes to fill us up. This had to be the cheapest meal anyone could think of. It was hard to eat three pancakes the size of your plate with nothing but brown sugar in between each one. The worst part was that my grandmother had a rule that you could only have one glass of water with your supper. "You don't need to wash your food down with water. And you don't need more than one glass. I can't have you filling up on water and then wetting the bed," she would tell us. "Crystal only washes once a week. I can't afford to have her washing your filthy blankets every time you wet them."

God help you if you *did* happen to wet the bed for any reason. She would blister you with her stick. You not only got a beating, you slept on the soiled bedding until the next wash day. She did not have extra bedding, which was really nothing more than threadbare flannel blankets. There were no such things as sheets, not even on my grandparent's bed.

But trying to get down three dry pancakes with only one glass of water was almost impossible. (I still can't look a pancake in the face!) After we were finished with supper on the nights we had pancakes, we were thirstier than usual – and that called for some creative thinking.

Eleven

IT WAS OUR JOB – TIM'S AND MINE – TO HELP MY grandfather clear the table. When he was home on vacation, his job was to wash the dishes while my cousin and I dried them. My grandfather always dried the pots and pans to give us a little time to play before going to bed. As for my grandmother, her day ended after she cooked supper. She would settle herself in her favorite chair in the backroom, working her crossword puzzles and listening to the radio. My cousin and I always tried to hurry and get the dishes done so we could play hide and seek in the house before going to bed. If we had been allowed to play outside after dinner, there were plenty of places we could have gotten a drink; but we were not allowed back out of the house after supper. Since we were also not allowed to have anything more to drink, playing hide and seek provided us with a possible way to get a drink of water.

My grandmother kept a large clay bowl full of water behind her chair for the dog and cat to drink from when they were in the house. Our strategy was to take turns hiding behind her chair. Then we could silently sip water out of the bowl. I don't know if she ever knew what we were doing and just said nothing, but I doubt it. Surely there would have been a lesson of some kind to teach us for drinking the water intended for the cat and dog. Occasionally though, she would show some curiosity. One night, she said,

"Edward, have you noticed the animals are drinking an awful lot of water lately? I wonder why."

"I haven't noticed," was his only comment.

"Of course not. You never notice anything," she said sarcastically.

My grandfather didn't reply and continued to read his newspaper in silence.

We also hid in the bathroom, but it was much harder to get a drink in there because the pipes to the washbasin usually had air in them. If you were not careful when you turned the faucet on, it would make a horribly loud sound that my grandmother could hear from where she sat in the backroom. The trick was to wrap your lips completely around the faucet and slowly turn the water on until it began to trickle into your mouth. If you turned the faucet on too fast, the pipes would howl as air rushed through them. The problem with this method was that after you had successfully turned the water on and were drinking the trickle that very slowly flowed into your mouth, you were silent for a fairly long period of time. When she could not hear you or see you, my grandmother always became very suspicious.

"What are you doing?" she would shout.

"Just hiding, Grandma," the one who didn't have his lips wrapped around the faucet would respond.

"Well, come out here where I can see you."

"Yes, ma'am."

We would try to finish drinking as quickly as possible and shut the water off before she got up to come check on us.

Another trick to getting a drink of water from the bathroom was to tell her that we had to pee. This was usually a good plan, as she wanted us to pee before going to bed. In her mind, it lessened the chance of us wetting the bed. But this was a difficult plan to execute. In order to save water, we were told to flush the toilet only once after we had both peed. This presented a problem because the toilet flush would only cover the noise from the washbasin for a very short period of time, so we had to hurry if we wanted a few sips of water.

The truth is that no matter what ploy we used to try and get a drink of water after supper, we really never did get enough to satisfy our thirst. At best, even after all our scheming, we would accomplish going to bed a little less thirsty, but thirsty just the same. And once we were in bed, we were not allowed out of it again until the next morning. To get out and get caught assured you of a beating. Usually the beating was severe and would leave huge red welts on your behind and legs and even your arms if you tried to shield yourself and they got in the way of the stick.

"Don't get out of bed. I don't want to have to get up and come in there," she always warned us. "If I do, I'll make you wish you had listened to me."

"Yes, ma'am," we always answered.

I hated having to go to bed so soon after supper. During the summer, it would still be light outside and I would hear other kids playing. I wanted to be out there with them, having fun. I don't think it bothered Tim very much though. He was usually asleep soon after going to bed, leaving me without anyone to talk to.

Twelve

IT WAS USUALLY VERY HOT WHEN WE WENT TO BED in the summer. There were only two fans in the house, and they were for my grandmother. She had one that blew on her when she sat in her chair in the backroom, and another one beside her bed that blew on her at night. My grandfather never seemed to mind the heat and didn't want a fan blowing on him.

One summer night I lay there in bed thinking of how I would give anything for a fan. I could feel the sweat running down the sides of my face, down my arms and off the sides of my chest. A mosquito buzzed around my ears, and I slapped at it. My chest and ankles itched where it had already bitten me. I must have had a bite on my right side as well, because it itched worse that my chest and ankles.

I lay there as still as possible. I didn't want to move, but I had to scratch the mosquito bites. I felt miserable. The sweat continued to roll off me, and the itching bites tormented me. The mosquito buzzed by my ear once more, and again I slapped at it, hoping to kill it. I didn't mind the bites half as much as I did that buzzing. I could have taken the bites, if only I didn't have to hear that damned mosquito in my ear. If I had a fan to blow on me, it would have kept the mosquitoes away, and I wouldn't itch like this. I wanted a fan. I wanted the mosquito to quit buzzing my ear. But most of all I wanted my mother. Where was she? Why didn't she come and take me away from this sweaty bedroom, and make the mosquitoes quit biting me? Maybe she would even buy me a fan. I lay there trying to picture in my mind what she looked like. But it was so hard, because I could only picture her with her back to me, as though she were walking away. No matter how hard I tried I could not see her face. Tears came to my eyes. Even though I tried to squeeze them back, they welled up rolled down my face. I couldn't tell what she looked like, but I knew she wasn't coming back. Finally I gave up. I forgot about the heat, the fan, the mosquitoes and my mother. My mind drifted back to the sounds outside.

I listened to the other kids playing. I could hear other sounds as well, like the Whitbeck's cow lowing in the pasture across the street from our house. I loved to hear that cow. Her lowing sounded so soft and gentle, as if she were happy to be walking through the pasture in the evening. I wondered what it would be like to walk there with her and hear her moo right beside me.

I could not see Whitbeck's farm from our yard. Between the far side of the road and his fence were huge oak trees covered with Spanish moss, black-eyed susan and kudzu vines. To actually look over into the Whitbeck's property, I had to climb up into the oak trees as high as I could and look over the fence into his fields. I was always disappointed though; there was never anyone there. I don't remember ever seeing anything growing in the fields, and I never saw his cow. The only way I ever knew she was even there was when I heard her lowing just before sundown. I wondered where she went during the day. Maybe she stayed in the barn, or maybe she had a shady place where she lay down to keep cool.

Even though there was nothing interesting to see in Whitbeck's fields, it was great fun to climb as high as I could in the oaks. Being up that high in the trees was almost like being a part of the sky. Sometimes I felt that if I could just climb a little bit higher, I would be able to actually grab one of the clouds. What would it feel like, I wondered, to touch a cloud? Would it feel like a marshmallow in my hand? Or would it just stick like cotton candy? In the still heat of my room, I lay unmoving and wished I was there, sitting peacefully out on the end of a high limb and gazing out at the sky and the clouds, and Whitbeck's fields, and my grandmother's house with the flagpole in the front yard, its flag flapping in the breeze.

The mosquito passed my ear again, and again I swatted at it. I knew the air would not cool off until the tide came in. So I waited, trying not to move. I listened for the tell-tale rustle of the palms, alerting me that the breeze was coming up. Once I heard the palm fronds begin to rustle, I would know the tide was coming in and relief from the heat was on the way. At first it would be just a slight rustle, but slowly it would become louder as the fronds banged against each other. The sound itself was cool and refreshing.

Puffs of cool air soon blew through my window and cooled down the room. The air dried the sweat on my body and caused a slight chill. As I felt sleep creep into bed with me, my room was filled with the soft sweet smell of gardenias that grew outside my window.

Contentedly, I rolled over on my side and pulled the flannel blanket up around my shoulders. It may seem strange to hear that we were sleeping with flannel blankets in the summertime, but they had been washed and scrubbed so many times by Crystal that they were threadbare and were probably not even as heavy as a sheet. In the winter, my grandmother would take heavier blankets out of a cedar chest where she kept them and give us each one, when she thought it was cold enough.

As I was finally drifting off, I thought again of my mother, and tried to remember her face.

Thirteen

THE FLAGPOLE HAD BEEN INSTALLED IN THE FRONT yard shortly after they bought the house. It was slightly higher than the roof. My grandmother had once said, "I want a flagpole in the front yard, and I want to fly the flag every day," and my grandfather had replied, "Alright, Henrietta. If that's what you want, I'll put one up." And he did.

Afterwards, whenever he was home, he would walk out to the front of the house every morning and raise the flag. And in the evening, just before supper, he would take the flag down and carefully fold it.

"Grandpa," I asked one day as I helped him fold it, "why do you always fold the flag in a triangle?"

"Well, that's the proper way to fold our flag. You know who George Washington was, don't you?" he asked.

"Yes," I said. "He was our first president."

"Well, do you remember what his hat looked like?

"Yeah, kind of," I stuttered, trying to remember what it looked like.

"Well, the next time you look at it, you'll see it has three corners. The proper way to fold our flag is in a triangle to represent the three corners of George Washington's hat."

"Why does it have to look like his hat?"

"Well, I'm not sure," he said. "One of these days, we'll have to go to the library and look it up."

"Can we go tomorrow?" I asked.

"We'll see. Now let's go get washed up for supper."

As we walked down the driveway toward the back of the house, he handed me the flag. I was excited and very proud that he let me carry it. I could hardly wait for Tim to see me. I knew he would be jealous.

"Just remember, Billy," he said as he put his arm around my shoulder, "our flag must always be honored and protected."

"Yes, sir," I answered as I held the flag tightly against my chest.

Back then, nearly everyone had a flag displayed somewhere on their house, either in a window or on a pole attached to the front porch. Some people had gold stars and candles displayed in their windows, too. Those were the families that had lost someone in the war. I loved seeing the flag flying in our yard. I was proud of it, and I was proud of my grandparents for flying it. I would climb the oaks along Whitbeck's fence and get as high as I could so I could look back at our house and see the flag flying. Being that high in a tree, rocking gently as the limb swayed back and forth in the breeze was exhilarating.

But if sitting at the top of the oak trees along Whitbeck's fence was exhilarating, coming down was even more so. Since the trees were heavily covered with kudzu, they acted like a huge net. I could jump off the limb and let myself fall ten or fifteen feet and land in the net of vines. I would climb to the top of the tree and jump off again and again. I loved climbing in the trees; it was great fun, unless Bobby James decided he wanted to climb with us. He could jump from limb to limb and from tree to tree with amazing ease. His goal was to go the entire length of Whitbeck's property line through the trees, without ever touching the ground. I think he must have gotten the idea from some *Tarzan* movie he had seen. He was very good at it, though. He jumped between branches with an athletic grace that made it look incredibly easy. The problem was that he thought Tim and I should be able to do it too.

"Come on," he said one day. "It's easy. Just jump. You'll make it."

I looked at the distance between the limb I was standing on to the one he was on. I knew it was impossible; I could never make a jump like that.

"I'm afraid I'll fall," I cried.

"You *won't* fall. Just jump," he shouted.

"I can't. I'll fall. It's too far."

"Don't worry. You won't fall. And anyway, if you do, the vines will break your fall."

I knew the vines didn't cover all the trees along Whitbeck's property. We had worked our way through several trees and from the limb I was standing on, I could see that there was hardly any kudzu below. Instead, there were lots of jagged branches. If I jumped and missed the limb Bobby James was standing on, I would crash through them and they might puncture my stomach or poke one or both of my eyes out.

"I can't," I whined again.

Bobby James jumped from his limb back to mine. "Jump, goddamn it," he said. "Or I'll throw you off this fucking limb. And if you're still alive when you hit the ground, I'll come down there and beat the shit out of you. Now jump."

He would always badger, threaten and punch Tim and me until we eventually attempted a jump that was nearly impossible. In the end, we had three possibilities: we could stand there on the limb until Bobby James threw us off and – if we survived that – we would then have the shit beaten out of us; we could go ahead and jump, miss the limb and fall, and – if we survived that – run home to get away from him; or we could jump and *somehow* make it.

"If you fall, the vines will catch you and break your fall before you hit the ground," he said again.

"But there aren't any vines in these trees," I whined.

"Sure there are. Look, there are two or three vines that go almost all the way to the ground. If you fall, grab on to one of them. But you won't fall. It's easy, watch." He jumped back to the limb he wanted me to try for. "Come on jump," he coaxed again. "If you don't, I going to come back over there and throw your ass off."

I still stood there, tears rolling down my face, too afraid to jump. Suddenly, Bobby James was beside me on the limb again, and I jumped – out of pure fear – and barely caught the other limb. I hung there, afraid of falling and knowing there were no vines below me, not even the two or three he had told me were there. I was in limbo, unable to pull myself up and too afraid to let go.

"Bobby James, there're no vines below me. If I fall, I'll crash into those jagged branches," I cried.

"Well, then pull yourself up, shithead."

"I can't. My hands are slipping. I'm going to fall!"

"See if you can swing your feet over to that little limb just below you. Then you can stand there and pull yourself up," he advised.

"I can't do it," I cried. "I'm going to fall."

"Okay, if you're too stupid to get your feet on the limb below you, go on and drop," he said. "Just let go. But I'm telling you, you're going to look like one of Whitbeck's cow turds when you hit the ground."

Snot was flowing out of my nose and my arms felt like they were on fire. I knew I couldn't hold on much longer. Finally, I made myself look down in search of the limb Bobby James told me to get my feet on. I saw it, but it didn't look big enough for both feet. I also knew I didn't have much time before my arms would give out and I would fall. I weighed my choices. I could either drop and take the chance that a branch would poke one of my eyes out, maybe even pierce my brain and kill me, or I could swing my body toward the limb below and try to get my feet on it.

I made up my mind, and with a superhuman effort I swung my body toward the little limb and caught it with my feet. Using it for leverage, it enabled me to push myself up a little higher. Immediately I felt relief from the pressure on my arms. I was able to lock them around the limb I had been holding. Slowly and painfully, I pulled myself up. Finally I was on the limb. I had made it. It was exhilarating. I was proud of myself.

"Great! You did it," Bobby James screamed. "Now jump back over here again."

The feeling of exhilaration evaporated immediately. I felt sick. No way was I going to jump back to the limb I had just jumped from. As quickly and carefully as I could, I climbed down out of the tree and ran home.

When Bobby James got involved, what was fun for Tim and me turned into a miserable time of being bullied. For some reason or other, Bobby James felt that Tim and I had to be able to do the same things he could do. It wasn't easy getting away from him, and he usually forced us to jump from limb to limb until one of us fell or until he got tired of picking on us. Sometimes I fell, and other times I made what seemed like an impossible jump. But if I didn't completely miss the limb I was trying for and could at least grab it before I fell, then either the fear of falling or fatigue decided my fate. If I were too afraid to let go and fall, I could usually manage to pull myself up onto the limb from which I was hanging. But if not, the pain from my fatigued and aching arms would take over, and my hands would lose their grip. Sometimes the vines would catch me, but sometimes there were none, and my fall would only be slowed by jagged branches as I crashed through them on my way to the ground. I would end up scratched, bruised and bleeding; how I never broke anything is still a mystery.

On the other hand, I don't remember my cousin ever successfully making a jump. He usually missed everything except the smaller limbs he broke off on his way to the ground. Usually two attempts – and therefore two falls – were enough to send him home crying.

My brother, however, would continue to jump back and forth among the trees with such ease that I would almost think I could do it too. I wanted to be able to make the same jumps, with the same ability. In my eyes, my failure to do so was just an indication that I was not as gifted as he. He loved leaping and swinging through the trees; I think he must have done it every day, so his ability only improved as time went by. When he wasn't jumping from tree to tree, he was jumping from the roof of the house to the roof of the shed and then the garage, and back again. I don't ever remember seeing him fall. He seemed to have a perfect sense of balance. He liked being at the center of attention and would do anything to be there. He really had no fear. I don't think it ever entered his mind that he might injure himself.

One of his favorite attention-getting stunts was to walk on top of the pipe railing that ran around the end of the Gulfport pier. He would jump up on top of the railing and either walk or run around it without ever falling. His balance was amazing. It scared me when I saw him do it, and I would beg him to come down before he fell. Any old ladies walking on the pier when he put on this show also begged him to come down before he hurt himself. He liked that. The old men fishing on the pier just referred to him as "a damn fool," which he was.

Fourteen

GRANDMA'S HOUSE WAS COMPRISED OF A FRONT room and a kitchen with a hallway joining them, two bedrooms (one for my grandparents and one for us kids), one bathroom, and the backroom. There was also a front porch and a back porch. We were not allowed in the front room, except for special occasions, which made it all the more attractive. Just because I was supposed to stay in bed after my grandmother put me there for the night doesn't mean that I did. Sometimes, usually out of boredom and being unable to sleep because of the heat, I would get up and silently slip into the forbidden front room.

This was where the good furniture was. It was reserved for use only when company came over or for opening presents on Christmas morning. There were several things in this room that seemed very interesting to me, perhaps because they were forbidden. One thing was a horsehair sofa that was as hard as nails and uncomfortable as hell to sit on. It was a bluish color with some sort of yellow flower design, but most important was that, despite being the most uncomfortable thing on earth, it was very cool to lie on during the hot summer evenings. Often I would sneak into the front room and lie on the cool surface of this sofa for a few minutes. I couldn't lie there for long. First, it didn't stay cool very long. It was just a quick fix. The other reason was that I could not take the chance of falling asleep on it and getting caught by Grandma if, for whatever reason, she decided to check on something in the front room or the front porch. She had a sixth sense about these things and would show up when you least expected her.

So my rule was to lie there for a few minutes, enjoy the cool surface of the couch briefly, and then get out. There was a fireplace in the front room, complete with a mantel, but it was never used. There was also a huge Philco floor model radio that my grandmother let us listen to sometimes on Sunday evenings. My cousin and I liked to listen to the Shadow; the Green Hornet; Nick Carter, Master Detective; Roy Rogers and Gene Autry. This was a rare and unusual treat, and we had to have been really good to get it. We didn't get it very often.

She also had a bookcase filled with novels. I used to look at the bookcase and see all the colorful, glossy paper covers on the books and wonder what it would be like to read one of them. Sometimes I would take a book off the shelf and try to pick out words I knew, like "a," "the," and "and." Sometimes I knew other words too, but I couldn't really read the books, and my grandmother had warned us that they weren't to play with.

Sometimes when I was wandering around the house at night, I would go out and sit on the front porch. I especially liked to do that when it was raining. It had wooden slats all around it that went about half-way up from the floor, and it was screened the rest of the way to the ceiling. It also had awnings that you could roll down in case the rain was blowing in. Otherwise, the awnings were never touched. The air was cool as I sat there listening to the rain and watching pools of water form on the front lawn. All of these excursions into the front room and front porch had to be short ones. I never really knew where Grandma was for sure, and I did not want to take the chance of her finding me out of bed.

Our bedroom was off the hallway that ran from the kitchen to the front room. It didn't have a door, just a pole across the top of the doorway with a curtain hanging on wooden rings. That meant getting out of the bedroom quietly was not difficult or noisy.

There was no door to open or close, and I didn't need to worry about squeaking hinges that might get me caught. I just had to slip through the curtain into the hall.

Although exploring the front room and the front porch when I was supposed to be in bed was fun, the real challenge was exploring the kitchen, the bathroom and my grandmother's bedroom. There was a screen door that opened into the hallway from the kitchen. The trick was to get the screen door open and close it again without making any noise, then walk through the kitchen without stepping on any boards that squeaked or creaked. Once I got to the bathroom, I could possibly get a drink if I was careful and used the method of wrapping my lips around the faucet and turning it on slowly enough to prevent any air rushing through the pipes to give me away. Then I would move into Grandma's room. There was a wooden door between the bathroom and her room, which was never closed unless my grandmother was using the bathroom, and only then if company was in the house.

Once I was in her bedroom, I could peer into the backroom where she and my grandfather would be sitting. When I entered from the bathroom, the doorway was just to my left. It was also covered with a curtain attached to a pole with wooden rings, like the one over our bedroom. It was across the room from my grandfather's bed, which was up against the window that looked out onto the driveway that ran along the side of the house. My grandparents slept in separate beds. I think my grandfather had violent fits that caused him to hit or kick my grandmother in his sleep, so to protect herself she made him sleep by himself. Her bed was across the room, perpendicular to my grandfather's, and also up against a window: this one looked out behind the house, where the chicken coop was.

Getting from my bedroom to theirs and watching my grandmother as she sat in her favorite chair, working her crossword puzzles while listening to the radio, was very exciting. But I also had to get back to my bedroom without getting caught. Sometimes I would lie on the floor in their bedroom, watching them and listening to the radio. My grandmother always played the radio in the evening. She had several programs she liked. Sometimes it was big band music or the war news or Gangbusters, or the FBI in Peace and War. Another program she liked was the Inner Sanctum, which was scary. I didn't like it. If she were listening to the Inner Sanctum, I would go back to my bed right away.

Walking around the house at night had other perks besides listening to the radio or getting a drink in the bathroom. Exploring the house was an opportunity to get something else to eat. But there was a problem. My grandmother counted every single item of food: every slice of bread, every piece of fruit, every piece of candy, and every cookie – everything was counted. She knew if someone had taken a piece of candy or a piece of fruit or a cookie because they were all recounted every single day. But I had discovered there was one thing she never counted: the dog biscuits she bought for Butchie.

There were two types. One box contained large biscuits in the shape of a bone, and the other had much smaller ones. It was better to take from the box of small bones, because there were a lot of them and a few missing here or there easily went unnoticed. And there was another reason: both sizes of bones were extremely hard and very, very dry, but it was harder to bite off pieces of the big bones. Plus it would have been impossible to get a whole one of those completely down without drinking a lot of water. As it was, the bones tasted like cardboard; but they were filling.

I could move around anywhere in my grandmother's house without making a single sound. I knew where every squeaky board was and just how to slip past them. I believe that if I had not learned how to move around in the house, I would have gone crazy lying there in bed every evening, listening to the other kids playing outside. I could hear their shouting and laughter, and I wanted to be out there with them. Tim might be able to get in bed, wrap up in his blanket, and go to sleep immediately; but I never could. I could not shut my mind down that way. It always seemed as though there were a million things going through my head that kept me awake.

Sometimes I went out through the front porch into the yard, but this was dangerous. It was too easy to get caught that way. It seemed that some of the neighbors felt it was their responsibility to report a mischievous child to their parents. If anyone happened to see me in the front yard in my underwear, they surely would have mentioned it to my grandmother. So exploring the house was about all I could do until I got tired enough to go to sleep. My brother, if he decided to come in the house, slept in the same bedroom with Tim and me. There was a set of bunk beds where my cousin and I slept – I had the top bunk – while my brother slept in the single bed on the opposite side of the room. He didn't have to go to bed when my cousin and I did, not just because he was older but also because my grandmother couldn't control him as easily as she controlled Tim and me. But he still had to be home for supper on time or he would not be fed. If he wasn't back in the house by bedtime – which, for him, was determined to be when my grandparents went to bed – my grandmother would lock him out of the house. She made it very clear that she wasn't going to get up at all hours of the night to let him in and that he would have to find somewhere else to sleep on those nights.

Fifteen

THE TRUTH IS THAT MY BROTHER REALLY DIDN'T CARE if he got locked out of the house. He could usually get back in when he wanted to, and he'd sleep in a tree someplace if he didn't want to. We only had screen doors on the front and back of the house, and they were only locked with a simple hook-and-eye type of lock. My brother could usually slip the blade of his hunting knife through the space between the edge of the door and the door jam and lift the hook out of the eye to let himself in. When my grandmother finally had my grandfather install hooks with pressure springs on them, he could no longer get in that way. After that, he would come around to the window in our room and have me unhook the screen so he could crawl in through the window. When my grandmother figured out what he was doing, she had my grandfather nail the screens shut on all the windows. Bobby James told me that from then on, he usually slept in a tree or, if it was raining, either in the shed, which didn't have much room, or under the house, which he preferred.

In the morning after sleeping outside, he may or may not appear for breakfast, but if he came back later in time for lunch or supper she always let him in. One time after being locked out of the house, he didn't come back for several days. I don't know where he stayed, but one day I was playing in the fields behind the oaks when I heard him calling me. I looked all around and finally spotted him sitting on a limb, at the top of one of the trees. When I waved, he came down and ran over to where I was playing.

"I'm hungry," he said. "Can you get something out of the house for me to eat?"

"No," I said, "you know Grandma has everything counted. And besides, she's in the house and would see me take something."

"What about the bird's bread?"

"She keeps it in a drawer in the credenza, in the backroom where she always sits. She would see me take it," I said.

"You could tell her you wanted to feed the birds, and then she wouldn't ask any questions," he said.

"I don't know. It's not time to feed the birds yet," I said. I was trying to think of excuses not to have to try and sneak any food out of the house, because I knew that if I got caught, my grandmother would blister me with her stick.

"What time does she usually feed the birds?" he asked.

"The quail come in around three-thirty, and about an hour later the doves come in."

"Okay, you ask grandma if you can feed the birds today, and then get the bread out of the credenza. Then when you feed the birds, keep some of the bread in your pocket and bring it to me."

"Why don't you just come into the house and eat at supper-time?" I asked.

"No, I'm never coming back in the house again. I'm going to run away and try to find Mom," he said.

"Do you know where she is?"

"No, not really, but I think she's in California."

"Where's that?"

"Out West someplace."

"Do you know what she looks like?" I asked.

"Of course I know what she looks like. What kind of question is that?"

"I don't know. I don't know what she looks like."

"Never mind what she looks like. Are you going to get me the bread or not?"

"Okay," I said. "I'll try."

"Good. You know where the Allen's oak tree is?"

"Yes."

"Meet me there when you have the bread." Then he turned and ran off across the field.

The Allens lived two blocks south of the Hudsons, and they had a huge oak tree in their front yard with a tire-swing hanging from one of the limbs. Mostly the older kids played over there with them. They were more my brother's age, maybe a little older. One of the Allen boys had been killed in the war, and the younger boys were just waiting until they were old enough to go and fight the Japs. It seemed like everyone was either fighting the Japs or wanted to. People didn't talk much about fighting the Germans. It was probably because we were winning in Europe and most people thought the war there would be over soon. Everyone was directing their attention to the Pacific and finishing off the Japs.

The Allen boys were mean, and I stayed away from them. If I happened to pass by their house when they were outside, they would chase me and threaten to beat my ass and steal my clothes. My brother just laughed and never helped me if they were after me. I don't know if he was afraid of them or just didn't care if they beat me up.

I didn't want to try and sneak the bird's bread out of the house for Bobby James, because I was afraid of getting caught. But I knew if I didn't, he would beat me up the next time he saw me. So I convinced myself there was a chance I could get away with it. Sometimes my grandmother would let Tim and me feed the quail and doves, which arrived in the yard every afternoon. I don't know how it really got started, but my grandmother would put feed and bread out for them, and they would come in every afternoon at their usual times, looking for the food. First the quail would come in at around three-thirty in the afternoon and eat for about half an hour. When they left, the doves would come in. It was interesting to me that they never came in together or got their schedules mixed up. The doves always waited for the quail to leave before they arrived in the yard. Both bevies, of about fifteen to twenty birds each, came to the same place in the back yard, by the picnic table area. My grandmother loved watching them and looked forward to seeing them each afternoon. We were not allowed to scare the birds or try to catch any of them. If she observed any of us trying to do either, it brought a quick, hard rap against the side of our head from one of her fists.

The bread my grandmother saved for the birds was bread that had either gotten stale or moldy and could not be used for toast or sandwiches. She kept it in a special drawer in the credenza in the backroom where she could keep an eye on it, but she didn't count the slices. She probably figured it was highly unlikely that one of us would eat a piece of bread with mold all over it. But, in fact, this was another source of extra food when we could get at it. We just tore the moldy part off it and ate the part that was left. But we had to be careful not to throw the moldy pieces back in the drawer. If we did, she would know what we had been up to, and it would certainly bring some form of punishment down on us. Our usual tactic was to volunteer to feed the birds, and while we were feeding them we would tear the moldy parts off to throw to the birds and then – as long as we had our backs to her – we would eat the part that was good.

I knew before I asked my grandmother that she might either say no or that I might not be able to get very much bread, so as I walked through the backroom to the kitchen I filled my pockets with a few dog biscuits from the box on the counter.

"Grandma, can I feed the birds today?" I asked her.

"If you want to," she replied without looking up from the crossword she was working.

I slipped several slices out of the drawer.

"Put some of that back. You don't need to give them that much," she said.

I swear she had some kind of special eyes. How could she see how much bread I had taken? I had my back to her and was taking the bread out directly in front of me. It was scary.

I put one of the slices back and took the rest with me. The birds were going to get cheated today. If I gave them much of the bread, there would be very little left for my brother. So I just tore off the moldy parts and fed those to the birds, and kept as much as I could for Bobby James, which was about three slices.

After the birds had been fed, I wandered over to the Allen's and met him by the oak tree.

"This is all I could get," I told him.

"This is fine," he said as he took the bread.

"I got you some of these, too." I pulled the dog biscuits out of my pocket.

"What are those?"

"Dog biscuits."

"What'd you want me to do with them?"

"Eat 'em," I said, "I do. They fill me up when I'm hungry."

"You eat these things?"

"Yeah."

"Well, you better quit, or you're going to start lifting your leg to pee," he said.

"Well, try 'em if you get hungry. I gotta go," I said over my shoulder. "Or I'm going to be late for supper." I left him there and ran back to the house.

Sixteen

SHORTLY AFTER I HAD SLIPPED THE BIRDS' BREAD OUT of the house for him, Bobby James decided not to runaway and came back to the house. A few days later, my grandmother had to drive my grandfather to the doctor in St. Petersburg. Crystal had already called my grandmother and to say her mother was sick so she would not be able to come to do the washing until the next day. My grandfather couldn't cancel his doctor's appointment, so they left the three of us at home alone.

We were playing in the trees in the back of the house when Buddy Allen came over to the house with a BB gun. He wanted my brother to go shoot birds with him and, as it happened, it was about the time for the quail to come into the yard. My brother and Buddy decided to shoot one and cook it, and after several unsuccessful shots, they hit one in the wing. It tried to fly away, but it was unable to get off the ground with its damaged wing. Terrified and determined to stay alive, it showed amazing speed as the two boys chased it around the yard until they finally caught it and killed it.

At first they were going to try and cook it outside, but my brother decided they could cook it faster if they used my grandmother's gas stove in the kitchen. They tore most of the feathers off the bird and then tore its head off too. Buddy Allen shoved a stick up its ass and out the hole where its head had been. Laughing and joking, they ran to the house to cook it on the stove. They turned on the gas burner and held the bird over the flames with the stick Buddy Allen had skewered it with, slowly turning it and trying to get it cooked on all sides. The bird's remaining feathers caught on fire and as they burned off, they floated over the entire kitchen, landing on everything.

The quail turned out to be very greasy and started dripping all over the stove as they tried to cook it. There was grease everywhere, and the stink from the burned feathers was nauseating. Pieces of meat from the bird fell off and stuck to the burner. Finally, they decided the bird was cooked enough and pulled its feet and wings off. But it was still raw inside and blood ran all over the front of the stove and down onto the floor. They tried to eat it, but it was a bloody, half-cooked mess.

"Jesus, Bobby James, this thing tastes like shit," Buddy Allen said. "I can't eat this shit."

"Yeah, me neither," my brother said. "Throw it away or give it to the dog. Billy, bring Butchie in the house. Maybe he'll eat this shit."

I went out to the back porch and called Butchie, and he came running in immediately. I think he could smell the bird cooking from outside. The dog ran into the kitchen and Bobby James gave him the half-cooked bird, and before I could take him back outside, he ran into my grandmother's bedroom and began eating it on the rug.

"Oh, Jesus! Get the damn dog outside before he makes a mess," my brother yelled at me.

I went into my grandmother's bedroom and got the bird away from Butchie and then threw it out the back door. He quickly followed it out the door, but he had already made a mess in the bedroom.

"My grandmother is going to kill me," my brother told Buddy. "Help me get this mess cleaned up before she comes home."

By this time, Buddy Allen was doubled over with laughter, which only made my brother angry.

"Shut up and help me, goddamn it," he yelled at Buddy.

But Buddy Allen wouldn't quit laughing, even though he took

a dish rag off the sink and tried to wipe up some of the bloody mess off the floor. Soon my brother was laughing too. They wiped grease, feathers and blood off the stove, and when they thought they had it pretty well cleaned up, they ran out of the house, still laughing, and disappeared into the field out back.

When my grandmother got home, all hell broke loose. She wanted to know what had been going on and who had tried to cook something on the stove. She took the stick off the top of the icebox and whacked both my cousin and me. Butchie had followed her into the house when she came home and the minute she hit us, he went right for her arm and grabbed it in his teeth. I don't think he bit her very hard. He just wanted to make her quit hitting us.

"Edward, come here and get the dog," she yelled at my grandfather.

He came and grabbed Butchie by the collar and took him outside while my grandmother continued to whack us with the stick. "Who cooked on my stove?" she yelled at us.

At first we tried to lie about it. "I don't know," we both shouted at the same time.

Whack! Whack! Whack! The stick continued to hit us, over and over. Finally, I broke.

"Bobby James and Buddy Allen did it," I cried.

"What were they cooking?" she demanded.

I saw Tim disappearing into our bedroom. "One of the quail from the back yard," I sobbed.

"How did they get a quail?" she yelled with her stick raised, ready to strike again. She grabbed me by the arm to make sure I didn't try to get away too.

"Buddy Allen had a BB gun, and they shot one of the quail. Then they took its feathers off and cooked it on the stove." I was crying. The welts on my back and legs were beginning to swell and hurt where she had hit me. I just wanted to get away from her.

She finally let me go and placed the stick back on top of the icebox. "Get to your room. Get your clothes off and get in bed," she shouted. "Tell Tim to do the same."

"Why, Grandma? We didn't do it. We didn't do anything. Why do we have to go to—?"

Before I could finish the question, she backhanded me, sending me reeling across the kitchen floor. I slipped on the quail grease on the floor and slid into the front of the stove.

"I said get your clothes off and get in bed. Now move!" she shouted.

Crying, I reluctantly went to bed. It was so unfair. Why did we have to go to bed? Why wouldn't my mother come and take me home with her? Why did I have to stay here with my grandmother? Instead of getting up into my bunk bed, I jumped into Bobby James' bed, crying loudly. The more I thought about the unfairness of it all, the more I cried, and the louder I got.

Suddenly my grandmother appeared over me, her face twisted in anger. "Shut up with that crying right now or I'll gag you," she snarled.

I was so startled to see her that for a second I stopped crying, but I was still sniffling. When she left the room, I thought about how unfair it was again, and the madder I got, the more I cried. Without warning, my grandmother was back in the room with some dishtowels in her hands. She tied both my hands to the iron frame at the head of the bed with two of the dishtowels she had brought with her, and then stuffed one of my socks into my mouth and tied a dish towel around my head to keep me from spitting it out. I glared at her with all the hatred I could muster.

"Don't look at me like that," she snarled at me. "I'll knock that look right off your face."

I could barely breathe. My nose was stopped up from crying, and I couldn't breathe through my mouth because of the gag. I began to panic and fear raked my body. I kicked and thrashed around on the bed. I couldn't breathe, and I was afraid she would leave me to suffocate. I kicked the wall and yanked on my bound hands as hard as I could, trying to free them. Snot poured out of my nose, and when I tried to breathe through it, no air could get through. I was thrashing wildly, trying to free my hands so I could get the gag out of my mouth. I knew if I didn't get it out soon, I was going to die.

She must have realized what was happening, because she took the gag out of my mouth and told me that if I cried or screamed again, she would be back with the stick. I gasped for air, trying to fill my lungs. I wanted to blow my nose, but my hands were still tied to the bed. As soon as she left the room, Tim ran over and untied my hands. I blew my nose on the dishtowels and threw them on the floor. I was terrified and could not quit shaking.

After my grandmother left my room, I heard my grandfather speaking to her as she entered the kitchen. "Henrietta, try to control yourself."

"Control myself? How can I control myself? I'm scared to death about what could have happened with the boys here by themselves and Bobby James turning on the stove. What if he had set himself on fire? What if he had set the house on fire with Tim and Billy in here? They're only five years old."

"I know, but Tim and Billy aren't to blame for what Bobby James did," my grandfather told her.

"I don't know what to do, Edward. I can't control Bobby James. He belongs in a reform school. I can't even put him back in Mary Help a Christian. Susan hasn't sent any money for his tuition, and they won't take him back until we pay the bill for his room and board. Even if we paid it, he wouldn't stay there. I just don't know what to do."

I knew what my grandmother meant about Mary Help a Christian. Every time she took Bobby James over to the boarding school in Tampa, he would run away. He usually ran away within a few minutes of being there, and on several occasions had beaten her back to the house in Gulfport. He would be sitting on the front steps waiting for her when she pulled into the driveway.

"I know how you feel, but you can't keep taking your fear and frustration out on Tim and Billy."

"I've had it with Bobby James, but I don't know what to do."

I was hoping my grandfather would tell her what to do, but he did not reply.

Seventeen

THE NEXT DAY WAS THE END OF MY GRANDFATHER'S vacation, and we took him to the train station in St. Petersburg where he left for Knoxville. A few nights later, completely frustrated and at her wits end, I heard my grandmother call my mother long distance. I had gotten out of bed and was listening to my grandmother's end of the conversation while I lay on my stomach in her bedroom, peering out from underneath the curtain that hung across the door.

"Susan, I told you, I've tried to put him back in Mary Help a Christian, but they won't take him back… What? I said, they won't take him back…. Why?" she shouted. "Because you haven't paid his tuition!" She was clearly exasperated. I watched her shift the phone from one ear to the other. "Look, I don't have the money for these long distance calls, and I certainly do not have the money to pay for Bobby James' tuition. You are going to have to send me the money, or God only knows what will happen to him. He runs off and doesn't come home for days. I don't know where he is, or whether he's getting into some kind of trouble. When he does come home, he gets up on the roof and runs back and forth all night. Then the next day he's gone again.… No, do not send it in a letter. Wire it to me. I'm still waiting for the last letter you were supposed to be sending me with money for the boys. Make sure you wire it to me. Yes, I need it here by tomorrow. Are you sure? Alright, I will be looking for it tomorrow. What? Billy is fine. I said Billy is fine. Alright, goodnight Susan. Don't forget I want the money by tomorrow."

She hung up the phone and sat there for awhile in silence. Her cat, Obie, jumped up onto the arm of her chair and began rubbing his head against her arm. Absentmindedly, she reached up and began rubbing his head and scratching him behind the ears. I could hear him purring all the way over where I was laying on the floor. Suddenly, my grandmother got up out of her chair, and I silently slid back from the curtain, crept through the bathroom, across the kitchen, and down the hall to my room without making a sound.

The next day, my grandmother was still in a bad mood. When no money came she became even angrier. She stomped around the house with an ugly scowl on her face. Tim and I gave her a wide berth and tried not to attract attention to ourselves.

The following day, however, she received a phone call from the Western Union office in St. Petersburg telling her that they had some money that had been wired to her from a Miss Susan Christian. In a much better mood, she loaded Tim and me into the car for the trip into St. Petersburg to pick up the money. When we returned home, I watched my grandmother as she wrapped a rubber band around a roll of bills and hid them somewhere in the back of her closet.

I didn't think that was a very good hiding place. I knew that my grandfather made grapefruit wine and let it ferment in glass jugs in the back of the closet. I was also aware that Bobby James knew about the wine and would slip in there and drink out of the jugs whenever he got a chance. I figured he probably looked for other things whenever he was in the closet as well, and that it would only be a matter of time before he would find the money. But the question was, where *was* Bobby James? He had been gone for several days and had not even returned to jump around on the roof at night. My grandmother was worried and went to the back porch several times to call him, but she got only silence in return.

"Do you boys know where Bobby James is," she asked Tim and me.

"No, ma'am."

Two days later Tim and I were throwing guavas at each other in the side yard, and I looked up to see Bobby James sitting on the limb of the grapefruit tree outside the window where my grandmother sat and worked her crossword puzzles. He smiled at me and motioned with his finger to his lips not to say anything.

But I ran over to him and said, "Grandma has been looking for you for days."

"I know," he said. "I've been sitting here in this tree everyday watching her do her crossword puzzles."

"Didn't you hear her calling you?"

"Sure, I did."

"Well, why didn't you answer her?"

He shrugged. "I didn't feel like it."

"What are you going to do now?"

"I'm hungry. Do you think she will let me back in the house?"

"I don't know. She's pretty mad."

"I don't give a damn if she's mad. I know she wants to send me back to Mary Help a Christian." Then he swung down out of the tree and put his arms around mine and Tim's shoulders. "Let's go in and get something to eat."

I was nervous about walking into the house with my brother. I didn't want my grandmother to think I had known where Bobby James was all the while she had been looking for him. There was no telling what she might do, but I was pretty sure it would be connected to the stick on top of the icebox.

As Bobby James walked into the house, he said, "Hi Grandma," as if he were casually walking into the room and had not been gone for over a week.

She did not look up or answer him. She just kept filling in words for her crossword puzzle. He walked over to her chair and said, "Hi Grandma," again.

Tim and I hung back by the door, waiting to see what was going to happen. She continued to ignore him and kept working the puzzle.

"I'm hungry, Grandma. Can I get something to eat?"

She still did not look up, but this time she answered him. "If you're hungry, you can wait until I serve supper. Now go get a bar of Octagon Soap out of the shed and wash yourself up with the hose outside. You stink."

Tim and I ran out the backdoor ahead of Bobby James, relieved that we had not gotten punished for somehow being connected with my brother being gone for so long. For the rest of the afternoon, we chased each other around the yard, laughing and squirting one another with the hose. Butchie was barking and running along with us, so we squirted him too. It was one of the rare times that I ever remember having fun with my brother.

The next day, my grandmother put Bobby James' things in a brown paper bag, made him put on clean clothes, combed his hair and took him back to Mary Help a Christian.

And for some reason, this time he stayed. Her problem seemed to be solved, and things began to settle down with just my cousin and me to worry about at the house.

But the peace was not to last. A few weeks later, on grocery shopping day, it was windy and rainy. The rain was coming down in torrents and was flooding the backyard and the roads. Sometimes it came straight down, and other times the wind would whip around and drive the rain against the windows so hard it sounded as though someone were throwing handfuls of BB's against the glass.

My grandmother decided to leave Tim and me at home by ourselves. "Alright, boys, I'm going to the store. You had better behave yourselves and stay out of trouble while I'm gone," she admonished.

"Yes, ma'am," we said together as she went out the back door.

We watched from the back porch as she waded through the

puddles on her way to the garage, and then moments later as she drove down the driveway. For awhile we sat on the porch, watching the rain.

"What do you want to do?" I asked.

"I don't know," Tim said. "I wish we could play with Jack and Johnny."

"Grandma would kill us if we went over there instead of staying in the house."

"I know. They probably couldn't come out anyway, but I sure had fun playing with that kerosene lamp they stole the other day," Tim said.

"Yeah, me too. That was neat, wasn't it?"

Jack and Johnny Wilson had stolen a kerosene hazard lamp, which the city maintenance crews had set out to mark a large pothole in the road on Beach Boulevard. They had it back in the brush behind their house, concealed by kudzu vines and palmettos. We had sat there with them and Sally Ann, well hidden from any prying eyes, and had stacked leaves and twigs around the kerosene flame until soon we had a campfire going. The air was cool and a light rain was falling, but it was warm and cozy under the palmettos with our little campfire. None of us had said very much as we sat staring at the flames. It was just fun to feed the fire and listen to the rain drops hitting the palmettos. Jack said it reminded him of a movie he had seen once where cowboys sat around the campfire at night drinking coffee. Johnny and Sally Ann said they were reminded of the movie too. No one could remember the name of it, but we all agreed that we wanted to be cowboys when we grew up. Except Sally Ann, but she said she might marry Roy Rogers or Gene Autry. When she said that, we all said "ugh" at the same time.

We continued to sit there feeding the small fire until the kerosene finally burned away and there was no more flame. We couldn't keep the fire going because we had used up all the dry twigs and leaves to be found under the palmettos where we were sitting, and the ones outside the palmettos were too wet to burn. Tim and I finally decided to go home, where I knew we were going to be in trouble.

"Look at you," my grandmother shouted when we got there. "You're all soaked. How can you be so damn dumb? Don't you have enough sense to come in out of the rain?"

I didn't see what the problem was. Who cared if we got wet? We always got wet at the beach. All we had to do was dry off with a towel. But I didn't say anything.

"Get out of those wet clothes," she shouted, "and hang them on the tub."

I didn't care if she shouted at us this time. I had had fun with Tim and the Wilson kids. Sitting around the kerosene hazard lamp and pretending it was a campfire out west was fun.

We talked about it a little longer, remembering the fun we'd had playing with the Wilson kids and the campfire we had built and looking out at the rain.

"You want to play cowboys and Indians?" I asked.

"Yeah, we can chase each other around the house and pretend we're riding our horses out west," Tim said eagerly.

We began chasing each other around the house, cocking our thumbs and pointing our forefingers as if they were pistols as we pretended to shoot at each other. We ran around, screaming like wild Banshees, and sometimes we trotted along as if we were riding horses. Then we decided it would be even more fun if we had a real campfire, just like real cowboys. We rolled up newspapers and pretended they were the logs of a campfire. I don't know whose idea it was to have a real fire. It was probably mine. Anyway, I thought that if we lit a couple of matches from my grandfather's pipe stand and laid them on the newspapers, it would look like a real campfire.

I lit two matches and put them on the newspapers, but they only burned for a couple of seconds and then went out. I tried it a few more times with the same results. Then I thought maybe if

I struck a whole book of matches and set it on the newspapers, it would burn a little longer and really look like a campfire. So I opened one book of matches and set it on the newspapers, and then got another book of matches and stuck a match to light the ones on the newspapers. It worked great! The flame lasted much longer. When that started to burn out, I threw the other book of matches onto the flickering flames.

They ignited immediately and the campfire was going again. I threw several other newspapers on it and by now we had a huge campfire going, right there in our own living room! Suddenly the flames were getting bigger and I began to feel nervous. I was afraid that the campfire might burn a hole in the rug, which covered most of the floor. I quickly began trying to put out the fire, and Tim helped by pouring water from the cat's water bowl over it. We got it out, but smoke was everywhere – and just as I had feared, there was a huge hole in the rug.

We got things cleaned up as best we could, but there was no way we could hide the hole. It was staring at us like a huge eye, waiting to see what we were going to do next. At first I didn't know what to do. Then it came to me. We could just cover the hole with newspapers so my grandmother would not notice it. We put the rest of the newspapers down on the floor, covering the hole.

"It looks pretty good," I said.

"Yeah, she'll never notice it," Tim said, sharing my optimism.

When we heard my grandmother's car roll up the driveway splashing through the puddles as she headed toward the garage, Tim and I were in our bedroom playing. A few minutes later there was a loud scream, and my grandmother shouted for us to come to the backroom immediately.

"What is this? Which one of you was playing with matches?" she shouted.

Neither of us said a word. We just looked at each other and at her as if we didn't know what she was talking about.

"How did you burn a hole in my rug?" she shouted. "You

could have burned the whole damn house down! What were you doing?"

We stood in silence, staring. We didn't know what to say. We were both shocked that she had found the hole burned in the rug so fast. We had fully expected it would be days before she found it, and that by that time we would not be connected to it.

"Answer me," she shouted.

We gave her blank looks, speechless. How *had* she found the burn so fast? And what was the big deal? We hadn't burned the house down, just a hole in the rug. That was all. This was a very confusing situation. The only thing that was clear was that we were certainly going to get one hell of a spanking for this. My grandmother was obviously very upset.

"Boys, don't you know how dangerous it is to set a fire in the house? The floors," she said, pausing a moment to take a deep breath, "are made of wood. This *whole house* is made of wood, and it could go up in flames in just a few seconds. What is even more dangerous is that Crystal cleans these floors with *kerosene*, so they are highly flammable." She stared at us, unblinking. "Who burned the hole in the carpet?"

Of course, we didn't know anything about the hole in the carpet.

"I think it must have been Bobby James," I said. "He likes to play with matches."

"Bobby James is not here," she shouted, her voice filled with exasperation. "He's at school over in Tampa. He couldn't have done it."

I had counted on his quail cooking episode to connect him to the burned rug. It hadn't occurred to me that this wouldn't work since he was in Tampa.

"Now tell me, who burned the hole in the carpet? I want to know," she said so calmly that I was lulled into stupidity.

"It was me, Grandma. I was trying to build a campfire." I couldn't believe that the words were coming out of my mouth.

What was I doing? I knew I was going to get spanked for it. Why hadn't I at least tried to blame it on Tim? Why had I taken the whole blame? We had both done it, but I had told her it was me, and I was willing to accept my spanking or whatever punishment she was going to give me.

"Go get your clothes off and get in bed," she told me.

She was still calm, but I could see tears rolling down her face. That was the only time I ever saw my grandmother cry. Neither Tim nor I got spanked that day.

Eighteen

MANY YEARS LATER, WHEN I WAS GOING THROUGH MY
mother's papers, I found a letter that my grandmother had written
to her about the fire in the backroom.

> *Dear Susan,*
>
> *I am no longer able to take care of Bobby James and
> Billy. In the past two weeks, both boys have come very close
> to burning the house down. Although Bobby James is cur-
> rently at Mary Help a Christian School in Tampa, I know
> it is only a matter of time before he will run away from
> there again. I cannot control him, and most of the time I
> have no idea where he is. To make matters worse, you do
> not send any money for their support on any regular basis.
> At best, I may receive something from you once every three
> or four months that does not begin to cover what I have
> had to shell out for them.*
>
> *I cannot afford the expense of taking care of them.
> They are your children, you had them, and you need to
> take responsibility for them. This letter is to let you know
> that I am putting both of them on a bus and sending them
> to you in San Diego. By the time you get this letter, they
> will already be on their way to California. They will ar-
> rive in San Diego at 7:30 PM next Sunday evening. Please
> make arrangements to meet them at the bus station. I am*

loaning you the money for the cost of their tickets and
meals for this trip. I fully expect to be repaid.
        As always,
        I remain your mother.

It surprised me that Tim and I did not get spanked for burning a hole in the rug, but I was even more surprised two days later when my grandmother brought Bobby James back from Tampa and told the two of us that she was sending us to our mother in California. It was just her style to wait until the last minute to tell us kids anything of importance though.

"If you need to know," she would say, "I'll tell you when it's time. Until then, stop asking me."

"Grandma, when is it going to be my birthday?" one of us would ask.

"I'll tell you when it's time. Until then, stop asking me."

And the birthday would just arrive: one day, when you woke up in the morning, she might have a present for you; and at supper, she would sing happy birthday while you blew out the candles on a cake she had made while you were at school that day. Until that morning though, you would have no idea when your birthday was coming.

The presents were never very much. For one of my birthdays, she gave me a small package of figs. I loved that present because the figs, all four of them, were mine, and I didn't have to share them with anyone. Usually though, we just got a birthday cake and no presents.

It didn't bother us that we didn't get any presents. We didn't even know you were supposed to get presents for your birthday at first. We thought a cake was all you got, and we were happy with that. A cake was a real treat. My grandmother didn't believe in spending money on sweets and there were not many in the house. The ones we did have were for the adults, and they were counted.

There was no time to pester her for details after she told us she was sending my brother and me to California. She told us we were going, put us in the car, and off we went to the Greyhound Bus station in St. Petersburg.

The idea of a bus trip from St. Petersburg to San Diego was exciting. My grandmother had given my brother some money for food during the trip and warned him not to spend it on anything else. The trip would take five days, she told us. We would have to change buses several times, and the first time would be in Marietta, Georgia. My grandmother was a little worried about us having to change buses in various places that neither of us had ever seen or even heard of before, but my brother reminded her he was thirteen years old and could handle it without any problem.

"I'm sure you can Bobby James, but Billy is only five. I'm warning you," she said, pointing her finger at him, "you had better take care of him."

Before we knew it, it was time for us to leave. My grandmother spoke to the bus driver and asked him to look out for us. He promised to look after us on the way up to Marietta and said he would make sure we had seats on the very front row, directly opposite of him, where he could keep an eye on us. Finally she kissed us goodbye, admonished us not to talk to strangers, and reminded my brother one more time that the money she had given him was to be spent on food only. And on the bus we went.

Nineteen

I DON'T REMEMBER VERY MUCH ABOUT THE TRIP from St. Petersburg to Marietta. I just remember that we arrived in the middle of the night. It was dark in the terminal area where the busses were parked, and my brother took me by the hand as we wandered through the parking area, looking for our next bus. Finally he spotted it. He talked to the driver, who – as it turned out – already knew about us and had reserved the same two seats in the front row for us.

I was amazed that Bobby James was able to find the bus among all those other ones parked in the terminal. To me, the parking area was filled with noise and confusion. All the buses had their engines running and the area was filled with diesel smoke and fumes. But it smelled good to me. It was exciting.

I don't remember very much about the early part of the trip from Marietta either. I slept off and on, usually just watching the countryside slide by as the bus rolled along the highway. We drove along the beach for what seemed like hours, and I wondered how far the beach went.

"Bobby James, does the beach go all the way to California?" I asked.

"No, stupid. Pretty soon, we are going to be in Texas," he said. "Then we're going to see some mountains."

"What do the mountains look like?"

"You'll see. When we get to Mom's house in California, we'll climb a mountain together. She lives right next to one," he said.

Somewhere out in Texas, or maybe before we got to Texas, the beach disappeared and I began looking for the mountains. But it was just mile after mile of flat ground. The road looked as if it went on forever.

"When are we going to see the mountains?" I asked.

"Pretty soon," he said.

Twenty

THE BUS MADE PERIODIC STOPS SO PEOPLE COULD GET off, stretch their legs and go to the bathroom. In the afternoon, we stopped at a place to eat lunch. In 1945, there was no such thing as a McDonald's or any other fast food place. The closest thing was the diners where the buses usually stopped. The diners knew the bus schedules and were always ready to serve the meal of the day when the bus arrived. You couldn't get anything other than the meal the diner was serving that day, but the food was served relatively quickly so the bus did not have to stop for more than thirty minutes.

That afternoon, when we got to the lunch counter, I saw the plates they were serving had something on them that looked like roast beef, mashed potatoes and gravy, spinach, and a half of a canned peach. When I saw this, all I could think about was that peach half. It made my mouth water, and I decided that was what I wanted.

"How much is the plate?" Bobby James asked the man behind the counter.

"One dollar for the plate, sonny," the man answered.

"Can I just get some meat and potatoes on a small plate for my little brother?"

"I want one of those big plates," I told my brother.

"No, you don't," he said. "You won't eat it all."

"I can give you a plate with just mashed potatoes and meat for fifty cents," the man said.

"No, I want one of those big plates," I shouted.

"No, you don't," my brother shouted back at me.

"Yes, I do. I want one of those big plates with the peach on it," I shouted.

"Can you put a peach on it for my little brother?" Bobby James asked.

"I'll have to charge you the full dollar if I put a peach half on it," the man said.

"You're only going to get the meat and potatoes," my brother told me.

"No, no, no," I shouted. "I want the big plate with the peach on it!"

"Hurry up, sonny," the man behind the counter said to my brother. "I've got other people to serve."

"I want the big plate with the peach on it," I kept shouting over and over.

"No, you don't," my brother shouted back at me.

"Yes, I do," I screamed.

"Give your little brother what he wants to eat," someone shouted at my brother.

Everyone at the counter was now looking at Bobby James.

"Listen," he bent over and whispered in my ear, "you better eat everything on that plate, or I'm going to take you outside and beat the crap out of you. Do you hear me?"

I knew he wasn't kidding. He was mad at me for causing a scene and for making the adults at the counter take my side.

"Alright," he said to the man behind the counter, "give us two of the special plates."

"About time," the man said as he slid two plates toward us.

My brother glared at me. "You better eat it all."

I immediately ate the peach half and began to pick at the rest of the food. I didn't want any of it. I only wanted that peach; and once I had eaten it, I didn't care about anything else.

"Ten minutes," the bus driver shouted at us in the diner.

"Ten minutes," he repeated.

I still hadn't eaten anything else on my plate.

My brother punched me in the side. "Eat that goddamned food," he growled.

I said nothing and continued to pick at the stuff on my plate.

He punched me again, but I continued to pick.

"Five minutes," the bus driver shouted in the diner. "Five minutes. We leave in five minutes!"

"Eat your goddamned food," my brother growled again.

"I have to go to the bathroom," I said.

"No, you don't, because I'm going to beat the shit out of you right here." He hit me in the arm as hard as he could.

"Stop hitting me," I shouted, starting to cry. "I have to go to the bathroom."

Another punch in the side.

"Ouch," I screamed through my tears. "I have to go to the bathroom!"

"You better eat that food," my brother said in my ear. "It cost a dollar."

"I don't want to eat anymore. I have to go to the bathroom," I shouted, crying as loudly as I could.

A woman came over to my brother and grabbed him by the ear. "Young man, leave your little brother alone. Don't hit him like that," she said.

"I have to go to the bathroom," I said again.

"Now take your brother to the bathroom like a good boy," the woman told Bobby James.

"Come on," he said as he jerked me by the arm.

He dragged me into the bathroom and locked the door. "I told you I was going to beat the shit out of you if you didn't eat that food."

He began slugging me with his fists and kicking me in the shins. It hurt like hell, and I screamed for him to stop.

Suddenly, we heard the bus driver banging on the door. "Come out of there, boys. It's time to go. All aboard," he shouted.

When we came out of the bathroom, the woman who had told my brother to stop hitting me was standing right there. "Did you hit your little brother again while you were in the bathroom?" she demanded with a stern look.

"No, ma'am," my brother said. "He slipped on the wet floor and fell down, and I tried to help him."

She glared at him. "You better not have."

"Come on boys, get on the bus. Let's go," the driver said.

Once we were back on the bus and it had pulled out onto the road, my brother leaned over and whispered in my ear. "If you ever pull anything like that again, I'll kill you and leave your body stuffed in a toilet."

I believed him, and I knew that he would do exactly what he threatened to do. But I had gotten that half of peach and it had been delicious. I could still taste its sweet syrup on my lips. It was well worth the punches.

We rolled on across Texas and still there were no mountains. It was getting dark and I thought we should have seen them by now.

"When are we going to see the mountains, Bobby James," I asked.

"Shut up."

"But you said we were going to see mountains. When are we going to see them?" I persisted.

"I told you to shut up. Now, shut up."

"But —" An elbow hit me in the side, and I decided not to ask about the mountains for awhile. I know we stopped someplace to eat that night, but I don't remember what we ate. I'm sure a peach half was not included

Twenty-One

THE NEXT MORNING WE ARRIVED IN EL PASO AND I saw my first mountain. It wasn't very big, but it was a mountain. I was not as impressed with the mountain or its size as I was with the fact that it had a big white letter "A" painted on it near the top.

"Why does the mountain have an 'A' painted on it, Bobby James?"

"Shut up," he said.

"Do all mountains have an 'A' painted on them?" I asked.

"I don't know why it has an 'A' painted on it; and if you keep asking me, I'm going to beat the shit out of you. Now, shut up."

I fell silent for awhile and stared at the big white letter on the side of the mountain. The bus pulled into the terminal.

"Alright everyone, thirty minutes for breakfast," the driver announced. "Be back in thirty minutes or you'll be left behind."

"Can we climb that mountain, Bobby James?"

"No."

"Why not?"

"Because we only have thirty minutes, and it takes longer than thirty minutes to climb a mountain."

"When can we climb one?"

"When we get to California."

"When are we going to get to California?"

"I don't know."

"Will Mom be there when we get to California?"

"Yes. Now shut up and come on."

I watched the other passengers going to get their meal. "Are we going to eat breakfast?"

"No, and shut up I said. Now, come on."

I was confused. "Why aren't we going to eat breakfast? Where are we going?"

He turned and put his face as close to mine as he could. "I said shut up. If you open your mouth again, I'm going to put my foot in it. Do you understand?"

I nodded my head, and he turned and began walking toward some stores beside the terminal. One of the stores had a big sign shaped like a cowboy boot over the door. In we went.

"I want to buy a pair of cowboy boots," my brother told the man inside.

"Who are they for?" the man asked.

"Me. They're for me," my brother answered.

The man looked at my brother's feet and then disappeared into the back of the store. When he returned, he had a pair of brown leather boots with him. There was some fancy stitching on the sides that looked like a cactus.

"Try these on," he said. "They're Tony Lama's."

"How come Tony Lama doesn't want 'em anymore?" my brother asked.

"No, *Mijo*, these boots are made by Tony Lama. Very good boots."

"How much are they?" my brother asked.

"Twenty dollars."

I watched as my brother took some money out of his pocket and counted it. "I only have eighteen dollars," he said.

"Let me look at those boots again," the man said. He walked around my brother, looking down at his feet. "Oh, yes. I think I made a mistake, *Mijo*. These boots are eighteen dollars."

My brother gave him the eighteen dollars and we started to walk out of the store.

"Just a minute," the man said. "You forgot your shoes."

"Throw 'em out" my brother said. "I'm going to wear my boots."

And we left the store.

"Ten minutes," the bus driver was warning the other passengers.

"Are we going to eat breakfast?" I asked.

"No. Go to the bathroom," my brother answered.

"I don't have to go to the bathroom," I said, glaring at him. I was hungry, and I wanted to eat breakfast. I had been thinking about fried eggs and toast and bacon, like Grandma used to make. The more I thought about it, the hungrier I got.

"Listen, unless you want me to beat the shit out of you, go to the bathroom so we can get back on the bus."

As I started to turn to go to the bathroom, the bus driver called out. "Hey boys, I've been looking for you. Aren't you going to San Diego?"

"Yeah, we're going to San Diego," my brother answered.

"Well, you've been rerouted. You're going to have to change buses here, and catch the one over there for Albuquerque. I've already taken your bags off this here bus and moved them over to the Albuquerque bus. That's it over there, in lane five. It'll take you through Albuquerque, Santa Fe, Gallup and Kingman. You'll change buses again in Kingman for Yuma, and then on into San Diego. You better get moving, now."

"How come they rerouted us?" my brother asked.

"I have no idea, son," the bus driver said. "They don't tell me why. They just tell me. Here's your new ticket." He handed the tickets to my brother. "I've already talked to the Albuquerque driver, and he's got seats for you up front, just like you've had all along. I got to get now. Good luck, boys."

Twenty-Two

WHEN WE GOT ON THE BUS TO ALBUQUERQUE, WE both flopped down into our seats in the front row, just inside the door. There was a bar that ran across the top of the bulkhead that passengers could hold on to when they climbed up the steps to board the bus. As soon as we were on board, my brother propped his feet up on the bar and began admiring his new cowboy boots.

"How do you like 'em?" he asked me.

"They're nice," I said. "Can I get some the next time we stop?"

"No."

"Why not?"

"Because I said no."

"But why? If you got some, why can't I have some too?"

"I don't have any more money."

"None? You spent *all* our money?" I asked in amazement.

"Yeah."

"What will Grandma say? She's going to be really mad."

"Grandma isn't ever going to know."

"Yes, she will. She told you that money was for our food. She's going to be really mad, and we're going to get spanked." I began to cry. I knew we were in a lot of trouble.

"Grandma will never know what I spent the money on."

"Yes, she will," I said.

"No, she won't. She's in Florida, and we're going to California to see Mom. We will never see Grandma again, and she will never know that I spent the money on cowboy boots. Now, shut up."

"But what are we going to eat?" I cried.

"Don't worry about it. Just shut up."

I was worried, and I was hungry; but I was afraid to say anything more. I knew if I kept asking him about the money, he would punch me again.

Twenty-Three

AT NOON, WE STOPPED SOMEPLACE IN NEW MEXICO for lunch. I had no idea what we were going to do. Since we had no money and couldn't eat, I wanted to stay on the bus, but I also had to pee.

"Thirty minutes for lunch," the bus driver shouted. "Be back on the bus in thirty minutes or get left behind."

I sat there.

"Get off, stupid," my brother said, and kicked me in the leg with the toe of one of his new cowboy boots. "Let's go. We got to get something to eat, and I have to take a piss."

"How are we going to eat?" I asked.

"Come on. Get off." he kicked me again.

We got off the bus, and my brother went directly up to the woman who had grabbed him by the ear in the diner. "Excuse me, ma'am. Can you help us?"

"What's the problem, young man?" she asked with the sweetest smile and the kindest voice I had ever heard.

"When I went to the bathroom back in El Paso, I gave our money to my little brother to hold while I was inside, but he lost it. Now we don't have any money to buy something to eat."

"Why would you give your money to your little brother to hold?" she asked.

"Because I was afraid someone might rob me if they saw me in the bathroom alone. You know, me being just a kid and all. So I told my little brother to hold it, but then he lost it. I think he must have pulled it out of his pocket by mistake."

"Oh, you poor boys," she said. "Come with me, and I'll buy you boys some lunch."

My brother looked back at me. "Come on," he said. "This nice lady is going to buy us some lunch." And he gave me a big wink.

When we got inside the diner, he said, "We have to go to the bathroom. We'll be right back."

"Okay," she said. "I'll save two seats."

As soon as my brother and I were in the bathroom, he said, "You better not tell her I spent all our money on these boots. If she asks, you stick with my story about losing it while I was in the bathroom. Do you understand?"

"But I didn't lose our money," I said.

"If you don't want me to beat the shit out of you, you better tell her you lost our money. Do you understand?"

"Yes."

"Good, now hurry up and take a piss so we can eat."

When we came out of the bathroom, we found the lady sitting at the counter. She had saved us each a seat, one on either side of her, as she had promised.

"Jump up here, boys, and let's get you some lunch. I'm Miss Priscilla Adams. What are your names?"

"I'm Bobby James, and this is my little brother, Billy."

"How far are you boys going?" she asked.

"We're going to see our mother in San Diego," my brother said.

"Oh, you poor boys," she said. "You're going all the way to San Diego and you don't have any more money for food? How will you eat?"

"I don't know," my brother said. He began to cry. I had never seen my brother cry before, not even when my grandmother spanked him, no matter how hard she hit him with her stick.

"Oh, now, now," the woman soothed. "Don't cry. I don't have much money, but I'm sure I can find enough so you boys will have something to eat until we get to San Diego. I'm going there too. When we get there, your mother can repay me," she said.

My brother and I ate our lunch in silence while the lady kept telling us how brave we were to make such a long trip all by ourselves.

"Five minutes! Five minutes, folks. The bus leaves in five minutes," the driver called out to everyone in the diner.

When we got back into our seats on the bus, the woman leaned over and kissed each of us on the top of the head. "Now, whenever we stop for meals, you boys just come and find me, and I'll make sure you get something to eat. It won't be much, but at least you won't go hungry." She smiled at us and moved toward the back to her seat.

My brother put his feet up on the rail again in front of our seats to admire his boots. I think he thought it made him look like a tough guy, to prop his feet up there on the rail. I was sleepy, but just as I was about to nod off, I heard a gruff voice say, "Take your feet off the bar, son. That's not what it's for."

We had changed drivers, and this one didn't seem as friendly as the others. My brother didn't move his feet; he just stared out the window and acted like he hadn't heard what the driver had said.

"I said, take your feet off the bar, son. That's not what it's for."

"What's it for?" my brother asked.

"Don't sass me, boy. Take your feet down like I told you."

"Just tell me what it's for, if it's not to put my feet on," my brother said.

"Son, put your feet down now, or I'll put you off the bus right here. This is the last time I'm telling you."

My brother took his feet off the rail and put them on the floor.

The driver glared at him and then got behind the wheel and pulled out onto the road. I was relieved. What if the driver had made my brother get off the bus? What would I do? How would

I know when I got to San Diego? I didn't even know where San Diego was. And how would I find my mother? I didn't even know what she looked like. I was glad Bobby James had put his feet down so he could stay on the bus. I just hoped he wouldn't put them on the rail again. I didn't want to be left alone.

Twenty-Four

AS WE DROVE UP THROUGH SANTA FE AND GALLUP, New Mexico, the mountains became much bigger and more beautiful than anything I could have imagined. They were different colors – brown and red and orange and purple – with long shadows that fell across the ground as the sun moved across the sky toward sunset. I kept looking to see if any of the mountains had an "A" painted on them, but none did. I was glad. Some of the mountains were very high, and others were long and flat. The bus driver told me the long flat ones were called *mesas*. He said it was a Spanish word that meant table. I agreed: they did look a lot like my grandmother's table in the backroom.

As the sun began to set, the sky began to turn a bright orange. I watched the mountains with the orange sky behind them and dreamed I was a cowboy, riding my pony across the mesas and down the copper colored canyons and out across the desert, among the cactus and the sage brush plants. I thought of how free that life would be. I thought the view I was seeing from the bus was the most beautiful sight I had ever seen, and I wanted it to last forever.

But I knew it was foolish for me to wish that it could last. My grandmother had told me that nothing lasts forever when I had asked her how old I was once. It had been raining, and my cousin and I were playing in the backroom since we couldn't go outside.

It wasn't raining hard, just a constant drizzle. The air was cool, and it was comfortable inside the house. It felt so good, because the weather had been so hot until the rain came and cooled things off. My grandmother had let us use some of the footstools and the chairs from the table to build a fort in the house. We had stacked them up against the credenza and could go underneath them or climb on top without getting in any trouble.

The rain was beating on the roof, and I could look outside and see huge puddles forming in the back yard. I knew the rain was going to last for a long time, and that I could play in the house all day, climbing on the stools and chairs with my grandmother's permission. I felt good.

"How old am I, Grandma?" I asked.

"You're four years old. Why do you want to know?" she asked.

"This is the best day of my life. I wish I could stay four years old forever."

"That's pretty stupid. Why would you want to stay the same age forever?"

"Because then I could always play with the stools and chairs and stack them and climb on them. And I would always be nice and cool like I am today," I answered.

"What makes you think every day would be just like this if you stayed four years old forever?"

"I'm really happy today. If I stayed four years old, wouldn't everyday be the same? Just like this one? Wouldn't I be happy?" I asked.

"Nothing stays the same. Everything changes, and no one is happy forever. You need to stop dreaming and start living in the real world."

"Oh," I said.

I wasn't really sure why each day couldn't be the same and stay just like this one: nice and cool and rainy. I didn't really understand why she was so sure things couldn't stay the same. Suddenly I wasn't quite as happy as I had been before I had asked how old

I was. I realized she was right. Her answer had changed things. I didn't quite understand how, but they had changed.

But had they? Or had something been taken from me? A cloud had descended upon me, because I knew I was going to have to take the fort apart, and put the chairs and stools back where they came from, and that the fort wouldn't be there tomorrow. The rain, the cool air and the cozy feeling would be gone, too. I no longer felt good. I felt sad. There was no point in wishing for anything.

As I rode along looking out from the window of the bus, I knew it was foolish of me to wish that I could be a cowboy and ride along those beautiful mesas and canyons and out into the desert to be forever free. Somehow I knew, without knowing how I knew, that I would never be free. Tears rolled down my face.I wanted my mother.

"We'll be passing near the Grand Canyon later this evening," the driver said. Then he added, "But you won't be able to see it."

"What's the Grand Canyon?" my brother asked.

"Well, you see those cliffs and canyons off to the right?" the driver asked.

"Yeah," my brother answered.

"Well, it's a lot like those, only it must be a hundred times wider and deeper. It's the largest canyon in the world."

"Wow," I said. "I wish we could see it. Why can't we see it?"

"Well, the road we are driving on doesn't go directly by the Grand Canyon. It's further off to the right, maybe fifty miles away. And even if we *were* on the road that goes right by it, I would still have to stop the bus so you could go to the edge and look down into it. It goes way down into the ground. I think there's a river at the bottom of it, but I can't remember the name of it."

I was trying to picture in my mind what the Grand Canyon looked like. All I could envision was a big hole with water in the bottom of it.

"It's a beautiful sight to see," he continued. "I saw it once, years ago before the war. It changes colors during the day and especially around this time of night, when the sun begins to set."

As hard as I tried, I could not figure out how a big hole in the ground could change colors. But the mesas and cliffs I saw from the bus were changing colors as the sun set. Maybe it was like that, although it was hard to figure out how all these mesas and cliffs could be down in a hole.

The road became very winding as we went through the mountains and it began to get dark. The bus driver was driving slowly as he went around every curve to make sure there were no oncoming cars on his side of the road.

"Why are we driving so slowly?" I asked the driver.

"I don't want to go over the side of one of these cliffs and kill us all," he said. "People are always going too fast on these curves; the next thing they know, they've lost control of their car and they plunge over the side and kill themselves."

"Did you ever see anyone go over the side?" my brother asked.

"Well, I ain't never seen anyone actually go over, but I've come along many times after it's already happened, and I seen their car burning down there at the bottom."

"Do you think we'll get to see anyone's car burning down in the bottom of one of these canyons tonight?" my brother asked.

"I hope not," the bus driver said.

We continued along at a very slow pace as the bus driver carefully made his way around every curve. I think I must have dozed off at some point, because I was suddenly being punched by my brother.

"Look," he said excitedly. "Look down there. There's a car burning in the canyon."

I looked out the window to where he was pointing and saw a fire burning below us. "What's burning?" I asked, rubbing sleep from my eyes.

"A car went over the side," my brother said excitedly.

"Did it just go over?" I asked.

"Must have been earlier," the driver said. "The police are already here."

There were one or two cars ahead of us, and each one stopped to talk to the policeman directing traffic on the road. He seemed to motion them along without answering their questions. Eventually our bus came up to where the policeman was standing and the driver stopped.

"Evening, officer. Anyone killed?" the driver asked.

"Don't know. Don't have the equipment to get down there yet. But I doubt anyone is alive. It looks like there's one body lying about ten feet away from the car. Must have been thrown out on impact. Hard to say in the dark. Just guessing from what we can see in the lights from the passing cars. Move it along now."

"Good night, officer," the bus driver said as he shifted, and we felt the strain on the gears as the bus lurched forward to continue our climb up the mountain road again. "Now you see why I'm driving so slow in these here mountains, don't you boys?"

"I wish we could have gotten out to see if there were any dead bodies," my brother said.

I felt very sad for whoever was in that car when it went over the side. It seemed hard to believe someone might be dead back there. I hoped there were no children in the car. I didn't want to die. I thought about all the beautiful and neat things I had seen on this trip, and I wanted to tell my mother about them when I saw her. If I were dead, I wouldn't be able to see her. I began to cry. What if I never got to see my mother? What if I never got to see what she looked like? I would be dead, and there wouldn't be anything she could do for me. She wouldn't even know where I was if the bus went over the side and crashed and I got killed. I started to sob out loud, and my brother punched me in the side.

"Shut up," he said. "Quit your damn crying."

The bus driver turned around and looked at us. "What are you boys doing? Are you hitting your brother, son?"

"No, sir. I don't know why he's crying. He's just a big baby. He cries all the time."

"Well, you boys better behave yourselves. I got enough to worry about while I'm driving in these here mountains without having to worry about what you two are doing. Do you hear me?"

"Yes, sir," my brother said. Then he leaned over to me and said, "Shut your mouth and stop crying before you get us in trouble."

I managed to stop crying, but I still felt very sad. Who was in that car, I wondered. I fell asleep trying to imagine what I would look like if I were dead.

I was awakened by the bus driver shouting. It was light outside and the bus had stopped.

"Kingman! Kingman, Arizona. Anybody for Kingman, Arizona, this is where you get off," he shouted. "Change buses here for Yuma. For the rest of you folks going to Los Angeles, you got thirty minutes to use the john and eat your breakfast. Thirty minutes!"

Twenty-Five

MY BROTHER AND I WERE THE FIRST ONES OFF THE bus. It felt good to be able to walk around. There were a few mountains in the distance, but nothing like I expected. "Where are the mountains?" I asked the driver.

"We left 'em behind in the night, son," he said. "For the next eight hours, you're going to be going through the desert. Nothing out there to see 'cept sand, some sage brush and lots of cactus."

The woman who had grabbed my brother by the ear back at the diner in Texas got off the bus, raised her arms high above her head as she stretched and then came over to us. "You boys go on in and use the bathroom, and I'll save you two stools at the counter so we can get some breakfast. We'll have to hurry, because we have to change buses here for Yuma."

I was hungry and breakfast sounded great to me. I could just see those scrambled eggs with toast and bacon in my mind. My mouth began to water.

"Come on," my brother said. "I'll race you to the bathroom." He took off running, and I followed.

Once we were out of earshot, I asked, "What's that woman's name who's buying our meals?"

"I don't know, Miss Priscilla something or other."

"Do you know her?" I asked.

"No, stupid. I never saw her before she grabbed me by the ear when you made a stink about that plate with the peach on it."

"Then how did you know she would buy our meals for us?"

"I didn't, but since she was alone, I thought I would ask her before anyone else."

"How did you know she would buy food for us though?"

"I *didn't* know for sure, but any other time I've pretended not to have any money, someone always took pity on me. The poor little boy with no money ... It works every time."

We finished in the bathroom and ran to the diner to meet Miss Priscilla and get some breakfast. I could hardly wait. When we got inside, she waved us over. I ran up to her and jumped onto one of the stools beside her.

"Did you boys wash your hands before leaving the bathroom?" she asked.

I started to tell her that no, we had forgotten, but my brother answered first.

"Yes, ma'am," he said quickly.

"Good. I hope you boys like creamed chipped beef on toast. Doesn't it look good? This will really hold us until lunch time."

I hardly heard anything she was saying. I was too disappointed to listen. I looked at the plate in front of me. "Where are the eggs and bacon?" I asked.

"Too hard to get eggs," she said. "They're still rationed. But this chipped beef will do fine. It looks delicious. Eat up, boys. We only have a little time before the bus leaves. We don't want to get left here in Kingman, now, do we?"

She sounded so cheerful, but I was miserable. I knew I couldn't eat that stuff. It looked like someone had vomited on a piece of toast, and it was making me feel sick. I gagged a little.

"What's wrong, little boy?" Miss Priscilla asked.

"I feel sick," I said.

"Oh, you poor thing. It must be all those hours on the bus. I know that must be hard on you."

"I think I'm going to throw up," I said.

"Listen, kid," the man behind the counter shouted. "If you're gonna puke, go outside and do it."

I looked up at him over the pile on my plate and started gagging again.

"I said, if you're gonna puke, get outside!" he shouted again and took my plate away. "I don't want you puking on my counter. Get outta here."

My brother was glaring at me, and I knew he was wondering how he was going to get out of eating the mess on his plate, too. As I jumped off the stool and ran towards the door, I heard my brother say, "I better go check on him. I think he's sick."

"You get outta here too, kid," the man behind the counter shouted at him.

We both ran outside and stood alone by one of the buses.

"That stuff was awful looking," my brother said.

"I really was going to throw up," I said.

"Too bad you didn't puke in your plate," my brother said, laughing. "They could have served it again to someone else. No one would ever have known the difference."

"What are we going to do, Bobby James? I'm still hungry and we don't have any money."

"Bend over and pretend you're puking," he said.

"Why?"

"Just do it."

I bent over and coughed as if I were puking while he patted me on the back.

"Here comes Miss Priscilla," he said. "Just keep pretending like you're puking."

I stayed bent over and kept coughing and gagging.

"How's your little brother, son?" I heard her ask as she approached us.

"I think he's going to be okay," my brother said. "I guess this long bus trip is too much just before you eat. You know, with us having to always hurry and eat and all."

"Oh, you poor boys," she said. "I know what you mean. Your stomach can get so upset when you have to ride in a car or a bus or train for a long time."

"Yes, ma'am. But I think he's going to be okay now," my brother said.

"I'm so sorry you boys didn't get a chance to eat. Are you still hungry?"

"Yes, ma'am, but we can wait 'til lunch time," my brother said.

"Listen, I have an orange I've been saving, but I'll give it to you, if you want it. Would you like to have it? You'll have to split it between you. I only have one."

"Yes, ma'am, we would," my brother said. "I'm sure it will make my little brother feel better. I can peel it for us."

"Okay then, just let me dig it out of my bag."

She rummaged around in the brown paper bag she was carrying and took out the orange. "Here you are boys. Now be sure and split it equally between the two of you."

She handed it to Bobby James and then smiled before turning to make her way back to the bus. My brother took the orange and began to peel it, throwing the peels on the ground.

"Pick up those peels and put them in the trash can over there, son. And don't throw anymore on the ground." We turned around. It was the bus driver.

"Yes, sir," my brother said and began picking up the peels. He walked over to the trash can and finished peeling the orange as he stood in front of it. On the way back to where I waited, he tore off pieces of the orange and popped them into his mouth. I watched as he ate the entire orange.

"How come you didn't save me any?" I cried.

"You were sick, and I didn't want you puking on the bus."

"I was not sick," I shouted at him.

"Shut up, you want to get us in trouble with Miss Pris? If you make her mad, she won't buy us anymore meals," he said.

I didn't want to make her mad, but I was hungry – and *I* was mad. "That was mean," I said. "I wanted some of that orange too."

"Here, you can smell my fingers," he said. "They smell like oranges."

He stuck his hands under my nose and I shoved them away.

"You're selfish," I shouted at him with tears in my eyes from anger. I think he was about to punch me, but just then two sailors who were also traveling to San Diego on the bus came up laughing. One of them slapped us both on the back. "You boys couldn't eat that SOS, eh?"

"What's SOS?" my brother asked.

"Shit on a shingle," the other answered, laughing. "The Navy serves it every morning for breakfast. It looks God awful, but it really ain't that bad, once you get used to it."

"It looks like somebody puked on a piece of toast," I said.

The sailors laughed again. One of them tousled my hair as he climbed aboard the bus.

A new bus driver followed them. "Come on boys, get aboard," he called. "We gotta get on the road."

Bobby James and I followed him onto the bus, and I slid into the seat by the window. To keep the hunger pains and my anger from making me cry, I looked out the window and tried to enjoy the scenery as we rolled down the highway. But there wasn't much to see. It was just sand and cactus, the way our last driver had said it would be.

My brother tested the new driver by putting his feet up on the railing in front of our seats.

"Nice boots, young man. Where'd you get 'em?" the driver asked.

"Got 'em in El Paso," my brother answered.

"Pretty proud of 'em, aren't you?" the driver said.

"Yep, I love 'em," my brother said.

"Well, if you want to keep 'em, you better take your feet off the rail."

My brother took his feet down immediately and said nothing.

"Are there any Indians out there?" I asked the driver.

"Oh, no, I don't think so," he said. "Not much of anything can live out there, 'cept snakes and lizards. It gets pretty hot during the day and pretty cold at night. Not much protection from the sun. No, I don't think you'll find any Indians out there."

"I heard Indians can live anywhere," my brother said.

"Well, maybe they can, but I bet it would be pretty tough going out there in this desert," the driver said.

Late in the afternoon, we stopped at a little diner in the middle of nowhere for lunch. The building was a light tan color from the dust that completely covered it. There was a wind blowing sand across the road and tumbleweeds rolled around the parking area where the bus stopped. The sand stung my face and I had to keep my head down to keep it out of my eyes.

"Over there on the right is the old wooden highway," the driver told the passengers. "The early settlers built that highway out of wood so they could cross these here dunes without getting their covered wagons stuck in the sand."

"Pretty smart idea, if you ask me," someone said.

"When are we going to get to San Diego?" my brother asked.

"We'll be there around eight o'clock this evening," the driver answered.

"Does that mean we'll see Mom tonight?" I asked my brother.

"Yep," he answered.

"How will we find her?" I asked.

"She's supposed to meet us when the bus gets in," he said.

"Do you know what Mom looks like?" I asked.

"Of course I know what mom looks like, stupid. Don't you?"

"No," I said. "Tell me what she looks like."

"She's really pretty, like a movie star," he said. "And she's really smart, too."

"I don't know what she looks like," I said.

"Sure you do. You've seen her."

"I know I've seen her, but it was a long time ago, and I can't remember what she looks like. She didn't come to see us at Grandma's house very much. Do you know why she stopped coming to see us?"

"She's busy. I think she has a job where she has to work all the time, so she couldn't come to see us very much."

"Why does she have to work?" I asked.

"Everyone has to work, stupid."

"Grandma and Grandpa don't work."

"Sometimes they do. Grandpa still has to work in Knoxville, and when he's home at Grandma's house he's always working around the house, building something or repairing things. You know, like that fence he's always rebuilding over by the Hudson's place."

I thought about that for a moment. "Why doesn't Grandma have to work anymore?"

"Because she's retired."

"What does retired mean?"

"It means you don't have to work anymore. Now shut up."

I wondered why my mother had to work and couldn't come to see me. I wondered what she looked like, and whether or not I would recognize her at the bus station. Maybe she wouldn't recognize me either.

After we finished eating, we got back on the bus. I was glad to get away from the diner. The wind blew dust and sand everywhere. It was all over the inside of the diner and even in the stew we had for lunch. The sand crunched in my teeth when I ate, but I didn't care. I was hungry and the stew tasted good.

Even Miss Priscilla got sand in her teeth. "My, my," she said cheerfully. "It looks like we got a little something extra with our lunch today, doesn't it, boys?"

I heard Bobby James groan. I don't think he liked Miss Pris, as he called her.

Twenty-Six

I LISTENED TO THE RHYTHM OF THE WHEELS ON THE road as the bus rolled across the desert, and at some point I fell asleep. I don't know how long I slept, but it seemed like only a few minutes before I felt my brother hitting me in the side with his fist.

"Wake up, stupid," he said. "We're here."

"Where are we?"

"San Diego, dip shit."

"Is Mom here?"

"I don't know. We have to go inside the terminal and see if she's there."

"What does she look like?" I asked.

"Quit asking me that. You'll see when we get inside."

"San Diego, San Diego. This is San Diego. Change buses here for all other destinations," Our driver sang out the information in a musical rhythm.

I could hardly wait to see my mother. I jumped off the bus and took off across the parking area toward the doors of the terminal with my brother right behind me.

"Slow down there, boys, before you fall and hurt yourselves," a passing bus driver cautioned us.

As soon as we got inside the terminal, Bobby James ran toward a woman I did not recognize and hugged her. She must be our mother, I thought. Then, as I looked at her, I *did* recognize her, and she was beautiful. But I couldn't run to her. I don't know why. I just stood there, staring at her, thinking how beautiful she was. For some reason, I wanted to cry. A very lonely feeling for my grand-mother swept over me, and I wished that she was there with me.

My mother came over to me, smiling. She stooped down in front of me and took me in her arms, and then she hugged me tighter than I had ever been hugged before in my life. Even when Johnny Wilson got me in a bear hug, it wasn't as tight as my moth-er was holding me. She smelled so good. I buried my face between her shoulder and neck, and I could smell her perfume. It was deli-cious. I was so glad to see her that I didn't want to let go of her. I wanted to stay there with my head on her shoulder and hug her forever.

Finally, she released me and stood up. "Let's get your suitcase, and then we'll take a cab to the hotel."

"What's a hotel?" I asked.

"It's a very tall building where we are living," she answered.

"Does it have a yard to play in," I asked.

She smiled. "There's a park that's like a huge yard you can play in, right across the street."

"Is there a mountain we can climb?" my brother asked.

"Well, there aren't any mountains close to the hotel, but there are some hills in the park across the street with lots of trees you can climb."

While we were waiting for our suitcase, Miss Priscilla Adams came over and introduced herself to my mother. "You certainly have two beautiful boys," she said extending her hand to my moth-er. "They're real gentlemen. I'm Miss Priscilla Adams. I met your two fine boys on the bus. It seems they had a little accident in El Paso and lost all their food money."

My mother was taken by surprise, but she took Miss Priscilla's extended hand and shook it. "You say they lost their food money?" she asked.

"Yes. I guess your older boy gave it to his little brother to hold so he wouldn't get robbed while he was in the bathroom," Miss Adams laughed.

My mother turned to give my brother a skeptical glance.

"Your little one must have accidentally pulled it out of his pocket and lost it someplace," Miss Adams continued. "I've been buying their meals for them."

"Oh," my mother said, "how much do I owe you for your kindness?"

"Well, I really hate to ask to be repaid, but I'm traveling on very limited funds myself."

"No, no, not at all," my mother answered. "It was very kind of you to help them. How much do I owe you?"

"Well, ten dollars should cover it," Miss Adams answered.

"Are you sure ten dollars is enough?"

"Oh, yes, ten dollars will cover it nicely," Miss Adams said shyly. "I really hate to ask you for it."

"Nonsense," my mother replied. "Thank you so much for helping them." She opened her purse and took out a ten dollar bill and handed it to Miss Priscilla.

"Well, goodbye boys, it was a pleasure to meet you." She bent down, kissed us both on the forehead and walked away.

Bobby James grabbed our suitcase and we all piled in a cab for the ride to the hotel. "Can we have something to eat when we get to the hotel?" I asked.

"Yes, you can. You can have anything you want," she said.

"Can we have some ice cream and a peanut butter sandwich?" my brother asked.

"Yes, you can. And we have lots of milk and bread and eggs. I'll fix you anything you want."

I was so happy I didn't know what to say.

"Can we go to the park tomorrow?" my brother asked.

"You and Billy can go to the park and play all day, if you want."

"Will you come with us?" I asked.

"No, honey, I have to go to work; but you can spend the day at the park, and we'll play together when I come home from work. How does that sound?"

"Oh boy, I can hardly wait," I said.

"Me, either," Bobby James said.

When we got to the hotel, my mother paid the cab driver, and my brother and I ran inside laughing and shouting.

"Where's our room?" we shouted together.

"Shh shh, you can't yell like that in the hotel," she said. "It disturbs the other guests."

I didn't see how we could disturb anyone. The place was loud and filled with soldiers, sailors and lots of other people. Everyone seemed to be talking at once in loud voices. But we were excited and could hardly contain ourselves. It was hard to be quiet. When we got to the room, we bolted inside and ran all around looking at everything. There was a small kitchen; a large living room with a table and chairs and a couch; a bathroom; and another room with the door closed.

"Don't open the door to the other room, boys," my mother called to us.

Bobby James and I ran to the kitchen and opened the refrigerator.

"Can we have some milk and a peanut butter and jelly sandwich right now?" I asked.

"Yes, you may," she said. "I'll fix it for you."

"Where do we sleep, Mom?" My brother asked.

"You and Billy can sleep together on the couch. It opens out into a bed. I'll make it up for you while you're eating."

She made us sandwiches and poured us each a big glass of milk. We sat at a small table in the living room near the couch. As we ate, she began unfolding the couch into a bed. The blankets and sheets were in a closet. As she was getting them out, my brother and I started laughing and jumping on the bed.

"Susan, can't you keep those brats of yours quiet?" someone shouted from the room with the closed door.

"Who's that?" I asked.

"It's Frank, isn't it?" my brother asked.

"Susan, I'm trying to sleep!" the voice shouted again.

"It *is* Frank," my brother said.

"Try to quiet down a little, boys, so he can get some sleep," she whispered. "I'll make up the bed, and when you have finished your sandwhiches, you can crawl in. I know you must be tired."

"Why are you whispering, Mom?" I asked.

"Because she's afraid of Frank," my brother said.

"Who's Frank?" I asked.

"He's a drunk," my brother said.

"Alright now, boys, your bed is all made up. Get your clothes off and hop in," she whispered with a smile.

We jumped into bed, and she bent down and gave us each a kiss. Then she turned out the light and disappeared into the other room. As soon as she closed the door behind her, Bobby James jumped out of bed.

"I'm hungry," he said. "Let's finish eating our sandwhiches."

"Who is Frank?" I asked my brother, following him out of bed.

"I said, he's a drunk," my brother answered with some agitation in his voice.

"Is he our father?"

"He may be your father, but he ain't mine," he said firmly.

"How do I know if he's my father?"

"Ask Mom."

"Where is your father?"

He shrugged. "I don't know. Mom divorced him a few years ago."

"What does divorce mean?"

"It means they aren't married anymore."

We wolfed down the rest of our sandwhiches, finished drinking our milk, and got back in bed.

"Are Mom and Frank married?"

"I don't know," he said irritably. "Ask Mom. Now go to sleep and leave me alone."

I could tell he was angry about something, but I didn't know what it was.

"What's a drunk?" I asked.

"It's someone who drinks too much whiskey."

"Why?"

"Why what?"

"Why do they drink too much whiskey?"

"I don't know. Mom said they have an illness or something," he said.

"Is Mom a doctor?"

"No, she's not. Why?"

"Well, if your father was a drunk and Frank is a drunk, and if it's an illness, maybe she's trying to make them all well again," I said.

"Go to sleep," my brother said and rolled over with his back to me.

Twenty-Seven

I LAY THERE IN THE DARK, TRYING TO UNDERSTAND what a drunk was and what kind of illness made people drink too much whiskey, and why my mother wanted to make them well again. Soon my thoughts drifted to other things. I began wondering what the park looked like. I wanted to go play there tomorrow and maybe go to the zoo. My mother told us in the cab there was a zoo in the park. Pretty soon I felt as though I were drifting and floating through the park, and I could see all the animals in the zoo, and I was asking my mother if I could pet them and she said yes.

"Get your hands off me and go to sleep," my brother murmured through a sleepy haze.

"I'm sorry," I said. "I thought I was petting the animals at the zoo. Can we go there tomorrow, Bobby James?"

"Yeah, we can go there. Now shut up and go to sleep before I smack you."

I began drifting off to sleep and soon I was dreaming again. My mother was happy to see me, and she was hugging me, and I could smell her perfume and was hugging her back. And then we were floating together and laughing. Then she began to float away from me, and I couldn't see her face again. I reached for her, but she was too far away for me to touch. I kept trying to remember her face, but I couldn't. All I could see was her back.

"Billy. Billy, wake up. It's time to get up." It was my mother, gently shaking me.

As I opened my eyes, I could see her face, and I wrapped my arms around her and hugged her tightly. "You're still here," I said.

"Of course, I'm still here. Where else would I be?" she laughed. "Are you hungry for breakfast?"

"Yeah. Can I have eggs and bacon and toast?" I asked.

"You sure can. I'll start frying the eggs while you go wash your face in the bathroom and get dressed. And don't go into the bedroom with the closed door," she said.

"Is Frank asleep in there?"

"Yes, and you mustn't wake him up."

"Is he a drunk?"

"Whatever gave you that idea?"

"Bobby James said he was a drunk, like his father."

"Well, you mustn't believe everything your brother tells you," she said.

"Is Frank my father?"

"You can call him Daddy if you wish. I'm sure he won't mind. Do you want to call him Daddy?"

"Okay. I don't know. I guess so."

I really wasn't sure how I felt about calling whoever was in that room Daddy. I had never even seen him, and I had never called anyone Daddy before. I just had a grandmother and a grandfather, my mother, Bobby James and my cousin, Tim. I knew the other kids had daddies though. Some of them had been killed in the war, and they weren't at home anymore. I always thought my daddy had been killed in the war, since I never saw him.

"Was my daddy killed in the war?" I asked.

"Oh, you have so many questions, don't you? Why don't you go wash your face and hands? When you get back, I'll have your breakfast ready. How's that?"

"Okay. Where's Bobby James?" I asked. "He didn't go to the park without me, did he?"

"No, of course not. I sent him down to the lobby to get a newspaper," she said.

"What's the lobby?"

"Do you remember that big room downstairs that we first came into when we got to the hotel last night? It had all those nice men in uniforms to help carry your suitcase?"

"I guess so."

I didn't remember anyone carrying our suitcase. But there were a lot of people walking around when we first got to the hotel. I guess that was the room she was talking about. "I remember," I said.

"Well, that's the lobby, and they have a stand where they sell newspapers. Bobby James has gone down to buy a newspaper for me. Frank likes to read it with his coffee when he wakes up."

"Is Frank— I mean, Daddy, going to the park with us today?"

"No, he won't wake up for awhile, yet."

"Are you going to the park?" I asked.

"Oh, no, honey. You remember, I told you last night I have to go to work? But I'll go downstairs with you and show you how to get to the park. You can play over there all day, until I come home from work tonight. How's that sound?"

"Okay, I guess. Does… Daddy have to go to work too?"

"Well, not today. He's on leave right now."

"What does that mean?"

"It means he has a few days to rest up before he has to go back to the war."

"Is he fighting the Japs in the war?"

"Well, he hasn't done any fighting yet, but he is going to soon."

"Why does he have to go fight in the war?"

"Oh, sweetheart, you have so many questions. Now run and wash up while I fix breakfast. We have to hurry or I'm going to be late for work."

"Okay."

I went looking for the bathroom, but I opened the door to the bedroom by mistake.

"Shut the *goddamned* door," a voice roared from inside the room.

I nearly jumped out of my skin and slammed the door shut.

My mother came running over to me in the hall. "Honey, you mustn't go in the bedroom when your daddy is sleeping. It makes him mad if you wake him up."

"I'm sorry," I said and began to cry.

"Oh, honey, don't cry. I know you didn't mean to wake him up. Come on now, this door is to the bathroom." She steered me to the next door. "I'll get you a wash cloth and towel."

When I finished washing, I went back into the kitchen where my mother had breakfast ready. The eggs and bacon smelled so good, my mouth began to water. My brother was already sitting at the table, drinking out of his cereal bowl.

"Don't drink out of the bowl, Bobby James. Use your spoon," my mother told him.

"Yes, Mom," he said and set the bowl down on the table.

"Here's your breakfast, Billy," she said.

"Can I have orange marmalade on my toast?" I asked.

"I don't have any marmalade," she said, "but I have some grape jelly. How's that?"

"Okay, I guess. I never tasted grape jelly before," I said.

"I'm sure you'll like it," she said. "Now you boys finish eating while I go and finish dressing for work." She walked toward the bedroom. "When you're finished, just put your dishes in the sink," she said over her shoulder.

I was expecting the voice from the room to yell at her when she opened the bedroom door, but no sound came out of there.

"Are you ready to go to the park and climb some trees?" my brother asked.

"Yeah," I said. "Are there any mountains in the park?"

"I don't think so. Mom said there were only hills there, but we can look and see."

"I want to go to the zoo, too," I said. "I want to pet the animals."

"You can't pet the animals in the zoo, stupid."

"Why not?"

"Because they are in cages and you're not allowed near them. They'll chew your hand off if you try to pet them."

"What kind of animals do they have?"

"All kinds. Lions and tigers and bears and zebras and elephants. All kinds."

I finished my breakfast. They were the best eggs and bacon I had ever eaten. My mother had cooked them for me, and I was happy. When she came out of the bedroom, she was all dressed for work and she had flowers in her hair.

"Why do you have flowers in your hair?" I asked.

"Do you like them?" she asked.

"Yeah. Are they real flowers?"

"No, they're not real, but I think they look nice. It's a little something different," she said.

"Can we go now, Mom?" my brother asked.

"We're ready," she said. "Did you boys go to the bathroom?"

"Yes," we both lied.

"Okay then, let's go."

As we left the room, my brother ran down the hall to the elevator and pushed the button. In a few minutes, a bell sounded and the elevator doors opened. There was a colored man, as black as Crystal, dressed in a black uniform and a white shirt and a black bowtie. He pulled the inside door of the elevator open for us and we all got in. I had never seen a colored man dressed so nicely before.

"Good morning, Joseph," my mother said to him.

"Good morning, Miss Susan. These here your children you been telling me was coming to see you?"

"Yes, they are. The little one is Billy and this is Bobby James."

"Good morning boys," Joseph said.

I couldn't speak. I was still in awe of a colored man in such a nice suit.

"You kinda shy, ain't you, boy?" Joseph smiled at me with perfect white teeth.

I didn't answer and I didn't move. I couldn't.

"They're going to the park to play today," my mother told him.

"That's real nice. You boys'll have a lot of fun over there," he said.

The elevator stopped with a slight jolt.

"First floor and lobby," Joseph sang out as he opened the door for us. "You have a nice day today, Miss Susan. And you boys have a good time in the park."

We filed out of the elevator and followed our mother into the lobby. I looked back and noticed the door to the elevator was still open, and Joseph was sitting on a stool, waiting for someone to ring for the car. He winked at me and smiled. For some reason, I couldn't wave or smile back. I just stared.

"Okay, boys, I'm going to give you fifty cents to spend at the park. Bobby James, you keep it in your pocket and make sure you share with Billy. This is to get something to eat and a soda." She took two quarters out of her purse and gave them to my brother, and then she bent down and gave us each a kiss on the forehead.

"I'll be home at five o'clock tonight. I want you boys to meet me right here in the lobby at five o'clock. Don't go up to the room until I come home. I don't want you to wake anyone up."

"There's only one person in the room," I said.

"I know," she said, "but I don't want you to wake him up."

"Come on, Billy, let's get to the park," my brother called to me. He was already at the edge of the sidewalk.

"Goodbye, mom," I said.

"Goodbye, sweetheart. Be a good boy today, and mind what your brother tells you. He's in charge. I love you."

Then she turned and walked away. She was wearing a tomato-red suit. I watched until she got to the corner where she turned to the right, out of sight.

"Come on," my brother yelled, "let's go."

Twenty-Eight

WE RAN ACROSS THE STREET TO THE PARK AND quickly headed for the trees.

"Come on, let's climb that one over there," my brother said, pointing to a large tree with lots of branches. We ran over to it and stopped at the base of the trunk.

"These don't look like the trees at Grandma's," I said.

"I know. They're different," he said.

I watched as he jumped up, caught the lowest limb with both hands, and gracefully pulled himself up into the tree. It looked easy; I was sure I could do it too. I ran and jumped to catch the branch the way he had. But it was too high. Instead of catching it, I smashed into the trunk, scraping my face and hands.

"Come on up," my brother shouted at me.

"I can't reach the limb," I said.

"Then just shinny up the trunk until you can reach it. After that, you can just pull yourself up."

I tried to shinny up the trunk, but it was too big around. Every time I tried, I would climb a few inches up the trunk and then slide back down, scraping my hands and legs even more.

"I can't do it," I shouted. "The trunk is too big for me to grab on to."

"You can do it. Just keep trying," he shouted back.

By this time, he was well up into the tree. He had quickly climbed from limb to limb, going higher and higher, until I couldn't see him anymore. I thought he might have jumped to another tree and left me there.

"I can't see you," I shouted.

"I'm right here above you."

"I still can't see you."

"Here, look up. I'm going to throw a twig down at you. Just look up and see where it comes from," he shouted.

I looked up and saw a twig floating down toward me, directly above my face, and just before it hit me, I saw his face peeking through the branches at me and laughing.

"Try again," he said.

I tried to shinny up the trunk again, but I kept sliding down. By this time, my hands and arms and the inside of my legs were raw. I wished I hadn't worn short pants.

"I can't do it," I cried.

"Okay, stop crying. I'm going to help you."

I watched as he jumped from limb to limb on his way down from the top of the tree. All his movements were graceful, as if he were part monkey and was born to climb trees. Things like climbing trees, playing football or any other sport were just natural to him. And because they were so natural to him, he couldn't understand why others couldn't do the same things, with the same ease that he could. In a few seconds, he was standing on the limb above me.

"I'm going to hang upside down and grab you to pull you up. Once you get to the first limb, the others are closer together and easier to climb. When I put my hands down, grab 'em, and I'll pull you up."

He wrapped his legs around the limb and swung down, holding onto the limb with his legs and extending his hands to me. I reached up, grabbed them, and then just hung on while he pulled me up to the limb.

"How am I going to get down?" I asked.

"Just jump. It's not far. It won't hurt you."

I looked down and it seemed like a long way to the ground. I was sure that it would hurt if I jumped or fell. "Don't worry about it right now," he said, "let's climb to the top. Just follow me and put your foot on the limbs I put my foot on, and you'll be okay."

I watched him climb easily up to the next layer of branches and then began to follow him. He was right, the branches were pretty close together, and the climbing was much easier than I expected. "Look over there," he said, "that's the zoo."

I looked in the direction he was pointing and could see several cages and buildings where the animals were kept.

"Can we go over there?"

"Sure, but first, let's climb some more trees. Let's see if we can find a really big one so we can climb to the top and see all over the place. I wonder if we can see the hotel."

We sat there for awhile, letting the breeze blow through the tree, gently moving the limbs where we sat. It was very peaceful and cool and my legs didn't hurt anymore from where they had gotten scraped.

"Look at that tree over there," he said, pointing. "I bet that's the biggest one in the park. Let's go climb it."

As we descended from our perch in the top of the tree, I slipped and crashed through several smaller branches before I finally caught myself on a larger limb and was able to stop my fall. But several twigs had gouged me in the neck, and I was bleeding a little bit. I wanted to cry, but I was afraid that if I did, my brother would get mad and run away, leaving me alone in the tree.

"How come these trees don't have any Spanish moss or kudzu?" I asked.

"That stuff only grows in Florida," Bobby James answered with authority.

"I wish it grew here so we could jump down on it without getting all scratched up."

"Be careful and don't let go of a limb until your feet are on the one below you," he warned.

I tried to pay attention to what he said, but sometimes the limbs were really slippery and I would slip before my feet were firmly balanced below. My arms and legs were completely raw, and I didn't want to climb anymore. Besides, it wasn't any fun if you couldn't jump and let the kudzu vines catch you.

Finally I got to the bottom limb – the one he had pulled me up on – and it was time to jump to the ground. But I did not want to jump. It looked too far, and I was afraid I'd get hurt.

"Go on, jump," my brother said. "It's not far. You won't get hurt."

But I couldn't move. I was too afraid. He tried to push me off the limb, but I hung on and wouldn't move.

"Okay," he said, "if you won't jump, I'll jump down first to show you that it won't hurt."

"Okay," I said, "you jump first, and I'll follow you."

He jumped easily to the ground.

"See, it didn't hurt at all," he said, looking back up at me. "Now you jump."

I couldn't move; I wouldn't jump.

"If you don't jump, I'm going to leave you here," he said.

I kept sitting there on the limb, afraid to jump.

"Look, if you're afraid to jump from there," he said, "just slide over the limb and hang by your hands. Then you can drop to the ground, and it won't be such a long distance for you."

But I still wouldn't move or jump.

"Okay, I'm leaving you."

He ran away to climb another tree somewhere. I don't know how long I sat there crying and sniffling, but it must have been a long time. I finally decided that Bobby James wasn't coming back to help me get down, and I was afraid he would leave me in the park, and my mom would be mad at me if I didn't come back to the hotel on time. I finally decided to try and drop to the ground, the way he had suggested. Slowly, I hooked my legs around the limb and then my arms. Then I let my legs drop off the limb while I held on with my arms. I continued to hang there, my legs dangling, for as long as I could. My arms ached as if they were on fire. Finally, I couldn't hang on any longer. I let go. I was surprised that it wasn't a very far drop at all. I barely felt it when I hit the ground. It was almost as if I had floated down. My brother was right. It must not have been as far as it looked. I scanned the area looking for him, but I couldn't see him anywhere. I called him, but got no answer. I stood by the tree looking in all directions, but he was nowhere to be seen. I called and called, but still there was no reply. I stood by the tree in silence for awhile, hoping I would hear him calling me, but the only sounds were the birds. Where could he have gone, I wondered. I knew he liked to hide from me and then jump out and scare me when I least expected it. I was sure that was what he was going to do. I sat down by the tree. He had to come back sometime. He had to come back this way to get back to the hotel. I sat there in silence for awhile. I don't know how long I waited, but I must have fallen asleep, because suddenly my body jerked and there was slobber on the front of my shirt. I wiped it off with my hands as I stood up. I looked around and called Bobby James again, but I still didn't see him and he still didn't answer me. How was I going to get back to the hotel? I didn't know the way. I thought I could see it from where I was standing by the tree, but I wasn't sure. I was getting hungry. My brother had the money for us to get something to eat. There was only one thing to do, sit there and wait for him to come back.

After awhile, I saw a man walking toward me, and I stopped him and asked him if he knew where the hotel was.

"I don't know, son. What's the name of your hotel?" he asked.

"I don't know. We just got here last night," I said.

"Well, there's a hotel across the street over there." He pointed in the direction where I thought I had seen the hotel. "Thanks," I said, "I think that's it."

"Do you want me to take you over there, son?"

"No, thanks, I can find it now. Thank you," I said.

"Okay, be careful," he said as he turned away and continued walking.

I could see the direction I thought was the way to the hotel, but I was afraid to leave the tree. What would my brother do if he came back and I was gone? So I sat down again to wait. I waited for what seemed to be forever. It began to get dark, and I began to get frightened. I had better start walking, I thought or I won't be able to find the hotel in the dark. Then I saw my mother walking toward me, and I ran to her and started crying.

"Where have you been?" she asked. "I've been looking everywhere for you. Why did you run off from your brother?"

"I didn't, mommy. He ran off from me when I couldn't get out of the tree, and I couldn't find him," I cried.

"Bobby James said you boys were playing hide and seek and you ran off and wouldn't come back when he called you."

"That's not true, mommy. He left me in the tree I had to get down by myself, and he was gone and I called him but he didn't answer," I said crying and choking on my snot as I poured out all the unfair things that had happened to me.

"Well, let's go back to the hotel. Have you had anything to eat today?" she asked.

"No, Bobby James had the money, and I couldn't find him," I said.

"Well, you shouldn't have run away from him," she said.

"I didn't, he ran away from me and left me in the tree."

I could tell that she didn't believe me; she believed my brother instead. I was mad and hurt.

"We need to get you cleaned up and ready for bed after we get you something to eat," she said.

"Can I have a peanut butter and jelly sandwich?"

"I've already fixed dinner for us in the hotel room. You can have a peanut butter and jelly sandwich tomorrow for lunch."

"What are we having for supper?"

"I made liver and onions with fried potatoes."

I hated liver and onions. I wanted a peanut butter and jelly sandwich. Suddenly I wasn't hungry anymore.

When we got up to the hotel room, my brother was already there, sitting on the couch that was also our bed.

"Frank's drunk," he announced as soon as we opened the door.

The room smelled like something old and dirty, like the place where we put our dirty clothes before Crystal came to wash them.

"Mommy, are there dirty clothes in here?" I asked.

"No, just let me open a window and air things out," she said.

"Frank's drunk," my brother said again.

"Okay, boys, go into the bathroom and wash your face and hands and get ready for dinner," she said, ignoring my brother's comment.

"I already washed my face and hands," he said.

"Good boy," she said and gave him a nod. "Billy, you go and wash up too."

I went into the bathroom and accidently turned the water on full blast. It splashed out of the washbasin onto the floor before I could get it shut off. Nervously, I got a towel and tried to wipe up the water, but there was too much.

"Mom," I shouted, "I need another towel."

But she didn't seem to have heard me.

"Mom, I need another towel!" I shouted again.

Suddenly, the door to the bathroom crashed open and a man stood in the doorway.

"Goddamn it, Susan, can't you keep these brats of yours quiet?"

Twenty-Nine

HE WAS STANDING THERE IN HIS UNDERWEAR, SWAY-ing back and forth on unsteady legs.

"Get out of here, goddamn it. I have to piss," he shouted.

As he staggered into the bathroom, he slipped in the water on the floor. The only thing that saved him from falling was that he grabbed me with one hand and the washbasin with the other.

"What's all this goddamn water on the floor?" he shouted.

"Shit, Susan, you can't keep your goddamn kids quiet, and you can't keep the goddamn water off the bathroom floor." He glared at me and slurred his words as he growled, "Get out of here, you little bastard."

I ran out of the bathroom and into the living room, where I ran smack into my mother. She was on her way to see what Frank was doing.

"What's going on," she asked.

"I spilled some water. I'm sorry. It just came out of the faucet really fast," I said.

"That's okay. Go into the kitchen and sit down with your brother. I'll be there in a minute, and we'll have supper."

I ran into the kitchen and found my brother.

"Is that Frank?" I asked.

"Yeah, he's drunk. He's always drunk. He gets real mean when he's drunk. I can tell you for sure, we ain't gonna be here long."

"Why not? What do you mean?"

"Frank doesn't want us around. We get in the way, especially when he's drunk. He just wants Mom to drink with him."

"Does Mom get drunk?"

"I only saw her drunk once, and she almost died."

"What happened?" I asked. "Why did she almost die?"

"I only know she drank a lot with Frank, and then she fell asleep and I couldn't wake her up. Frank was going to leave us both in the hotel room, but I made him get a doctor."

"How did you make him?"

"I got a knife from the kitchen and told him I would kill him if he tried to leave us there alone."

I couldn't imagine telling anyone I was going to kill them. If I said something like that to my grandmother, she would have knocked me down. "What happened," I asked.

"He finally called the hotel doctor, and then he tried to leave again. I told the son-of-a-bitch I'd kill him for sure if he tried to leave before the doctor came. So he waited until one showed up."

"Was Mom going to die?"

"She could have, if a doctor hadn't come. The doctor said she was poisoned by drinking too much whiskey."

"You mean Frank poisoned her?"

"No, he didn't poison her, but she wasn't used to drinking that much whiskey and it made her sick, like she had been poisoned."

Just then my mom came into the kitchen and said, "Okay, everything is fine. Now, we can eat. Who's hungry?"

Neither my brother nor I answered her. We just sat there while my mom put liver and onions along with some potatoes on our plates.

"Come on now, boys, you have to eat. I made this especially for you because I knew you would be hungry after playing all day."

We sat there looking at our plates. I hated liver and onions, but I was afraid I would have to eat it for breakfast if I didn't eat it now. If Butchie had been there, he would have helped me. I could have slipped it to him under the table and he would even have eaten the onions. I missed him. I sat staring at my plate, and finally my brother got up and left the table.

"I'm going down to the lobby and buy a comic book, Mom," he said, as he went out the door of our hotel room.

"What's the matter, Billy? Why aren't you eating? I made it especially for you," she said.

"I don't like liver and onions," I said.

"You don't?" she sounded surprised. "Grandma told me that you always eat all your liver and onions."

Tears started streaming down my face. "That's because she'll make me eat it for breakfast if I don't eat it for supper."

"Oh, come on now, she would never make you eat liver for breakfast. I know better than that."

"Yes, she does. Am I going to have to eat it for breakfast tomorrow morning?"

"No, of course not," she said.

"Can I have a peanut butter and jelly sandwich, instead?"

"Liver is good for you. Just try a little bit. I'm sure you're going to like the way I cooked it," she coaxed. "Here, I'll cut it up for you, and you can just try a small piece."

She began cutting the liver, and I managed to eat about half of it and all the potatoes. It was all I could do to keep from gagging. I thought I was going to throw up. "I can't eat any more, Mom," I pleaded.

Suddenly the bedroom door banged open and Frank was standing there, wobbling back and forth in the hallway. "Susan, where's my goddamn bottle?" he yelled.

"Frank, please don't drink anymore," she begged him.

"Where's my goddamn bottle? Get my goddamn bottle right now," he shouted.

"It's on the sink, Frank, where you always leave it."

He stumbled into the kitchen and farted when he passed the chair where I was sitting. The stink was terrible. Between the liver and his fart, I puked on the table and the floor.

"What's the matter with your goddamn kid? He's made a fucking mess in here. What are your goddamn kids doing here anyway? I don't want them here, Susan. I told you that. They're in the way. Send 'em back to your goddamn mother in Florida."

"Frank, now is not the time to discuss this. Please go back to bed. We can talk about it when I come to bed."

"Look at this fucking mess," he said, wobbling back and forth and trying to steady himself on the edge of the sinkboard. "You need to clean this goddamn mess up before we all get sick," he slurred.

"You're very drunk. Now, please go back to bed."

I was frightened, and I tried to clean the puke up with napkins, but it seemed like it was spreading around even more. The more I tried to wipe it up with the napkins, the bigger the mess became.

"That's it kid, clean up this goddamn mess. Your fucking mother won't do it."

"Come on, Frank," my mother coaxed, "get your drink and go back to bed. I'll be in there in a few minutes."

"You need to clean this mess up, Susan. It stinks," he slurred. "Your kid's puke stinks."

Someone started knocking at the door to our room.

"Go let your brother in," my mother told me.

"Bobby James? Is Bobby James here?" Frank bellowed. "I told you that kid could never come back here again, no matter where we were," he shouted. "He's just one big fucking problem, and I don't need another fucking problem right now. I told you that, Susan. I told you, I don't need another fucking problem." He was swaying back and forth and I thought he might fall.

"Frank, we talked about it, and I told you my mother was sending the boys out here because we weren't sending her any money for them, and she couldn't take care of them anymore. You said it was okay. Now please go back to bed. We can talk about this later, when you're sober."

I went and opened the door for my brother.

"What happened to you? You look like someone puked all over you," he said as he strolled into the room.

"Is that you, Bobby James?" Frank called from the kitchen. "Because if it is, I don't want you here. I don't know why your mother brought you here."

My brother turned and ran down the hallway toward the elevators. I ran after him, but he threw his comic book at me and ran down the stairwell. "Leave me alone," he shouted.

When I returned to the room, my mother was walking Frank back to the bedroom. I could hear him farting – long, loud, disgusting farts. I didn't want to go back in the room, because I was afraid I would get sick again, but there was no place else to go. When my mother came back from putting Frank to bed, she didn't say anything. She just started cleaning up the kitchen. I tried to help her, but she didn't want any help.

"That's okay, honey," she said. "Go into the bathroom, take your clothes off and wash up. Be careful not to turn the water on too fast. I'll be in there in a minute."

"Bobby James went downstairs," I said.

"I know. I'll go down and find him when I finish cleaning up here."

"Do you want me to go downstairs to the lobby and look for him?"

"No, dear. Just go in the bathroom and clean up. I'll be in there in a minute. I won't be long."

After I washed up in the bathroom, I went back in the living room and sat on the couch in my underwear. I didn't know what to do with myself. There was a *LIFE* magazine on one of the end tables, and I began looking at the pictures. There were lots of pictures about the war. I really didn't know what the pictures were all about, other than that they were of the war. But the explosions and fires in the pictures had such vivid colors, they mesmerized me. I couldn't quit looking at them – especially the aircraft carriers. There were bellowing clouds of orange flames with thick black smoke, and sailors trying to put out the fires on the decks where Jap pilots had either crashed or where pieces of their planes had been shot off and landed on the deck in a scorching inferno. There were hundreds of men in the images, all fighting the fires and trying to save their ship. Some appeared to be badly burned, but I found out later they were just covered in oil. I was so engrossed with the pictures that I never heard my mother come in from the kitchen, and I didn't even realize she was there until she began rubbing my head.

"Well, I got everything cleaned up in the kitchen," she said. "I'm going downstairs to find your brother. You stay here and look at the magazine. Please remember to be very quiet."

"Can I go with you?"

"No, you just stay here. I won't be long."

"What if Frank gets up while you're gone?"

"Don't worry honey, he won't. He's asleep now and he won't wake up for a long time. I'll be back as soon as I find Bobby James."

She left, and it was several hours before she returned with my brother. He had a roll of candy with him.

"You want a Lifesaver?" He offered them to me.

"What's a Lifesaver?" I asked.

"It's candy," he said. "A G.I. downstairs in the lobby gave them to me. Only guys in the service can get candy. It's rationed to everyone else."

I didn't understand what it meant for things to be rationed, except that they were hard to get; but I knew everyone had a ration book. Even Tim and I had one. Grandma took our ration books to the store whenever she went shopping. She would give some of the stamps to the man at the grocery store or to the man where she bought gas. If she didn't have enough stamps, she couldn't buy certain groceries, nor could she buy gas or anything else that was rationed. It seemed like there was so much stuff rationed during the war that it was hard for some people to get things they needed.

"I'm sorry, Mrs. Christian," the butcher would say. "You don't have enough stamps for the meat. Save 'em up and come back next month."

I wasn't sure how it worked, but I learned that ration stamps were as valuable as money – and both were scarce at my grandparents' house.

"I don't know how we're going to make it, Edward," my grandmother would say to my grandfather. "There simply is not enough money to make ends meet."

"Henrietta," he would reply, "we'll make it. We're simply going to have to tighten our belts a little more. The boys are going to have to keep wearing hand-me-downs. They can go without new shoes for another year, and we'll all have to eat a little less. We have plenty of eggs, and we still have at least a dozen hens if we need to eat one now and then."

"I wish that damn rooster would do what he's supposed to do," I heard her say. "We should have some chicks by now. That damn rooster attacks me whenever I get near the hens in the chicken yard. If I don't see some chicks soon and he keeps that up, I'm going to wring his neck."

"Well, I suppose we could eat him; but in the long run, it may not be in our best interest. As I said, we'll just have to tighten our belts. Maybe you can save up some of the ration stamps and make them stretch a little further."

"What the hell is that supposed to mean? Don't you think I'm doing everything I can to make the stamps go further?"

"I only meant it as part of the solution, not as a criticism of what you are doing, Henrietta," my grandfather replied and immediately went outside to do something in the shed with his tools.

I suppose I was too young to understand the value of the stamps, but I was fascinated by them. I liked the colors. Some were green, some were red and some were blue. One day, when my grandmother was outside watering the plants, I was exploring the shelf next to her chair where she sat each night after supper. Not wanting her to catch me going through her things, I watched through the window, keeping one eye on her as she moved from flower bed to flower bed with her hose while I rifled through the papers, crossword puzzle books and other magazines on the shelf. I wasn't looking for anything in particular. I was just curious. Then, as I continued to search along the shelf, I found a treasure.

Just behind her radio and a stack of old crossword puzzle books, I discovered a candy box. Hoping there might be some candy inside, I opened it. But what I found was not candy; it was our ration books, tightly bound together with a rubber band. Quickly, I pulled the rubber band off the books and looked through them, marveling at the different colored stamps. They reminded me of the ones I had seen my grandmother paste on envelopes when she mailed a letter. Suddenly, I had a great idea. I could paste these stamps into my scrapbook.

Forgetting about my grandmother watering the plants outside, I ran to my room to get it. I felt around under my brother's bed where I kept the scrapbook and the jar of library paste until my hands finally found what I was looking for. I fished them out. Kneeling beside the bed and filled with excitement, I flipped through the book, looking for a blank page on which to paste the stamps. This was going to be beautiful.

As I ripped stamps out of the ration books and pasted them into my scrapbook, I was pleased with my work. They looked beautiful, all the different colored stamps pasted together in the center of a page all their own.

Whack! I felt the sting of my grandmother's stick hit me across my back.

"What in damnation are you doing?" she screamed.

"I was just pasting these stamps into my scrapbook, Grandma."

"Those are my ration books you're tearing up," she screamed at me again. She lashed out with her stick, hitting me across the chest. It stung so badly, I felt the wind go out of my lungs, and I nearly fell to the floor. But I knew that if I fell, she would continue to hit me with the stick. She was furious, and I knew I had to get away from her.

I regained my balance and tried to slip past her, but she smashed her fist into the side of my head, knocking me to the floor. I saw the stick start down to hit me again, and I rolled under the bed as fast as I could. I was crying and I ached all over. Blood was trickling out of my nose and pooling on the floor, but I knew I was safe for the moment.

My grandmother was too big to crawl under the bed to get me.

"We don't have enough money as it is, and now you you've gone and ruined my ration books!"

"I'm sorry, Grandma, I didn't know they were ration books," I lied. I lied because I didn't know what to say. It didn't seem that serious to me.

"Can't you just take the stamps back out of my scrapbook and use them?"

"No, the stamps have to be in the book to be any good."

"I'm sorry," I said again. "I didn't know, Grandma."

"What were you doing going through my things, anyway?" she shouted, full of anger.

"Nothing," I said, still crying and wishing she would go away.

"Come out from under there," she growled. "I'm not through with you, yet."

She began jabbing at me under the bed with the stick and got me sharply in the side and chest. I tried to get against the wall, but she got on top of the bed and jabbed at me between the bed and the wall. Before I could get out of the way, the end of the stick came down on my shoulder and opened up a gash. I screamed. I could see that it was bleeding, and before I could roll the other way to get under the middle of the bed, she slammed the stick down on my head. I screamed at the top of my lungs.

Then I heard my grandfather. "Henrietta, what are you doing? Stop it! Stop it right now! Give me that stick. What's wrong with you? You're going to injure the boy."

"He deserves it. He's ruined the ration books," she shouted.

"I don't care what he's done. You can't treat him like that."

My grandmother began screaming at him now. "I don't know what I'm going to do! How I can afford to keep things going? We don't have enough money to feed and clothe all of us, and I can't stretch things any further. I'm at my wits end!"

My grandfather stooped down and peered at me from the side of the bed.

"Come out here, Billy. Let me look at you," he said gently.

I could see my grandmother's feet beside the bed and I knew she was still in the room. "Is she going to hit me again?" I sobbed.

"No, no one is going to hit you. Come out here and let me look at your shoulder."

I rolled out from underneath the bed and moved as far away from my grandmother as I could get.

My grandfather put his glasses on and examined my shoulder. "It doesn't look that bad," he said. "I think the bleeding has stopped. Just sit here on the edge of the bed and wait for me. I'll be back in a few minutes to put some iodine on it. You'll be fine." Then he turned to my grandmother and gently said, "Let's go in the kitchen and talk, Henrietta."

They left and went into the kitchen. I moved to the door so I could hear what they were saying.

"Now, tell me what's going on here," I heard my grandfather say calmly.

"We simply do not have enough money to keep things going here."

"What about the money Jessica sends for Tim, and the money Susan sends for Bobby James and Billy?" he asked.

"You know damn well they rarely send any money. The fact is they haven't sent any money for nearly a year."

"Why didn't you tell me?"

"You're always in Knoxville, working. What good would it have done? What can you do about it? You don't even know where they are."

"Well, yes I do. They're working in Washington, D.C., in the war effort."

"Edward, you're such a fool. How do you expect to find them in Washington?" My grandmother sounded tired and defeated.

"I don't know. Regardless, you cannot take your anger and frustrations out on the children."

"Well then they better learn to behave themselves. I have enough problems with Bobby James. That boy belongs in reform school. And that's just where I'm going to send him if he doesn't straighten out."

As I stood in the hotel room staring at the Lifesavers, I remembered how angry my grandmother had been, and the terror of being beaten with her stick. A shiver went over my body.

"What's the matter with you?" Bobby James said. "Do you want one or not?"

"Sure," I said, collecting myself. "Thanks."

When my brother and I went to bed that night, we talked for a long time, mostly about Frank and him being drunk all the time.

"Why does Mom like him?" I asked. "He's mean."

"I don't know."

"Will he always be drunk like tonight?"

"No, not always; but most of the time."

"Is he always mean?"

"Yes, especially to me," my brother said. "He hates me."

"Why?"

"I told you, because I threatened to kill him, stupid. He's hated me ever since then. I think he would kill me if he could, but Mom won't let him touch me when she's around. That makes him hate me even more."

"Aren't you afraid of him?"

"Nah, I'd kill the bastard before he could kill me, if I had to," my brother answered.

"Does he hate me?" I asked.

"I don't know if he does now or not, but if Mom spends more time with you than him, he'll hate you – and probably try to kill you. If he sees Mom hugging you or kissing you, he'll probably try to kill you for that, too. He wants Mom all to himself, and we are only in the way. He has no use for us."

I started to sob. I wanted Mom to hug me and kiss me, but what if he saw her? I didn't want him to kill me.

"Why are you crying?" my brother asked me.

"I don't want Frank to kill me," I said, and my sobs became louder.

"Shut up and stop crying you big crybaby, or you'll wake up Frank and he'll kill you right here and now."

I began to cry even louder. I was afraid Frank would come out of the bedroom and try to kill me. I could practically feel him grabbing me.

"Shut up," my brother said. "I was just kidding. Mom would never let Frank kill you or me. I was just kidding."

"You sure he won't try to kill me if Mom hugs me?"

"He won't try to kill you. I was just kidding. Besides, he wouldn't even be able to find you when he's as drunk as he is right now. All you would have to do is keep running in circles, and he would fall on his ass," my brother laughed.

"Are you sure?"

"Yep, I'm sure. Now shut up and go to sleep."

Sleep finally caught up to me, and I dreamed of Frank standing there in his underwear, wobbling back and forth, farting loud, stinking farts and telling me that he was going to kill me. I tried to run in circles like my brother had told me to, but I was frozen in place and couldn't run. He laughed at me and his face was huge, and he yelled, "I'm going to kill you, you little bastard."

I screamed and sat up in bed, kicking and trying to get away from him. My brother jabbed me with his elbow. "Lie down, you're having a bad dream," he said.

Thirty

THE NEXT MORNING, I AWOKE TO THE SMELL OF coffee brewing. I loved that smell, even though I wasn't allowed to drink it. I didn't care. I didn't like the taste anyway. Once, when my grandmother wasn't looking, I tried some from her cup, but it was so bitter I couldn't even swallow it. I never wanted coffee again after that, but I always thought the smell of it brewing and of bacon frying were the best smells in the world to wake up to. It seemed to guarantee everything was going to be good that day. And today was one of those days. I could smell the coffee and the bacon, and I was suddenly very, very hungry. I had only had some liver and onions since breakfast yesterday and I had thrown most of that up last night. I jumped up, ready to eat.

My brother was already at the table, fully dressed. My mother was cooking eggs and was dressed for work with an apron on over her dress. I ran into the kitchen, only to get the shock of my life when I saw Frank sitting there at the table, fully dressed in an army uniform. He was drinking a cup of coffee and reading the paper, which my brother had probably brought up from the lobby. A plate of toast sat untouched in front of him.

"Are you going to want some eggs, Frank?" my mother asked him.

"No, I'll be fine with just the toast and coffee," he answered without looking up from the paper.

When my mother turned around from the stove, she said,

"Well, good morning sleepyhead. I see you finally woke up. Do you want some eggs and bacon?"

"Yes, ma'am," I said.

"Okay, run and wash your face and hands and get dressed. I'll have your breakfast ready when you get back," she said.

"See if you can keep the goddamn water off the floor this time," Frank snarled without looking up from his paper.

My mother came over and tousled my hair as she gently guided me toward the bathroom. As I was leaving the kitchen, I saw my brother make a sign with his hand like he was slicing his throat. I started to tremble, and my mother said, "You must be getting a chill. Hurry, now, go wash up and get your clothes on."

Breakfast was wonderful. I had two eggs, sunny side up, two slices of bacon, two pieces of toast with grape jelly, a glass of orange juice and a big glass of milk. I couldn't believe all there was to eat. It was wonderful.

"Are you boys going to play in the park again today," my mother asked.

"Yeah," my brother answered, "we're gonna go to the zoo, too."

"Don't run off from your brother today," my mother said.

I wasn't sure if she was talking to me or to Bobby James. Even after I had told her that he had run off from me, she still seemed to believe him. Maybe she was telling us both not to run off, since she really didn't know who was telling the truth.

In the elevator, my mother greeted Joseph, the same as she had the day before.

"Good morning, Joseph," she said.

"Good morning, Miss Susan."

"You boys going to the park again, today?" he asked.

"Yes," we answered.

"Good morning, Mister Frank. You all dressed up in your uniform. You goin' to the Army Base, today?" Joseph asked.

"You know I can't tell you where I'm going, Joseph," Frank answered with a flat, uninterested tone.

"Yes, sir, I knows dat. I's just making conversation, Mister Frank, you know."

I noticed that Joseph's English changed when he answered Frank.

Frank made no reply and we rode down the rest of the way to the lobby in silence. When we reached the lobby, we all went out to the sidewalk in front of the hotel, and Frank told the doorman to get him a cab. The doorman put a whistle in his mouth and gave a loud, shrill blast on it. Soon a cab appeared at the curb. As we stood there, watching, Frank got in and was gone without saying anything to any of us, not even to my mother.

When he was gone, my mother leaned over and kissed both of us on the forehead. "I'll see you this evening, boys. Have fun in the park today. Bobby James, make sure you stay with your brother and be back at the hotel by five o'clock."

"Okay, mom, we'll be here at five o'clock. I promise."

She smiled and walked away toward the corner of the street, the same direction she had taken the day before. Again, I stared at her back as she walked away. For one panicky moment, I wondered if she really were coming back tonight.

As soon as she was out of sight, my brother yelled. "Come on, dip shit. Let's go."

We ran across the street to the park and began roughhousing with each other. Bobby James was much bigger than I, and he knocked me down easily, but it was fun to run and laugh and make as much noise as we wanted. We had had to be quiet in the hotel room so we wouldn't wake up Frank, but out here we could be as loud as we wanted. It was like being back at my grandmother's house, where we played outside in the fields and climbed trees or swam at the beach. All of us kids hollered at each other when we played and never thought anything about it. No one in the neighborhood ever told us to be quiet or stop our hollering.

At last, my brother and I collapsed on the ground and lay on our backs, looking up at the sky. It was a beautiful light-blue color, dotted with fluffy white clouds of all sizes and shapes. We each took turns describing what each of the clouds looked liked to us. Then we lay there in silence for a long time, each with our own thoughts. I wondered what Grandma and Grandpa and Tim were doing back in Gulfport. I hoped Tim had someone to play with, since I wasn't there to play with him. Then I thought about my mother and the way she looked when she had walked away from us this morning when she left for work. It was exactly how I had pictured her whenever I thought about her at Grandma's house. She was always walking away from me; I could never see her face. Even as I lay there on the ground with my brother, I tried to imagine what her face looked like, but I couldn't make it out. I could only see her back as she walked away.

Suddenly, Frank's face appeared in my mind. It was the face I had seen last night, when he was standing over me in the bathroom. I could see him clearly as he stood there, wobbling back and forth and yelling at me to get out of the bathroom so he could take a piss.

"Where did Frank go this morning?" I asked my brother.

"I don't know, probably out to the Army Base. I think he's stationed out there in the Quartermaster Corps or something like that."

"What's the Quartermaster Corps?"

"I don't know. I think it's something like a person who sends things to the army overseas."

"What kind of things?"

"I'm not sure, but I think it has to do with food and boots and uniforms… and guns, things like that. That's how come Mom gets all that food we have in the hotel. No one else can get it, but Frank always brings it home with him."

I was awed at his knowledge. "How do you know all this stuff?"

"'Cause every time I'm with Mom and Frank, she always tells me he's going to bring a lot of food home, and he does."

"Have you been with Mom and Frank a lot?" I asked.

"Not a lot, but you know when Grandma gets tired of me being there, she sends me back to Mom. But I don't stay for long. Mom either sends me back to Grandma or she puts me in a boarding school someplace. That's how I got in that school over in Tampa. You know, Mary Help a Christian."

"Didn't you like that school?"

"No, I hated it. I always ran away from there. Sometimes I tried to find Mom, but when I couldn't find her I just went back to Grandma's house. But Grandma didn't want me there either."

"Why not?"

"Because Mom never sends her any money to help take care of me, and Grandma can't afford to have me there unless she gets some money from Mom. That's why she doesn't like it when I show up there again. But mostly she doesn't like it because I won't do what she tells me."

"How many times has she sent you back to Mom?" I asked.

"I don't know… lots. Why do you think we're here with Mom, now? She doesn't want us here, and Frank doesn't want us here either. The only reason we're here is because Mom didn't send Grandma any money, and because *you* tried to burn the house down."

"I didn't try to burn the house down. That was an accident."

"What were you doing, anyway?" he asked.

"Tim and I were trying to build a campfire with some newspapers and some matches from Grandpa's pipe stand. It got too big, and before I could put it out, it burned a hole in the rug. I didn't mean to do it."

"You were lucky you didn't burn the whole damn house down. You know the kerosene stored in the shed that Grandpa uses to heat the house in the winter?"

"Yeah."

"Well, that's what Crystal uses to clean the floors in the house. She puts it on her dust mop to pick up all the crap on the floor. Those floors have years of kerosene soaked into the wood. I bet if you had let the fire burn just a little longer, the whole house would have gone up in flames. I really would have liked to have seen that." He laughed, and we lay there in silence for awhile.

"Come on, let's go to the zoo," he said. "We may as well enjoy it while we can, because our stay here ain't going to last very long."

"What do you mean?"

"Frank will make Mom send us back to Grandma's pretty soon. I guarantee you. We won't be here very long. You heard him last night telling Mom he didn't want us here."

"What if Grandma won't take us back?"

"Don't worry. She will. She always does."

"I don't want to go back to Grandma's. I want to stay with Mom."

"I know. I do too. But that ain't going to happen. Come on, let's go to the zoo."

"Do you know where the zoo is?"

"Yeah. Now come on and quit asking questions."

We ran across the field together. I followed behind my brother, because he knew the way. He knew everything, and I believed him that we probably were not going to be here with Mom very much longer. I had heard Frank last night say he didn't want us here, but I hadn't heard my mom say the same. Maybe she could convince Frank it was okay for us to be here, and we wouldn't have to go back to Grandma's house. I didn't want to go back. It was fun here, and I didn't have to eat liver for breakfast. I didn't even get spanked for spilling water on the bathroom floor. It would be good if we could stay here with Mom. I crossed my fingers and wished with all my might that we could.

That afternoon, we went to the zoo and saw all the animals. I had never been to a zoo before. We ate cookies and drank Coca Cola; that was a real treat for me. Later we climbed in the trees and ran around the park, chasing each other. When it was time to go, we went back to the hotel. Bobby James had not run off and left me all day.

When we got to the hotel, I saw Mom just as she was getting back and I wondered if Frank was there too. "Hi, boys, did you have fun in the park today?" she asked, smiling at us.

"Yeah," I said. "We went to the zoo too and saw all the animals. I saw lions and tigers and giraffes and elephants and monkeys, too. We went together."

"Wow, it sounds like you saw a lot. Did you boys have anything to eat?"

"Yeah, we had cookies and Coca Cola," my brother said.

"Well, tomorrow is Saturday," she said. "I think they have pony rides in the park every Saturday. Would you boys like to go and ride the ponies?"

"Oh boy, yeah, we would," I said.

Thirty-One

FRANK CAME BACK TO THE HOTEL LATER IN THE evening, and my mother cooked dinner for us. She made corned beef and cabbage with boiled red potatoes. We had ice cream for dessert. My mom let us have all we wanted to eat. I could hardly believe it. For the first time that I could ever remember, I wasn't going to have to go to bed hungry. After dinner, my brother and I were looking at *LIFE* magazine together while my mother and Frank talked in the bedroom. They talked in hushed voices, and we couldn't make out everything they were saying. But every now and then we could pick up a word or two of their conversation.

"Okay then, next Sunday morning… I don't know what mama will say… what about Bobby James?… Washington, D.C."

We didn't know what it meant, but we tried to listen. We had stopped talking so we could hear better, but they must have realized that we were too quiet, because one of them closed the bedroom door.

"What do you think they're talking about?" I asked.

"Probably how to take us back to Grandma's."

"Why do we have to go back? Why can't we just stay here?"

"I told you this afternoon, they don't want us here. I don't think they are even going to be here much longer anyway."

"Why not?"

"I think Frank is being sent overseas to someplace in Europe."

"Can't we go with them?" I asked.

"No, stupid, we can't go fight in the war."

"Is Mom going to fight in the war?"

"No, stupid, women don't fight in the war, only men."

"Why can't we stay with Mom then?"

I felt like I shouldn't have to ask these questions. It seemed obvious to me that Mom should keep us with her, the way other kids' mothers did.

"Because she has to work and she can't take care of us and work too. That's one of the reasons she leaves us with Grandma," my brother said in an exasperated tone.

"But, I don't want to stay with Grandma. I want to stay with Mom."

"Too bad. We can't."

"Where does Mom work?"

"I think she might have a new job in Washington, D.C."

"Where is that?" I wanted to know.

"I don't know. Someplace a long way from here. Now go to sleep and leave me alone."

Somewhere, between worrying about being sent back to Grandma's and wondering where Washington, D.C. was, I fell asleep.

The next morning when I got up and entered the kitchen, I found my brother sitting at the kitchen table alone, eating a bowl of cereal.

"Where's Mom?" I asked.

"She's gone to work already. She said you could have cereal when you woke up."

"I thought we were going to ride the ponies in the park today," I whined.

"Afraid not. She decided to go to work."

"Is Frank still asleep?"

"No, he left with Mom this morning." Bobby James picked up the Kellogg's PEP cereal box and poured some into a bowl for me.

"Was he drunk?" I asked.

"I don't think so, but he will be soon, I think. He gets drunk every chance he gets."

"Why does Mom like drunks?"

"Who knows? Eat your cereal. Here's the milk."

As I began to eat my cereal, I wondered what was going to happen to Bobby James and me. I wondered how we would get to Grandma's house, and whether Mom would put us on a bus to go back, the way Grandma had done when she sent us out here.

"Will we go on the bus again, when we go to Grandma's house?" I asked my brother.

"I don't know. I don't think so. After you went to sleep last night, I listened outside their bedroom door. I heard them say something about a car and driving to Washington, D.C., but they didn't know if they would have enough gas. Frank is going to see if he can get some kind of letter from the Army saying he can buy gas for the trip."

"Are we going to leave today?"

"No, I think they are talking about some time next week."

For the next few days, my brother and I played in the park and occasionally went to the zoo and walked around. One of the days it rained, so we stayed in the hotel room and looked at magazines or ran up and down the hallway, trying to hide from each other, until someone from the hotel told us to stop or they would tell our parents. We usually stopped long enough for the person to get out of sight, and then we were off and running again. We tried to get Joseph to take us up and down in the elevator, but he told us it was for the guests in the hotel and not for us to play in. We begged and begged him, but he said he would lose his job if he let us play in the elevator. We pestered him so much that he finally said, "Get the hell outta here! I ain't got no time for your foolishness."

I don't know why he didn't have time. Whenever I saw him, he was just sitting on his stool inside the elevator, waiting to take some passenger up to one of the floors in the hotel. Running up and down the hallways was fun for awhile. Then it became boring. My brother couldn't stand staying in the hotel any longer, so he sneaked out of the hotel to play in the rain, and left me there. I didn't see him for several hours, and when he came back, he was soaking wet.

It didn't bother me to sit in the room or just walk around the hotel. The hotel maids were always friendly and talked to me while they made up the rooms. Sometimes they would give me a piece of candy that one of the soldiers left behind in the room. There were always a lot of soldiers in the hotel. I don't think all of them had a room there, because I would see them in the lobby, sleeping in chairs and on the floor. Soldiers were everywhere, and most of the time they were drunk like Frank, but they were never mean. They were always friendly, and sometimes they would give me money to get them a newspaper or a sandwich.

I thought all soldiers must drink a lot, like Frank. But as I look back on it, I guess they were just trying to have a good time before they had to go off to war. Most of them told me they were going to fight the Japs. I never saw any of them for very long. It was usually just a few days, and then they would be gone and new ones would take their place. I always wondered how the ones who had left were making out fighting the Japs and hoped I would get to see them again. But I never did, and I never found out how they made out.

Thirty-Two

THE DAY FINALLY ARRIVED THAT BOBBY JAMES AND I were dreading. My mother told us she was going to take us back to grandma's on the train, then she and Frank would continue on by train to Washington, D.C. Just as my brother had predicted, she told us that Frank was going overseas to fight the Germans and he had found a job for Mom at someplace called the Pentagon, in Washington, D.C. I didn't want to go back to my grandmother's house. I wanted to stay with my mother, and I begged her to take me with her.

"Please, Mom, I promise I'll be good. Please take me with you. I don't want to stay with Grandma," I sobbed.

"I can't take you with me, honey," she said. "I have to work, and I don't have anyone to take care of you. Grandma can take good care of you, and I'll know you're safe."

I had not been spanked or slapped once the whole time I had been there with my mother, if you didn't count the times my brother punched me. I wanted to stay with her forever. She was very gentle, and I loved being with her.

"I don't want to go back to Grandma's house," I cried. "I want to stay with you."

"Oh, honey, I can't keep you with me. No one will be able to take care of you."

"I promise I'll be good. I won't cry, and I won't get into any trouble. I promise."

"I can't take you and Bobby James with me," she said.

"Please, please Mommy! Please take me with you. Please don't make me go back to Grandma's house. I promise I'll be good. I won't cause any trouble. I promise."

She held me in her arms and hugged me tightly. I could smell her perfume, and I just loved her so much, I didn't ever want to leave her. I was sobbing, and she was rubbing my back and speaking in such a soft, soothing voice – and along with the smell of her perfume, I felt as though I were in heaven. Even today, if I try hard enough, I can still smell her perfume.

"There, there, sweetheart. Everything's going to be fine. You'll have Tim and Bobby James there to play with. I know Tim is going to be happy to see you. Grandma tells me he has really missed you while you've been out here. Everything's going to be okay."

I continued to press up against her in her arms, not wanting to move. I was afraid that if I moved I would never have this time with her again.

"Now, dry those tears and let's have dinner," she said, gently pushing me back off her shoulder.

"Let me see a big smile, now, sweetheart."

She was smiling, and I tried to smile, too.

"There you go," she said. "Just think, it won't be long, and you'll be back playing with Tim."

"When are we going to Grandma's house?" I asked.

"We leave in three days. We're going to take the train. Won't that be exciting? It will be your first trip on a train. You're going to love it. There will be lots of soldiers for you to talk to."

Finally, I resigned myself to the fact that I was going back to Grandma's house. I thought about seeing Tim again and playing with the other kids, Ronnie and Donny and the Wilsons, and I began to feel better about going; but I was still sad that I couldn't stay with my mother.

But then, something happened. Two days before we were supposed to leave on the train, my brother ran away. He had gone down to the lobby to buy a newspaper, just as he had done every day since we got there, but he didn't come back.

Then Frank shouted at my mother that all the money he had on the dresser was missing.

"Goddamn it, that little bastard stole three hundred dollars from me!" He was on a rampage. "He's done this before, Susan. He's stolen money and run away before. He's never going to change, and you know it. I told you we should have put him in Boy's Town a long time ago. He's a thief and a major problem. Your mother doesn't want him back there. She can't control him, and she's told you that. I'm telling you, when we find him this time, we're sending him to Boy's Town. Maybe they can straighten him out."

My mother was crying. I tried to comfort her by rubbing her back but she just kept crying.

"Please don't cry, Mommy. I'll help you find Bobby James," I said.

"Do you know where he might be?" she asked.

"Maybe he's at the zoo," I said. "We go over there whenever it's not raining."

"Frank, I'm going to walk over to the zoo and see if Bobby James is there," she said.

"I don't give a good goddamn what you do. I don't give a damn if he never comes back. Whatever happens to him serves him right. He's nothing but a fucking problem."

My mother didn't answer. She just got up and got ready to leave. I ran after her to the door.

"No, honey, you stay here. I'll be back soon," she told me.

"But, Mom, I know where he likes to go in the zoo. I can help," I pleaded.

"No, thank you for offering, but I need to go alone so I can walk fast and not have worry about you too."

"But I ..." She slipped through the door and was gone, and I was alone in the room with Frank. I didn't know how long she would be gone. I just sat on the couch, worrying about where she was and whether she was okay. I was afraid, after the way Frank had talked to her, that after she found Bobby James she wouldn't come back, and I would be alone with Frank forever. I began to worry. Frank was going away to fight the Germans, and he couldn't take me with him. Where would he leave me if my mother didn't come back? Would he take me back to my grandmother? Maybe he would just leave me here in the hotel? I felt like crying, but I didn't want Frank to see me cry. I didn't want him to tell me to shut up. Suddenly, my thoughts were interrupted by the sound of the phone ringing. It startled me. I hadn't even realized there was a phone in the room.

Frank answered it. "Hello? Yeah, yeah. So he's okay, then? Where did they find him? I see. Well, just tell 'em to keep him there overnight, and we'll get him out in the morning. No, I'm serious, Susan, he needs to be taught a lesson. Let him stay there overnight. Now come on back to the hotel."

Frank hung up the phone and lit a cigarette. I hated it when he smoked in the room, because the smoke made me choke and I had a difficult time breathing.

"That was your mother," he said to me. "The cops found your brother, and they have him at the police station. He's going to stay there overnight. We'll get him in the morning."

"Why does he have to stay there overnight?" I asked.

"Teach him a lesson. Maybe if he spends the night in jail, he'll learn how to behave himself." Smoke curled out of his nose as he talked.

I couldn't figure out why Bobby James had to stay in jail overnight. Jail was for people like the Muncies, not for Bobbie James. He was just a kid. I was sure he wouldn't have broken any law. I sat there wondering what it would be like to be in jail. I wondered if there were people like the Muncies in there with him. Maybe someone would have a knife, like that Muncie boy who threatened to cut my dick off if I told my grandmother he had thrown the fish heads in our yard.

I don't know how long I sat there. At some point, Frank had gone into the bedroom and shut the door behind him. I must have fallen asleep, because the next thing I remember was being awakened by the sound of the key in the door.

The door opened, and my mother walked into the room with Bobby James. I was so happy to see them that I jumped off the couch and ran over to hug them both. My mother had come back, just as she had promised. And she had Bobby James with her. He didn't have to stay in jail overnight after all.

"Get ready for bed, boys," she said as she walked into the bedroom where Frank had gone. She shut the bedroom door, and within a few minutes a loud argument broke out between them.

"I thought you had to stay in jail tonight," I said.

"Mom said no. She wouldn't leave me there. I don't think the policeman wanted to keep me there either, but they tried to scare me."

"Were you scared?"

"Nah, there's nothing to be scared about. They treat you really good. They gave me Coca Cola and ice cream."

"Was Mom mad at you?"

"Yeah, she was pretty mad. She wanted to know why I ran away."

"Why did you?"

"I told Mom I wasn't going back to Grandma's, and if she tries to make me I will run away again."

"What did she say?"

"She started crying and said she didn't know what to do with me. She said she couldn't take care of me in Washington, D.C. and the only place she had to send me was Grandma's. But I told her I wasn't going back to Grandma's, and if she wouldn't take me to Washington with her, I would run away."

"What did she say? Is she going to take you to Washington?"

"I don't know. She's talking about it with Frank right now."

We could hear their raised voices in the bedroom. They were

both mad at each other. Frank was mad because my mother had brought Bobby James back instead of leaving him in jail, and my mother was mad at Frank for wanting to leave Bobby James there.

"He's only thirteen years old. There is no good lesson that he could learn by being left in jail overnight," she shouted.

"Goddamn it, Susan, I'm not going to put up with him running away all the time and doing whatever he damn well pleases. He needs some discipline. If he were old enough, I'd put him in the Army. You've got to do something about him or I'm going to leave you. By the way, where's the three hundred dollars he took? Did you get it back from him?"

I heard my mother crying. She started to plead with Frank. "I don't know what to do with him. I don't know why he acts the way he does. If I did, I would try to fix it; but leaving him in jail overnight is not the answer."

"Goddamn it, you either do something with him or I'll leave you here."

"What do you want me to do, Frank?"

"Put him in Boys Town, right now. I'll call Father Flannigan tomorrow and make the arrangements, otherwise you can do whatever you damn well please, but I'll leave you." There was a lull in the conversation, and the only sound I could hear was my mother crying.

Finally, I heard her say. "Okay, Frank, make the call to Father Flannigan tomorrow."

She was sobbing as she spoke. "They say he works wonders with boys that have problems. Maybe that is the best thing to do."

I could hear her crying and crying. I didn't want to hear it. It hurt me too much.

"Did you get the three hundred dollars back?" Frank asked.

"The police said he didn't have any money on him when they picked him up," my mother answered.

"Well, somebody stole it," Frank shouted.

"Check your other pants, maybe it's in there," my mother said calmly.

I looked at my brother. "Did you take Frank's three hundred dollars?"

"Yeah, I took it," he said.

"What happened to it?"

"The policeman took it away from me when he picked me up. He gave it to Mom when she came down to the station to get me."

"Mom has the three hundred dollars?"

"Yeah."

I considered that for a moment, confused. "How come Mom didn't tell Frank she got the money back?"

"She's afraid he'll drink it up, and they won't have any money for the trip or to give Grandma when we get there."

The next morning, Frank made the call to Father Flannigan; and a day later, Bobby James was on a bus to Boys Town, Nebraska. It would be many years before I would see my brother again.

Once, I heard from my grandmother that Bobby James had run away from Boy's Town, and Frank had pulled some strings to get him into the Army. Later I found out Frank had convinced my mother to lie about Bobby James' age and sign the papers required for the Army to take him.

Thirty-Three

THE DAY AFTER BOBBY JAMES LEFT FOR BOYS TOWN, Mom, Frank and I boarded a train for St. Petersburg. There were soldiers everywhere – G.I.'s, my brother had called them. The train was crowded and hot. My mother had a ticket for me, but it wasn't for a seat. She had to hold me on her lap. Frank spent most of his time drinking with the G.I.'s, and we saw very little of him.

At first I thought I would love sitting on my mother's lap and having her all to myself. But it quickly became impossible for both of us. No matter how much I twisted or turned, I couldn't find a comfortable sleeping position. When I did fall asleep, I was awakened a few minutes later when my mother shifted her position, trying to get comfortable.

"Please don't move, Mommy. I want to go to sleep," I murmured.

"Honey, can you stand up for a few minutes? I think my legs are asleep," she said.

I slid off her lap and stood in the aisle, rubbing the sleep out of my eyes, while she rubbed her legs, trying to get the circulation going again.

"Ma'am, why don't you take my seat for your son?"

It was the G.I. sitting in the seat next to us.

"Oh, no, I couldn't do that. We'll be fine. Thank you for offering," my mother answered.

"Please, I insist. I'm going up to the next car to see some of my buddies," he said, sliding out of his seat into the aisle beside me. He smiled at me. "Whatta ya say, Sport? You wanna save my seat for me while I visit my buddies?"

"Yeah," I said, eager to crawl into his seat and go to sleep.

"Great, don't let anyone sit in it, now. You promise?"

"I promise, thank you," I said.

"You're welcome. By the way, Sport, you like chewing gum?"

"Yeah, I do."

"What kind you like?"

"Juicy Fruit," I said.

"Well, you're in luck. I just happen to have a pack of Juicy Fruit right here. I'll give it to you for saving my seat."

"Gee, thanks."

"You're welcome, Sport." He pushed his way through the crowded aisle toward the next car and shouted over his shoulder, "Don't forget now, don't let anyone take my seat!"

"I won't," I shouted back. I crawled into his seat and immediately fell asleep. Sometime later, I awoke to the sound of my mother's voice. She was talking to a G.I. sitting on the arm of the seat across the aisle from her.

"Would you like a drink ma'am?" the G.I. asked, pushing a brown paper bag in her direction.

"No, I don't think so. Thank you, though."

"You're welcome. You know, this is a troop train. You're not supposed to be drinking on a troop train. But there ain't much else to do 'cept maybe play poker," he said. "I hope I didn't offend you, ma'am."

"No, not at all. Where's your home?" I heard her ask before sleep engulfed me again. I don't know how long I slept, but when I awoke again the G.I. who had given me the gum to watch his seat was sitting in my mother's seat, and the soldier she had been talking to earlier was stretched out asleep in the aisle.

"Hey, sleepyhead, you finally woke up. Have a nice nap?"

"Where's my mother?" I asked.

"She's gone to the dining car, Sport. She'll be back in a few minutes."

Suddenly, I was really hungry, and I wished she had taken me to the dining car with her. I rubbed my eyes and stretched.

"Why do you call me Sport?" I asked the G.I.

"Oh, I don't know. Just a habit I have, I guess. What's your real name?"

"Billy," I answered.

"Okay, Billy. That's what I'll call you from now on. No more Sport."

"I don't mind if you call me Sport. I just wondered why. What's your name?"

"Smitty," he answered. "You can call me Smitty."

Just then my mother returned from the dining car carrying a glass of milk and a sandwich. Smitty practically jumped out of the seat when he saw her. "Here you go, ma'am. Here's your seat back."

"Thank you for watching Billy for me while I was gone."

"You're welcome ma'am. He's a real nice kid. Well, I'm going back up to the next car to see my buddies," Smitty said as he stepped over the soldier in the aisle.

My mother gave me the sandwich, and I gobbled it down and drank the milk as if I hadn't been fed in days. I handed my mother the empty glass and sat back in my seat. I was glad I didn't have to sit on her lap. Suddenly Frank appeared out of nowhere. At first he just stared at me but didn't say anything. He was smoking a cigarette and seemed unsteady on his feet. He turned his gaze on my mother.

"Where have you been, Frank?" she asked, and I detected a combination of hurt and anger in her voice. "I thought you were going to stay with us."

Before Frank could answer, the soldier in the seat across the aisle jumped up. "Here, Captain, you can have my seat so you can be with your wife," he said.

"No, that's okay, son. Keep your seat. I have to get back to my friends in a minute." Then he turned to my mother. "Let me have twenty dollars, Susan. I'm out of money."

"I gave you fifty dollars when we got on the train. What did you do with it?"

"Are you sure you don't want this seat, Captain?" the soldier across the aisle asked again.

"Son, this is the last time I'm going to tell you. Keep your goddamn seat."

"Yes, sir," the soldier said and slid back into his seat, mumbling something I couldn't hear to the G.I. sitting beside him.

"Susan, don't give me any shit. Just give me twenty dollars," Frank said, raising his voice.

"Frank, please don't make a scene. We don't have much money and if I give you twenty dollars, it's going to put us short."

Frank stood there, swaying back and forth and staring at my mother, pursing his lips as though he were trying to think of something to say. Then he just walked off without saying anything more. I could tell by the look on my mother's face that she was angry. She was looking straight ahead, and I saw a tear roll down her cheek.

"I love you Mommy," I said stroking her arm. But she didn't answer. She just kept staring straight ahead and more tears rolled down her cheek. "I love you, Mommy," I said again, continuing to stroke her arm.

She turned to me, her eyes red and full of tears, and took me in her arms. "I love you, too, sweetie," she said as she held me, rocking back and forth. Then she sat up, took a tissue out of her purse and dried her eyes.

"Why are you crying, Mommy? I don't want you to cry."

"I'm not crying, sweetie. I'm just a little tired."

She smiled and tousled my hair, then hugged me again.

I fell asleep with her holding me, and when I awakened sometime later, she was asleep. I watched her sleeping for awhile and then I looked out the window at the fields as they flew by. There was a two-lane road between the train and the fields, and every now and then I saw a car. Several times a train passed us, going in the opposite direction. I tried to see the people in the passing train, but it was traveling too fast and was more of a blur than a train. On two occasions, we spent an entire day on a train siding, waiting for other trains to pass. My mother stopped a colored porter named Steven coming down the aisle. She knew him because he had offered to go to the dining car a few times for her to get sandwiches so she wouldn't have to leave me alone when Smitty wasn't around.

"Steven, why are we stopped on this siding?" my mother asked. "We've been here all day."

"Waitin' on da other troop trains, ma'am."

"How come we have to wait for them?"

"They's got da priority, ma'am. All dem troop trains headed to da west coast gots da priority. They's taken our boys to go fight dem Japs. We has to wait 'til all dem priority trains pass. Then we can go again."

"How long do we have to wait here?"

Steven shook his head. "They don't tells me dat, ma'am."

Just then a soldier with a whiskey bottle in his hand pushed past Steven.

"Get rid ah dat der bottle, son," Steven said to the soldier. "I don't want no drinkin' in dis here car."

The soldier saluted Steven and the bottle disappeared. Steven turned back to my mother.

"Can I gets you anythin', ma'am?" he asked.

"No thank you, Steven. We're fine."

"Okay, ma'am, if you or your boy needs anythin', you just tell me." Then he moved toward the other end of the car, joking with some of the G.I.s standing in the aisle. We hadn't had a bath or been able to change clothes in many days. My mother had a couple of washcloths she would dampen in the bathroom so we could "freshen up," as she would say.

I hated using the bathroom on the train. There was always a

long line to get in and if it wasn't stopped up or overflowing, someone had puked on the floor or worse, in the washbasin.

"This place is full of flies and it stinks, Mommy. I think I'm going to puke."

"Here, honey, wipe your face with the washcloth. It'll cool you off."

I tried to hold the washcloth over my nose while I was in the bathroom so I couldn't smell the stench, and I got out of there as quickly as I could. I wondered if the trip was ever going to end.

After ten days without getting off the train, we finally reached St. Petersburg. It was nearly midnight, but my grandmother was at the station to meet us. My mother and I got off together, and Frank found us on the platform about a half hour later. He was drunk, slurring his words and staggering when he walked.

"Susan," my grandmother said, "you and Billy can come to the house, but Frank cannot. I'm not going to put up with a drunk in my house."

"Oh, Mama," my mother said, "he's not drunk. He's just tired. He'll be okay."

"He is drunk! I can smell him all the way over here. He cannot come to the house. I'll take Billy, and you are welcome to come too, but not Frank. Make up your mind."

I knew my grandmother meant business, and I was glad. It was nice not having Frank around on the train, and I didn't want him to go with us to my grandmother's house. I was afraid my mother might convince Grandma to let him come, but I didn't have to worry. It soon became clear that my grandmother was not about to let Frank come with us.

"Mama, listen, we're only going to be here a couple of days and then Frank and I are taking the train to Washington. Just let him stay there at the house until we leave," my mother pleaded.

"I said no, and that means no," my grandmother said firmly.

"Mama, this is war time. I'm sure we can't find a hotel room, especially this late at night."

My grandmother said nothing, but the look on her face could not be mistaken. Frank was not welcome.

"Listen, Susan," Frank slurred, "you go on to the house with your mother. I'll find a hotel room."

"No, Frank, I don't want to leave you," my mother said and turned back to face my grandmother.

"Mama, you take Billy, and I'll go with Frank. We'll see you tomorrow."

"Don't bother to come if you have Frank with you. I don't want him in the house."

My mother leaned down and kissed me on the forehead.

"I'll see you tomorrow, sweetie," she said holding my chin in her hand.

I stared at her back as I watched her walk away with Frank.

"Get in the car," my grandmother said to me.

I got into the back seat and my grandmother drove us home in silence. It seemed strange to be sitting back there by myself. We kids always had to sit in the back whenever my grandmother drove us anywhere. She said it was safer for us to be back there. This was the first time that I could remember sitting back there by myself; usually Tim and Butchie sat back there with me. When we got to the house, my grandfather was still up and waiting for us. He seemed happy to see me, but I don't think my grandmother was happy at all. If she was happy about anything, it was that my brother hadn't come with us.

"Where's Susan?" my grandfather asked.

"She's staying in a hotel with the drunk," my grandmother replied.

"Where's Tim?" I asked.

"He's asleep. You need to get to sleep too. Go to the bathroom and get in bed, and don't wake Tim up."

"Can I have a drink of water?"

"No, you cannot," my grandmother said. "I don't want you wetting the bed."

"My mother let me have a drink if I wanted one," I said.

"I don't care what your mother let you do," she snapped. "She's not here."

"But, Grandma, I didn't wet the bed when she let me have a drink at night."

"You heard me. Now, get yourself in bed."

I knew that was her final answer. If I said anything more, I might get a rap in the mouth. As I went to the bedroom, I slammed the screen door between the kitchen and the hallway. In less time than it took me to take the five steps from the screen door to the door of the bedroom, my grandmother was there with the stick from the top of the icebox in her hand. She gave me a whack on my backside before I ever knew what happened.

"Now, do you want to slam that door again?" she demanded.

"No," I said.

"Good, now get in bed and don't wake Tim up."

Nothing had changed. The bunk beds in our room were still there. I had wondered if Tim had taken the top bunk since I had been gone, but when I looked at the beds, he was asleep on the bottom bunk as usual. I was happy that I at least still had the top one. I wanted to wake Tim up to let him know I was back, but I was afraid my grandmother might hear us talking and come into the room with her stick again.

I'll talk to him in the morning, I thought to myself as I slowly climbed the ladder to my bunk.

As I lay there in my bed, trying to go to sleep, I wondered whether Whitbeck's cow still lived across the street, and whether my cousin would be glad to see me again. I also wondered if my mother would really come to the house tomorrow, or if I would ever see her again. I thought about a Navajo Indian boy I had seen riding along the road on his pinto pony in New Mexico. I remembered how he waved at us as we passed. I thought about how free he seemed to be, riding his pony in the desert. I thought about the desert and the changing colors in the canyons and on the mountains as the sun began to set. Exhausted I slowly closed my eyes, and sleep swiftly swept over me.

That night, I dreamed about the Indian kids I had seen on their ponies, riding along the side of the road as we passed by on the bus. I wanted to be with them, and suddenly I was riding my own pony through a shaded canyon. Then I came out onto the desert where there were cactus and tumbleweeds. I wondered where the Indian kids had gone. I saw a red mesa in the distance and rode toward it. As I rode toward the mesa, it kept moving away from me. I rode and rode, but the mesa got smaller and smaller as it moved further and further away from me, until I couldn't see it anymore. Then I saw my mother waving to me. I tried to see her face, but I couldn't. As I got closer, I saw that she wasn't waving to me. She had her back to me. And I realized I didn't know what she looked like anymore.

Suddenly I jerked awake and I was crying. A feeling of loneliness swept over me. I rolled over on my stomach and, with tears running down my face, I fell asleep wondering if I would ever see my mother again.

Thirty-Four

THE NEXT MORNING I WAS AWAKE BEFORE TIM, AND I slipped out of my bunk and down the ladder to wake him. "Hey Tim, wake up," I whispered and shook him gently. I didn't know what time it was, but it was light outside so I figured he should be awake by now. "Wake up," I said again and gave him a stronger shake.

Suddenly his eyes opened and he smiled at me. "I heard you slam the screen door last night," he said.

"Why didn't you say something?"

"I didn't want Grandma to hear me talking. I was afraid she would whack me if she heard us."

"What have you been doing since I've been gone?"

"Not much," he said. "You haven't been gone that long."

"So who have you been playing with?"

"I play with Ronnie and Donny a lot. They're fun."

"Have you been playing with the Wilsons?"

"Sometimes, but mostly I play with Ronnie and Donny. They're more fun. They have a game called Pick Up Sticks that we play on their front porch."

"How do you play it?" I asked. "Do you have to go out in the yard and find a bunch of sticks or something?"

"No, the sticks are in a can. You throw them in a stack on the floor and then you try to pick up each one, one at a time, without moving any of the other sticks."

"Let's go outside and climb trees. You want to?"

"Okay, yeah," he said.

We got dressed and slipped out the back door, and then we raced each other to the oak trees in the back yard. Butchie heard us and came out from under the house where he had been sleeping. I stopped to hug him to let him know how happy I was to see him. He licked me all over my face when he saw me and kept jumping all around me. We ran to the trees and he bounced along beside us.

"I think he's glad you're back," Tim said.

"I think so, too. I know I'm sure glad to see him."

After we had been playing for awhile, Grandma called us in for breakfast. I was looking forward to eggs, sunny side up, with bacon and toast; but she had fixed poached eggs instead. Next to eggs sunny side up, I loved poached eggs the best – and I liked the way my grandmother fixed them. She would fill one of her frying pans with water and once it was boiling she would break an egg and drop it in. It would float there and boil. When the yolk was just turning purple, but before it got hard, she would use a large, flat ladle with holes in it to scoop the egg out of the boiling water and lay it on a piece of toast. It was almost like having an egg sunny side up.

When I cut into the egg, the yolk broke and soaked into the bread. It was delicious. And there was bacon, too. Maybe she was glad I was back after all.

After we ate, we went back outside to play. I wanted to find Jack and Johnny and tell them about all the things I had seen on the bus trip. I wanted to tell them about the park and the zoo, and the train trip back to St. Petersburg, and all the soldiers I met. Their father was a marine in the Pacific someplace, fighting the Japs. Tim and I ran across the field to the edge of their property. I called out to them, but there was no answer.

We slipped into the thick brush and made our way among the bushes and palmettos. The kudzu vines hung from the trees like curtains we had to pass through as we moved deeper onto their property. After we had walked about thirty feet, we passed under one of the huge oaks. Suddenly, loud screaming and yelling surrounded us. Jack jumped out of the oak tree and pretended to be shooting at us with a rifle, which was as big as he was. Johnny jumped out of some bushes and began shooting at us with his cap pistol. He was wearing a steel helmet painted olive drab. Then Sally Ann jumped up from the ground right beside us. She had been hiding under a pile of brush and leaves, and began throwing sticks at us. She was wearing the olive drab liner to the helmet Johnny was wearing. All three of them were wearing web belts with canteens on them.

"You guys are dead," they announced. "You walked right into our ambush, and you're both dead," Johnny shouted.

It was true. They had been so well hidden we never saw them until we walked right up on them.

"Where did you guys get all this stuff?" I asked, indicating the rifle and the rest of the military gear they were wearing.

"Our dad brought it back from the war. This is a real Jap rifle," Jack said proudly.

"What's your dad doing back from the war? Is it over?" I asked.

"Nah, it ain't over, yet. Our dad got wounded and got to come home. He's only got one eye now."

"Can he still see?"

"Yeah, he can see okay," Jack said. "But they won't let him fight anymore. I think he got hurt in the head too. He says he's got a steel plate on one side."

"He's got some metal in his hip too, and he has to walk with a cane," Sally Ann added.

"He brought all this stuff back with him," Johnny said.

"This is really neat," I said. "You guys were completely hidden. Can we play war with you?"

"Sure, but you guys have to be the Japs and try to find us before we shoot you," Jack said.

"How do you like all the stuff our dad brought back from the war?" Sally Ann asked.

"It's neat. Can we play with some of it too?" I asked.

"No," Jack and Johnny said at the same time. "Our dad said we couldn't let anyone else play with it. He wants to keep it, and he's afraid it'll get lost."

I noticed Jack had a long knife in a scabbard attached to his webbed belt. "Where'd you get that knife?" I asked.

"It's a bayonet my dad took off a Jap, after he killed him."

"Neat. Can I see it?"

"Sure, but you have to give it right back. And be careful, it's really, really sharp," he said as he took the bayonet out of its scabbard and handed it to me.

I looked at the bayonet for a long time, wondering if the Jap had ever used it to kill an American before Jack's father had killed him. It was a weird feeling, standing there holding a bayonet that had belonged to a Jap soldier who was now dead. I thought about all the soldiers I had met in the hotel in California and on the train, and I wondered whether any of them would get killed, and whether some Jap kid would be playing with *their* stuff. I couldn't explain it, but holding the bayonet gave me a feeling of overwhelming sadness.

"Come on, give it back," Jack said. "Are we gonna play war or not?"

"Okay," I said. "Let us go home and get our guns, then we'll be back to fight you."

Okay, but don't forget, you have to be the Japs and try to find us in here," Johnny reminded us.

Tim and I ran back to our own yard.

"We don't have any guns," Tim said when we got back to our house.

"We'll have to find some," I said. "We can use some wood that looks like a gun and just pretend."

We went to my grandfather's wood pile in the chicken yard,

behind the shed. I began looking through pieces of wood, and I soon found two pieces nailed together that looked like a pistol, if you used your imagination a little.

"Do you want this for a pistol?" I asked Tim.

"No, I found a rifle. Look at this." He showed me a long thin piece of wood that had been cut so one end was wider than the other. If you looked really hard, you could see where the wide part could be the stock of a rifle.

"Okay, let's go get those guys," I said.

We took off running across the field and into the brush on the Wilson's property. As soon as we came to the kudzu vines, I slowed and looked around to see if we could spot them. I was sure they would be in the same hiding places they used when we walked into their ambush a few minutes ago.

"Tim, you run over there where Sally Ann was hiding earlier and start shooting at her. I'll stay here and cover you. When they start shooting at you, we'll know where they are, and we can get 'em."

Tim ran over to Sally Ann's old position, but she wasn't there. "She's not here," he shouted at me.

"Okay, I'm coming. We'll have to find them."

We began creeping forward, looking in the trees and bushes and in the clumps of palmettos where we thought they might be hiding. Just as we were passing under the oaks, all three of them jumped out of the trees from different directions. Before we could think to shoot any of them, they snatched our guns away from us and ran deeper into the brush, toward the back of their house, shooting at us as they ran yelling, "You dirty Japs are dead."

I was mad. I was mad because they had taken our guns, and because we hadn't thought to look in the trees. "Come on, give us our guns back and we'll try to find you again," I shouted.

"We won't give you your guns back," they shouted from somewhere in the brush. "We captured them. You have to go home and get some more."

"You better give us our guns back," I shouted at them.

"Oh yeah, what are you gonna do if we don't?" Jack shouted.

"My grandmother is a policewoman. You better give our guns back, or I'm going to tell her," I threatened.

"What's she gonna do, come and arrest us?"

"Yeah, and she'll take you off to jail too!"

"Okay, go ahead and tell her!" Johnny called out. "We don't care."

I knew it was an idle threat. My grandmother would just laugh at me if I told her to go arrest them because they took our guns away from us. She would say it served us right for being dumb enough to let them do it.

Just as Tim and I were about to leave and go back to our own yard, Sally Ann came running up and gave our guns back. Jack and Johnny were right behind her.

"Do you guys still want to play?" Johnny asked.

"Yeah, we still want to play," I said. "But you can't take our guns away from us anymore. We don't have any of that neat stuff like you guys."

"Okay," Jack said. "You two pretend you're Japs. Go hide, and we'll count to a hundred and then come and find you."

Tim and I bolted into the brush. We could hear Sally Ann counting as we searched for a place to hide. Just as she was about to reach one hundred, we quickly decided on a small clump of palmettos that we could hide under. We saw that if we lay flat on our stomachs, they wouldn't be able to see us. We would let them get right on top of us and then we would open fire with our make-believe guns and kill all three of them.

We lay there as quiet as possible, and in a few minutes we saw them coming through the brush. Tim saw them first. He tapped me on the shoulder and pointed at the movement behind some kudzu vines. We were both a little giddy, certain they hadn't seen us. We knew we had them and would easily be able to surprise them.

Suddenly, a rotten grapefruit crashed through the palmettos and landed between us. It broke apart and exploded all over us with the stinking smell of rotted fruit.

"KA-BLOOIE!" Jack and Johnny shouted together. "You guys are dead. We just blew you up with a hand grenade."

"Hey, you guys changed the rules," I shouted. "That's not fair. We're supposed to shoot each other."

"My dad says everything is fair in love and war," Jack shouted back.

For the rest of the day and for many days following, we played war with each other, shooting, hiding, ambushing and throwing rotten-fruit hand grenades into each other's hiding places. Maybe being back wasn't so bad.

Thirty-Five

MY MOTHER AND FRANK ONLY STAYED THREE DAYS before they left for Washington. My mother came to the house twice, but Frank did not come with her. I was glad. It was nice seeing my mother, but the time with her was painfully short and all too soon it was time for her to leave. The night she left, I hugged her for as long as I could before she finally pried my arms from around her neck.

"I want you to be a good boy, honey. Do what your grandmother tells you to, and I will see you when I get back."

"When are you coming back, Mommy?"

"As soon as I can, sweetie. Now promise me you'll be a good boy."

"I'll try," I said with an empty feeling in my stomach, trying to hold back the tears.

"I know you will," she said and kissed me on my forehead.

Tears filled my eyes and rolled down my cheeks. She kissed me again on the forehead before she stood, picked up her suitcase, and followed my grandmother out to the car. I ran to my bedroom to look out the window, hoping to see her and wave to her as my grandmother backed down the driveway. As the car went by, I waved, but she didn't see me. Then she was gone.

For several days after she left, I felt a loneliness I hadn't known before. The days dragged by, and for awhile I held out hope that she would change her mind and come back. But after a few weeks, I knew that wasn't going to happen. My cousin and I climbed trees or played in the fields with the Wilson kids or with Ronnie and Donny. Sometimes we spent the entire day at the beach, fishing, swimming and crawling under the Casino, looking for money. My grandmother never made us come home for lunch on the days we went to the beach.

"If you boys want lunch, be here at twelve noon. If you're not here, you won't get anything until supper time. And if you miss lunch, you better be home for supper at four o'clock. Is that clear?"

"Yes, ma'am," we answered as we ran out the door.

We usually stayed at the beach all day and counted on finding enough money under the Casino to get something to eat. Sometimes we got lucky and found enough change for us each to get a nickel root beer and an order of French fries to share, but that was rare. We usually went hungry and drank out of the water fountain in the picnic area on the beach.

One day as we were emerging from under the Casino from an unsuccessful search for change, I saw my grandmother pulling into the parking area between the beach and the road. I watched her, waiting for her to get out. I figured she had come to get us for some reason. But she stayed in the car.

"Come on Tim, let's go over to the swings and climb on the monkey bars for awhile," I said and started running toward the swings.

I didn't want my grandmother to know I had seen her, because I was afraid she was going to make us go home with her. We each crossed the monkey bars a couple of times. Tim had not seen my grandmother's car, and I didn't mention it; but I continued to watch her out of the corner of my eye. She was still in the car. I wondered why, but I still wanted it to appear as though we hadn't seen her, lest she catch our eye and motion for us to come get in the car.

"Come on, Tim. Let's go back in the water. I'll race you." And off we ran, hitting the water as fast as we could. It was a game we played to see how far we could run into the water before we fell. Since neither of us knew how to swim, we stayed in the shallow water, splashing each other and rough housing, trying to dunk one another. After a few minutes, I glanced up to see if my grandmother had gotten out of the car yet. I fully expected to see her watching us and beckoning us out of the water. But her car was gone.

Why had she been there, and why had she left? I wondered if we were in trouble for something and were going to get punished when we got home. Maybe she had seen us coming out from under the Casino. I had never mentioned that we went crawling under there to my grandmother, and now I wondered if we were going to get punished for it. If we were, I wondered why she hadn't made us go home right then. I was starting to worry about it when Tim suddenly jumped on my shoulders, trying to pull me under water. I quickly forgot about the possibility of getting punished, and we began playing again.

Periodically, one of us would run up on the beach and check to see what time it was with some of the elderly people sitting at the picnic tables. To get home by four o'clock, we had to leave the beach by three thirty.

As it turned out, we did not get punished for anything when we got home. My grandmother did not mention that she had been parked at the beach, and I did not tell her I had seen her. I did wonder why she had been there though, and I made a mental note to be careful not to let her catch us crawling around under the Casino, just in case she disapproved.

Thirty-Six

A FEW WEEKS LATER, CRYSTAL DECIDED TO TAKE TIM and me to have lunch with her and R.C. Kitchen at our favorite place behind the Porpoise Inn, where R.C. worked.

"Don't you boys forget dem fishin' poles, now," she said. "We needs you to catch some of dem shiners so R.C. can fry up 'em for lunch."

My grandfather had made us each a fishing pole out of bamboo or, as he called it, cane. It wasn't anything fancy: just a bamboo pole with some fishing line, a hook, a lead sinker and a bobber. When we walked to the beach, we would wind the fishing line around the pole and carry them over our shoulders, like a soldier would carry his rifle. People called us Tom Sawyer and Huckleberry Finn when they saw us.

Having our own fishing poles was one thing, but we had to find a penny somehow before we could fish. We needed to buy a shiner for bait. The easiest way to get the penny was to find an empty soda pop bottle thrown along the side of the road. That was worth two cents when we turned it in at the Casino for the deposit. If we were not lucky enough to find a pop bottle before we got to the beach, then we would crawl under the Casino to look for change. If that came up dry, we would walk out on the pier and wait for someone to catch a shiner, and ask them to give it to us before they threw it back. Sometimes that was a pretty hard way to get bait because other kids were trying the same thing.

"Hey, mister," one of us would yell, "can I have that shiner before you throw it back?"

 "Sorry kid, I already promised it to that kid over there."

Sometimes it was a kid we knew from school, and we would ask him to let us cut off a couple of pieces of the shiner so we could bait our hooks. Once we got the bait and could get our hooks in the water, we were almost guaranteed to start catching more shiners right away. Then we had our bait for the rest of the day and we could start catching more to sell to Sonny or take over to R.C. to cook up for our lunch.

The one thing you had to be careful about was making sure the shiners didn't die before you could get them to the bait house. Sonny only bought live ones. He kept them alive by throwing them into a large tank that floated in the water under the bait house. Fishermen going after bigger fish like mackerel or flounder bought them from Sonny. If you left the shiners you caught lying on the pier in the sun, they died immediately. The best way to keep them alive was to keep them in a bucket of seawater until you had ten of them. Sonny only bought them ten at a time and only paid a half a cent a piece for a shiner. He said he didn't want to mess with pennies. So to get a nickel, you had to have ten shiners. Tim and I never had a bucket, so we would ask one of the old men fishing on the pier if we could keep our shiners in their bucket until we had enough to sell.

One day, we really got lucky. I asked one of the fishermen if we could put our shiners in his bucket to keep them alive.

"What are you gonna do with those little fish, kid?" he asked.

"We're gonna sell 'em to the bait house when we get ten of 'em," I said.

"Okay, sure, you can keep 'em in my bucket," he said. "Let me know when you get ten of 'em."

Within a few minutes we had ten, and I told him we were going to take them out and sell them. But when I started taking them out of the bucket, they started flapping all over the place and Tim and I couldn't hold all ten of them at the same time.

"Can I borrow your bait bucket to take them in to Sonny and sell 'em?" I asked. "I promise I'll bring it right back."

"How many you say you have in there?" the man asked.

"Ten. We can only sell them ten at a time," I said.

"Tell you what," he said, "why don't you just leave them in the bucket for me, and I'll give you a nickel a piece for 'em."

I couldn't believe my ears. A nickel a piece meant we would have fifty cents, a quarter a piece, to spend. We had never gotten more than ten cents at the most for selling shiners before.

"You sure, mister? Sonny only gives us a half a cent a piece."

"I know, but I'll give you a nickel a piece for them if you sell them to me. You boys have been working really hard this morning. Do we have a deal?" he asked.

"Yes, sir," I said. "We sure do, mister."

He gave us our money and off we ran to spend it on hot dogs and sodas at the Casino.

"Hey, boys, don't forget your fishing poles," he yelled.

We ran back, picked up our poles, and started for the Casino again. We couldn't believe our luck. We had enough money for us each to have a hotdog, a bag of potato chips and a soda.

"After we finish eating, maybe we should find that guy again and try to sell him some more shiners," I said.

"Yeah, I might want another hotdog after this one," Tim said.

"Yeah, me too," I grinned.

We sat there and slowly ate our hot dogs, chips and drank our sodas. This had been our lucky day, and we were in no mood to move off the porch of the Casino. But pretty soon it was time for us to go home. I didn't want to go. I just wanted to sit there on the porch looking out at the bay and watching the kids jumping off the diving dock, which the City of Gulfport had built. It was about a hundred yards off shore and was a long way to swim. If you were like Tim and me and didn't know how to swim, you could usually get one of the older kids to take you out there on his back. But that limited you, because you could only get out there when some older kid would take you, and then you had to stay out there until that kid or some other kid was ready to come back to the shallow water.

Whenever Crystal took us to the beach, we had lots of fun with her and R.C. Today – going to have lunch with her and R.C – was going to be as good as that day when we sold the shiners for a nickel each. I had my pole over my shoulder, and I was happy. The three of us walked along in contented silence. Tim and I tried to keep from burning our bare feet on the hot sand in the road while at the same time staying out of the sandspurs on the side of the road. Crystal seemed to be immune to both the hot sand and the sandspurs as she padded along in her bare feet.

Tim and I followed in single file behind her, keeping our eyes peeled for a soda pop bottle. She had a long stride and sometimes we had to run to keep up with her. My mind began to wander, and I thought again about the day I had seen my grandmother sitting in her car at the beach. I decided to ask Crystal about it.

"Crystal?" I called to her.

No reply.

"Crystal?"

"Wha'chu wants child?" she asked without looking around or breaking her stride.

"I want to ask you a question."

"Well, go on then and aks me."

"The other day, when Tim and I were at the beach, I saw Grandma sitting in her car. She didn't get out and she didn't say anything to us. Do you know why she would do that?"

"Child, don't you know anytime you and Tim goes to the beach alone, yo grandma drives down dare to check on ya'll? She always be goin' in da morning, and if you two ain't showed up fo' lunch, then she done goes down dare again in the afternoon."

"Why does she do that?" I asked.

Crystal stopped walking and turned around to face me.

"'Cause she be worried 'bout you, boy. Don't you knows that? Also, she's a poleese woman, and it's her job to check on the beach too."

"How can she drive the car so much? Isn't gas still rationed?"

"I don't know nothin' bout no gas ration and yo grandma's car. I only knows she drives to the beach to check on you boys when ya'll is there."

"She checks on the beach?" Tim asked.

"Das right."

"What does she do to check on the beach?" I asked.

"She makes sure no one be causin' no problems."

"What kind of problems?"

"She makes sure nobody ain't gettin' drunk or loud or doin' no fightin'."

"What does she do if she sees a drunk or someone fighting?" Tim asked.

"She makes 'em leave the beach. She sho does," Crystal answered, shaking her head with admiration.

"How do you know she does that?" I asked.

"'Cause sometimes she makes me go with her. I sits in the back seat and I don't get outta the car or nothin', but I can sees what's goin' on."

I knew why Crystal never got out of the car. Colored people weren't allowed on the beach, and there would be trouble if anyone saw her there.

"Did you ever see my grandmother stop someone from fighting?"

"I ain't never seen her stop no fight, but I done seen her make a drunk leave the beach one time."

"What happened?" Tim and I both asked together.

"Well, we done drove down to the beach to check on you boys. I guess we done been sittin' dare 'bout thuty minutes watchin' the people. Then this drunk man come staggerin' 'cross the beach from the Casino carrin' a beer bottle. He ain't got no shirt on or nothin'.

And, oohie, he be so sunburned. He look like one a them crabs after R.C. done boiled it. I ain't never seen a body so sunburned. He be yellin' at people and tryin' to put his arm around dem young girls. Yo grandma, she done seen him staggerin' our way, and she watch him tryin' to put his arm around dem girls. So, she done reached in the pocket of her dress and pulled out her poleese badge and pins it on the front of her dress. Then she gets outta the car and walks over to him. And he aks her, 'Whaddaa ya want old woman?' And I sees him staggerin' toward her, and I be thinkin', oh lawd, don't let that drunk man hit yo grandma with no beer bottle."

"Was she afraid?" I asked.

"I don't rightly know. She didn't act like she was afraid. She just started talkin' to him and pointin' toward the Casino."

"Then what did he do?" Tim asked.

"Well, at first he be standin' dare, swayin' back and forth. Then he looks back toward the Casino where yo grandma is pointin'. Then he turned back to yo grandma and tried to put his arm 'round her. She done brushed his arm away. I couldn't hears what she done tol 'em, but I sees her pointing toward the Casino again. 'Bout that time this woman in a bathin' suit walks up and puts her arm around the drunk man, and she's talking to yo grandma. I sees her shakin' her head and sayin' okay, like she gonna do what yo grandma done tol 'em. Then they just starts walkin' toward one of dem cars parked further down the beach near the Casino. Yo grandma, she just stood dare watchin' em 'til they gets in theys car. When theys gone, yo grandma come back to her car and aks me, 'Do you see the boys anywhere?' And I says, 'Yes, ma'am, Miss Christian. Them boys over by the swings. Theys fine.' Then we leave, and she drives back to the house."

"Wow. Does my grandmother have a gun?" I asked.

"No, she ain't got no gun, child. You grandma don't like no guns. She don't need no gun. She got that badge. She be real proud of that badge."

We started walking again, Crystal leading the way. "Come on

now, we's gots to hurry. R.C. gonna be lookin' for us. Maybe he think we ain't coming and he eat by hisself."

We continued walking and within a few minutes Tim spied a soda pop bottle in the grass about ten feet off the side of the road. Now we wouldn't have to waste time crawling under the Casino. We could get our bait and start fishing right away.

As soon as we got to the beach, Tim and I ran over to the Casino to cash the pop bottle in for the deposit. When we went back to the restaurant to tell Crystal we were ready to go fishing, R.C. gave us a big tin can to keep the shiners in so they wouldn't die.

Together that day, Tim and I caught twenty shiners, and R.C. cooked them up with French fries. We didn't have enough money for sodas, so R.C. got us all ice water to drink. When it was time to go home, I didn't want to leave; but Crystal said she had to get us home so she wouldn't miss the last trolley car to St. Petersburg. As we were leaving, I heard R.C. tell her he would see her later, and I saw her smile.

Thirty-Seven

ONE NIGHT, A FEW MONTHS AFTER RETURNING FROM California, I was lying in bed as still as I could, trying to cool off while I listened to the other kids laughing and shouting as they played outside. Every now and then, in between their shouts, I could hear Whitbeck's cow lowing. It was such a soft, sweet sound and I wondered what she was trying to say. I decided that I wanted to go and see her. I wanted to see what she looked like, standing in that field just before sunset.

I slipped down the ladder from my bunk to the floor as quietly as I could. Tim was already asleep, as usual. I slipped out of our bedroom and into the hallway and then into the front room. Tim would not know I was gone, unless he had heard me get out of bed. If he hadn't heard me, he would just assume I was still in my bed above him – a major advantage of having the top bunk. I could always lean over the edge of my bunk and look down to see if Tim was there, but he had to get out of his bed to check on me; and he was too afraid to do that once he had been put to bed at night.

Slowly, I slipped through the front room, across the front porch and into the front yard. It was still light, so there was a chance someone might see me. I had a moment when I almost lost my nerve and went back inside, but I had come this far. I might as well go all the way across the road to the trees where I could climb up high enough to maybe see the cow.

I mustered all my courage and ran all the way from the front porch to the road and up a tree before I even took a breath. I climbed to the top as quickly as I could. It was much harder to climb in my bare feet. I kept jabbing the soles of my feet on the jagged twigs that stuck out of some of the tree limbs. At last, I was at the top –and I could hear the cow again.

I had never been able to see her any of the other times I looked over the fence, even though I could often hear her. I had always been disappointed, and I was afraid I would be again. But on this day, I was finally rewarded. I was so surprised, I almost fell out of the tree.

She was large and tan. She reminded me of Elsie, the Borden's cow I had seen in magazines advertising Borden's Milk. As I watched her, she slowly walked along, eating grass. Then she stopped, raised her head, and let out a long, soft moo. Then she started walking again, with her head down, eating more grass. She repeated this behavior over and over, and I just watched from my perch in the oak tree. I thought her moo was such a beautiful sound, and I loved watching her walk through the field, eating grass and stopping to moo every few steps. Something about that fascinated me, but it also made me lonely for my mother.

I don't know how long I stayed in the tree watching her, but it was dark when I finally decided to climb down and return to the house. Using the vines like ropes, I slowly lowered myself hand over hand. Once on the ground, it was much darker than it had been at the top of the tree. I quietly moved to the edge of the trees and was about to make a run for the house when I saw a shadow moving in the center of the road. Oh my God! My heart raced and I began to sweat uncontrollably. My legs started shaking so badly I thought I was going to collapse. My grandmother must have discovered I was not in bed and had come out to look for me. What could I do? I was trapped. If she caught me, I knew she would use her stick and God knows what other punishment she might think of.

I stared, trying to make out which direction she was going. Maybe I could sneak around her and still make it back to the house without being seen. As my eyes began to adjust to the dark, I noticed that the form was still moving, but it wasn't going anywhere. How could that be? I rubbed my eyes and strained to focus them on the shadowy form in front of me. It didn't look as big to me as it had when I first saw it. What was going on?

I looked closer and suddenly I realized it wasn't my grandmother at all. It was the Hudson's dog, Skipper. He was lying in the middle of the road, licking himself, and he was directly between me and my grandmother's front door. The panic I had felt just a few minutes earlier quickly subsided, but I had another problem now. How was I going to get around that damned dog? He hated me. If I tried to run past him, he would jump up and attack me. I envisioned him pulling me down and could practically feel his teeth as he tore into my arms and legs. This was serious trouble. I wasn't sure which was worse, my grandmother or the dog.

I was trapped outside. My grandmother might decide to check on me at any moment and I was in danger of being attacked by that stupid dog and maybe even being seriously injured or even killed. At the least, the noise would surely bring my grandmother out to see what was going on. If Skipper didn't succeed in killing me, my grandmother would definitely finish me off. For a second, I wished that Butchie were out and would come find me so I could have him kill Skipper. But I knew that was foolish. Butchie was in the house. I had to figure this out for myself.

I quickly and quietly withdrew back into the cover of the brush around the oaks while I tried to pull myself together and figure out how I was going to get out of this. As I moved up against the tree, I stepped on the jagged edge of a rock, which sent a sharp pain all the way up my leg. Damn, I thought, everything is going wrong. What was that stupid dog doing out there anyway? Butchie should have killed him a long time ago. I reached down and picked up the rock to get it out of the way so I wouldn't step on it again.

Then I had an idea. I felt around on the ground for another rock. In a few minutes I found one. Slowly and as quietly as I could, I crept back to the edge of the road and saw that Skipper was still there, licking his balls. With the rock in my right hand, I took careful aim. This had better work, I thought. If I miss, Skipper will surely figure out where the rock came from and charge into the brush after me. I knew I would not have time to make it to the safety of the oak tree if he did. I would be dog food. Slowly I drew my hand back, trying to remember what my brother had taught me when we threw rocks at tin cans. "Keep your eye directly on your target," he had said, "and when you bring your arm forward to release the rock, throw it as hard as you can, letting it follow your line of sight. You'll hit the target every time."

I slowly cocked my arm behind my head and then – as I brought it forward with all my might – I continued to look directly at Skipper's head. As soon as I let the rock go, I knew it was a good throw. It smacked Skipper with a hard thud on the side of the head. He immediately jumped up with a yelp, looking stunned and confused. He had no idea what had hit him or where it came from. While he stood there, looking up and down the road and periodically shaking his head, I shifted the rock I had been holding in my left hand over to my right hand. Again I slowly cocked my arm and this time drew a bead on Skipper's side. I wanted to hit him in the ribs as hard as I could. I hoped it would send him running home. I kept my eyes directly on his rib cage and let the rock fly. Again, my aim was perfect; I thought I heard the air go out of his lungs when the rock hit him. He staggered for a minute and then let out a series of yelps as he ran down the road to his house.

Once I was sure Skipper wasn't coming back, I ran for the front door of my house, hoping my grandmother had not noticed I was out of bed. The chances of her checking the top bunk were slim, because she was too heavy and would not climb up the ladder to look in my bunk. But I also knew you could never be too sure. Just about the time you thought you were safe was when she would catch you. I knew she hadn't caught me if I got to the front porch and the screen door wasn't locked. If she had discovered that I was out of bed and out of the house, she would have locked me out. We only had screen doors on the front and back of the house, and my grandmother never kept them locked unless she was locking my brother out. Since he was not living with us anymore, there was no reason for the door to be locked.

Ten feet from the door, I heard a vicious growl and saw Skipper racing full speed across the yard from his house, headed directly for me. I prayed I wouldn't trip. The growl was deeper, more vicious and much closer. I was sure he knew that I was the one who had hit him with the rocks. If he caught me, he would kill me. Two feet from the door, I prayed out loud, "Please dear God, don't let him catch me."

I jumped directly to the top step, and I could hear his paws on the grass behind me. My heart was pounding. Was it locked? "Please dear God, please don't let it be locked." I grabbed the handle, the door swung open and I slipped inside, closing it behind me just as Skipper hit the top step.

I stood there staring out at him. His growl was a low, nasty sound and saliva hung from his mouth in long, thick streams, dripping on the steps. His upper lip curled back exposing ugly, yellow teeth and his head jerked sideways each time he growled as if to emphasize how much he hated me. I stood as close to the door as I could get without touching it, and then I peed through the screen, hitting Skipper in his mouth and nose. He stopped growling and began to sneeze. I kept the stream of pee on him until he finally turned away and ran back to his own yard.

Once Skipper was gone, I stood there on the front porch for a few minutes, shaking and covered in sweat. When I finally recovered and knew I was safe, I walked as quietly as I could through the front room, back to my bedroom. Even though the adrenalin was still rushing through my body, I tried to be as quiet as possible. There was no reason to let myself get caught now.

I slipped back into my bed and quickly fell asleep, happy and exhausted. Pissing on Skipper and hitting him twice with a rock was almost as good as getting to see the Whitbeck's cow. I never sneaked across the street again to see that cow; I didn't need to. After that night, whenever I was lying in bed with the sun going down and heard her lowing in the field, I could see her in my mind's eye as she strolled through the field, eating grass, stopping now and then to raise her head and let out a long soft moo. It was a nice picture and a wonderful sound to fall asleep to.

Thirty-Eight

AFTER AWHILE, I FORGOT HOW LONG IT HAD BEEN since my mother had left for Washington. The war ended in August 1945, and summer came to a close. I thought surely my mother would be coming back to get me. Every day I asked my grandmother if Mom would be coming soon. For awhile she said she didn't know. Then she told me to quit asking, and eventually I did.

Over the next two years, Tim and I went everywhere together. People often asked us if we were brothers. They asked us if our mother had died, and they always asked us if our father had been killed in the war. In the summer of 1947, Tim and I were spending nearly every day at the beach – and that was the year we finally learned how to swim. At last, we would no longer be prisoners to the shallow water near the shore. I was tired of splashing around with the little kids and their mothers. I wanted to get out to the diving dock, which was about a hundred yards off shore, so I could jump off like the big kids. One afternoon I got up the nerve to ask one of the older boys to take me out to the diving dock on his back.

"Why don't you swim out to the dock by yourself?" he asked.

"I don't know how to swim," I said.

"I'll teach you," he told me. "It's easy. Can you dog paddle?"

"I don't know. What's a dog paddle?"

"Like this," he said. And he started swimming around me, keeping his head just above water like a dog does when it swims, using his paddling hands to pull him along. Occasionally, he kicked his legs to help keep afloat.

"Just pull yourself along in the water with your hands and kick your feet. If you hold your head up like this, you can swim all the way out to the dock anytime you want, and you can come back without having to wait for someone to bring you."

I tried it and immediately went under water, but he grabbed me and pulled me up so my head was above the water again. "Look, I'll hold you up with my hands on your stomach while you paddle around and get the hang of it," he said.

"Okay," I said, not too sure if that was going to work.

"Lay out straight, like you're going to do the dead man's float, and I'll put my hands on your stomach to hold you up. Don't worry, I won't let you go. Are you ready?"

I had learned to float in the shallow water, and I wasn't afraid to do the "dead man's float" with my face in the water, because I knew I could touch bottom if I started to sink. I stretched out, fully extended, with my face in the water and floated. I felt him put his hands underneath my stomach and heard him say, "Now pull your head out of the water and begin paddling with your hands and kicking your feet, the way I showed you."

I splashed and coughed, but soon I was paddling around, safe in the knowledge that he had his hands under my stomach and I wouldn't sink.

"Good, good, you're doing great," he said.

I never felt him let go of me as I paddled around. Suddenly, I noticed he was a few feet away from me. I was about to panic and sink, but I heard him say, "Look, you're doing it. You've been swimming all by yourself without me even having to hold you."

"I have?" I asked, surprised.

"Yeah, look where you are. You're way over there. I never had a chance to hold you up. You just started paddling and took off. Now you know how to swim."

It was that quick. I never thought it would be that easy. I was happy because now I knew that I could swim out to the dock and come back whenever I wanted. It was as if I had been set free.

"Thanks," I shouted. "I can go out to the dock by myself now!"

"You're welcome. I would practice some more in the shallow water where you can stand up before you go all the way out to the dock by yourself, though. When you're ready to go out there, let me know, and I'll swim along beside you the first time to make sure you get there."

The boy swam off to join a group of girls swimming nearby. I looked around for Tim. I wanted to show him what I had learned and teach him to swim, too. That way we could both swim out to the diving dock together.

"Tim, I can swim," I shouted at him when I saw him splashing and floating in the shallow water.

"You don't know how to swim," he said. "Show me."

"Yes, I do, look." And I dog paddled around him.

"Your feet are touching the bottom."

"No, they're not, look, you can see me kicking them while I paddle with my hands."

He watched me for awhile and finally believed that I was really swimming. "How did you learn?"

"Some boy taught me because he didn't want to swim out to the dock with me on his back. He said I could swim out there by myself, if I knew how to do this dog paddle thing. I can teach you, too. Just do the dead man's float, and when you feel me put my hands on your stomach, just start paddling around like this and then you'll be swimming too. You want to try it?"

"Yeah, but don't let go of me. You promise?"

"Yeah, I promise. Come on, do the dead man's float."

He floated, and I stood beside him with my hands on his stomach, like the older boy had done for me. He began to paddle and kick his feet.

"You're swimming," I said, "keep paddling."

Tim learned almost as quickly as I did. The only reason it took him a little longer was because he didn't trust me the way I had trusted the boy who taught me. He would stop paddling to make sure I was still holding my hands on his stomach. But he soon caught on, and I let him go just the way the boy had let me go. He was as surprised to find himself swimming as I had been. Soon, we were both paddling around in the shallow water, and we decided to try for the diving dock.

"The older boy said he would swim along beside me when I was ready to swim out to the dock," I said. "But I don't see him around anywhere."

"We don't need him. We can do it," Tim said. "Let's just go together. If anything happens when we get in deep water, we can help each other."

That sounded reasonable to me.

"Okay," I said. "Let's go."

We began paddling out to the diving dock, secure in the knowledge that we had each other to help if anything happened. It never occurred to either of us that we would both probably drown if one of us got in trouble and the other had to help. Whether or not either of us could actually help at all didn't matter. It was because we knew we had each other there that gave us the confidence to try for the diving dock, and thankfully, we made it.

A few years after we had learned to swim, we got up the nerve to swim from the fishing pier to the diving dock. I had never seen anyone do it before, but I was sure we could. By then, we were confident swimmers and were no longer doing the dog paddle. We had learned to do something called the Australian crawl. It was much faster and smoother, and it didn't tire you out anywhere near as much as the dog paddle did.

I didn't want to swim alone, because I thought that if a shark was going to attack and there were two of us, it might attack Tim instead of me. If I were swimming alone, I would be the only choice. Never mind that no shark – other than the little sand sharks that hung around the bait house – had ever been seen at Gulfport Beach, I didn't want to swim alone. I never told Tim my reason for asking him to swim with me, and after much cajoling he agreed to try it too. As it turned out, no sharks appeared and it really wasn't much of a challenge. It was a couple of hundred yards from the pier to the diving dock, and it only took a short time to cover the distance. Tim and I had become excellent swimmers, and soon we were swimming back and forth between the pier and the diving dock routinely.

We would also swim under the pier around Sonny's Bait House and dive down to look at the shiners Sonny kept in the cage under there. We swam under water all around the cement pylons supporting the pier, and sometimes we would see a large fish hanging out. Once, Tim jerked hard on someone's fishing line. I know the guy must have thought for a moment that he had hooked a whopper.

Thirty-Nine

IN FEBRUARY, 1948, I TURNED EIGHT YEARS OLD. WHEN I came home from school on my birthday, my grandmother gave me a package that she said had come in the mail from my mother. I was surprised, because she had never sent me a present before. I was excited and tore it open immediately. Inside were three small wooden boats, each painted a different color: one red, one yellow and one green. Each one had a black smoke stack. I couldn't quit staring at them. I hadn't seen my mother since she and Frank had left for Washington nearly three years ago. Suddenly I was over-come with sadness and tears filled my eyes. No one noticed. My grandparents were busy talking about some letter that my grand-father had gotten in the mail. He had retired a few months ago and was now living with us full time. Before he left Knoxville, he had rented out the house he and my grandmother still owned up there.

"It seems Mr. Holms has lost his job and can no longer pay the rent," my grandfather said. "He and his wife are going to have to move out. They're going to go live with her mother."

"Well, that's just fine," my grandmother said. "What are we going to do? We've been counting on that money. Without it, I don't know how we can afford to keep Billy and Tim living here. Neither Susan nor Jessica have sent us any money in years."

"I'm aware of that, Henrietta," my grandfather replied in his usual calm voice.

"Well, what are we going to do?"

"I don't know yet. I'll have to think about it."

"You do that," my grandmother said sarcastically.

"I suppose I should go up to Knoxville and check on the house and see if Mr. and Mrs. Holms are okay. I feel badly for them," my grandfather said, almost absentmindedly.

"You better start feeling badly for us instead," my grandmother snapped.

"I know this is serious, Henrietta. I'll figure something out."

My grandmother didn't answer. I could tell she was angry. As usual, she had never looked up from the crossword puzzle she was working during the conversation. It was as if she had decided the problem was not hers. It was for my grandfather to solve; therefore, it didn't warrant any eye-to-eye contact during the conversation.

Several days later, my grandfather caught the train for Knoxville. Occasionally, Tim and I would wonder when Grandpa was coming back and would ask Grandma, but she would just say, "I don't know." I happened to find a letter one night when I was snooping through the things she kept on the shelf by her chair in the backroom. She had gone to a town council meeting and left Tim and me at home by ourselves. I read it out loud to Tim.

> *My Dear Henrietta,*
>
> *I arrived safely in Knoxville and have visited with the Holms. They will be vacating the house tomorrow afternoon. They have made arrangements to live with Mrs. Holms' mother until Mr. Holms can find a job. It seems that Mrs. Holms' mother has been sick and will welcome them moving in with her. Her husband passed away several months ago and although he left her very well off, she has not really been able to accept his death and has been steadily deteriorating in health.*
>
> *The house is in excellent shape. They have taken good care of it. As Mrs. Holms told me, they treated it as if it were their own. Mr. Holms has made several minor re-*

pairs, and I have reimbursed him for the work. At first he wouldn't accept the money, but after I insisted, he took it. He seemed very appreciative.

I also visited Darst Coal Company yesterday and spoke with Mr. Darst. He was very pleasant and seemed genuinely glad to see me. He said he hadn't been able to find a decent bookkeeper since I left. I asked him if he would be interested in hiring me back. He said he couldn't pay me what I made before I retired, but if I were willing to take a reduced salary he might be able to. I told him I would think about it, but I have not committed to anything yet. However, I think I should seriously consider it. The money would help us with the boys, and I could live in the house. It would only be a short walk to work. All the furnishings are still there, as you know, so there would not be any added expense. I could probably take the train down to Florida for a visit every three months or so. That way living apart again would not seem as bad.

I will write again tomorrow. As always I remain your faithful and loving husband.

Edward

It was clear Grandpa had taken the job and would be away for months at a time. Tim didn't seem to care about the letter. He had the ability to just put things out of his mind that he didn't want to think about. Just like at night when we went to bed. He could fall asleep immediately, but my mind would still be racing with the day's events and it would take forever to go to sleep. When I could hear the other kids shouting and laughing as they played outside until well after dark, I would lie awake wondering what it would be like to be out there playing with them. But not Tim; he could get in bed, pull the blanket up around his shoulders – regardless of the temperature – and be asleep within seconds. I suppose that was his way of dealing with our abandonment.

One day, many weeks after we had found the letter, Tim and I came home from school and were surprised to see my grandfather at the house. We hadn't seen him in a long time. He and my grandmother were walking around the property. We hung around as she showed him all the plants she had added to flower beds in the backyard since he left. Then she showed him the condition of the chicken coop, the shed and the back porch. All three needed repairs, she told him. And there was also a step that had rotted out on the back porch, which she wanted fixed first.

The following day, my grandfather began making the repairs. By the time we came home from school, there was a new board where the rotted step had been; the wire around the chicken coop had been pulled up tight and nailed to the cross boards at the top; and my grandfather was standing on the top step of a ladder inspecting the roof of the shed.

"Looks like it's going to need some shingles replaced," he was telling my grandmother. "But first I'll need to pull up the old ones and see if any of the boards are rotten. If they are, I'll replace them and then put some tar paper down and re-shingle the roof."

"Well, I want you to get it done before it rains again," my grandmother told him. "And don't forget to paint that step tomorrow." Then she turned and went in the house.

At the dinner table, the conversation was between my grandmother and grandfather. Neither Tim nor I said a word while they were talking. We would never have interjected ourselves into an adult conversation. My grandmother would have rapped us across the mouth with her fist. So we just listened. I had eventually discovered that you could learn as much by listening as you could by asking questions anyway. The questions that formed in my mind were almost always answered somewhere in their conversation, if I just paid attention and listened long enough.

Evidently, my grandfather had sold the house in Knoxville after all, and would be moving the furniture down to Gulfport. The problem was where to put it. My grandmother already had furniture in the house and there was no room for anymore. As they talked, I learned that they were planning on building a new shed so they would have a place to store the stuff. This was very exciting to me. Where were they going to build the new shed, and what did the furniture look like? All too soon we were finished with dinner and it was time to do the dishes and go to bed. I wasn't ready. I wanted to hear more about the furniture and the new shed.

My grandmother went outside to the henhouse to tell the chickens goodnight and see if they were happy with the repairs my grandfather had made. I hated to think what the consequences would be for my grandfather if the hens told her they didn't like the repairs for some reason. My cousin and I helped clear off the table and we dried the dishes while my grandfather washed them. When my grandmother came back into the house, I managed to convince her to let Tim and me stay up long enough to play hide and seek for a while.

I wasn't as interested in drinking out of the cat's water bowl tonight as I was in hearing more of the conversation about the new shed. But they didn't talk about it anymore, and I went off to bed disappointed.

As I lay there, I wondered why my mother had never come back to see me and if she were ever coming back again. I wondered why I couldn't live with her, and why I still had to live here at Grandma's house. As always, I tried to picture what she looked like in my mind; but I couldn't. I just couldn't see her face. It was always that same view of her back as she was walking away from me, except now she was always wearing the tomato-red suit I had seen her wear to work in San Diego. Then I began wondering what the shed would look like. If it looked like the one we had next to the henhouse, I thought, it won't be very big. I didn't see how it could hold any furniture. However, there was a small chest of drawers in the shed where my grandfather kept his tools and some old rags that he used when he was painting. I hated to open the drawers of that chest, because once when I opened the drawer a rat had jumped out and scared the daylights out of me, and I was afraid another one would jump out and bite me.

When I had opened the drawer and slammed it shut again in fright that day, I thought I had seen other rats crawling around inside it, and so I ran into the house, yelling to my grandmother that the chest drawers were full of rats.

"Shut up, with that screaming," she said. "Edward, go out there and see if there are any rats in the chest."

I went with him, and when he looked in the drawer we discovered a nest of baby rats in the rags. The rat that had jumped out must have been the mother, and what I had seen after she jumped out were these five or six baby rats crawling around.

My grandfather took all the babies out and put them in one of the many tin cans he kept in the shed. He dug a hole in the field out back of the oak trees, put the can of baby rats inside it, and then filled the hole with water. He finished by covering it up with dirt. "Don't dig these rats up," he warned, "I want them to stay in the hole to make sure they're dead."

When we returned to the house, my grandmother snapped, "Edward, I want you to clean out that shed and make sure there aren't any more rats in there."

We didn't see any more, but we could tell they had been behind some of the lumber he had stacked along the wall. There were rat droppings everywhere. My grandfather moved the lumber out of the shed and stacked it behind the chicken coop, out near the wash tubs where Crystal washed our clothes. Then he swept out the shed and put rat poison and rat traps all around the edges and in the corners.

"You boys stay out of here now unless I'm with you. I don't want you getting any of that rat poison on you," he told us. "Maybe we'll get that mother rat when she comes back looking for her babies."

I didn't mind staying out of the shed at all. I was afraid of rats, and I was afraid one might bite me. I went back behind the chicken coop where my grandfather had stored the lumber and poked at it with a stick to see if any rats came out, but none did. Then I walked around where the washtubs were hanging on nails to see if there were any rats back there. I knew that mother rat had gone somewhere when she jumped out of the drawer, and I was afraid that she might still be around, hiding, waiting to get back in there. "Grandpa, what will happen when the mother rat comes back again?" I asked him.

"Well, hopefully she'll get caught in one of the traps or eat some of that rat poison I put out, and we'll be rid of her."

Forty

I DON'T REMEMBER EVER SEEING ANY RATS IN THE lumber where the washtubs were, but I did see a snake from time to time. I don't know what kind they were, but my grandfather would kill them by cutting them in half with the shovel. I worried that Crystal might get bitten by a snake when she was washing out there, but she never seemed to worry about it.

"Crystal, if you saw a snake out here, what would you do? Would you be scared?" I asked her once.

"Nah, there ain't no snake scares me. I just leaves 'em alone and they leaves me alone."

"Would you shoot it with your pistol?"

"Boy, don't you be tellin' yo grandma I got me a pistol. You hear me?" she said.

"I haven't told her."

"I shoulda' never showed you that pistol," she said. "You just forget you ever seen it. You hear me?"

"Okay, I won't tell anyone. Why are you afraid I might tell my grandmother?" I asked. But I already knew the answer to that. My grandmother would have run her off, and she would never be allowed to come back again. I loved Crystal, and I didn't want her to get in any trouble with my grandmother.

"Your grandmother don't like no pistols 'round here; she would fire me and send me home."

"But you would come back wouldn't you?" I asked.

"No, sir, child. Yo' grandmother would never let me come

204

back, and I needs the two dollars a week I gets for this here job. So you just forget you ever saw what you saw; 'cause if you ever tell your grandmother, I'm going to switch you good before I leave. You hear me?"

"I hear you," I said. "I won't ever tell, I promise."

"Okay, you go on and play now. I got lots a work to do."

When Crystal washed our clothes, she built a fire in the chicken yard between some bricks my grandfather had put there for her. The bricks were stacked about a foot high on three sides and had some iron bars that my grandfather had cemented across the top so Crystal could set a washtub full of water on it. She would put sticks and twigs and paper under the tub and light a fire. Once the fire had started and was burning well, she would add pieces of wood from the pile of lumber my grandfather kept behind the henhouse. Then, when the water was boiling, she would ladle some out with a large tin can and pour it into the washtub with the scrub board in it, along with some cold water. She would only scrub the clothes when she was satisfied with the water temperature. Once the clothes were clean, she would move them to a third tub of cold water to rinse them. Then she would wring them out and throw them into a basket and hang them on the clothes line in the side yard, where the guava trees were.

In the afternoon, Crystal would take all the washing off the line and put it in a basket. Some of the clothes she would fold and put away immediately, like our pants and shirts and underwear. The things that she needed to iron were left in the basket until the next day, when she would come back to do the ironing.

When she was scrubbing the clothes, she stood on a wooden platform, about four inches off the ground, which my grandfather had built for her. She almost never wore shoes, but on wash day she always wore them. She said it hurt her feet to stand there all day on the boards scrubbing clothes. To get the clothes clean, she scrubbed them in one of the washtubs with a scrub board and a bar of Octagon soap. This was a large brown bar of soap with eight sides, and it tasted terrible. My grandmother used it to wash out my mouth whenever I said a bad word or sassed her. When the soap got down to small pieces that she could no longer hold in her hands to scrub with, she would throw the pieces into a gallon tin can and collect them until the can was half full. Then she would put the can over the fire and melt the soap down to liquid and pour it into her wash water to make more suds. Nothing was wasted.

On the day that Crystal ironed, my grandmother usually had a Home Demonstration Club meeting or a Garden and Bird Club meeting to go to, and she would leave Tim and me home with Crystal. Crystal would set her ironing board up in the backroom with a soda bottle full of water that she used to dampen the clothes. I was fascinated watching her iron. She would plug the iron in and test it to see if it was hot enough by spitting on her finger and then touching the iron. She could tell when it was hot enough if it made just the right sizzling sound when her wet finger touched it. To dampen the clothes, she would take a swig of water from the bottle and then squirt it through her teeth on the shirt or whatever it was that she was ironing.

"Why do you squirt the water onto the clothes through your teeth, Crystal?" I asked her one day.

"'Cause it's faster, and it comes out on the clothes evenly so I can iron 'em up nice. Don't you tell your grandmother I's spittin' on her clothes though. She don't like that. She wants me to dip my hands in the water and sprinkle it over the clothes. But that don't work so good as spittin.'"

On the washing and ironing days, Crystal was also supposed to look after us while my grandmother was at whatever meeting it was that she went to that day. We always had fun with her. When she got through washing or ironing, she would lie down on the bed in our bedroom, the one my brother used to sleep in when he lived there with us, and smoke a cigarette.

"Don't you go tell your grandma I been smokin' in here, now. She don't like it when I smokes in the house."

I liked being secretive with Crystal. I felt she trusted me, but the truth is I don't think Crystal really cared what my grandmother thought about her smoking. She always took good care of Tim and me, and my grandmother knew it. My grandmother would run her off if she knew Crystal carried a gun, but I don't think she would do anything just because she was smoking. Anyway, I didn't want Crystal to go away, so I never said a word.

Sometimes Crystal would fall asleep and the ash would fall off her cigarette and nearly burn a hole in the blanket. Whenever she fell asleep, I would lie there on the bed with her so I could wake her up when I heard my grandmother drive up the driveway. The driveway ran along the side of the house our bedroom was on, so it was easy to alert Crystal before my grandmother could get in the house. She would get up and meet Grandma in the backroom, so she wouldn't come into our bedroom and smell the cigarette smoke. She would immediately tell my grandmother something about the ironing she had done that day, and soon they would be talking about the clothes. Then it would be time for Crystal to leave so she could catch the 4:45 trolley car into St. Petersburg.

Forty-One

ONE DAY, THE MYSTERY OF WHERE THE NEW SHED WAS going to be was solved. Some men came to the house and told my grandfather they were ready to start building. My grandfather took the men out to the garage and told them he wanted the shed attached to the back of it.

"How long will it take you to build it?" my grandfather asked the man in charge.

"Oh, it shouldn't take too long, I don't think," the man answered.

"The longest length of time will be pouring the cement and waiting for it to dry. After that, things should go pretty fast. Tell me, are you going to want a door going from the garage into the shed?"

"No, I only need one door, here on the side," my grandfather told him.

"How about windows, you gonna want windows in it?"

"I don't need any windows," my grandfather said, "just a door here on the side. It's just going to be a shed."

"Why you puttin' a cement floor in, then?"

"Because we're going to store furniture in it, and I want to make sure it's well up off the ground so everything will stay dry."

"Furniture, eh," the man in charge said thoughtfully. "Then I suggest you let us put a shingle roof on it to keep the roof from leaking when it rains. We can snug it right up against the garage and make sure no water leaks in from there."

"I want you to snug it up against the garage, as you suggested, but I also want you to put a slight slope on the roof so it slants downward from the garage toward the back. That way, when it rains, the water will run off into the backyard and not collect on the roof," my grandfather said.

"Good idea," the man in charge said. "Anything else?"

"When can you start?"

"We'll start building the foundation for the floor today. Shouldn't take too long to do that. Next week we can have the cement truck here to pour the floor. Now, can we bring the cement truck in the back way? We won't be able to get in from the front of your garage, not enough room between the house and the garage."

"Yes, I don't see why not," my grandfather said.

"Good, then we're ready to start."

The men backed their truck into the driveway, and I watched them unload lumber and carry it around behind the garage.

"You a carpenter, son?" one of the men asked me.

"No," I said.

"Aw, that's too bad," he said. "If you were a carpenter, I would let you help me carry some of this lumber."

"I'll help," I said eagerly.

"No, sorry. If you're not a carpenter, you might drop it."

"I won't drop it," I said.

"Well, okay, here. Take these pieces around back and stack 'em with the rest," he said, handing me several short pieces of wood with pointed ends.

"What are they used for?"

"I don't have time for you to stand around asking a bunch of questions," he said. "I got to get this truck unloaded; so if you want to help, go stack those pegs out back."

"Yes, sir."

"By the way, son, we're gonna use those pieces to lay out the frame for the foundation, where the floor will be," he said, smiling at me.

The men worked steadily, and by late afternoon the frame for the cement floor was complete.

"Mister Christian," the man in charge at the back door called out to my grandfather, "you want to come outside and see what we've done before we leave?"

My grandfather went outside with Tim and me following him.

"I've built a frame for a cement step right here, where the door is going to be," the man said. "We'll pour that when we pour the foundation."

"Looks good to me," my grandfather said. "What day will you be here to pour the cement?"

"Well, let's see. Today is Wednesday… I can have the truck here Monday. How's that? After we pour it, we'll give it about two weeks to dry, and then we can start putting the frame up."

"Okay, I'll see you on Monday, then," my grandfather said.

This was exciting. I could hardly wait for the cement to be poured and the building to start. The time between Wednesday and Monday dragged by, and I wished each day would hurry and end so Monday would come sooner. I wanted to watch them pour the cement for the foundation; I had never seen cement poured before. I had seen a cement truck going down the road with its huge barrel turning, but never up close. I was sure the men on the cement truck would let me help them the way the carpenters had.

Every day, I waited for the truck. Early on Monday morning it finally arrived. I was the first one to see it rumbling across the field behind our garage, its wheels digging into the ground, churning up sand and grass as the cylinder full of cement slowly turned. It was huge with five wheels on either side. Eight of the wheels were on the back of the truck, and there were two sets of double wheels on each side. I was mesmerized as the giant beast swung around and began backing toward the garage. Less than two feet from the frame, the driver stopped, opened his door and jumped to the ground.

"Morning, you must be Mr. Christian," he said to my grandfather, extending his hand and smiling. "I got a load of cement for you. The name's Jake Taylor. Good thing it ain't rained lately," he continued. "Heavy as this truck is, I wouldn't have been able to drive 'cross your field."

"Everything's ready," my grandfather said, shaking hands.

"The carpenters already laid out the frame for you."

"I see that," the driver said.

Four other men appeared from a car that had rolled up and parked in our driveway.

"Mr. Christian, let me introduce you to my helpers, Willie, Joe, Sam and Dave. They're gonna help spread and smooth the cement."

"Pleased to meet you gentlemen," my grandfather said, stepping forward to shake their hands. "Do you think you can get this all poured today?"

"Oh, sure we can. This ain't that big of an area to do. If these boys don't take a nap on the job, we'll be out of here by noon," Jake said, smiling.

The four had already moved toward the back of the truck and were beginning to unfold the metal parts that made up the trough the cement would follow into the frame.

"Okay, boys, go ahead and extend that trough as far back toward the garage as it'll go. We'll work back to front," Jake yelled at his helpers.

"Okay, boss," one of the men yelled back.

The men worked quickly and soon the metal trough extended from the truck to the back of the frame. The end of the trough had little wheels on it so the men could move it back and forth to direct the cement where they wanted it. They worked as a team, with Jake operating levers that started the flow of the cement down the trough. One man monitored the flow and occasionally used something that looked like a large wooden paddle to keep the cement moving. As they poured the cement, the other three men wearing rubber boots worked inside the frame: two had huge iron rakes and they spread the cement and made sure it was consistently the right height as they worked from the back toward the front; and the third man worked with a long pole with a flat wooden blade on the end, which he used to smooth the top.

When the frame was completely filled, the two men who had been spreading with rakes also picked up long poles with flat blades and helped smooth the top. As they worked, excess water was scraped off the top and spilled onto the ground in gray streaks and puddles along the side of the frame. The driver folded the metal trough back up and secured it to the truck again.

"Okay, Mr. Christian, these boys will finish smoothing the top and getting rid of the excess moisture. I just need you to sign these papers, and I'll be out of here."

My grandfather used Jake Taylor's back to rest the papers on while he signed them. When he was finished signing, he handed them back to the driver and shook hands with him.

"We sure appreciate your business, Mr. Christian. Good luck with your new shed," the driver said, and then he swung himself up into the truck and drove across the field the same way he had come in.

Tim and I continued to watch as the men smoothed the cement. Pretty soon the job was done, and the surface of the cement looked like a shiny gray lake. I wondered what it would feel like to walk on it in my bare feet. One of the men must have read my mind.

"You boys stay away from this wet cement, now. We don't want you getting stuck in it," one of the men cautioned.

"What happens if I get stuck in it?" I asked.

"We'll have to leave you here, and the carpenters will have to build the shed around you. You'll have to spend the rest of your life standing out here in the shed," he told me.

"Oh," I said.

"'Course, if you don't want to stand out here in the shed the rest of your life once the cement dries, we'll have to cut your feet off to get you out," he continued.

I decided to stay away from the cement until it dried.

Forty-Two

THAT NIGHT I LAY IN BED THINKING ABOUT WHAT IT would be like to get stuck in the cement and what it would be like not to have any feet, if they had to cut them off to get me out. How would I get around? I wondered if I would have to stay in bed forever, because I didn't have any feet and couldn't walk. It was hot and I was sweating, and I think I was sweating even more than usual because of the picture I had of myself without any feet.

Mosquitoes buzzed in my ear. I swatted at them, trying to kill them, but they only returned a few minutes later. I had mosquito bites everywhere, and they itched worse than I could ever remember. They only added to my misery as I thought about my feet. I continually checked them to see if they were still attached to my legs. They were. I resolved once again not to walk on the cement until it was dry. But what if I walked on it by accident and got stuck? It wouldn't be my fault, but I would still have to have my feet cut off. I shuddered.

The sweat running off my body only made the mosquito bites itch all the more. No matter how still I lay, I could not cool off. I listened hopefully for the rustle of the palms that would signal the coming in of a breeze. But the palms were silent, the sweat kept rolling off and the mosquito bites kept itching. I finally decided to sneak into the front room and lie on the couch. It might be hard as nails, but it would be nice and cool for a brief time.

Quietly, I slipped out of bed and into the front room and lay on the couch. It was hard, as I knew it would be, but it was also cool. I scratched my mosquito bites, except for one that was on the soft flesh of my penis. It was too difficult to scratch, so I began rubbing it. Right away, I felt relief from the itching. But I felt something else, too. My penis started getting bigger and harder. The only time that I could remember it being like that was when I woke up in the middle of the night, needing to pee. But right now I didn't have to pee, and it was getting hard. God, I hoped I hadn't done something to it. How would I explain it to my grandmother? I quit rubbing it and it became soft again. I was relieved, but soon the itching returned. I rubbed it the way I had a few minutes ago and the relief from the itching was immediate, but my penis started to swell again. This time I didn't care. I just wanted relief from the itching.

But as I continued to rub the bite, I began to feel something far more than just relief from the itching. It was wonderful, and I kept rubbing. It was a feeling I had never experienced before. I continued rubbing, and suddenly I felt as if my whole body had suddenly gotten very warm. Out of nowhere, I thought of Sally Ann Wilson. I felt so good I didn't want the feeling to stop. The harder and longer I rubbed, the better I felt. Then, it was over. That wonderful feeling was gone. The mosquito bite didn't itch anymore, and my penis was no longer hard. I knew I had discovered something wonderful. I could make the itching stop and feel really good at the same time. I thought I was really lucky to have a mosquito bite like that. I was so excited about what I had discovered that I wanted to tell Tim.

I rolled off the couch and went back into the bedroom. I tried to wake him up so I could tell him what I had experienced, but he was dead to the world and wouldn't respond, even when I shook him as hard as I could.

The next night when we went to bed, I tried to tell Tim what I had discovered so he would know what to do if he ever got a mosquito bite on his penis. But he wasn't interested. He fell asleep while I was talking to him. Didn't he have anything to think about before he went to sleep? How did he do it? I wondered.

I climbed up to my bunk and lay there wondering if my mosquito bite was going to start itching again. It did, and again I slipped into the front room and lay on the hard couch to rub it. Again, I experienced that wonderful feeling, and again I thought of Sally Ann Wilson. I felt like I loved her, but I didn't know why rubbing a mosquito bite would make me think of her. I didn't purposely think of her. She just popped into my mind out of nowhere. We only played together occasionally, but I also played with Ronnie occasionally, and she didn't pop into my mind while I was rubbing the mosquito bite. Why did Sally Ann? True, she was in the same class as me at school, and she walked home from school each day with Tim and me and her brothers, Jack and Johnny. But I never had any feeling for her. I couldn't figure out why, when I rubbed the mosquito bite, I felt like I loved her. I was puzzled, but soon the mosquito bite was gone; there was no need to rub it anymore, and my love for Sally Ann was quickly forgotten.

Forty-Three

TWO WEEKS LATER, WHEN THE CEMENT WAS thoroughly dry, the carpenters arrived and worked steadily for nearly a week. I liked the smell of the new wood and the sound of their hammers driving nails into two-by-fours and plywood. I wanted to help. I knew I could hammer nails if they would let me, but whenever I asked, I always got the same answer: "Beat it kid, before you get hurt out here."

Then one day the shed was completed, and the men were gone. I don't know what I expected, but it wasn't just a big room with a concrete floor and no windows. My grandfather had the electricians put a light switch inside, with a place for a light bulb in the middle of the ceiling, but there was no bulb in it, yet. When the door was shut, it was pitch black inside. I asked my grandmother if Tim and I could play inside the shed, and much to my surprise, she said yes. It was cool, and the cement floor felt good on our bare feet. We only took our shoes off when Grandma wasn't around. She would spank us if she caught us barefooted. Most of the other kids always went barefooted when they weren't in school. Tim and I also wanted to; but my grandmother said we would catch something from the dirt if we ran around without our shoes. I don't remember any of the other kids ever catching anything, but that argument held no water with her. She had said we couldn't go barefooted and that was that.

A few weeks later, a truck full of furniture arrived at the house. The driver and two other men unloaded the furniture and put it in the new shed. It was stacked everywhere; there was no order to how it got put in there. Anywhere the men could find a place to set something was where it went. Furniture was stacked on top of furniture, along with barrels and trunks. There were two cedar chests full of linen and clothes and other stuff. It smelled wonderful when the chests were opened.

Soon, everything was unloaded and stacked in the shed, as my grandfather called it, or the "store room," as the men on the truck called it. My cousin and I had fun climbing on the stuff and dropping down among the tables and chairs into what we pretended were caves and tunnels. We could crawl underneath the benches and chairs stacked in there and get into lots of places where we could be completely hidden. It was great fun to play in there and hide from each other, and then pop up out of a hiding place when the other least expected it.

My grandmother let us play in there whenever we wanted. That was until I locked Tim in there one day and wouldn't let him out until Grandma called us in for supper. As soon as I let him out, he ran into the house crying and told my grandmother I had locked him in the shed all day and he had wet his pants. I got a spanking and was sent off to bed without my dinner. Needless to say, we were not allowed to play in the shed anymore.

As I lay in bed after that episode, I began to think of all the ways I could get even with Tim for telling on me. At some point I must have fallen asleep, because I suddenly jerked awake when Tim came in to go to bed. It was dark outside, and I didn't hear any kids playing.

"What time is it?" I asked him.

"I don't know. Grandma let me stay up a little longer because I had to sit in the shed all day by myself."

"She let you stay up late because of that?" I asked in disbelief.

"Yeah, she said I really didn't get a chance to play today."

"I can't believe that," I said. "You wet your pants and I got spanked and sent to bed without any supper. That's not fair."

I was mad that I had gotten a double punishment, while he had gotten to stay up late. I was tempted to smack him in the face for being such a baby.

"Why did you have to go and tell Grandma I locked you in the shed?"

"Because I had wet my pants, and I was afraid I was going to get spanked and have to wear them on my head."

Grandma made us wear our pants on our head if we wet them while we were playing outside.

"You can just see what it smells like," she would say. "There's absolutely no reason for you not to come inside and use the bathroom when you have to go. Now, pull those pants down over your face and sit there on that chair until I tell you to get up."

Then she would make us sit on a chair where she could see us. I guess that was to make sure we didn't take them off and therefore escape the real punishment of smelling them. Actually, I didn't mind the smell. Maybe I was just used to being hot and dirty all the time. It was the humiliation of having to sit there with my underwear on my head that I hated.

Forty-Four

DURING THE SUMMER, WE GOT OUR BATH EITHER BY going swimming at the beach or my grandmother would turn the hose on us in the yard before supper. I liked it when she turned the hose on us, because it helped cool us off before going to bed. In the winter we only got a bath on Saturday night because Grandma didn't want to waste water. She would fill up the tub with water, put some soap powder in it to make lots of suds, and give us a bar of Octagon. The oldest person got to use the tub first. When one was finished, the next one would get in. We all used the same tub of water so as not to waste it. I was sure my grandmother put the soap powder in the water to make a lot of suds so we couldn't see how dirty the water was when it was our turn to get in the tub.

When we were finished bathing, we would let the water out of the tub and scrub it clean. I was amazed at the filthy ring that formed around the tub by the time we were finished washing. When my brother was living with us, after every bath he would tell us he had peed in the water. I was never sure whether or not to believe him, but just the same, I never washed my face with the water.

"I'm going to tell Grandma," I said once after he had told me that he peed in the water.

"If you do, I swear I'll beat the shit out of you." Then he pulled out the hunting knife he always carried and said, "If you tell Grandma I peed in the tub, I'll cut your tongue out with this knife. You understand?"

"Yes," I said, because I felt for sure that he would cut it out and somehow I also knew he wouldn't care what happened to him for doing it.

He never seemed to care what kind of trouble he got into. It was almost as if the more trouble he was in, the better he liked it. I don't think he really liked anyone or anything. He was always throwing rocks or grapefruit at the house. When he didn't come home for supper and my grandmother locked him out, he often just stayed nearby and threw rocks at the house now and then. He wasn't afraid of anything or anyone – not even my grandmother. I, on the other hand, was afraid to sleep outside overnight. I thought some mean man like one of the Muncies from next door might grab me. I was never sure what I thought they might do to me, but I always stayed away from them anyway, and I never slept outside. I didn't want to take the chance that one of them might grab me in the dark.

I think my brother was friends with some of the Muncies and used to go with them to poach alligators. At least, he told me he did. Hanging around with them is probably where he learned to be so mean and belligerent. The Muncies acted the same way. They would get drunk and fight out in the middle of the street in front of the house until the police came to arrest them, but they never seemed to care. My brother was the same way. He didn't care about anything and had no fear of being punished. That was the reason it was impossible for my grandmother to control him and didn't want him around. I knew she was very glad my mother had sent him off to Boys Town in Nebraska, and knowing he was there was likely the only reason she agreed to let my mother bring me back to her house. I think my mother also promised to send money regularly to help her feed and clothe me, but I don't know whether she sent any or not. I guess she must have because I was still there, waiting for her to come back.

Forty-Five

IF MY GRANDMOTHER WAS GLAD THAT MY BROTHER wasn't coming back to live with her, I was even happier about it. Now I got the tub first when we bathed on Saturday night; and best of all, there wasn't anyone around to beat the shit out of me every chance they got. I was the oldest kid in the house now, and ever since my cousin told on me for locking him in the shed, I began to hold my status over him. I would threaten to beat the shit out of him if he told on me or didn't do what I wanted him to do.

It worked for a while, until he got to be bigger than I was and began to fight back. He couldn't always beat me when we got into a fight, which was often; but it was not as easy to intimidate him as it had been for my brother to intimidate me. So we had a kind of easy truce that basically boiled down to an agreement that neither of us would tell on the other one. It got to the point that when one of us lied to my grandmother about something, the other one swore to it. For awhile, it left her a little confused and not sure which one of us to punish, so she punished us both – unless, of course, she caught you red-handed. Then you alone bore the brunt of the punishment.

One thing about being punished together and getting sent to bed, we could lie there and talk to each other until Tim fell asleep. Then I would continue to lie there awake, listening to the sounds outside, waiting for the tide to come in and planning what I was going to do the next day when I went out to play. Sometimes I would get up and make my routine rounds of the house, usually out to the front room to lie on the couch and cool off. I soon discovered that I didn't need a mosquito bite to enjoy that wonderful feeling.

Sometimes I would go the other direction in the house, into the bathroom to get a drink or sometimes into my grandmother's bedroom. Sometimes I would pick up some dog biscuits if I was hungry after supper or if I had been sent to bed without my supper. I became very skilled at walking around the house without being detected. Sometimes I would pretend I was an Indian sneaking through the forest as I moved through the house..

One of the things I really liked to do was sneak into my grandmother's bedroom when she was listening to the radio, especially when she was listening to the music of the big bands. One night I had slipped into her bedroom and was watching her from behind the curtain that covered the doorway between her room and the backroom. The radio was playing music from one of the big bands performing in some ballroom somewhere. I could see my grandmother sitting in her chair, working one of her beloved crossword puzzles. I couldn't see my grandfather, but I could see puffs of smoke coming from the direction of his chair. He would be sitting there, smoking his pipe and reading the newspaper. I could picture in my mind's eye the little stand by his chair where he kept his smoking supplies, matches, tobacco, pipe cleaners and the like. After the dishes were done in the evening and Tim and I were in bed, this was how they relaxed: one working her crosswords, the other reading the paper and smoking his pipe.

My grandmother's cat, Obie, was sitting on the arm of her chair, his favorite place in the evening. From time to time he would rub his head against her, wanting her to give him some attention. She would stop working on her puzzle for a few minutes to rub him under his chin or behind his ears. Then she would go back to her puzzle. This routine would go on for hours as they sat there together every evening.

As I lay on the floor, peering out at her through a thin space between the edge of the curtain and the door jam, I felt giddy. It was exciting to be this close to danger without her knowing I was there. It was thrilling to be so close to being caught and getting a severe beating for being out of bed. And it was the thrill that I liked. Then, suddenly, the thrill was swept away by fear. Obie had shifted his position on the arm of my grandmother's chair and looked directly at me. I was sure he had seen me and was going to tell my grandmother I was there in the doorway of her bedroom. I struggled to overcome the panic rising up in me. I wanted to bolt from the room, but I knew I couldn't run; for if I did, I would surely make enough noise to attract her attention and get myself caught. The result would certainly have been a beating.

As I mustered the willpower to calm myself, I kept an eye on the cat. Obie kept looking at me, and I waited for him to give me away. I had seen him do it to Bobby James once before. Obie had been sitting on the arm of Grandma's chair one evening while she alternated between stroking him and rubbing his head. Suddenly, she stopped and began to study him, more closely.

"Obie," she cried. "Who cut your whiskers off? Someone has taken the scissors and cut your whiskers off." Her tone was one of complete disbelief. "Who cut your whiskers, Obie?"

Without hesitation, Obie had turned and looked directly at my brother.

"Bobby James, did you cut the cat's whiskers off?" my grand-mother asked.

"No, ma'am," my brother answered.

"Obie, did Bobby James cut your whiskers off?" she asked the cat directly.

Once again the cat turned and looked straight at my brother.

"You *did* cut the cat's whiskers," she shouted at my brother. She got up out of her chair, grabbed Bobby James by the ear, and dragged him into the kitchen, where she took the stick from on top of the icebox and began to give him such a severe beating that huge red welts rose up on his legs and arms.

"Don't you ever cut that cat's whiskers again," she shouted as she continued to beat him with the stick.

Finally, he managed to break free of her and ran outside.

"Fuck the cat," he shouted over his shoulder as he ran.

She grabbed a bar of Octagon from the sink to wash his mouth out with for his language, but he was long gone. When she turned and looked at me, I disappeared as quickly as possible, lest I get my mouth washed out just on general principles. It was two days before my brother came back again. And when he did return, he told my grandmother he was sorry he had cut the cat's whiskers. "I was just playing," he said. "I didn't mean to cut them completely off."

My grandmother didn't answer him. She was still mad, but she let him back in the house anyway.

Now Obie was staring at me as I lay there, peeking around the curtain. I was afraid to move a muscle, wondering if the cat was going to give me away. I stared back at him and remained as still as I could. He kept looking at me, blinked his eyes a few times, and then turned away. The look he gave me as he turned away was almost as if to say, "I see you there; I just don't feel like giving up my head rub right now so she can beat your sorry ass." Sometimes, I hated that cat.

Forty-Six

I LET OUT A LONG, SILENT BREATH AND RELAXED again. I don't know how long I lay there listening to the music. I must have fallen asleep at some point, because I was suddenly awakened with a sharp sting on my leg. Whack! Another sting bit my leg. Whack! Whack! Whack!

I was fully awake now and could see my grandmother standing over me with the stick. Whack! The stick caught me on the shoulder. I was trying to get up off the floor.

"What are you doing out of bed?" she shouted at me as the stick caught me on the leg again.

"I don't know," I cried.

My legs were really beginning to hurt. I could hear Butchie outside at the back door, barking and trying to bust through the screen.

"I asked you a question. What are you doing out of bed?"

"I was listening to the music on the radio. I just wanted to hear the music," I cried.

Whack! Whack! The stick came down on my legs and backside again. I could hear Butchie clawing at the screen, trying to get in to help me; and I wished with all my heart as I tried to get away from her he would bust through the screen and tear my grandmother's throat out. I heard her yell to my grandfather. "Get that dog away from the screen door before he tears it off."

I ran to my room and got in bed. I lay there terrified that she was going to come in the room and hit me again. I was shaking, I ached all over, and I wanted my mother. I began to cry. My grandmother had recently moved me off the top bunk and into the double bed where Bobby James used to sleep. It was the same bed where Crystal and I would take a nap in the afternoons that she watched us while my grandmother ran her errands. It was much cooler on that bed. I rolled over in my blanket, still crying, wishing that my mother would come and take me away from this place forever. But I knew she wasn't coming.

I hated my grandmother. I didn't want to be there anymore. I understood for the first time why my brother was always running away. I wanted to run away too. But where would I go? My brother was eight years older than I, and he knew how to take care of himself. I was afraid to stay out all night, and I didn't know where my mother was, so I couldn't go to her. I decided that tomorrow, I was going to run away. I didn't know where I was going, but I hated my grandmother, and I hated this house.

Forty-Seven

THE NEXT MORNING, I TOLD TIM ABOUT MY PLAN TO run away. He was excited and wanted to go with me. We began making plans to run away as soon as possible, but we didn't know what to take with us. Where would we get food? What would we drink? Where would we go? We had to make some kind of a plan.

"Maybe Ronnie and Donny can tell us what to do," Tim suggested.

"Their father lets them camp out in their front yard all the time."

"That's a good idea," I said. "Let's talk to them."

We asked Grandma if we could go over to Ronnie and Donny's to play. When she said yes, we ran across the field to their house and banged on the screen door.

"Can you guys come out to play?" we shouted.

They came outside together.

"We need to ask you something," I said. "Since you guys camp out all the time, what do you need to sleep outside for a long time?"

They looked at each other with confused expressions.

"Why?" Ronnie asked.

"Because Tim and I want to sleep outside, maybe for a week, but we don't know what we need."

"Why do you want to sleep outside for a week?" Donny asked.

"Because we're going to run away," Tim blurted out.

"No, you aren't," Ronnie said. "Your grandmother would kill you."

"We aren't going to tell her," I said. I was mad at Tim for telling them why we wanted the information. I was afraid that if anyone knew, they might tell Grandma. But since he had already let it out, I figured we might as well get as much help from Ronnie and Donny as we could. "We're just going to leave and go someplace where she can't ever find us, but we don't know what we need to take. Since you guys camp out in your front yard all the time, we thought you could tell us what to take so we can sleep outside."

"Wow, that's neat. Are you really going to run away?" Donny asked.

"Yeah, we are," I said.

"Wow!" they both said at the same time.

"So tell us what we need," Tim said.

They shrugged their shoulders and looked confused.

"We just sleep outside sometimes. We ain't got no food or nothin," Ronnie said.

"What do you use when you sleep outside?" I asked.

"We just make a tent with a blanket over a rope. My dad ties it to two sticks in the ground, and my mom gives us a couple of blankets and a pillow to sleep on in the tent. That's about it. We ain't got no food or nothin' like that."

"Well, what do you eat when you sleep outside?" I asked.

"Sometimes my mother gives us cookies and a soda pop or somethin."

"Don't you cook eggs or anything?"

"No, we don't know how to cook. And besides, we're not allowed to play with matches," Ronnie said.

"Okay," I said, "guess you can't help us."

"Sorry," Donny said. "You guys wanna come up on the porch and play Pick-Up Sticks with us?"

"Yeah," my cousin said excitedly.

I think he had already forgotten about running away. I was disappointed. I wanted to run away the way my brother had and get away from my grandmother. I was tired of getting spanked or beaten for everything I did, but it seemed hopeless to me. I decided to go in and play Pick-Up Sticks too, although I kept thinking about running away.

The idea began to fade as the days dragged by. I would still lie in my bed and think about my mother. I always wondered where she was and what she was doing, but I didn't cry about it anymore.

"Tim, do you ever think about your mother and wonder where she is?" I asked him one day.

"No," he said. "I can't remember what she looks like, so I never think about her much. I remember she gave me candy once. But that's about all I can remember."

Forty-Eight

ONE DAY WHEN WE CAME HOME FROM SCHOOL, MY grandmother and grandfather were going through some of the things they had stored in the new shed. The shed where the furniture was stored had become known as the new shed, while the shed where the rat had jumped out at me a couple of years ago became known as the old shed. They had the two cedar chests out on the lawn and had been taking things out of them. My grandmother was folding some of the linens she had found in the chest and placing them on a wooden bench nearby. As she got near the bottom of one of the chests, she took out two small, olive-colored hatchets.

"What are those, Grandma?" I asked.

"These are Girl Scout hatchets. One belonged to your mother, and one belonged to Tim's mother. They used them when they went camping with the Girl Scouts. Would you boys like to have them?" she asked.

"Yeah," we both shouted at once.

We could hardly believe our grandmother was giving us each a hatchet. My mind was racing a hundred miles an hour, thinking about all the things I could do with it. Now we could chop wood, or throw them at a tree like Indians, or use them to cut limbs to make a fort.

"I'll let you have them," she said, "but you can't throw them. You can't cut limbs off any of the trees, and the first time I catch you doing what I told you not to do with them, I'm going to take them away from you. And you won't see them again. Do I make myself clear?"

"Yes," we said, together.

I didn't like the rules, but I knew I had to agree to them in order to get my hands on one of the hatchets. I still planned to do what I wanted to with it. I couldn't see the point of having a hatchet if you couldn't throw it at something or cut some limbs off a tree to make a fort. I just had to make sure I didn't get caught.

The hatchets were wonderful. We played with them every day and were careful not to break any of the rules my grandmother had laid down, at least not where she could see. We would go over to Jack and Johnny's yard where there were a lot of bushes and palmettos to cut down. Their parents didn't care what we cut down, as long as we didn't cut each other. They figured stuff would grow back. And it did, very quickly. We cut green fronds off the palms and sharpened one end to a point to make swords. The green fronds made great swords, because they had a row of sharp teeth on either side. Jack had a pocket knife and he would whittle out a handle on one end so we could hold them without cutting our hands on the sharp teeth. Then we would have sword fights and try to draw blood by hitting someone on the arm or leg with the teeth on the side of the frond.

We all practiced throwing the hatchets at the oak trees to see if we could make them stick in the tree like an Indian tomahawk. Most of the time, they just glanced off the tree in some weird direction and landed in the brush someplace. Every now and then, one of us would hit the tree perfectly; and the hatchet would stick there just like an Indian had thrown it. Whenever that happened, we would all shout with glee and dance around the tree, hollering and screaming like wild Indians.

One day, Tim and I were playing in our yard and had our hatchets with us. I had mine tucked into my belt while I climbed high up in one of the oak trees. My cousin was on the ground below me, and I thought it would be funny if I dropped my hatchet down from where I was in the tree, so that it would hit the ground beside him and scare him. I took careful aim at a spot right beside him on the ground and let the hatchet go.

Just as it left my hand, he moved toward the spot I had aimed for. There was no time to warn him. The hatchet was on its way, and he was moving right into its path. I was afraid to shout at him, thinking he might look up just in time for the hatchet to hit him square in the face.

Fortunately, it only hit him a glancing blow on the top of the head. But he screamed bloody murder, and I knew I was in trouble; I wasn't going to get out of this one, and I would probably never see my hatchet again.

Quickly, I climbed down from the tree to where my cousin was lying on the ground. Blood was everywhere, and he was screaming at the top of his lungs. My grandfather came running.

"What happened?" my grandfather shouted.

"I think Tim fell out of the tree," I said. I had already picked up my hatchet and stuck it back in my belt.

"Did you fall out of the tree?" my grandfather asked him.

"No," he screamed. "I wasn't in the tree."

"My God, there's blood everywhere. Let's get you into the house," my grandfather said.

"What happened?" my grandmother demanded to know when we got to the house.

"He's got a bad gash on the top of his head," my grandfather told her. "I'm going to clean it up and see if I can put a bandage on it to stop the bleeding."

"How did you cut your head?" my grandmother asked Tim.

"I don't know," he said. "Something hit me. I don't know what it was."

"Did you see what hit him?" my grandmother asked me.

"No, ma'am. I was up in the tree climbing around when I heard him start screaming," I said.

"Did you fall and hit your head?" she asked Tim.

"No, I was just walking around, and something hit my head," he cried.

"Well, something just doesn't hit you in the head from no-where," my grandmother said.

"Maybe a limb broke off and hit him while I was climbing," I offered.

"It would have to be a pretty big limb to cause a gash like this," my grandfather said. Then he added, "I didn't see any limbs on the ground that could have caused this kind of wound."

"Are you sure you don't know anything about this?" my grandmother asked me.

"No, ma'am. I was up in the top of the tree."

"Did Billy hit you with something, Tim?" my grandmother asked him.

"I don't know. I didn't see what hit me," he said. He was be-ginning to calm down as my grandfather washed out the gash on his head with warm soapy water. Then he put iodine on it and a bandage.

I was amazed that I could lie my way out of this situation so easily, and that I was not even a suspect. Whenever my grand-mother asked questions about what had happened, I said I didn't know and continued to be as helpful as I could in trying to solve the mystery of what had hit Tim.

Looking back, I think the reason I was able to lie my way out of it so easily was for two reasons: fortunately, Tim didn't know what hit him, so he couldn't point the finger at me; secondly, we were so used to lying about anything and everything to keep from getting a beating or incurring some other type of punishment that lying had become so natural to us we could lie with a straight face any time we needed to. The only time it didn't work was when we were caught red-handed, as my grandmother liked to say. Even then, we would still try to lie our way out of it and make up some kind of fantastic story to justify our actions.

I think there was also one other reason I was able to lie my way out of this one so easily. It was because I was up in the tree; and it never occurred to either my grandmother or my grandfather that someone would actually drop a hatchet on another person's head from that height without either killing them or splitting their head wide open. But my innocence was not to last for long.

Forty-Nine

EVERY NIGHT AFTER WE WERE FINISHED WITH THE dishes, my grandfather would wash out the gash on Tim's head with warm water at the kitchen sink, put iodine on it, and apply a clean bandage.

"I think this is getting infected," he said as he examined Tim's head one evening.

"Why do you say that?" my grandmother asked from her chair in the backroom.

"I think I see some pus in it tonight," he said. "I've been trying to keep it clean, but we may have to take him to the doctor and have some stitches put in it to close it up. I can't keep it clean because it keeps opening up again. I can't get the gash to close up properly."

"We don't have any money to go to the doctor to have stitches put in his head."

"Well, Henrietta, if we can't keep the infection out of the wound, we're going to have to take him to the doctor," my grandfather said, his voice expressing mild exasperation.

The conversation was making me nervous.

"Maybe if we take him to a doctor, he can tell us what caused this gash; and I'll know better how to keep it clean," my grandfather said.

Now I was getting very nervous. If the doctor could tell that a hatchet had made the gash, then I was the only one who could have done it. And I knew I would be in a lot of trouble if it went that far.

"Grandpa," I said in a shaky voice, "I know how Tim got that cut on his head."

"You do? Well, why haven't you told us how it happened?" he asked.

"I was afraid," I said.

"How did it happen?" He was looking directly at me, but without any anger in his face.

I decided that I needed to tell the truth, or at least some version of it. I might still feel the sting of the stick kept on top of the icebox if I told him this version; but if I told him exactly what happened, I would surely have my hatchet taken away from me.

"Tell me," he said very gently.

"Well, I had my hatchet in my belt, and I was climbing in the top of the oak tree, and when I was hanging upside down, the hatchet slipped out of my belt and hit Tim. I tried to warn him, but he didn't hear me."

"So it was an accident?" he asked.

"Yes, I didn't mean to do it."

This was partially true. I really didn't mean to hit Tim when I dropped the hatchet.

"Why didn't you just tell us what happened? We understand accidents happen. You should have told us the truth," he said in a kind and gentle voice.

I was very thankful that my grandfather was a gentle man and not prone to losing his temper the way my grandmother was.

"I was afraid I would get in trouble. Is Tim going to be okay?" I asked.

"Yes, I think so," he said.

"Are we going to have to take him to the doctor?" I asked.

"No, I don't think so. Now that I know what really happened, I think I can fix it up okay with iodine and a bandage."

I felt relieved. He didn't need to know how it had actually happened. He accepted that it was an accident and that was good enough for me, as far as a confession went. Some years later, when I was thinking about it, I wondered if my grandfather had already suspected that I was the one to blame for the gash in Tim's head and had started the conversation about going to the doctor to see if I would own up to it. I'll never know, because I never asked him.

Just as I feared, the hatchets disappeared the next day, and neither my grandmother nor my grandfather had any idea what had happened to them, when we asked where they were. Or at least they professed to not know anything. But I'm sure they knew exactly what happened to them, and where they went. In any case, we never saw them again. I wasn't surprised.

Fifty

CHRISTMAS MORNING AND CHRISTMAS DAY WERE always exciting at my grandmother's house. She loved Christmas. She loved having a tree put up with lots of colorful bulbs and lights and tinsel on it. She loved Christmas carols and having some of her close friends over for Christmas Day dinner. She always had lots of nuts and raisins and apples in bowls throughout the house, along with holly and pine wreaths hanging on the walls in the hallway.

The combination of smells from the wreaths and fruit were incredibly delicious. The raisins, which were in the bowls with the apples, were still on their stems and came in bunches like grapes. It was easy to sneak a few without getting caught, because you could pick some off the inside of the stem so it was not obvious any were missing. You couldn't eat the apples though, because they were counted and she knew exactly how many she had in each bowl. Christmas morning was the most exciting. My grandmother always got up first and would wake up everyone else in the house while it was still dark outside. She would come through the house singing "Hark! The Herald, Angels Sing" at the top of her voice while she pulled vigorously back and forth on her concertina. While she played and sang, Butchie would be jumping and running beside her, howling at the top of his voice, and Obie would meow as loudly as he could, winding in and out of her legs, as she marched across the kitchen, down the hall past our bedroom and into the front room. It was a wild parade, and no one could sleep through it. But who would want to? It was Christmas morning.

The Christmas tree and presents were always in the front room. As she passed our bedroom, we would jump out of bed and join the parade, adding our shouts of glee to the din as we all marched into the front room. Stockings were hung on the mantel of the fireplace. They were old nylon stockings that she had saved during the year instead of throwing them out when they got a run in them. On Christmas morning, each one had a name on it, and we always ran to the stockings first. They would be stuffed with nuts and candy and apples and the most delicious tangerines. There was never a toy in them. The toys were always under the Christmas tree, and my grandmother was always the one in charge of handing out the presents. She would stoop down, pick out a present, call out the person's name on the tag and give it to them.

One particular Christmas I sat there on the floor full of excitement as she passed out the presents, waiting for my name to be called. Tim got his, my grandfather got his, and even Butchie and Obie got theirs. Finally, all the presents under the tree had been handed out, but my name had not been called.

"Grandma, I didn't get a present," I said in disbelief.

"That's right," she said.

"But why? Everyone else got one."

"Do you remember the time I told you not to get out of bed again or you wouldn't get anything for Christmas?"

"Yes, ma'am," I said weakly.

"Well, you got out of bed, didn't you?" she reminded me.

"Yes, but—"

"But nothing. I said you wouldn't get anything for Christmas if you got out of bed again. Apparently you didn't believe me. Maybe this will teach you a lesson for the future."

I was devastated. I couldn't believe it. Even at the table when we were having Christmas dinner, I kept expecting my present. But it never came.

Usually Christmas dinner was a fun time. My grandmother always had each place set at the table with a little green Christmas tree. The little trees were about four inches high and were frosted, as if snow had fallen on them. I loved those trees, and I looked forward to the pot roast, white rice and gravy my grandmother always prepared for dinner on Christmas Day. She made the best brown gravy, and it was especially delicious poured over the rice. For desert, she usually made a pineapple upside down cake. Everything was made from scratch; she spent nearly all day cooking.

But that year, dinner was no fun and nothing tasted good. Not getting a present that Christmas was one of the worst times of my life. I've never forgotten it.

Fifty-One

MY FAVORITE OF MY GRANDMOTHER'S FRIENDS WAS a man named Gordon McCray and his wife, Squirrel. I'm not sure why she was called Squirrel, except that her face did look somewhat like a Squirrel. He was an explorer who had traveled all over the world and written books about the places he had been. I loved to go to their house, because it was decorated with all the things he had brought back from different parts of the world. There were spears from Africa, blow guns from South America, knives and shields from India and other unusual things, like the headdress from a tribal chief in Africa.

When we would go to their house for dinner, he always cooked an exotic dish he had learned from somewhere during his travels. My favorite was curry. It smelled so good when he was cooking it, and it tasted even better. We could have all we wanted to eat whenever we went to his house, and I always asked for seconds, ignoring the evil eye I got from my grandmother.

"You act like you've never had anything to eat before," she would say to me as she grabbed me by the earlobe on the way to the car when it was time to go home. But I didn't mind, even though my ear felt like it was a foot longer by the time we got to the car. It was worth it to get seconds on lamb curry with mint chutney.

Gordon McCray also played the bagpipes, and he always brought them with him when he visited and played them for everyone after dinner. Sometimes when we were at his house, he would also dress up in his kilts and march around the house, playing the pipes. I loved it, and I would beg him to play over and over again. Usually he would play as long as anyone wanted to listen. I was always sad when it was time to go home. The time passed too quickly, and I wanted to stay there and listen to him forever. The same was true when he came to our house and it would eventually be time for him and Squirrel to leave. He was so much fun that I wished with all my heart that I could live with them.

My grandmother's strict rule that you were to be punished whenever you disobeyed her was always in force. Getting my ear pinched on the way to the car for eating too much was only the precursor of what was to come when we got home. Usually I would get a good swat from the stick to remind me to remember my manners in the future, but her punishment could take on other forms as well. Nonetheless, I was always running afoul of her idea of how I should behave. No matter how hard I tried, it seemed as though I always wound up getting punished and missing out on fun things.

Fifty-Two

ONE YEAR A GAY 90s DAY CELEBRATION AND PARADE was held in Gulfport. People dressed up the way they did in the 1890s and paraded down Beach Boulevard to the Casino. There were pony rides at the beach, old cars and lots of good things to eat, like hamburgers, hot dogs, cotton candy, saltwater taffy and peanuts. During the day, there would be hydroplane boat races on the bay; and at night, there was a huge fireworks display. I didn't get to go. I wound up having to stay home in bed. I don't know why I just couldn't behave myself, but for some reason it was impossible, and as a result I didn't make it to the Gay 90s Day celebration. That I didn't get to go wasn't that big of a deal; it was par for the course with me. For some reason or other, whenever something special was coming, I just couldn't behave.

But being left at home all day by myself was not all that bad. Even though I was warned not to get out of bed when they left, as soon as my grandmother's car was out of the driveway, I would get up and walk around the house, helping myself to the dog biscuits and drinking water out of the faucet, not giving a damn about the air in the pipes or the noise it made. I made sure I flushed the crumbs from the biscuits down the toilet. Even if I were to get caught up walking around the house, which I never did, I always had a good excuse ready. All I had to say was that I had to go to the bathroom. My grandmother would accept that as a valid reason. That is, unless she caught me in the front room. It would be a little difficult explaining what I was doing in there rubbing mosquito bites in the front room if I had to go to the bathroom.

During these times, I would explore the entire house without fear of being caught. It was complete freedom. It was the only times that I could do anything without sneaking around in fear of being punished. I still had to be careful not to leave any evidence that I had been into anything, but I loved the freedom.

Maybe that was the reason I always misbehaved before a special event. I don't know for sure, but one thing I do know: often, when everyone else got to go to a big event, I had to stay home.

Fifty-Three

IN APRIL OF 1950, WHEN I WAS TEN YEARS OLD, TIM AND I arrived home from school one afternoon to discover a new problem had shown up at my grandmother's house. It was a pretty, little four-year-old girl with curly blond hair and big brown eyes. Her name was Allyson, and – as I was to find out shortly – she was my half sister. When Tim and I arrived at the house, my grandmother was arguing with a woman I didn't immediately recognize. But before my grandmother even said the woman's name, I heard her voice and realized who it was: my mother. My mother, who I hadn't seen in five years, was actually standing there in my grandmother's house. They were in the middle of the room, facing each other in a heated discussion.

"No, Susan, you can't leave her here. We cannot afford it. You've already dumped two of your kids here. Now you want to dump a third one. What's wrong with you? Why can't you take responsibility for your own kids?"

The little girl saw me looking at her and quickly hid behind my mother's skirt.

"Mama, it will only be for a short time while Frank gets settled in his new job. We'll pay you."

My grandmother was mad. She had been glad when my brother was sent off to Boys Town, and although she wasn't happy that she still had my cousin and me to take care of, with my brother gone the burden had been a little less, and she had begrudgingly accepted the fact that she was stuck with us.

"Susan, you haven't contributed one thin dime toward the support of Billy. Your father and I are running through our life savings to feed and clothe him. You haven't even been here to see him in five years. Now you show up wanting to dump Frank's brat on me."

My grandmother never missed an opportunity to remind everyone how much she hated Frank. She thought he was a good-for-nothing drunk and could not understand why my mother stayed with him. As far as she was concerned, Frank was an alcoholic, and that's all he ever would be. He didn't send any money to help with my care, and as long as my mother stayed with him, she was not even looking after her own kid. But worst of all, Allyson was Frank's kid, and my grandmother made no attempt to hide her intense dislike for anything connected to him. Instead of my mother coming to take me to live with her, she was just there to drop off another kid. I was devastated.

How my mother was ever able to talk my grandmother into taking Allyson – or "Frank's brat," as my grandmother called her – is somewhat of a mystery. She didn't want her there and made it clear from the moment she arrived. Somehow my mother had convinced my grandmother that it was only a temporary arrangement until she and Frank could get settled in Texas. My mother went on and on about Frank. She said he had gotten a job as a reporter with the *Houston Chronicle*, and it seemed that for the first time since the war, Frank was going to have a real job, and they were going to have a real home and were making solid plans for their future – and all they needed was some time to get settled. Then my mother would come back and take both Allyson and me to live with them in Houston.

In the end, my mother must have given my grandmother some money, because Allyson stayed. I think my grandfather may also have had something to do with it. He always saw the good in everyone, and he really loved my mother. No matter how my grandmother may have acted toward him, he would never have allowed her to turn my mother away with a four year old little girl. He just wasn't made that way.

Since my grandmother wouldn't allow Frank in the house, he and my mother rented a hotel room on one of the Gulf beaches. They didn't stay very long, and my mother never spent the night with us while they were there; she always returned to the hotel to be with Frank at night. She did bring me a present. It was a carving of three wooden geese in flight, which had been made out of a single piece of mahogany and could be hung on the wall. I wished that she would take me with her at night when she went back to the hotel, but she never took me – only Allyson. I suspected this was because Frank was drinking heavily and didn't want me there. After all, I wasn't *his* kid – but since Allyson was his daughter he didn't mind having her in the hotel with them.

Even though Allyson was actually my half-sister, just as Bobby James was my half-brother, I immediately started thinking of her as my sister. I really didn't know what it meant to be a half-sister or half-brother, so I simply thought of them as my brother and sister. Bobby James and I had never referred to each other as our half-anything, just as brothers – and now we had a sister.

Three days after arriving, they left again, but Allyson stayed with us. She was confused and didn't understand why she couldn't go with her parents, and she began to cry. I knew that if my grandmother heard her crying, she would either gag her or give her something to cry for, which translated into a severe spanking. I took Allyson back to our bedroom and told her not to cry or she would get in trouble.

"What kind of trouble?" she asked, sobbing and wiping the tears out of her eyes.

"Grandma will either gag you with a dishtowel, or she'll spank you," I said.

"I really miss Mommy and Daddy. Why couldn't I go with them?" she asked me.

"I don't know," I said. "I don't think they want us."

"Why?" She was crying so hard her whole body shook, and I didn't know how to make her stop. I was afraid my grandmother would hear her and come in the room and spank us both. Tim didn't say anything. He just put his arms around Allyson and patted her on the back, trying to comfort her. We had barely gotten her to stop crying when my grandmother suddenly appeared in our room.

"Here are a couple of blankets for you," she said, throwing the blankets at Allyson.

"Is Allyson going to sleep on the top bunk now, Grandma?" I asked.

"No, she is not. She's too little to sleep on the top bunk. She can sleep on the floor. That way she won't be falling out of any bed. Supper is ready. Get yourselves to the table." Then she turned and left the room.

That night we had rutabaga and green beans with garlic. My grandmother prepared the rutabaga by boiling it, then mashing it with a potato masher, as if she were making mashed potatoes. In fact, it looked like orange mashed potatoes. She seasoned it with black pepper and brought a mound of it to the table in a huge bowl. Both Tim and I liked the green beans, but we hated the rutabaga. It was going to be hard to get rid of it without getting caught, because Butchie wouldn't touch it and my grandmother was keeping a close eye on all three of us while we ate. We couldn't even wrap it up in our napkins and throw it in the trash.

Allyson looked at her food, took one bite of it, and began to cry.

"What are you crying about?" Grandma demanded.

"I don't like this orange stuff or the green beans," she said.

"That's rutabaga. It's good for you, and so are the green beans.

Now eat them. You're not leaving this table until you eat everything on your plate."

Huge tears rolled down Allyson's face, and she started to cry even louder.

"Either you stop your crying, or I'm going to give you something to cry about," my grandmother told her.

Allyson tried to stop crying, but the tears just kept flowing. Every time she tried to eat the rutabaga or the green beans, she would gag. I thought she was actually going to throw up on the table. My grandmother must have thought so too.

"You better not throw up that food," she warned

By now my grandmother was totally preoccupied with my sister, so I took the opportunity to pick my rutabaga up with my napkin and stuff it in my pocket. I was relieved that I had gotten it off my plate and into my pocket without getting caught. Now I would not have to eat it for breakfast in the morning.

My cousin was still sitting there with a big pile of the orange mess on his plate. He wasn't crying, but I was sure he was going to wind up having it for breakfast. I couldn't understand why he hadn't taken the opportunity that I had to get rid of it in his napkin and stuff it in his pocket. Instead, he just sat there staring at it. I waited for a few minutes and then excused myself from the table, picking up my plate and heading for the kitchen.

"Hold it. Let me see your plate," my grandmother ordered.

I showed it to her so she could confirm that I had eaten everything on it, and then I marched off to the kitchen. Once there, I immediately pulled the napkin out of my pocket and dumped the rutabaga in the sink where I washed it down the drain, under the pretense that I was rinsing off my plate. Then I threw the paper napkin in the trash. On previous rutabaga nights, I had just thrown the whole mess in the trash, but once my grandmother had discovered it and it had appeared again for my breakfast.

"What are you doing with the water running?" she yelled from the table.

"I'm just rinsing my plate," I answered.

"Well, turn it off and quit wasting water," she growled.

"Yes, ma'am," I said.

I was overjoyed that I had gotten away without having to eat the rutabaga. My cousin and Allyson were still at the table, and my grandmother was not letting them go anywhere. I knew that she would make them sit there until it was time for us to dry the dishes, and if they hadn't eaten their food by then, she would gather it up and save it for their breakfast. A half hour later, my prediction was fact.

"Alright," I heard my grandmother say. "It's time to do the dishes and get ready for bed. You'll have what's left on your plates for breakfast in the morning. We are not going to waste food in this house."

My grandfather announced that Allyson would not have to help dry the dishes because she was too little.

"That's not fair," I said. "Tim and I had to dry the dishes when we were her age. How come she doesn't have to help?"

"She's smaller than you boys were at that age; and besides, we don't need three people in the kitchen drying dishes," my grandfather said.

"Why can't we take turns, then?" I asked.

"I'm not going to say anymore about it," my grandfather told me.

I knew that was the end of the discussion. My grandfather didn't take a stand very often; but when he did, it was final. To continue arguing only risked bringing my grandmother's wrath down on me, when she had had enough of hearing me. So the subject was dropped, and Allyson didn't have to dry the dishes.

Fifty-Four

THE NEXT MORNING WAS SATURDAY. FOR BREAKFAST, I had a bowl of raisin bran with a banana and milk, while Tim and Allyson sat there staring at the leftover rutabaga from the night before. I was so happy that I had escaped their punishment that I almost laughed out loud. I didn't have to face the challenge they were facing: how to get rid of that stuff without eating it. Fortunately for them, this morning my grandmother had also fixed them some toast and eggs to go with the rutabaga.

"If you mix the rutabaga in with your egg, it will be easier to eat," I offered.

Tim began mixing his in with his egg and put salt on it. Soon he was eating it, and he had it down before he knew it.

Allyson just sat there, staring at the food in front of her with tears rolling down her cheeks. "I want my mommy," she cried.

I didn't know what to say to her. Our mother wasn't here, and she wasn't coming back. She couldn't help us.

"Try to eat your egg and toast," I coaxed.

Slowly she picked up her fork and began to eat the egg. She picked up the toast and began to eat that, too. But she still didn't touch the rutabaga.

"Try mixing it in the egg yolk," I offered again, but she ignored me.

Soon she had eaten all of the egg and the toast, but the orange pile was still in front of her. My grandmother came in from her bedroom and glanced at Allyson's plate.

"You better eat that rutabaga," she said. "We don't waste food in this house."

My sister said nothing. She just sat there with tears still streaming down her face.

I finished my cereal and started to take my bowl to the kitchen when my grandmother suddenly grabbed my sister's face in one hand, forcing her mouth open. With the other hand she took a spoon, scooped up some of the rutabaga and jammed it into Allyson's mouth. When Allyson started to gag and throw it up, my grandmother held her mouth shut so she couldn't spit it out.

"Swallow, right now," my grandmother demanded in a low, threatening voice. "Swallow it right now, or I'll ram it down your throat."

My sister held it in her mouth as long as she could, but the pain from my grandmother's grip on her jaws was too much. Finally, she swallowed it; and as soon as she did my grandmother jammed another spoonful into her mouth. Then she held Allyson's mouth shut again until she swallowed it. This process continued until all the rutabaga was gone.

"Next time, maybe you'll eat what's put before you," my grandmother told her as she picked my sister's dishes up off the table to take them to the kitchen. "Now go outside and play, and don't come back into the house until I call you for lunch."

We all ran out the back door, glad to be away from the table and away my grandmother. Allyson ran straight to one of the flowerbeds and puked up her breakfast.

At lunch time, my grandmother called us in from the backyard and gave us each a peanut butter and jelly sandwich with a glass of milk. We all liked that lunch and had no trouble eating it. For the next few weeks, my grandmother didn't serve us anything that was on our hated-food list, and we got through the meals without too much trouble. But we were always still hungry when we left the table. My sister didn't seem to mind it as much as my cousin and I did. Maybe it was because we were older and bigger and needed more food than she did. Or maybe she just wanted to go home.

Fifty-Five

A COUPLE OF MONTHS WENT BY AND WE ALL managed to stay out of trouble and not get spanked too often. However, I did slam the screen door one day.

"Come back here and open and close that door quietly one hundred times," my grandmother shouted. "And count out loud while you do it."

I was already in a hurry to go and play outside, which is why I had slammed it in the first place, so I didn't want to spend all day counting to a hundred while I opened and closed the door with each number. "One, two, three, ten, eleven—"

"Start over," she quietly told me.

"One, two, three, four, five, nine, ten, thirteen—"

"Start over," she told me again.

This time I got all the way to seventy before I started skipping numbers again. It wasn't that I didn't know how to count; I just wanted to shortcut the process.

"Seventy-five, eighty, eighty-five—"

"Start over," she said, as she sat there working her crossword puzzles.

Now I was really mad. I began counting from one again, only this time I counted in a very low voice, almost a whisper, thinking I could skip numbers and she wouldn't catch me.

"Start over and count so I can hear you," she said.

This time I counted from one to a hundred without skipping

any numbers, but when I got to one hundred, I slammed the door as hard as I could.

"Start over," came her voice. "And if you don't do it right this time, you'll find yourself in bed without your supper." So this time I counted from one to one hundred without skipping any numbers and loud enough for her to hear me. When I reached one hundred, I gently shut the door.

"Can I go outside now?" I asked.

"You can go. Next time don't slam the door."

The next day, when she was outside watering the plants, I went in the house to go to the bathroom and slammed the door as hard and as loud as I could. She didn't hear. I felt great.

Fifty-Six

ON ONE OR TWO NIGHTS DURING THE WEEK, WE might have a meatless supper, but on Friday nights it was *always* meatless. My grandmother wasn't Catholic. In fact, I don't think she subscribed to any particular religion, so there couldn't have been a religious reason for not eating meat on Fridays. I think it was a habit left over from the war years when meat was rationed and everyone was expected to go at least one day a week without eating any.

As far as religion or religious training went, we kids were whichever church had the best offer that week. When the First Baptist Church had a hayride to recruit new members, we were all Baptist that Sunday. We loved getting on the hay wagon pulled by two huge plow horses from Jim Demby's Jim Dandy Ranch. When the Presbyterian Church gave out pictures of Jesus with a little poem on the back that said "Jesus wants me for a sunbeam," we were all Presbyterians that Sunday.

My favorite church was the Methodist Church. They had a Sunday school teacher by the name of Miss Kent who always held the Sunday school classes outside underneath the pine trees. We would sit on the ground, in the pine needles, while she sat on a small chair reading Bible stories to us. She was the kindest, gentlest woman I ever knew. When I would crawl under the church to hide from her, she would find me and beg me to come out and join the Sunday school class again. I would refuse until she promised to hold me on her lap and read me a story about Jesus. She always kept her promise, and she never told my grandmother about me crawling under the church or hiding from her. I loved that woman and I felt a terrible loneliness when she died suddenly from a heart attack one day while she was mowing her front yard.

Why my grandmother had elected Fridays as the day to go meatless, I don't know. But on many of those Friday nights, she would serve fried eggplant instead. It looked like chicken fried steak when it came to the table because she always dipped it in a batter of eggs and cornmeal and then fried it in leftover bacon grease. Even though it looked like chicken fried steak, the disappointment when you bit into it and discovered it was just slimy eggplant was enough to make you want to puke. All three of us kids hated it; it was almost as hard to choke down as rutabaga. Thank God when Butchie was in the house on those nights. He would wait under the table for any food that might drop on the floor, and if we were careful, we could usually slip the eggplant off our plates and feed it to him. Unlike rutabaga, he always gobbled it down. It must have been the cornmeal and bacon grease that delighted his taste buds.

One particular night, Butchie was not in the house when we sat down to supper. I don't know if my grandmother left him outside because she suspected somehow that we were feeding him our eggplant, or if he just wasn't around when dinner was served. In any case, he was missing; and we all three sat there staring at the eggplant on our plates, Tim and I wondering how we were going to get rid of it, and Allyson, who had no idea there *was* a way to get rid of it, in complete misery. Every time she tried to eat it, she gagged and nearly puked.

"Don't you throw that food up," my grandmother cautioned.

"You better eat every bit of it."

I knew my sister was in for a hard time. She hated the stuff as much as Tim and I did, but obviously she remembered the ordeal with the rutabaga. She tried to eat it, but it made her gag again.

"Eat your eggplant," my grandmother told her, "or I'll feed it to you." She stood over Allyson, glaring at her. It seemed that for some reason, my grandmother had become obsessed with making my sister eat the eggplant immediately. Usually she would warn you a few times, and then if you still hadn't eaten it while you were at the supper table, it would show up again for breakfast. It was easier to get rid of at breakfast. You just had to make sure Butchie was in the house when you sat down to eat. But tonight my grandmother seemed determined to make my sister eat it before she left the table.

As a result, she was paying very little attention to me or Tim. This gave me the opportunity to slip the eggplant off my plate and into my napkin, which I then quickly stuffed in my pocket. That night, as I watched my grandmother force Allyson to succumb to her will, I realized just how much she hated my sister. I made a mental note to remember it and see if I could use it to my advantage some way in the future.

A few weeks later, we had rutabaga again, and I decided to test what I had learned regarding my grandmother's obsession with bending Allyson to her will. At the table that night, my grandmother was watching all three of us like a hawk, and it was almost impossible to slip the rutabaga off my plate and into my napkin without being caught. Finally, after sitting there for awhile, I made my move.

"Grandma, Allyson hasn't eaten anything on her plate," I said.

My grandmother's attention was immediately diverted to my sister, and she began berating her for not eating what was put before her. I took the opportunity, while my grandmother's attention was focused on Allyson, to slip the rutabaga off my plate and into my napkin. My sister looked at me with such pain and hurt on her face, as if she couldn't believe what I had just done to her.

I had betrayed her, but I didn't care. I had gotten rid of the hated food on my plate, and it wasn't coming back in the morning. The hurt on my sister's face made no difference to me. I had discovered a way to divert my grandmother's attention away from me, and I would use it again and again. My cousin sat there staring at his food, and I knew it would be back again in the morning for him to stare at some more. Allyson began crying, and my grandmother threatened to shove the food down her throat if she didn't eat it immediately – a threat I knew all too well she would make good on. I had heard and experienced it many times myself. I sat there watching everyone at the table, smug as could be with my clean plate.

It amazed me that my grandfather never saw me slipping the food off my plate and into my napkin. Maybe he did see and just decided not to say anything in an effort to keep the peace, however he may have defined the peace. My grandmother had a way of intimidating him whenever he tried to intervene in her disciplining of us. She intimidated everyone. He just stayed out of it for the most part, unless he thought the punishment had gone too far or was too harsh or dangerous. Usually he just kept peace with himself and quietly smoked his pipe. I liked my grandfather. I always thought he was a good man. He was weak and quiet, but he was basically a good man. I just knew that I could never count on him to help me out of any trouble with my grandmother. He would rarely interfere. That's just the way he was.

My sister finally choked down the rutabaga, but I'll never know how she did it without throwing up. I knew I would have thrown up if I had to eat it without mixing it with something like my eggs in the morning. Maybe it was because she remembered how my grandmother had jammed the spoonfuls of rutabaga in her mouth before, and she simply didn't want to have to go through that again. I began to feel ashamed that I had betrayed her, but then I figured that I had to look out for myself first; and the feeling of shame quickly disappeared.

Fifty-Seven

FROM THAT DAY FORWARD, I BEGAN TO DODGE MOST punishment from my grandmother by blaming everything I did on Allyson. I would steal a banana from the bowl on top of the icebox, eat it and throw the peel in the trash. If my grandmother didn't notice and therefore said nothing about the missing banana, I said nothing. But if she noticed that something was missing – a banana, an apple, cookies or a piece of candy – then I would tell her Allyson had taken it.

"I want to know who ate the banana I had on the counter," my grandmother would say.

The first line of defense was to always deny that you knew anything about it. It was always better to play stupid and try to come off as innocent by being totally ignorant of what had happened. We all used that defense often, and usually we merely shrugged our shoulders and said "I don't know" when confronted.

However, sometimes one of us would say something like, "I didn't even see a banana by the sink," without realizing we had added an extra fact, which could be costly.

"How did you know I meant on the counter by the sink?" my grandmother would ask.

At that point, if you had already supplied too much information, a shrug of the shoulders, an "I don't know" or an attempt to look as innocent as possible wouldn't get you out of it. It was always better to just not know anything from the start.

My grandmother always picked up on a slip like that. "You're the one that ate it," she would quickly conclude. "Otherwise, how would you know where it was. Go get yourself in bed. You don't need any supper tonight."

It was important that you not give any more information in your answer than she had provided in her question, even if you were, indeed, completely innocent. You could still be branded the guilty party just by appearing to know more about the incident than she had let you know. These tactics must have come from being a policewoman.

Allyson didn't understand this subtlety when answering my grandmother's questions and usually said too much, so she often wound up branded as guilty, even though she was innocent 99% of the time. She found this very confusing, especially when she hadn't done anything. I found it a good strategy to be quiet as long as I could and simply let Tim or Allyson entrap themselves.

Sometimes I could talk Tim into taking the blame so we could get out of bed and go back outside and play, but that only worked if we had been sent to bed in the morning or early afternoon. If it was later in the afternoon or just before or just after supper, he didn't care about getting up again. He just went to sleep, and then he was gone for the rest of the night. Allyson would never voluntarily take the blame for anything. She was already being blamed for too much as it was, and volunteering for further punishment probably didn't make any sense to her.

One day, when my grandmother was in the backroom talking on the telephone, I noticed a cookie that had fallen partially out of a bag on the counter by the icebox. I quickly snatched it up and ate it on my way to the bathroom. My grandmother must have been doing something with them at the time, probably counting them, when the telephone rang and interrupted her.

When she was finished with her call, she went back to the kitchen. Within moments, we were all called to the kitchen for interrogation.

"Which one of you ate one of the cookies I had here on the counter?" she asked, pointing to the open bag.

No one knew. We all shrugged our shoulders and gave the same answer. "I don't know. Not me, Grandma."

"You had to have just eaten it. I only left them here to answer the phone. Now which one of you did it?"

Still no one knew. We were all innocent.

"Maybe Butchie got up on the counter and ate the cookies, Grandma," I offered, trying to be helpful and send her attention in another direction.

"The dog is out. He's been out all morning. Now which one of you ate the cookie?" she demanded again. "Somebody better own up to it, or all three of you are going to find yourselves in bed."

We all knew that was just a trick. We had fallen for it before: whoever owned up to the offense got just as bad a beating as they would have if they had kept quiet until the very last second before being discovered.

"Alright, open your mouths," she demanded, and I knew I had been caught. As soon as I opened my mouth, she would see some of the cookie on my teeth or on my tongue. When she got to me, I wouldn't open my mouth, so she forced it open by squeezing my mouth between my upper and lower jaw until I had to open it. When I did, chocolate colored saliva ran out of my mouth and down the front of my shirt.

"I thought so," she said as she jerked me over towards the ice-box. She reached up and took down her stick. As she whacked me over and over, I tried not to cry. I held it as long as I could, but it only intensified her anger, and she increased the severity of the whacks on my back and arms. Whenever she spanked us, it was as if she couldn't control her anger; the stick would come down harder and harder until we could manage to break away from her. As soon as I started getting beaten with the stick, Allyson and Tim quickly ran outside to get away from her wrath. None of us ever stuck around to see the others get spanked. It was too scary and we always wanted to be as far away from what was going on as we could get.

Fifty-Eight

BLAMING THINGS ON ALLYSON MADE MY LIFE EASIER, but it made her life a living hell. She got the blame for nearly everything I did. The more I got away with, the more I blamed on her. She was in so much trouble all the time that my grandmother was convinced she had another problem-child like Bobby James on her hands – and she was determined to control this one. The fact that Allyson was Frank's daughter only provoked my grandmother all the more and intensified the anger she unleashed on her. It was as if she were looking for things Allyson had done just so she could find a reason to punish her. That was why it was so easy for me to blame things on her.

My sister knew I was the reason she got punished for everything, and I didn't care that she knew. As long as I could steal food and escape unpunished by blaming Allyson, I was going to continue doing it. But the thing I had a hard time understanding was that even though she was getting punished because of me, she still looked up to me and always wanted to play with me when we were outside. She followed me wherever I went. If we got in a rock war with the Wilson kids, she was always on my side, and she would hang in there and throw rocks even after she had been hit and was bleeding.

I always tried to clean her up and make sure she wasn't bleeding before we went back in the house. I didn't want my grandmother to know that she had been throwing rocks with us. My grandmother was very old fashioned in that respect. Little girls played with dolls; they did *not* throw rocks. If she found out, I would get the blame for getting her involved in these games and not protecting her.

Maybe Allyson wanted to play with me and was willing to throw rocks because she didn't have very many toys to play with. I don't know. She always thought of me and shared whatever she had with me. No matter how mean I was to her or how much stuff I blamed on her, she always brought me something from wherever she had been, whether a friend's house, a birthday party or even an event at school. Sometimes it was just a couple of pieces of candy she had saved and kept in the pocket of her overalls until she came home, other times it was food. Once, one of her friends had a birthday party out by the Davis Causeway, a bridge that connected St. Petersburg with the beaches out on the Gulf of Mexico. They were going to dig for clams and then cook them on the beach and celebrate the little girl's birthday with ice cream and cake.

That evening when she came home, she had a bandage on her left heel. The little girl's father explained to my grandmother that Allyson had stepped on an oyster shell in the water and had sliced her heel open.

"We managed to get the bleeding stopped," he said, "and we've put iodine on the cut and bandaged it up. I don't think she's going to need any stitches, but you'll probably need to change the bandage tonight and put more iodine on it. It's a pretty bad slice, so you will want to make sure it doesn't get infected."

When Allyson came in the house, she was hobbling, walking only on the toes of the foot that was bandaged. She refused to cry or let my grandmother know how much it hurt. Instead, she came straight over to me. "This is for you," she said, handing me a little package. "I brought you some birthday cake from the party."

Fifty-Nine

ALLYSON'S GENEROSITY AND KINDNESS WAS A mystery to me. One day, when we went to the grocery store with my grandmother, she made her usual stop at the drugstore and bought us each an ice cream cone. Of course, there was one for Butchie too. I was holding my ice cream in one hand and Butchie's cone in the other while he licked it. My ice cream dropped off my cone and into my lap. Butchie ate it in one gulp before I could retrieve it.

"Grandma, I dropped my ice cream and Butchie ate it," I whined.

"Too bad, you should have been more careful."

"I didn't get any ice cream," I continued to whine, and I noticed that my cousin was eating his cone much faster now. Obviously, he didn't want to take the chance that my grandmother might tell him to share it with me.

"Next time, hold it correctly and you won't lose it," she advised me.

I was mad that I had lost my ice cream and was about to eat the rest of Butchie's cone, but he gobbled it out of my hand and finished it off before I could take a lick. I'm sure he knew what I was thinking.

"Here, you can have the rest of mine," my sister said as she offered her cone to me.

She always ate her cone very slowly, and as a result there was almost the whole cone left.

"Thanks," I said. I took it and began licking it as fast as I could, before she changed her mind and wanted it back.

There was no end to her kindness, and there was no end to the things that I tried to blame on her. It never occurred to me to ask her why she was being so kind. I just thought it was something I deserved. I was older. I let her play with us, and I always told her I was sorry whenever she got spanked for something I did. It never occurred to me that she was kind to me because she loved me. No one loved me. No one loved Allyson or Bobby James either. Why would they? We were animals. We were in the way. My grandmother sure didn't love any of us or even want us around. She was just stuck with us. And it was clear that she resented it. I fully expected that one day we would all be sent to Mary Help a Christian the way Bobby James had been.

Despite the fact that Tim, Allyson and I had each other to play with, along with the other kids who lived around us, I was lonely. I couldn't understand why my mother didn't want me or Allyson. She had seemed to love me when Bobby James and I had visited her in San Diego a few years ago, but if she did, why didn't she come to get me? I pondered this all the time, mostly at night before I fell asleep. Sometimes I even thought about it during the day when something would happen to remind me of my mother and how much I missed her.

One day, when all of us kids were playing in the road that ran in front of Ronnie and Donny's house, Jack and Johnny's mother and father came driving up the road in their old Ford car. They were coming home from shopping in St. Petersburg. I thought their car was neat because it had a rumble seat in the back. When they saw all of us in the road, they pulled up and stopped.

Their father was driving, and I could see the black patch he always wore over the eye he had lost during the war. Jack and Johnny ran over to the passenger side of the car where their mother was riding

"Hello, buckaroos. Give me a kiss," she yelled out the window.

"Hi, Mom," they said as they jumped up on the running board to kiss her.

"You boys hungry for some lunch?"

"Yeah," they both shouted.

"Well, jump in the rumble seat and we'll go home and fix some," she said, smiling at them.

They both scrambled to the back of the car, piled into the rumble seat and away they went. As I stood there in the dust, watching their car drive down the road toward their house, I wished with all my heart that my mother would drive up and give me a kiss and ask me if I were hungry for some lunch. Maybe she would call me buckaroo, too. Soon all I could see was a dust cloud from their car, but I continued to stand there and wonder what it would be like if that were my mom.

"Come on, Billy, let's go over to my house and play in the mulberry tree."

It was Ronnie. She was standing there in a dusty hand-me-down dress from her mother with huge sweat stains under the arm pits. Ronnie always wore her mother's old dresses, and they usually hung down to her ankles. Most of the time she was barefoot, but in the winter she often wore an old pair of her father's shoes. Even though she was a girl and wore dresses, she was nice and fun to play with. She liked to throw rocks and climb trees with the rest of us, and she never complained if she got hurt. Ronnie was as tough as any one of us boys, but she was also very kind.

As we walked toward her house, she put her arm around my shoulder and said, "Don't be sad, Billy."

Sixty

ALTHOUGH RONNIE WAS TOUGH AND COULD THROW rocks as hard as any of us boys, Allyson could be just as tough, especially when we got into any rock wars with the Wilson kids. She had a good eye and a good arm. Even when she got hit and was cut and bleeding, she didn't cry or complain. She hung right in there, throwing rocks just as hard as Tim and I.

The rock wars sort of evolved out of the games we used to play with the Wilson kids when we played war and were pretending to be Japs and Americans fighting against each other. In the beginning, we just threw rotten fruit at each other. But at some point, when we didn't have any rotten fruit to throw, someone threw a rock. At first it began with gently throwing small rocks into the bushes where someone was hiding and then it progressed into throwing bigger rocks at each other across the property line, which was defined by the Hudsons' ruts.

It was always hard to see the Wilsons because of all that vegetation on their side of the line. They could throw rocks at us from their hidden positions before we even knew they were there. We, on the other hand, had an open field on our side. And although it had high weeds to hide us, we had to stand up and expose ourselves to throw a rock. This meant that we usually got pelted much worse than they did, but it also taught us a couple of lessons. It was hard to see where they were hiding, and we could only get a small glimpse of where they were when a rock came flying our way. The best way to get at them and roust them out of their hiding places was to throw a huge number of rocks at their position as fast as we could. It also meant we had to get closer, but when we did, we left ourselves open to getting hit. The second lesson we learned was that we needed some sort of shield to help protect us to get close enough to make our rock throwing effective.

Our first attempt at shields were to use the lids from the corn and grain chicken-feed cans, and they worked very well; but as soon as my grandmother saw what we were using, she put a stop to it. That meant we had to find some other type of shield to protect us. It took us several days to solve this problem. Walking home from the beach one day, the answer was suddenly staring us right in the face. As we walked up a street where workmen from the city were trimming fronds from some royal palms, I noticed that the fronds closest to the trunk of the palm, which were wide at the top and narrow at the bottom, would be perfect for a shield. And they were, except there wasn't any way to hold on to them with one hand. Then Tim got the idea to take my grandfather's hand drill and make two holes in them, which we could run some twine through and use as a handle. It worked. The first time we used them, we were able to rush Jack and Johnny's position and pelt them good with rocks.

At first we were a little afraid to hit Sally Ann with a rock because she was a girl, but after she nearly knocked me senseless with a rock one day, she became fair game. We rousted them out of their hiding places and drove them all the way back to their house, hitting them regularly with rocks until their mother came out and made us stop.

Both Jack and Johnny liked our shields. Jack was a very good artist and could draw birds beautifully. He wanted to draw cardinals on our shields to make them really fancy. We all thought that was a good idea. Jack asked us where we kept our shields at night. He promised to come and get them, paint them that night, and then leave them waiting for us in the morning. We were so excited at the possibility of having really neat shields that we were more than happy to show him where we kept them, under our back porch.

The next morning we ran outside after breakfast to see our newly painted shields. We wanted to use them to raid Jack and Johnny's position again, but to our surprise there were no shields under the porch. Immediately, we ran over to the property line and yelled at them to come out and give us our shields back. We heard laughter and rustling around in the bushes, but no one came out. We picked up rocks that were lying on the ground from yesterday's battle and began throwing them into the bushes where the laughter had come from. Right away, we were met with a barrage of rocks as Jack and Johnny came running out of the bushes holding our shields with the beautiful head of a cardinal painted on each one.

I was sick. They had stolen our shields and painted them for themselves, and they were beautiful.

They should have been ours. I was so mad I began throwing rocks at them as fast as I could. Tim and Allyson were mad too, and they were also throwing many rocks, but Jack and Johnny fended off the rocks with the shields and rushed us. They chased us back into our own yard, hitting us repeatedly with rocks until we were crying. I don't know if I was crying from the pain of getting hit or because I was so mad at myself for telling them where we kept our shields. They continued to throw rocks at us in our backyard until our screaming brought my grandmother outside so see what was going on.

"Go home right now," she shouted at Jack and Johnny.

"Grandma, they stole our shields. Make 'em give 'em back to us," I cried.

In the meantime, rocks were continuing to rain down on us. We tried to pick some up off the ground and throw them back, but without the shields we had no protection.

"Go home, get out of here," my grandmother continued to shout at the boys. "Get off this property right now. Go on home."

"But, Grandma, make them give us our shields back. Those are our shields. They stole them from underneath our back porch," I pleaded.

Jack and Johnny finally quit throwing rocks and just stood there, laughing at us. I was furious. I rushed at them, trying to grab the shields before they could leave, but they turned and ran for home before I could grab them.

"Grandma, they stole our shields," I cried again.

"Too bad," she said. "You shouldn't have left them out where they could find them. Maybe next time you'll know better." With that she went back in the house.

I had an idea.

"Grandma, can Tim and I go to the beach?"

"Yes, but be home by four o'clock."

We ran to our room to put on our swim suits and then ran out of the house toward the beach. If my plan worked, we would be back way before four o'clock. I told Tim that all we had to do was go back to where the men were trimming the palms the other day and get new shields. He thought that was a great idea, and off we went. I was excited. We would get new ones, and this time we would hide them in a place where Jack and Johnny couldn't find them.

I was so excited, I ran all the way to where the men had been trimming the palms a few days ago, without checking to see if Tim was keeping up with me. But when I got there, they were gone. All the palms were trimmed, and everything had been cleaned up and taken away. I was crushed. We were not going to get new shields. I began walking back home, dejected and fiercely disappointed. Soon I ran into Tim. He was still walking toward the place where we first found the shields.

"Why did you run away from me?" he asked.

"I'm sorry," I said. "I thought you were with me."

"Where are the shields?"

"I don't know. Everything was gone. The men weren't there."

Tim began to cry.

"You mean we won't get a new shield?"

"I guess not."

"Maybe we can steal them back from the Wilsons," Tim said.

"Yeah, maybe we can. Let's go see if we can sneak up on them and find out where they keep them hidden."

We raced home and changed out of our swim suits and back into our play clothes. As soon as we had changed, we ran over to the property line and slipped into the bushes on the Wilson's property. We were sneaking through the brush and palmettos toward their house, trying to be as quiet as we could.

Suddenly Sally Ann yelled out. "Hey, what are you guys doing here?"

The rocks began to rain down on us from Jack and Johnny's hidden position. Then they were running at us, throwing rocks and chasing us back into the field on our property. We stood there in our field, wondering what to do and not wanting to get in a rock war without shields. We all realized that the introduction of the shields into our rock wars had changed the game. When both sides had no shields, the game was even. But when one side had shields, it had a huge advantage over the other side. We were going to have to get new ones somehow.

As we stood there, Sally Ann came running out of the brush and set a tin can down in Hudsons' ruts. Then she disappeared back into the bushes. Tim and I wondered what the tin can was for, but we didn't want to go pick it up for fear of getting pelted with rocks.

"Pick up the tin can," Johnny shouted from the cover of the thick brush.

"No," I said.

"Why not," he shouted back.

"Because you'll throw rocks at us if we do," I shouted.

"No, we won't. We promise. There's a note inside the can. Read it."

"You promise not to throw rocks at us if we come get the can?" I asked.

"Yeah, we promise. We won't throw rocks at you. Read the note."

Tim and I sent Allyson over to get the can, just in case the Wilsons were lying. Better that she get hit instead of us. She ran over, picked up the can and brought it back to our position. No one threw any rocks. I took the note out of the can and read it out loud.

"We're sorry we stole your shields. We will give them back if you leave 15 cents in the can."

I wanted the shields back, but we didn't have 15 cents. There was a pencil in the can. I wrote on the back of the note that we didn't have 15 cents, and we didn't know where to get it. I sent Allyson back with the can to set it in the ruts where she had found it.

Soon Sally Ann came out, picked up the can and ran back into the bushes. I figured that she had been sent out to place and retrieve the can for the same reason we had sent Allyson. As much as I wanted to throw a rock at her while she was such an easy target, I didn't because they hadn't thrown any at Allyson.

Soon Sally Ann was back out in the open with the can. We sent Allyson once more, and read the new note.

"Try to find the 15 cents by tomorrow. Ask your grandmother for it."

I almost wanted to laugh. I knew my grandmother didn't have 15 cents either; and even if she did, she wouldn't give it to me to get our shields back. She had already said it was our own fault for leaving them out, and she wouldn't change that opinion, I knew. The note also said to let them know by tomorrow if we had the 15 cents.

I knew it was useless to even try. My grandmother never gave us money for any reason, let alone to get something back that we had lost due to our own stupidity. And there was never any money lying around that I could steal. I don't think I ever saw any money, except on the days that my grandmother went downtown to get groceries.

We weren't going to get our shields back, and there was no use having a rock war without them. The three of us decided to go back to our house. The shields and the 15 cents were soon forgotten.

Sixty-One

WHEN WE REACHED THE HOUSE, ALL THREE OF US SAT on the back steps in silence. We were dejected, and I was still mad at myself for letting Jack and Johnny steal our shields. Several minutes went by and Allyson wandered off to go play somewhere else.

"What do you want to do?" I asked Tim.

"Let's go over to Ronnie and Donny's and play with them."

"Okay, let's go ask Grandma if we can go," I said. I ran into the house with Tim right behind me.

Inside, we found her in her usual place. Her cat, Obie, was sitting in his spot on the arm of her chair. My grandmother had my grandfather build a folding platform on the right arm of her chair so the cat could sit there with her. He was a huge, tiger-striped tabby, and when he would jump up on the arm of her chair he used to crowd my grandmother. She couldn't write properly with him pushing up against her arm, so my grandfather built the cat the platform and had even put hinges on it so she could fold it down on the side of the chair when the cat wasn't sitting there.

"Grandma, can we go over to Ronnie and Donny's to play?"

"Yes, but be home for lunch when you hear the siren blow."

Every day at noon, the Gulfport fire department tested the air raid siren. You could hear it all over town, and my grandmother used it as a marker for when we were to be home for lunch. She usually gave us about five minutes, ten at the most, after the siren sounded for us to make it home. If she could see us coming and knew we were on our way, we usually didn't get in any trouble for

277

being a little late; but if we missed it by more than ten minutes, we didn't get any lunch, and we usually had to sit on a chair in the kitchen thinking about being late until she said we could get up again. Asking her if we could get up would only extend the time we had to sit there. So we just sat there, waiting for her to give us our freedom. On those days, lunch was out of the question.

Sometimes, for some odd reason, I couldn't sit there quietly until she let me go, and the punishment would be ratcheted up until I either got spanked or sent to bed or both. Sometimes, when I couldn't sit quietly, it was because she wouldn't let me do what I wanted, and I just could not accept that. I would wind up sitting on the chair in the kitchen for some offense I had committed, and after only five minutes, I would ask, "Can I get up now?"

"No, I'll tell you when you can get up," she would say.

Five minutes later, I would ask again. "Can I get up now?"

"No. If you ask me again, you'll spend the afternoon sitting there."

Knowing that I was testing her, I would only last five more minutes. "Can I get up now?"

"No. You just sit there until I tell you to get up."

"I have to go to the bathroom."

"Go, and then get back on the chair."

This exchange would take place while she was sitting in her chair in the backroom, working crossword puzzles, and I was in the kitchen, sitting on the punishment chair. After she gave me permission to go to the bathroom, I would skip in there and wrap my lips around the cold water faucet in the washbasin to get a drink. Sometimes, if I weren't careful, she would hear me turn on the water. "Turn that water off and get back on the chair," she would shout from the backroom.

"Yes, ma'am," I would say, and keep on drinking.

Sometimes, if I took too long, I would finish drinking and turn to find her standing there behind me with the stick in her hand. "I told you to turn off that water and get back on that chair, didn't I?"

"Yes, ma'am."

"Why didn't you do what I told you?" she would ask, peering down at me.

That always seemed like a trick question to me, and I wondered if she asked it just to hear what I would say. I thought the reason was obvious. I didn't do what she had told me, because I didn't want to. But I was careful not to say that.

"I don't know," I would always say, whether I really knew why or not. It was much easier and safer to tell her I didn't know than to tell her the real reason. If I had told her it was because I was thirsty or because I really didn't know why I had to sit on that damn chair anyway, she would either force my mouth open and sprinkle red pepper on my tongue or shove a bar of Octagon soap in it.

But sometimes, even when I knew what the safest reply was, I still couldn't resist telling her exactly how I felt. And she would make me pay for it.

"I'll teach you not to sass me," she would growl before punishing me. Of the two punishments, I always preferred having my mouth washed out with the soap. You could at least get that out of your mouth by using your shirt to wipe your mouth out, but the red pepper was impossible to get out, no matter what you did. If you tried to rub it with your shirt, it felt as though you were only rubbing it deeper into your tongue. Sometimes it went down your throat, as if you had swallowed a ball of fire. The only sure way to get it out of your mouth and throat was with water; and my grandmother made sure you did not have access to that once she had put the red pepper on your tongue.

"One of these days, maybe you'll learn your lesson. But I doubt it," she would add, "you're just too stupid." And then she usually sent you to bed as well.

After awhile, we generally knew what the punishment was going to be for our crimes, and we weighed the consequences against whatever it was we wanted to do. Then we either went ahead and did it, or – if we thought better of it – we just waited for another day when we might not get caught. Sometimes we just said to hell with it, full steam ahead, and were prepared to accept the consequences no matter what they were; but that was not often, especially if I didn't think I could give myself an out by blaming it on Allyson or Tim.

Since Allyson's arrival, it was rare that I blamed anything on Tim; but I continued to blame whatever I could on Allyson, because I knew my grandmother wanted to believe that Allyson was bad.

Sixty-Two

THE MISSING FRUIT, CANDY AND COOKIES I WAS stealing from my grandmother and blaming on Allyson caused my grandmother to put a hook on the screen door between the kitchen and the hallway that led to our bedroom. She was convinced we were getting up in the middle of the night to steal the food, so she put it on the side of the door facing the kitchen. Once we were put to bed, she would latch the screen door so we couldn't get into the kitchen. That way, we would be locked in our bedroom until she unhooked the door in the morning and let us out. In her mind, that should put a stop to the stealing.

It may have kept us from getting into the kitchen at night and taking food, but it also meant that none of us had access to the bathroom if we needed to use it in the middle of the night. But that didn't matter to my grandmother, because she didn't feel that we needed to go to the bathroom after we were put to bed. We were only allowed one glass of water with our supper at night and nothing more to drink until the next morning. Therefore, as long as you went to the bathroom before you went to bed, you wouldn't need to get up again. Sometimes even that precaution wasn't enough, and my sister would wet the bed every now and then. But it was rare, and when she did, my grandmother made sure she spanked her.

Of course, by drinking out of the cat's water bowl at night, my cousin and I had more than our allotted amount of water; but going to the bathroom wasn't a problem even when the screen door was locked. To unlock the screen door, we just slipped a piece of paper between the door and the door frame and gently lifted the hook out of the eye. We were both experts at opening it without a sound and making our way to the bathroom in silence. To muffle the sound of our peeing, we just peed on the side of the bowl. Then we would slip back to bed, and she never knew we had been up. This was fairly easy to do because we were never supposed to flush the toilet when we peed. That was a waste of water. My grandmother may see the pee in the toilet bowl, but she never knew when it got there or who did it. It could have been there all day – unless someone had pooped. If you pooped, you flushed – but otherwise, my grandmother just flushed the toilet one last time before she went to bed.

Most of the time, we kids avoided the bathroom during the day. If we were outside playing, we just peed out there, wherever we were. That applied to pooping, as well. If you had to go, you just walked back into some bushes or weeds and went, used leaves or weeds for toilet paper and went on playing. Of course, if someone pooped and it was a really big one, then we all gathered around to look at it and poke it with a stick. We were fascinated at how quickly the huge, green shit-flies would collect on it. Tim was the champion pooper. No one could leave a turd as big as Tim's. We were all in awe of its size. It was as long and as big around as our forearms. Everyone always had to go and see a Tim turd.

Even though he was the champion pooper, he didn't seem to be very excited about it. Everyone always wanted to know what he had had to eat, and how long it had been since he last pooped. Nevertheless, we all poked it with a stick and sometimes we would try to flick pieces of the turd on each other with our sticks. Everyone laughed uproariously, especially if you managed to get a really big piece of shit stuck on someone's clothes. That unlucky person usually had to roll in the grass until they got it off.

It may have been easy to unlock the screen door, but it was impossible to lock it again after we had returned from our sojourn around the house. The first few times my grandmother noticed the door unhooked in the morning, she thought she had forgotten to hook it. But when it became a regular routine, she changed the lock to a spring-loaded hook, and it became impossible for us to unlock.

It ended our running around the house at night for awhile, but it didn't matter to Tim and me that we could no longer go to the bathroom after we went to bed. If we had to go, we just peed through the screen on the window in our room. We couldn't open the screen because my grandmother had made my grandfather nail them all shut, but peeing through it became routine. We thought nothing about it until one day my grandmother noticed that the screen was rotting out. She had asked my grandfather to replace all the screens on the house in the spring, so she was probably surprised to find one rotting out so fast. She examined the screen more closely.

"You've been peeing out the window, haven't you boys?"

Uh-oh, here comes trouble, I thought. How could she tell? I was convinced we had been caught because of her training as a policewoman. How else could she have figured it out? But I wasn't too worried. I knew that if she wouldn't let it go, I could just blame in on Allyson.

"Look here," she said pointing to the screen, "I can see exactly where you have been standing and peeing through the screen. It has a pattern in this area here and nowhere else. If the screen were defective and rotting out, it would have rotted everywhere, not just in this pattern right here."

"Grandma, I didn't want to say anything because I didn't want to get her in trouble, but I think Allyson is the one that's been peeing out the window at night," I said helpfully.

"Oh, no you don't," my grandmother shouted. "Allyson may do a lot of things, but she is not equipped to pee out the window. Now which one of you boys has been doing it? I want to know right now."

"Grandma, it's Billy. He pees out the window every night after we go to bed," my sister informed her.

I was shocked. My sister had never told on me for anything before. I couldn't believe it, and I just stared at her in disbelief. What had she done? Why had she done it?

I was still in shock and trying to figure out why she would tell on me, when I heard my grandmother's voice.

"That's what I thought." She left the room only to return almost immediately with the stick from the icebox. It was close quarters in our bedroom and hard to get away from her. I took a pretty good beating that afternoon.

Afterwards, through my tears, I told my sister in a low menacing voice that I would get even with her. And I meant it.

She just looked at me without blinking or walking away. There was no fear in her eyes. The only thing her expression conveyed was that she was not afraid of me. We stared at each other for what seemed to be forever, until I finally walked away.

Sixty-Three

IN 1950, WHEN I WAS TEN YEARS OLD, MY GRAND-
father gave both Tim and me a brand new pocket knife.

"I always carry one," he said, "and I think you boys are old
enough now to have one of your own. You never know when you
might need one. You can use it for almost anything: cut bait on the
pier, whittle sticks, or cut string and rope with it."

"Thank you, Grandpa," we both said together.

"You're welcome," he said. "All I ask is that you use it properly and take good care of it. If it gets dull, just bring it to me; I'll
sharpen it on my whetstone."

When we were alone, my cousin and I asked each other why
Grandpa had given us a knife. We rarely ever got a present, even
on our birthdays. Although we were somewhat confused, we were
delighted. The pocket knife was even better than the hatchets we
had a few years ago. We could carry our knives in our pockets
wherever we went and even bring them into the house at night.
We had always had to leave the hatchets in the old shed at night.

Right away, we wanted to throw them and see if we could
make them stick in the ground, blade first. Allyson became our
target. We didn't want to hit her with the knives when we threw
them; we just wanted to throw them at her and make them stick in
the ground beside her. She would stand with her legs apart and we
would throw our knives at her, trying to make them stick between
her feet.

"Don't move when we throw our knives at you," I cautioned.

"We might accidentally hit you if you move. Stand as still as you can."

She never moved, and she never asked if she could throw the knife at us. She just stood there, a willing target. Most of the time, our knives landed in the dirt a few feet in front of her. Sometimes they would go astray and fly off to the side or land somewhere behind her.

"That's why we don't want you to move," I reminded her. "If the knife slips out of our hand when we throw it, we don't always know where it is going to go, and it could hit you. You could be moving directly into its path." I remembered how Tim had moved directly into the path of my hatchet several years ago. God help us if my grandmother or my grandfather ever caught us throwing our knives at Allyson. Not only would we surely get beaten, but we would never see our knives again

One day, when my grandmother and grandfather had gone out, we invented a new game to play with the knives in our bedroom. We were still not allowed to go outside when they left us alone, but usually we did, as long as we knew it was too soon for them to return unexpectedly. One afternoon, however, we had to stay in the house because it was raining. We were playing in our bedroom, when one of us – either Tim or I – came up with the idea that we could use our knives to pin Allyson's feet to the floor. We thought it would be neat to drive the knife through the edge of her shoe into the floor, so she would be pinned there and couldn't move.

I'm not sure how we convinced Allyson to go along with this game, but she did.

"Now, don't move," I cautioned her, "because I don't want to miss your shoe and drive the knife into your foot."

"Okay. You promise you're not going to stick my foot with the knife?" she asked.

"I promise, but make sure you don't move."

"Okay." She stood there as still as she could.

"Are you ready?" I asked.

"I think so. Just promise you'll be careful."

"I promise," I said as I cocked my arm to bring the knife down as hard as I could so it would go right through her shoe and into the floor. I brought the knife down overhand, aiming for the edge of the sole. The first few times I missed her shoe completely. I decided not to raise my hand so high, because there was no accuracy when it came down. It was usually wide of the mark.

"Let me see if I can just chip it into your shoe," I said, and I began chipping at her shoe as if I were using an ice pick to chip ice. Finally, I got it barely through the edge of her sole on the side of her shoe, but it didn't stick in the floor.

"I think I've almost got it," I said. "This time ought to do it."

I raised my hand and brought it down as hard as I could, and the inevitable happened: the knife went into the side of her foot. She screamed with pain and tears began rolling down her face.

I quickly pulled the knife out of her shoe. Scared and shaking, I told her to take her shoe off so I could see how badly I had stabbed her. As soon as she managed to remove it, I pulled her dirty sock off and examined her. There was a tiny bit of blood on the side of her foot where the knife had nicked her, but there wasn't any big cut. The knife had glanced to the left when it hit the shoe leather and had just barely nicked the skin, causing it to bleed a little.

"It's just a tiny nick. Please don't tell Grandma," I pleaded.

"I won't tell Grandma, but I don't want to play this game anymore," she said, wiping her eyes. Bubbles of snot were coming out of her nose, and she wiped them off on the sleeve of her shirt.

"I don't either," I said. "Let's play something else." But we all sat there, not talking to each other. I think we were all afraid of what had nearly happened.

We heard the clock in the backroom strike nine, and it was time to go to bed. The next morning when we awakened, none of us mentioned what had happened the night before, and it was quickly forgotten.

Sixty-Four

THE DAYS OF SUMMER FLEW BY. WE WERE OUTSIDE playing every day, all day long, except when it rained. We were still put to bed almost immediately after supper, and we would still lay there in our sweat, listening to the Whitbeck's cow, the other kids outside, and the cooing of the turtledoves in one of the trees near our window as we waited for it to cool off. Sometimes we could hear the scurry of rats running across the attic or a dog barking somewhere in the distance, which Butchie would answer. Then the other dog would bark again, and Butchie would answer back, and both dogs would continue until my grandmother went out into the yard and brought Butchie into the house.

As always, when darkness began to fall, the sounds would fade and I would lay there fighting sleep. I still never wanted to go to sleep. I wanted to be outside playing or talking or listening to the radio. And in these times, as always, I thought about my mother and tried to remember her face, or I imagined myself riding that Pinto pony through the desert canyons or stopping on top of a mesa to watch the colors of the mountains change as the sun went down. Despite the time that had passed, the colors were no less vivid.

I would still wait for that rustle of the palms to know the tide was coming in – the gentle breeze creeping through the window, cooling the room and bringing with it the sweet smell of gardenias from the bushes outside the window. I never knew exactly when I shifted from daydreams to night dreams; no matter how hard I tried to stay awake, sleep always won out. Often I would get up and walk around the front room just to keep from falling asleep as long as I could. I hated being in bed, and I hated having to go to sleep.

One evening I got out of bed after Tim and Allyson had fallen asleep and walked through the front room to the front porch. I noticed that my grandmother had put the colored card in the front screen of the porch to tell the ice man how much ice to leave when he came by the next day. The card had four amounts on it, and each amount color-coded so the ice man could clearly see what size block to deliver. The yellow side was twenty-five pounds, the blue side was fifty pounds, the red side was seventy-five pounds, and the green side was one hundred pounds. It was placed behind the screen on the porch, with the desired amount of ice at the top of the card.

My grandmother had a small icebox and usually never got more than twenty-five pounds of ice at a time. As I sat there on the front porch, I began fooling around with the ice card, absent-mindedly turning it over, first one way and then another. When I decided to finally return to bed, before sleep trapped me on the front porch, I set the card back on the ledge. I returned to my room and immediately slipped into sleep.

The next morning after breakfast, we kids were outside playing when my grandmother yelled for us to come in immediately. "You kids get in here right now!"

I knew we were in trouble by the tone of her voice, but for the life of me I couldn't figure out what we could have possibly done. I didn't like it when I didn't know why we were in trouble, because I wouldn't have an excuse or a story ready when she confronted us.

"Sit down over there at the table, all three of you. Now, I want to know who was playing with the ice card on the front porch. And what were you doing on the front porch anyway?"

Right away, Tim and Allyson were taken completely by surprise. Neither of them ever went out on the front porch, and Allyson probably hadn't even heard of an ice card, much less know what it was. We three sat there in total silence.

"Answer me," she said. "You've cost me a lot of money by playing with that card, money I don't have. I put it there with twenty-five pounds showing. One of you changed it to seventy-five pounds, and I have to pay for it."

Still there was no answer from any of us. "I'm going to ask you one more time to tell me who was playing with the ice card?"

Still, there was no answer. All three of us sat there without moving or saying a word.

"Alright, all three of you go get yourselves in bed. And you can stay there until one of you tells me who did it."

We all got up slowly from the table and went to the bedroom, relieved that she hadn't gotten her stick off the icebox and tried to beat it out of us. Anything that cost my grandmother money was definitely cause for a beating. We got in our beds and lay there in silence for some time. Finally, I asked Allyson and Tim if either of them had played with the ice card.

"No," they both said.

"I wonder how it got turned around," I said, pretending not to know anything about it either.

"Are we really going to have to stay in here all day?" my sister asked.

"I think so," I said, "unless the one who turned the card around owns up to it."

I was still pretending that I didn't know anything about it. It was safer that way, in case my grandmother was listening to our conversation. It was never a good idea to admit you had actually done the deed or knew anything about it, even if you thought she wasn't around. That way, you could keep from trapping yourself if she overheard your conversation and confronted you. This was one of the many lessons learned from living with her for over ten years.

"Tim, we're not going to get out of bed unless one of us admits we played with the ice card," I said. "Since none of us had anything to do with it, why don't you tell Grandma you did it, and that it was an accident and you're sorry," I continued.

"Why me?" he asked angrily. "Why don't you tell her you did it?"

"If I tell her I did it, she won't believe me. She thinks I lie about everything, and she'll think I'm lying now if I tell her it was me," I reasoned.

"And she'll just think I'm lying if I tell her I did it," Tim said.

"No, she won't. She knows you seldom ever lie about anything," I said, which was true. Tim didn't lie very much. He just took his punishment and forgot about it. I think it was because he didn't lie very often that Grandma never spanked him as hard as she did me. To her, it was just a minor offense when Tim did anything, and his punishment didn't need to be as severe as mine. At least that's how I saw it.

"If you tell Grandma you did it, she probably won't even spank you."

"Why not?" he asked.

"Because she will be so happy you decided to tell the truth, she'll just let us up, and then we can go back outside and play."

"I'm afraid she'll spank me anyway," he began to whimper.

"She won't spank you. I promise. She'll just be happy that you told her the truth."

"You promise?" he asked.

"I promise. Are you going to tell her so we can all get out of here and go outside and play?"

"Okay."

"Grandma," I yelled.

"What do you want?" she yelled back.

"Tim has something he wants to tell you," I volunteered. I wanted to make sure Tim didn't change his mind now that he had agreed.

"What does he want to tell me?" she yelled back again.

"He said he's the one who played with the ice card, and it was an accident, and he's sorry he put it back in the window the wrong way," I said, trying to get as much information out to her as I could before Tim changed his mind.

A few seconds later, she was in the room with the stick in her hand "Is that right, Tim, you were the one who played with the ice card?" she asked.

Tim was still lying on the bed and hadn't noticed the stick yet. "Yes, ma'am, it was an accident. I'm sorry."

My sister and I were already getting up. "Can Allyson and I go back outside and play, Grandma?" I asked.

"Go on," she said, and then she turned to Tim.

"What were you doing in the front room?"

"I don't know," I heard him say weakly as we fled the room as quickly as we could.

By the time Allyson and I reached the back door, we could hear the stick coming down on his backside.

"I thought you said she wouldn't spank him," my sister said.

"I didn't think she would," I lied. But I reasoned that it was better that he got spanked than me. I had had enough spankings, and I was tired of getting spanked for every single thing I did wrong. I wished that we could just have some fun for a change, instead of being punished all the time.

Sixty-Five

ON LABOR DAY, THE LAST DAY OF SUMMER VACATION before school was to start again, my grandmother took us all to a picnic at the Community Center in Gulfport. It was one of those rare times that we all actually got to go someplace fun. All three of us were excited and looking forward to having a good time. It was the type of picnic where everyone brought food, and you could have as much as you wanted to eat. There was plenty. My grandmother took a huge pan of Boston baked beans and a huge bowl of potato salad she had made especially for the picnic. I loved her Boston baked beans. She baked them in the oven with molasses and brown sugar, and put cloves and strips of bacon on top. She baked them all day long, and the house smelled delicious while they cooked. She loved potato salad and made it in the same large mixing bowls she had used to mash up the Oleo bars during the war. Everyone always told her she made the best potato salad. Even my brother, when he was living with us, used to say her potato salad was the best.

The picnic turned out to be great fun. We got to play outside all day, only going inside the Community Center when we wanted another hot dog or some more of my grandmother's baked beans. There was plenty to eat, and we could fill our own plates. I took lots of potato chips and hot dogs. The adults were either playing cards at tables set up inside, or they were outside playing shuffleboard on the courts behind the Community Center. In the evening, there was going to be a cakewalk; and my grandmother told me it was alright if I entered it, and even gave me a dime to buy a ticket. If I were standing on the number drawn when the music stopped, I could win a cake.

Someone had used chalk to draw a circle at one end of the Community Center. The circle was made up of about twenty squares and each square had a number in it. The cake I wanted was a huge chocolate cake with white icing. It was the biggest of all the cakes. It had red and yellow flowers on it with green leaves. It was beautiful, and I wanted to win it.

"Alright, ladies and gentlemen, it's time for the cakewalk," a man with a booming voice named Mr. Kenney finally announced. "You know how it works. Let's have the first twenty people get on a square in the circle. When the music starts, walk around the circle. When it stops, you stop. I'll draw a number from the bowl up here on the cake table, and if you're standing on that number, you win a cake of your choice from the table up here. It's that easy."

Nearly everyone in the Community Center was headed for the circle, and I was afraid I wasn't going to get a square. I ran through the crowd as fast as I could to get one before they were all taken. I made a desperate jump for the final square and barely made it just ahead of another kid who was also trying to get there. He tried to shove me off the square, but an old lady on the square next to me told him to behave himself and wait for the next walk.

Mr. Kenney's voice boomed out again. "Okay, let me wind up the old Victrola here and we'll get started. Here we go. Good luck."

The music started and we all began to march around the circle on the floor to the tune of *Stars and Stripes Forever*. When the music stopped, I was standing on a square with the number twelve in it.

"Okay, folks, look at the number in the square where you're standing. I'm reaching into the bowl, I'm pulling out a ticket, and the number is… twelve! If you're standing on twelve, shout it out and claim your cake."

"It's me! It's me! I'm standing on number twelve," I shouted.

"Sounds like we have our first winner," Mr. Kenney announced. "Will one of you ladies from the cake table check that young man's square and confirm that we have a winner?"

An old lady pushed her way through the people standing around and came over to check my square. "Yes, sir, Mister Kenney, we have a winner over here. This young man is standing on number twelve," she said.

"Congratulations, young man. Come on up here and pick out your cake."

I was so excited, I could hardly believe it. I was the first winner, and I could pick the very cake I wanted. I skipped all the way up to the cake table. When I got there, I saw my grandmother up there talking to Mister Kenney in hushed tones. As I neared, I caught a little bit of their conversation. She had heard me called as the winner, and was certain that I must have cheated somehow.

I was crushed. I wanted that cake so badly. I had won, and the very cake I most wanted was within my grasp. Now my grandmother was trying to ruin it all, and I might not end up with any cake, much less the one I wanted, especially since it was the biggest and most beautiful one on the table.

Was Mister Kenney going to make me forfeit the cake because of what my grandmother was saying? I tried to listen.

"The boy won the cake fair and square, Henrietta. Let him have it. He won it"

"Alright," my grandmother said. "I just wanted to make sure."

"Okay, son, pick out one of these beautiful cakes from the table."

"I want that one," I said, pointing to the big one with the flowers, which I had chosen in my mind before the cakewalk had even started.

"The young man has picked this beautiful cake so graciously

donated by Miss Sadie Weaver. Here you are young man." Mister Kenney gave me the cake, but it was too big for me to hold and I was afraid I might drop it.

My grandmother stepped forward to take it from me. "I'll hold it for you," she said.

"Okay. I'm going to try and win another one," I said.

"No, you're not going to try and win anymore cakes," she said. "One is enough. The cakewalk is not for children. It's for adults, and they don't want kids winning everything. You just go on about your business, now."

I was disappointed, but I knew better than to argue. Besides, I had won the cake I really wanted, and I was happy. On the way home that night, my grandfather held the cake on his lap, while the three of us sat in the back seat in silence, dreaming of eating a piece when we got to the house.

My grandmother broke the silence. "In all the years I've been going to the picnic, I've never won anything. And now you win a cake on your first try." There wasn't any malice or anger or even any jealousy in her voice. It was as if she were really proud that I had won. I think she thought it was amazing that a kid could win something like that. I know I was amazed.

We all fell silent again and finished the ride home without another word. Tim fell asleep on the way, but as my grandmother stopped the car to let us out before pulling into the garage, he woke up.

"Did you really win that cake, Billy?" he asked.

"You know I did. I already told you that. What do you think we've been talking about all the way home?" I answered.

I was feeling pretty cocky and was thoroughly enjoying being thought of as somewhat of a hero by Tim and Allyson. All three of us ran and skipped into the house full of excitement and ready for a piece of the cake.

"Alright," my grandmother said, "it's late. Get your clothes off and get yourselves in bed."

"But, Grandma, aren't we going to have any cake tonight?" I asked.

"No, it's too late, and you kids have to get up early for school tomorrow. You can have some tomorrow night for dessert after supper."

"But—" I began.

"You heard me, now march."

"But, Grandma—" I began again.

"Don't make me tell you again," she said in a stern voice that meant one more word out of me and she would get the stick off the icebox.

We all went to bed filled with disbelief and disappointment. I was angry. It wasn't fair. How could she expect us to see that cake and not want any? I had planned to get out of bed and get some later, but she had locked the screen door to the kitchen and I couldn't get in there. That night, I fell asleep thinking about the cake and vowing not to get into any trouble tomorrow. I didn't want to get punished and lose another opportunity to taste it.

The next day, we walked to school with Jack and Johnny and their sister, Sally Ann. We talked about the cake and how we weren't allowed to have any last night.

"That's not fair," Jack said.

"No, it ain't," Johnny chimed in. "If I had won a cake, my mother would have let us have some before we went to bed."

"Do you think she'll let you have a piece tonight?" Sally Ann asked.

"I hope so," I said. "If we can stay out of trouble, she said we could have a piece for dessert after supper."

"Well, eat a piece for me," Jack said, "and let me know how it tasted."

As we continued walking to school together, we talked about other things, but the cake was never far from my thoughts. Even though I felt a little better when the Wilson boys and Sally Ann confirmed that not getting any cake last night was not at all fair, it was still a long day at school. I thought about the cake and how badly I wanted some all day. I could almost taste the sweet frosting and the soft, moist cake. I was going to ask my grandmother to cut me a big piece with one of the red and yellow roses on it. I wanted to see what they tasted like. I wondered if the roses would be sweeter than the rest of the frosting.

That afternoon we ran all the way home from school, anxious to have supper and get to the cake.

"Is supper ready yet?" I shouted as we raced into the house.

"No, not yet. Go outside and play. I'll call you when it's ready," my grandmother said, not even looking up from her crossword puzzle.

We all three turned toward the back door to go back outside to play.

"Not so fast," she said. "Go change out of your school clothes before you go outside." She still hadn't looked up. It was as if we were minor annoyances, not worth her full attention.

We raced to the bedroom to change our clothes. I never understood why we had to change before we could go outside and play. The clothes we wore to school and the clothes we played in were the same clothes; we just wore them on different weeks. The clothes we wore to school this week would be our play clothes next week, and our play clothes this week would be our school clothes next week. They were rotated on wash day.

On our way out of the house, I stopped at my grandmother's chair where she still sat working her crossword puzzle. "Grandma, why do we always have to change out of our school clothes before we can go outside and play? Our school clothes look just like our play clothes."

"Your school clothes are clean. Your play clothes are dirty," she said without looking up.

"Oh," I said and ran out to the backyard where Tim and Allyson had already started playing with Butchie. I considered her explanation. I guess it makes sense, I thought. All my clothes looked the same, as did the clothes Tim and Allyson wore. I wore Bobby James' hand-me-downs, Tim wore my old hand-me-downs, and Allyson wore Tim's old hand-me-downs, which were really mine, except that they had a lot more patches in them than the ones I had on right now.

I quickly quit worrying about the difference between school clothes and play clothes and started playing with Butchie too. We were throwing a stick for him to fetch and bring back. It was a game we could all take turns at and that Butchie never got tired of playing. He did all the running, and we stayed close to the back door, waiting for the call for supper.

Finally, it came. "Billy, Tim, Allyson, get yourselves in here and wash up for supper," my grandmother called from the back porch.

I hoped we weren't going to have eggplant or rutabaga or anything else I hated that might keep me from getting my dessert. I knew if I couldn't get that stuff off my plate, there would be no cake for me.

We all ran into the bathroom together and got our hands under the water faucet at the same time. That way we didn't waste any water. My grandmother had a towel on a hook by the washbasin for us to dry our hands with. She always checked it to make sure there weren't any dirty hand prints on it, because if there were then we hadn't washed our hands well and had unnecessarily dirtied a clean towel. To make sure we never got it dirty, we always dried our hands on our own pants to remove any dirt that still might be there after washing them. It worked, and the towel never became a problem for us.

That night we had fried fish, cornbread and green beans for supper. It was one of my favorite meals, and it assured me that I wasn't going to have any problem finishing my supper, and I would get my cake. My grandmother placed a platter in the center of the table piled high with fried fish and served us each one piece, leaving an almost equal amount on the platter.

We wolfed down our food, and then my cousin asked the inevitable question – the one he asked after every meal. And he got the inevitable answer – the one he always got.

"Grandma, can I have seconds?"

"No."

"Are we going to have some of the cake for dessert?" I asked.

"Just hold your horses until everyone is finished," she said.

I always wondered what she meant by that. I didn't have any horses, and I didn't know why she was always telling me to hold them. I mean, I knew it meant that I shouldn't be in such a hurry; I could figure that out. But why was she telling me to hold my horses? Why didn't she just say, "Don't be in such a hurry"? I kept thinking about it as Tim and I helped my grandfather clear the table and put the dishes in the sink to be washed.

My grandmother took the cake out of the oven where she had stored it overnight to keep it from drying out. My cousin and I hovered around her, watching every move she made.

"Go sit down at the table and get out of my way," she snapped.

"Can I have a piece with the flowers on it?" I asked as I ran back to the table.

"Me, too," Tim shouted as he ran with me.

My grandmother did not reply. We sat down at the table and waited for what seemed to be an eternity. Finally, she emerged from the kitchen with a tray in her hand.

"Here you go," she said as she set the tray down on the table with five plates of cake.

Each one of us got a plate with the smallest piece of cake I could ever have imagined. It was barely more than a sliver, and there were no frosting flowers on the pieces she served us. I was so disappointed, I wanted to cry. The only reason I didn't was because I didn't want to get sent to bed.

"Is this all we get?" I asked.

"That's all you get," she said. "It's plenty for you."

"But, Grandma, I wanted one of the frosting flowers on my piece of cake," I said.

"Me, too," my cousin chimed in.

Allyson said nothing. She was already eating her piece of cake. I thought about the piece of birthday cake she had brought me from the party where she had sliced her heel on an oyster shell. That had been five times bigger than the piece my grandmother had just served me, maybe even ten times bigger.

"Grandma, why can't we have a bigger piece?" I asked.

"One more word out of you and I'll take that piece away from you, and you can just do without."

I knew she meant what she said. I sat there debating whether or not to complain again and let her send me to bed without any, but in the end I decided this little piece was better than not having any at all, and I ate it in three bites. It was the best cake I ever tasted.

After supper, we helped my grandfather dry the dishes. I was still mad about the cake, but I didn't complain. It wouldn't have done any good anyway.

Sixty-Six

THAT NIGHT WAS TUESDAY NIGHT. MY GRAND-
mother and grandfather were going to a city council meeting after
the dishes were done. We would be left alone in the house.

Just before they left, my grandmother put us in bed and
warned us not to get up while they were gone. As we lay there,
I began to formulate a plan in my head that would get me another piece of that cake. But I would need Tim's help to pull
it off.

"Tim. Tim, wake up," I said.

"I'm awake. What's wrong?"

"Nothing. I think I know how we can get some more cake
tonight. Do you want to help me?"

"What if we get caught?"

"We won't."

"How are we going to get more? The screen door to the kitch-
en is probably locked," he reminded me.

"I thought of that," I said. "All we have to do is go out the front
door, walk around the house and come in the back door. We'll go
into the kitchen, take the cake out of the oven and eat a little bit
of it."

"Grandma will know because some of it will be gone," he reasoned. "She'll know we ate it."

"No, she won't. We can save a little bit of the frosting from
where we cut a hole in the side of the cake. We can eat the cake out

of the hole and then smooth the frosting over the hole when we put the cake back, and she'll never know."

"Why do I have to help you? Why can't you go and get some cake and bring it back for us?" Tim asked.

"I thought of that. I was going to go get the cake and bring it back to surprise you, but I don't think I can lift it out of the oven by myself without dropping it. I need your help to get it out."

He was silent for a long while, and I thought he had gone to sleep, "Tim, wake up," I said.

"I'm awake. Okay, I'll help you," he said.

So off we went, out the front door, around through the side yard to the back of the house, in through the back door and into the kitchen. We opened the door to the oven and there it was, sitting on a thick piece of cardboard just slightly larger in diameter than the cake itself. Between the cake and the cardboard was a white paper doily. All we had to do was get it out of the oven, cut a hole in the side, eat what we wanted and then cover the hole again with frosting.

Carefully, we removed the cake from the oven. Each of us took one side of the cardboard plate, lifted it, and then slowly inched our way toward the counter. Then disaster struck: the weight of the cake seemed to shift, the cake started to slide, and we lost hold of the cardboard. It landed upside down on the kitchen floor.

A wave of fear swept over me and Tim immediately began to cry. I couldn't believe what had happened. Not only was the cake now upside down on the floor, it had broken apart into several pieces. There was no way we could ever get it back in the same condition it had been in before we took it out of the oven. We were doomed, and there was no way around it.

"What are we going to do, Billy?" my cousin asked. He was crying, and I could tell from his voice that he was on the verge of panic.

"There's only one thing we can do, and that's pick it up and put it back," I said.

"But Grandma is going to know. We're going to get the daylights beat out of us." His voice was breaking and he was filled with fear.

"Look, here's what we do," I said. "We pick it all up and put it back in the oven on the cardboard plate. Then, when Grandma comes home, we tell her we think Allyson tried to get the cake out of the oven and dropped it."

"Are you sure that will work?" He was practically bawling at the top of his lungs now.

"Yes, but we have to stick together and swear that Allyson was the one who tried to get the cake out. We have to say we tried to stop her, but we couldn't – and then she dropped it. Remember, we have to stick together."

"Okay," he sobbed.

We began picking it up off the floor and putting it back on the heavy piece of cardboard that served as its plate. The pieces we picked up were covered with dog and cat hair and dirt. Every time we tried to pick up a big piece of the cake, it would crumble and fall apart. Finally, we had as much as we could pick up with our hands piled on the cardboard, but the floor was a mess. We decided to get the broom and dust pan to sweep up the rest of the crumbs and pour them over the pieces we had already picked up. As we put it back in the oven, pieces fell off and littered the inside of the oven. We finished cleaning up the floor as best we could, but the cake was completely unrecognizable.

I closed the oven door, got one of the kitchen chairs, climbed up and unhooked the latch on the screen door. There was no need to walk through the yard just to come in the front door to get back in bed. Someone was going to get blamed for destroying the cake, and if shifting the blame to Allyson didn't work, we were all going to get the daylights beat out of us, no matter what. Even if my grandmother really believed our story about Allyson being the one that dropped the cake, there was still no guarantee that we all wouldn't get a beating.

As I lay there in the dark waiting, I was terrified. There was no way to lie about the cake and pretend we didn't know anything about it. The cake had been fine when she and my grandfather had left for the council meeting. We were going to have to face her, and the only way Tim and I could save ourselves was to blame it on Allyson, and be convincing about it.

Sweat came flowing out of every pore in my body. Even if I didn't get a beating for getting into the cake, I would probably get one anyway just because of the way I was sweating. It was going to look like I had wet my bed. Finally, the moment I had been dreading arrived: I heard the tires of my grandmother's car on the oyster shells in the driveway, and I saw the headlights go past our window as she headed to the garage.

I figured Tim would already be asleep, but I thought I would try to warn him anyway. "Tim, Grandma just got home," I whispered.

"I know," he said. "I heard the car in the driveway."

I was surprised that he was awake, but I was glad. "I'm going to tell Grandma as soon as she comes in the house," I said.

"Okay," came his weak reply from the direction of his bed.

"Are you ready?"

"I guess so," he said, again weakly.

"Don't forget," I warned, "Allyson is the one that got into the cake, and we had to help her pick it up."

"Okay."

I slipped out of my bed and went into the hallway and stopped by the screen door so I could hear her when she came in the house. I wanted to tell her the moment she came in. I felt that no matter what the punishment was going to be, it would be better if we got it over with as soon as possible. I heard her voice as she said something to my grandfather, and I knew they were in the house.

"Grandma," I called.

No answer.

"Grandma," I called again, louder this time.

There was still no answer. I got up the nerve to call her as loud as I could.

"Grandma," I called a third time, much louder than before.

Suddenly, out of nowhere, she appeared on the other side of the screen door. "What are you doing out of bed?" she asked.

I had trouble finding my voice. Her sudden appearance had unnerved me.

"I asked you what you're doing out of bed. And how did this screen door get unhooked?" she demanded.

"Tim and I have something we need to tell you," I said.

"Well, what is it? It had better be the explanation for why this screen door is unhooked." She stared at me through the screen. "Speak up, I'm tired of waiting."

"While you were gone, Allyson got out of bed and got into the cake in the kitchen," I finally said.

"How did she get into the kitchen? I had the screen door locked so none of you could get in here."

She opened the screen door and came into the hallway where I was standing. I began to shake with fear, and my bowels felt loose. I was afraid I was going to make a mess in my underwear.

"I asked you how Allyson got the screen door unhooked," she said. Her calm, even voice was terrifying.

"Sh-she-she didn't unhook the screen door," I stammered.

She stared at me, unblinking and expressionless. "Then how did she get into the kitchen?"

"She went out the front door and then around to the back door and came in that way."

"How do you know she did that?" my grandmother asked.

"When she asked Tim and me to help her pick up the cake, I couldn't get the screen door open to get in the kitchen. So I asked her how she got in, and she told me she had gone around."

"What do you mean, pick up the cake?" she asked in the same flat tone. Her expression still hadn't changed. She continued to stare until I was sure her eyes were going to bore a hole clear though me.

"She-she was trying to get it out of the oven, and it dropped on the floor," I sputtered.

"Allyson! Come in here," my grandmother shouted as she charged back into the kitchen and opened the oven. Now the rage she had been holding back boiled over and filled the room like a clap of thunder.

The other two arrived in the kitchen at the same time.

"What were you doing, taking the cake out of the oven after I put you to bed?" my grandmother shouted in Allyson's face.

"I didn't touch the cake," she cried. "Billy and Tim dropped it, and they're blaming it on me."

Before I could open my mouth to protest, my cousin shouted at Allyson. "You did so take the cake out of the oven! And when you dropped it you asked Billy and me to help you pick it up."

I was shocked that he had said anything. Usually he just kept quiet and only opened his mouth if my grandmother asked him a direct question.

"That's right," I said. "You aren't blaming that on us."

"How did you boys get into the kitchen with the screen door hooked?" my grandmother asked. "Allyson isn't tall enough to un-hook it, even if she stood on a kitchen chair."

"We went around, the way Allyson did," I answered. "After we helped her pick up the cake and put it back in the oven, I stood on a chair and unhooked the screen door so we could go back to bed without having to go outside again."

"Grandma, I didn't get into the cake. Billy and Tim did, and now they're trying to blame it on me," Allyson pleaded. Tears were rolling down her face as she tried to convince my grandmother that she had nothing to do with this fiasco. But it was no use. My grandmother simply believed it was Allyson who had dropped the cake on the floor. Allyson could not win, and I knew it. Tim and I were going to escape this time.

"You boys get back in bed," my grandmother said as she reached for the stick on top of the icebox.

"Please, Grandma, I didn't do it," my sister pleaded as we turned and ran back to the bedroom.

Whack! Whack! Whack! Over and over, we heard the stick hitting her legs and backside, and in between she screamed for our mother. "Mommy, mommy, help me!"

But my grandmother's anger had boiled over, and she continued to give Allyson a terrible beating. Eventually we heard my grandfather's voice as he intervened, and the noise stopped. This intervention probably prevented my grandmother from injuring Allyson severely.

When my sister returned to our bedroom and lay down in her bed on the floor, she was sobbing uncontrollably and calling out for mommy. I was sorry I had gotten her in trouble, but I couldn't change it. My grandmother would never believe me now, even if I did tell her the truth; and besides, there was no way to erase the beating my sister had already gotten. I decided there was no use in telling my grandmother the truth.

"Allyson," I called softly to her in the dark.

There was no answer.

"Allyson," I called again.

"What?" I heard her say between sobs.

"I'm sorry we got you in trouble," I said.

"No, you're not," she sobbed. "You and Tim planned it before Grandma got home that you were going to blame it on me. I heard you."

"I know we did," I whispered, afraid my grandmother might overhear our conversation, "but I never thought she would spank you that hard. I'm really sorry."

"No, you're not, and I hate you."

Her words cut through me. "You don't really hate me, do you?"

"Yes, I do," she sobbed. "I'm going to hate you forever. Don't talk to me anymore." Her sobs turned into full crying, and I heard her saying, "Oh mommy, please, please, come and get me." I was worried because I had violated my rule of never admitting guilt in case my grandmother overheard and learned the truth. I held my breath, waiting to see if Grandma had heard me and was returning to punish me over the cake as well.

I fell silent and listened to Allyson's crying, and soon sleep overtook me and I floated away into a sea of bad dreams and nightmares. My sister hated me, and in my dreams I could see her floating away from me and I knew that just like my mother, she wasn't coming back.

The next morning when we went to the table for breakfast, Tim and I had a bowl of raisin bran and milk at our places. Allyson had a bowl of the cake crumbs we had swept up off the floor the night before, complete with dirt and hair from the cat and dog.

"You wanted that cake so badly," my grandmother told her, "you can have it for breakfast." Then she turned and went into the bathroom.

My sister sat there staring at the bowl of cake crumbs and its filthy content, huge tears rolling down her face.

"You better eat every damn bit of it," my grandmother called from the bathroom, "or you'll find it there again for supper." Allyson sobbed openly. She couldn't bring herself to eat the mess in the bowl. "It has hair in it," she said, loud enough for my grandmother to hear.

"You should have thought about that last night before you dropped it on the floor," came her reply.

Tim and I got out of our chairs and walked over to see what the stuff in the bowl looked like. There was a lot of cake and icing in the bowl, but we could see the dog and cat hair stuck to it. I picked up some of the frosting on my finger and licked it off. It didn't taste bad. In fact, it was pretty good. I tried some more, pulling some cat hair out of my mouth. Tim tried some too, and he also thought it was pretty good.

"Do you want us to help you eat some?" I whispered in her ear.

She glared at me with the meanest, most hateful look she could muster and said between her teeth, "You can eat it all. I will still hate you."

Neither Tim nor I paid any attention to the hair stuck to the cake and icing, except to pull it out of our mouths when there was too much to swallow. We both quickly scooped up the mess in Allyson's bowl and ate it all in just a few minutes. Then we returned to our seats at the table and finished our cereal.

On the way to school, we joined up with the Wilson boys and their sister, Sally Ann. Soon, Ronnie and Donny had joined up with us too.

"So how was the cake last night?" Jack asked.

"We didn't get very much," I said.

As we walked, we told them the whole story of how we had dropped it on the floor and blamed it on Allyson, and how my grandmother had served the cake crumbs to Allyson for breakfast. We told them how Tim and I had eaten the crumbs for her.

"You mean the cake had dog hair in it?" Sally Ann asked.

"Yeah, and cat hair, too," Tim said.

"You and Tim dropped the cake on the floor and blamed it on Allyson?" Ronnie asked.

"Yeah, we blame everything on Allyson," I said. "That way Tim and I get away with a lot more without getting spanked for it."

"What happened after you blamed Allyson for dropping the cake?" Sally Ann asked.

"Grandma beat the daylights out of her," Tim answered, with a laugh.

"That's wrong. Why do you blame things on your sister? She's just a little girl," Sally Ann said.

"It's easy," I said. "We blame everything on her. There's nothing she can do about it. Our grandmother hates her."

Sally Ann and Ronnie fell back to where Allyson was trailing along behind us and walked beside her with their arms around her. Tim and I continued on our way to school, talking about other things with Donny and the Wilson boys.

That night at supper, I fully expected that Allyson would have another bowl of cake crumbs in front of her. But she didn't. Apparently the cake was gone, and I was not about to ask Grandma where it went. Later, I looked in the trash, but I didn't see it there. Tim said he was pretty sure he had seen it in the chicken yard. I guess my grandmother had cleaned it out of the oven and thrown it in the chicken yard for the hens to eat.

The meal that night was actually pretty good. It was what my grandmother called a hot weather meal. It consisted of sardines, potato chips, sliced tomatoes and juicy red onions. She even had iced tea with lemon and sugar. I loved it, but even though I was still hungry when I left the table, I knew better than to ask for any more. I was glad the cake issue was behind us; I didn't want to invite any further trouble.

When I went to bed that night, I tried to talk to my sister again, but she wouldn't answer me. The next morning when we were getting ready for school, I tried again, but still she just ignored me. She wouldn't speak to me or even look at me. She was the same way with Tim. She had been so happy for me when I won the cake, but now she hated me. The cake turned out to be nothing but a problem from the very beginning, and I secretly wished that I had never won the damned thing.

Sixty-Seven

AFTER THE INCIDENT WITH THE CAKE, WE ALL THREE managed to stay out of trouble for the most part for several weeks. Then one evening after supper, Allyson, Tim and I were playing hide and seek and taking turns sneaking a drink out of the cat's water bowl. Somehow, in trying to get behind my grandmother's chair to get a drink, I accidentally stepped on the cat's tail. Obie let out a shriek louder than any human I had ever heard. I know he did it intentionally, so my grandmother would punish me. I really hated that cat.

"What are you doing to the cat?" my grandmother demanded as she got up out of her chair to investigate.

"Allyson stepped on the cat's tail," I automatically told her.

"I did not," she shouted. "Tim did. I didn't."

Actually Allyson was in the process of getting a drink, and was no where near the cat, but for some reason she must have thought Tim was the one who stepped on Obie.

"I didn't step on the cat's tail," Tim said and began to cry. I knew why he was crying. None of us wanted to be blamed for stepping on the cat's tail, because none of us wanted my grandmother to grind the heel of her shoe into our instep.

"You did so," my sister shouted.

"Yeah, Tim," I shouted at him, quickly trying to get the blame focused anywhere but on myself. "Why didn't you watch where you—" But before I could finish my sentence, Tim hauled off and

313

socked me in the face. I stumbled backward into my sister, knocking her over, and we both fell over the cat's water bowl.

Before I could get up off her, Tim hit me in the face again and Allyson bit me on the back of my arm, breaking the skin and sinking her teeth deep into the flesh. She would not let go. I began yelling and crying, twisting away from her and kicking at Tim. He jumped on me and continued hitting me while my sister bit down as hard as she could. I swung around with all my strength and managed to hit her in the head, forcing her to release her bite.

All three of us were punching and kicking, biting and scratching – doing anything we could to try and hurt each other. There was water all over the floor from the cat's water bowl, and Butchie was barking and jumping all around us. The cat had jumped up on the table to watch the show from a safe place.

My grandfather leapt in the middle of us, trying to break it up, and my grandmother appeared with the stick, which she had apparently fetched from the kitchen, and began whacking all of us with it. I think she even whacked my grandfather a few times – maybe not by accident. They finally got us apart, and we each got several whacks from the stick across our backsides.

My grandfather took me in the bathroom to wash out the wound where my sister had bitten me. He put some iodine on it, but no bandage. The iodine stung like hell, and I screamed; but he kept putting it on the bite where the flesh had been torn away.

"I know it hurts," he said, "but we have to get it completely cleaned out. A human bite is the easiest to get infected."

I didn't care. I was willing to take the chance with getting infected if he would just quit touching it. "I don't care if it gets infected," I shouted.

"You will if you get lockjaw," he said.

"What's that?"

"It's when your wound gets infected, and it affects your muscles and makes it so you can't open your mouth anymore."

"It would serve him right," my grandmother shouted from the other room.

"You mean I wouldn't ever be able to open it again?"

"That's right, never again," he said as he poured more iodine on the torn flesh.

"How would I eat?" I screamed at him, half out of fear and half out of the pain in my arm.

"That's the rub," he said. "You couldn't eat, and you would die."

Now I was really upset. I didn't want to get lockjaw and die, and I was in a lot of pain both from the iodine and the bite itself. I knew I was going to get even with my sister for biting me; I just didn't know how yet.

"Stop that screaming," my grandmother shouted at me from the other room, "or I'll come in there and really give you something to scream about."

Sixty-Eight

THAT NIGHT AFTER WE WENT TO BED, I LAY THERE wide awake long after Tim and Allyson had fallen asleep. My mind was racing as I thought about all the injustices I had had to suffer. I wanted my mother to come and take me home with her. She could leave Allyson here for all I cared, but if she would take me home, I knew I could be good and not get in so much trouble all the time.

Suddenly, I felt the urge to pee. With all the commotion going on, I had forgotten to go to the bathroom. My arm was killing me, and I had to pee in the worst way. At first I thought about peeing out the window through the screen, which my grandfather had replaced after we were discovered last time. I was afraid to do it again, because my grandmother might be checking it every day to see if Tim or I had returned to our old ways. I knew the screen door to the kitchen was locked and I wouldn't be able to slip through the kitchen to the bathroom. I thought about going out to the front porch and peeing off the front steps, but that was too risky. One of the neighbors might see me and tell my grandmother. Then I got an idea.

Quietly I got out of bed and walked over to where Allyson was sleeping on the floor. I watched her sleeping for a few minutes, listening to her even breathing, and then I peed in her bed. I was surprised that she didn't wake up screaming right away. When I finished, I woke her up.

"Allyson. Allyson, wake up. You wet your bed," I said.

Slowly, she came out of a deep sleep and got up. At first she just stood there, not really comprehending what I had said. It was almost as if she couldn't believe she had actually wet the bed.

"You're really going to be in trouble now," I whispered to her. "Grandma is going to beat the tar out of you."

She said nothing. She just stood there looking at the puddle in her bed. Soon, tears began to roll down her face as she tried to figure out how she could have wet her bed. She turned to me, and I could see that her face was completely wet with tears. I noticed that her lower lip was quivering, and I knew she was frightened. Her lower lip always quivered when she was afraid. Now the tears came gushing out and she began to cry out loud. "Please don't tell Grandma," she begged. "Maybe it will dry by morning and she won't know I wet the bed."

Suddenly I realized that I could either get her spanked or keep it a secret. I felt powerful.

"Please don't tell her," she begged again.

"I won't," I said. "Go back to sleep."

"It's all wet. Where can I sleep?"

"Try to sleep on the edges," I said, trying to sound as helpful as I could. "I think it's still dry around the edges."

She lay down on the edge of the blanket and fell asleep again.

I got back into my own bed, and lay there thinking how glad I was that I had peed in her bed.

But I wasn't satisfied. She wouldn't get spanked if her bed clothes dried out by morning and my grandmother never found out she had wet the bed; she could escape punishment all together. My arm was still killing me where she had bitten me. She needed to be spanked for what she had done to me, I thought to myself. What if the bite got infected and I did get lockjaw and died because I couldn't eat any more? She would be the one responsible for killing me, and she would never be punished for it. That wasn't right. I wanted her punished before I died.

I continued to lie there for awhile, thinking about getting

lockjaw and how Allyson might not get punished. I could hear my grandmother's radio playing. The song was "Daddy's Little Girl" by the Mills Brothers. And as the music floated into my room, it reminded me of Frank, and of how much I hated him. I hated him for taking my mother away, and I hated him for bringing Allyson to my grandmother's house. By the time the song was over, I knew what I was going to do.

Slowly I got out of bed and went out into the hallway to the screen door.

"Grandma," I whined in my most sorrowful voice.

"What are you doing out of bed?" she shouted from the back-room.

"Allyson wet the bed and it stinks in here," I said.

I heard her slam her crossword puzzle book down and get out of her chair. She was furious. I could tell by the way her heels dug into the floor as she crossed the kitchen, stopping briefly at the icebox on her way to our bedroom.

"Now, what's the problem in here?" she demanded.

I could see the stick in her hand, and I wanted to make sure that I was well out of her reach in case she turned her anger on me for making her come in here. "Allyson wet the bed," I said again, "and it stinks in here."

My grandmother couldn't see where Allyson had wet the bed because she had removed our light bulb from the fixture on the ceiling after we kept forgetting to turn the light off when we left the room. She wanted to teach us a lesson for wasting electricity. We had been without a light bulb for so long that the three of us had become accustomed to dressing and undressing in the dark and thought nothing about not having one. But now it was too dark in the room for Grandma to see, and she couldn't switch the light on.

By now, both Allyson and Tim were awake.

Allyson began to cry. "You promised you wouldn't tell," she cried out at me.

My grandmother jerked Allyson out of bed and dragged her into the hallway by her hair. "Let me see your pajamas," she yelled. "Look at you, you're all wet!" She whacked Allyson several times with the stick.

"You promised you wouldn't tell," my sister screamed through her tears.

I just smiled at her, as if to say, "Now we're even for the bite." I was glad she was getting spanked. She deserved it. But I wasn't prepared for what my grandmother did next.

"Pick up those stinking blankets and come with me," my grandmother shouted at Allyson. "I've had enough of you. I've had it with all of you."

My sister picked up her wet, dirty blankets, and my grandmother grabbed her by the hair again and dragged her down the hall and into the kitchen. "Maybe if you sleep out in the shed tonight, you'll learn your lesson."

Now I was frightened for my sister. I couldn't believe my grandmother was going to make her sleep outside in the shed. I wondered if she meant the new shed or the old shed. The thought of sleeping in either one of them frightened me, but if it was the old shed it would be horrible. There were always rats in the old one, and I was afraid one might bite Allyson.

I got back into bed, pleased that she had gotten spanked but very worried about her having to sleep outside in one of the sheds. I had only wanted her to get a spanking. I never dreamed my grandmother would make her sleep outside.

"What happened?" Tim asked.

"Nothing," I said. "Just go back to sleep."

It seemed like hours that I lay there in the dark before I finally fell asleep. I don't really remember when I finally dozed off. I just remember being suddenly awakened the next morning by my grandmother as she rummaged through the stack of dirty clothes on the floor in the closet, looking for my sister's clothes.

"Get up and get ready for school," she growled at me. As she left the room with some of Allyson's clothes, she said over her shoulder, "Make sure you get Tim up too."

I woke Tim up and we dressed hurriedly and went out to the backroom for breakfast. My sister was already sitting at the table eating a poached egg on toast. I went over to where she was sitting at the table.

"Are you okay?" I asked her.

There was a big red welt on the side of her face where my grandmother had hit her last night. She just looked at me. There were no tears and no expression of any kind on her face. "You're a liar," is all she said.

A chill passed over me. I felt as if something bad were going to happen. I wanted to run away. My mother was never coming back and my sister hated me. And I hated her. I hated Tim. I hated my grandmother and my grandfather. I hated myself. We lived like animals, I thought. We treated each other like animals. We *were* animals. We were caged animals, and there was no escape.

I don't remember how long my grandmother made my sister sleep in the shed. I think it was about a week before she let her sleep in the house again. As it turned out, she had been sleeping in the new shed, not the old one. I tried to talk to her to find out what it was like out there at night, but her answers were short and she only answered the specific questions I asked her.

"Are there any rats in the new shed?" I asked.

"I could hear them running around, but I couldn't see them."

"Were you afraid?"

"The first two nights I was."

"Was it dark in there?"

"Yes."

"Why didn't you turn the light on when you were in there at night?"

"Grandma took the light bulb away."

When my sister was allowed to sleep inside the house again, it was in my grandmother's bedroom. She had made up a bed for

Allyson on the floor beside her own bed. "How come you're sleeping in Grandma's room now, instead of in our bedroom?" I asked.

"I told her I didn't want to sleep in the room with you anymore," she said and looked at me coldly, without emotion.

"Why not?"

"Because."

"Because why?" I persisted.

"Because, you're a liar," she said and walked away. I felt the
chill again and I shuddered.

Several days later, when Tim and Allyson and I were out in
the back yard, I tried to talk to her again. "Why won't you talk to
me anymore, Allyson?"

"Because you're a liar, and I don't believe anything you say.
I will never believe anything you say, ever again. But mostly it's
because I hate you."

"I'm sorry," I said. "I didn't mean for you to have to sleep in the
shed. I thought you would only get a spanking. I'm really sorry."

I didn't really mean what I was telling her. I wasn't sorry. In
fact, I really didn't give a damn anymore if she had to sleep in the
shed. I just hated that she wouldn't talk to me. It was making me
feel lonely and confused. I knew that I had lost something that
I could never get back. The feeling of loneliness crept over me
again and hung on. I remembered all the times she had brought
me something or thought of me when she didn't have to. I would
never admit it to her, but it had always made me feel special. I had
felt as though I had a special place in her heart, and it had made
me feel good.

Now I had lost that. She didn't think I was special anymore.
I didn't care about the loss of the candies or the odd piece of cake
she used to bring me. She didn't look up to me anymore. I couldn't
bear the thought of having lost that special connection with her.

"Please talk to me, Allyson," I begged.

"I don't want to talk to you. You don't like me. You get me in
trouble all the time, and you're a liar."

After that day, we didn't play with Allyson much anymore. We still walked to school together, but Allyson always trailed behind and kept to herself. Even Sally Ann and Ronnie couldn't talk to her. They tried and they were always nice to her, but she just walked along in silence. Ronnie and Sally Ann never seemed to like me or Tim anymore either. After we had told them how we blamed things on Allyson, they quit talking to us and never played with us anymore.

I tried to tell myself I didn't care, but I really did. I would have given anything if I could take back all the mean things I had done and all the times I had gotten Allyson in trouble. But I couldn't. I was miserable, and sometimes I thought that if I didn't still have Tim to play with, I would have died.

Sixty-Nine

THE DAYS CAME AND WENT. I STOPPED STEALING FOOD, and I stopped blaming things on Allyson. But she still hated me and very seldom spoke to me. Mostly she just played with a doll Crystal had given her for her birthday one year. It was all dirty now and was missing one arm, but Allyson carried it around and talked to it. Sometimes I saw her hold it close to her heart and whisper things to it. She hardly spoke to anyone else.

I think Crystal was mad at me too, but she never said so. Maybe she really wasn't mad, but I was sure she was disappointed that I had become so mean. Tim and I became much closer and were practically inseparable. We went everywhere together: we climbed trees together, went to the beach together and talked about what it would be like when we were old enough to leave Grandma's house. We swore a pact that we would leave together as soon as we could, and we would stay together and watch out for each other forever.

Then one day, out of nowhere, my Aunt Jessica showed up at my grandmother's house to say she had come to take Tim home with her. I was devastated. If Tim left, I wouldn't have anyone to talk to or play with. I could probably play with Donnie and the Wilson boys, but that wasn't going to be much fun. It wouldn't be the same. We never played with them very much anymore anyway. Tim and I were always too busy playing together in our own yard, or we were at the beach swimming together or fishing off the pier. But now he was going away to live with his mother.

"Aunt Jessica, is my mother coming to get me, too?" I asked her.

"I don't know, Billy. She's never said anything to me about it."

"Do you know where she is?" I asked.

"I think she and Frank live in Texas, somewhere. I'm not sure though."

"Can I go with you and Tim?"

"No, honey, you have to stay here."

"Why can't I go with you?"

"Because I have a very small apartment. It's only big enough for Tim and me."

"I want to go with you," I whined. "Please take me too. Tim, tell her to take me with you."

"I wish I could take you, Billy, but I can't. And besides, your mother might not be very happy if I took you with me."

"She won't care," I pleaded. "She never comes here anyway."

"Well, I can't take you, honey, and that's that."

"Okay," I said. I didn't know what else to say.

I felt the chill that had become so familiar again, and my entire body shook. A feeling of emptiness swept over me. I felt completely alone. I couldn't understand why, but every time I felt it, I shuddered violently, as if a blast of cold air had hit me.

It took a few days for my aunt to get everything organized for taking my cousin with her to wherever it was that she lived. Somewhere up north, I think.

As she was packing my cousin's clothes, I heard her laughing as she talked to Tim. "We're going to have to get you some new clothes. These are all patched and too small for you."

I couldn't figure out why she was laughing about his clothes. He was wearing the same clothes he always wore, and they looked fine to me.

"Look at your shoes," she scolded. "The toes are all scuffed out of them. I'm going to have to buy you some new ones."

It was true; Tim was hard on shoes. My grandmother always

said so. I could make my shoes last forever, it seemed. But Tim, for some reason, scuffed the toes out of his shoes almost as fast as he got a new pair, which wasn't very often. They had to be falling off your feet before my grandmother would spend the money for a new pair.

I was hoping Aunt Jessica would take me with her when she went to buy Tim his new shoes. Buying new shoes was fun, and we didn't go very often – maybe twice that I could remember. I remember on one shopping trip, we went to Sears in St. Petersburg. The best part was when trying the shoes on. We got to stick our feet into an x-ray machine so the salesman and my grandmother could see if the shoes would fit or not. It was really neat because when I looked through the viewer, I could see the bones of my feet inside the shoes. Some years later, when it was determined that too many x-rays were bad for you, all the foot x-ray machines disappeared.

While we were in Sears, we walked through the department that had bathroom sinks and toilets on display, and my cousin stopped in front of one of the display toilets. Before anyone realized what he was doing, he had peed in it. I waited for my grandmother to knock him into next week, but she didn't. In fact, everyone in the store thought it was funny. Even though I'm sure my grandmother was embarrassed, I'm pretty sure I saw a hint of a smile cross her face, although she rarely smiled, so I can't be sure.

My aunt stayed at my grandmother's house for less than a week, and then she was gone – and Tim was gone too. He actually cried when he hugged my grandmother goodbye. He didn't hug me. He just said, "Bye." He said nothing to Allyson, and she said nothing to him.

We watched as they got on the train. We could see them walking along inside the car as we watched from the platform. Eventually they found their seats, and Tim slid in next to the window and waved at us. I saw a porter stop by their seats, and my aunt gave him some money for two pillows. How exciting, I thought, to be going on a trip. Memories of the trip my brother and I had taken on the Greyhound buses many years ago – across the country to California – flooded back into my mind. That really was out west, I thought.

I missed my brother. I hadn't thought about him for years. I couldn't remember how long it had been since he and I had gone across the country together, but I thought it must have been about seven or eight years or so. I wondered where he was and what he was doing. I wondered if he still had his cowboy boots.

"All aboard," the conductor shouted.

The train began to slowly pull out of the station. I watched as the conductor caught the handle on the side of the train car and gracefully swung himself up onto the step of the car. We waved our good-byes as the train picked up speed, and all too quickly they were gone. We stood on the platform for a while, watching the train move further and further down the track. I heard it blow several blasts on its whistle as it neared a crossing, and then it was out of sight. People began to drift away, and red caps began moving the baggage wagons back into their proper places on the platform, ready for the next train's arrival.

We slowly made our way back to the car. I tried to talk to my sister, but she continued to ignore me – so we all walked in silence.

As we rode home, I tried to imagine what it was going to be like without Tim. Who was I going to play with? Even when we threw rocks at the Wilson kids, no matter how many times we got hit or cut with a rock, we always had each other to play with when we came back into our own yard. I'm going to be lonely going to the beach without Tim, I thought as I looked out the window. Why couldn't my mother have come for me instead? We rode in silence until lightning flashed across the horizon.

"Looks like we might get a storm this afternoon," my grandfather said.

No one else bothered to comment, but little raindrops began

to hit the windshield. My grandmother turned on the wipers, and we all rolled up our windows. Almost instantly, the rain was coming down in torrents. The windows fogged over, and it was nearly impossible to see the road. My grandmother slowed down as she strained to see. She tried to wipe the fog off the inside of the windshield.

Lightning flashed and thunder rolled across the sky in loud rumbling crashes. Some other cars had pulled over to the side of the road to wait for the rain to let up so they could continue without stalling out in the low areas. But my grandmother crept on, slowly driving toward home.

When she turned onto the street that ran passed the front of our house, there were huge puddles in the road and some places were so flooded we could not tell where the sides of the road began or ended. The street was not paved and the city had not put down any oyster shells to give people traction in the sand yet. My grandmother was afraid we would get stuck and need someone to come and pull us out.

Usually the neighbors would come out with shovels, boards and gunny sacks whenever anyone got stuck in the sand on our street. Once the sand was dug out from around the wheels, and once the boards and gunny sacks were slipped under the tires, everyone would push and rock the car backward and forward until the tires finally caught and gained enough traction to move the car out of the rut. Sometimes the process would have to be repeated several times before the person finally got their car on more solid ground, but other times the people just had to leave their car there in the road until the rain stopped and the water drained off. Then the same process would be used again, because the person had usually spun their wheels until their car was up to the axel in sand.

As a result, the road always had deep ruts whenever it rained, and the best way to navigate it was to go slowly enough to drive around them. Driving into the ruts was a guarantee you would get stuck.

"Try driving on the edge," my grandfather suggested. "Maybe we can get some traction where the road is a little higher on the edges, where the lawns come down to meet it."

My grandmother eased the car over to the right hand side of the road and took advantage of the higher ground, as my grandfather had suggested. She was able to avoid getting stuck, even though I was hoping we would so we would have to wait there until someone came along to pull us out. I was in no hurry to get home.

My sister had not said anything on the way home, but I could tell she was a little frightened of the low clouds, and the thunder and the lightning that sometimes seemed as though it were crashing nearly on top of us.

I reached over and touched her hand. "It's going to be okay," I said. "We're safe in the car."

But she jerked her hand away from me and said nothing. I hated her for not wanting to talk to me. I felt like punching her, but I didn't. That would have only invited the wrath of my grandparents.

The distance we had to drive, once we were on our street, was a short one. We were the third house from the corner, and my grandmother made it home without incident. As we passed by the Muncie's house, I looked in. One of the Muncie men was sitting on the toilet in the living room with his pants down around his ankles. He waved to us as we drove by.

When we turned into the driveway, it was flooded, too. But there was no danger of getting stuck here. My grandmother always made sure that it was completely covered with oyster shells. Once, many years ago, she had gotten stuck about half way down the driveway as she was backing out during a particularly bad rain storm. My grandfather was in Knoxville at the time, and back then the driveway was just a sandy path from the road to the garage. In trying to get unstuck, she had kept spinning the wheels, and the more they spun, the deeper they sunk into the sand. Finally, when there was no hope of her getting out, two of the Muncie men had come over to help her.

They brought the usual tools, shovels, gunny sacks and wooden planks to put under the tires. Once they had her dug out, they got in front of the car and pushed and rocked it while my grandmother gave it the gas. Finally the tires caught on the gunny sacks and planks, and the car moved backward out of the rut. She got stuck two more times before eventually making it to the end of the driveway. The Muncie men told her she should put oyster shells down in the driveway, the way the city did sometimes on the road in front of the house.

"That way the water will drain off through the shells and you'll always get traction," they told her.

I think her pride was hurt that she had to have the Muncies help her. Aside from her constant battle with them to get them to quit throwing their fish heads and other entrails into our yard, she also knew that they were aware she was the leading proponent for getting rid of the outhouses in Gulfport. She looked at them as the enemy and was sure that they looked at her in the same way. I, myself, don't think they saw her as the enemy so much as just a crazy old woman who was more or less a pain in the ass. But the next day, a truck arrived at our house full of oyster shells to be spread out in the driveway. And from that day forward she was never in danger of getting stuck in her own driveway again.

She let us out, as always, just before she pulled into the garage. There was very little room to open the doors once the car was inside and she didn't want us kids, or even my grandfather for that matter, banging the doors on the side of the garage.

"I wonder why Butchie hasn't come running to meet us," I said. "He's usually right here."

"He's probably under the back porch trying to keep dry," my grandfather said.

"I'm going to go get him and take him into the house so he

won't get wet," I said. I ran toward the back porch. The rain was coming down harder now and the backyard was flooded. I wanted to get Butchie – and myself – inside as quickly as possible. I heard my sister running right behind me, and I was determined to beat her to the house. Just as I got to the porch, I stopped. Allyson crashed into me and fell down in the water, getting mud and grass all over her soaking-wet clothes. Immediately, she started yelling and tried to kick me, but I paid her no attention. I turned and ran back to the garage, yelling for my grandmother and leaving Allyson there on the ground.

"Grandma! Grandma! Hurry, come quick, something's happened to Butchie. He's on the back porch. There's blood everywhere, all over the ground and the porch. Something's happened to him. Hurry, hurry, please hurry," I shouted.

"What's wrong?" she asked. "And stop that screaming, right now."

By now my sister was screaming at the top of her lungs. "Billy knocked me down!"

"I did not," I shouted, completely surprised by her accusation. "I wasn't anywhere near her. Grandma, Butchie's hurt. I think he's hurt bad. There's blood everywhere."

My sister was still screaming that I had knocked her down.

"I didn't knock you down. Shut up!" I screamed at her.

"You did so," she screamed at the top of her lungs. Her face was beet-red and her eyes were flashing with hatred.

"I did not."

"You did so. You stopped right in front of me when I wasn't looking!"

By now my grandmother was out of the garage and headed toward the house. She didn't say a word. She just went directly to the back porch.

"Alright, get up," my grandfather told Allyson, as he held out his hand to help her. "I'll speak to you in the house," he said to me.

My sister kept screaming that I had knocked her down. I

wanted to hurt her – I wanted to punch her in the nose and make it bleed, maybe even break it. It was all I could do to control my rage and not attack her right then and there. I tried to ignore her; I was more concerned about what had happened to Butchie.

My grandmother was at the back porch now, looking at Butchie. I ran up beside her and saw that while his eyes were open, he wasn't seeing anything. He was dead.

"What happened to him, Grandma?" I said, and then I started bawling, unable to hold it back any longer.

"Keep quiet. I don't know," she said.

"Let's all get in the house," my grandfather said calmly.

I was constantly amazed at how calm my grandfather always remained. No matter what was going on, I never heard him raise his voice or use a swear word. I think he really did believe that men should always conduct themselves as gentlemen. He promoted that philosophy all his life. He wouldn't even come to the supper table without his coat and tie, even when the weather was so hot and humid you could cut the air with a knife. My grandmother thought he was crazy for it and often told him so, but I guess the heat didn't affect him the way it did her. On the days when it was really hot and humid, my grandmother wore sleeveless dresses and was always rubbing Mexana Heat Powder on her neck and arms to keep from getting a rash.

When we got in the house, my grandmother said, "Billy, I've noticed the way you've been treating Allyson lately, and I'm sick of it. And Allyson, you whine and snivel about every single little thing. I'm sick of you, too. I'm sick of the both of you, and I'm going to use this stick on you every day until you straighten yourselves out. Do I make myself clear?"

"Yes, ma'am," I answered.

My sister said nothing. She just glared at my grandmother.

"Wipe that look off your face or I'll wipe it off for you," my grandmother told her. But Allyson said nothing; she just kept glaring.

"I'm not going to tell you again to wipe that look off your face."

Still my sister didn't say anything, and she didn't change the look on her face. I slowly started to move away toward my bedroom, hoping my grandmother's preoccupation with my sister's facial expression would spare me any further punishment.

"Come back here, you," she snapped at me. "I'm not finished with you yet."

I stopped shifting away and moved back beside my sister. Suddenly my grandmother lunged past me and hit my sister so hard across the mouth that it knocked her down. I turned and looked down in surprise. Blood was running from the corners of Allyson's mouth, but she didn't start crying, and nor did she say anything. She got up and glared at my grandmother again. If this was going to be a test of wills, I knew my sister couldn't win. My grandmother would eventually reduce her to tears, either by hitting her with her fists or the stick. For a few seconds I stared at my sister, wondering why she would test my grandmother this way. Just as I was about to turn and look at my grandmother, I felt the stick whack me across the back.

"You think it's funny to push somebody down in the water, do you? Maybe this will teach you a lesson." The stick caught me two more times in rapid succession across the arms and back. I tried to move around her and run to my bedroom, but she blocked my path and whacked me on the side of the legs. I fell to the floor and rolled past her. I thought of Butchie lying dead on the back porch. He would never again be able to try and stop my grandmother from hitting me.

"I wish Butchie were alive," I shouted at her. I began to scream and cry at the same time. "He would tear your arm off. I hate you!" I wanted Butchie to be alive, and I wanted him to tear the screen door off and rip my grandmother's throat out.

She raised the stick to hit me again, but there was a loud

pounding on the back door. "Hello, Mrs. Christian? Hello, can anyone hear me? I know who done shot ya'll's dog."

My grandmother immediately put the stick back on the icebox and went to the back door. "Who are you?" she asked.

"I'm Tom Muncie from next door. I know who done shot ya'll's dog."

"Is that what happened to him? Someone shot him?" she asked.

"Yes, ma'am, it was a police officer."

"A police officer? Why would a police officer shoot my dog?"

By now my grandfather had joined my grandmother at the back door. Allyson had gone to my bedroom, but I watched and listened from a safe distance in the backroom. I was afraid of the Muncies, and I wasn't too sure about one of them being at our back door. I didn't like the idea of him being on our back porch while Butchie was still lying out there in the rain, covered with blood. It didn't seem right to me. I don't think a Muncie had ever been in our backyard before.

"Yes, ma'am, it was a police officer. Before the rain started there was a city crew out on the street in front of your house. They was cuttin' some limbs off the trees around the power lines. They had 'em a nigger workin' with 'em, and your dog tried to attack the nigger. They tried to hit your dog with an ax, but he kept dodgin' 'em and going after the nigger. The guy in charge went over to the Hudson's house and used their phone to call the police."

"Did you see all this?" My grandmother asked.

"Yes, ma'am, I was sittin' on the crapper drinkin' a beer, watchin' the whole thing. I was hopin' your dog would catch that nigger. But then the police came. They tried to put a rope around your dog, but he kept slippin' around 'em and goin' after the nigger. When it looked like he was goin' ta get 'em, the police officer done pulled out his gun and shot ya'll's dog. I didn't think he was hurt too bad, 'cause I seen him limp off toward your backyard. I came over to see how bad he was hurt, and I seen him draggin' himself up on the back porch. I sure am sorry, ma'am, but I thought you would want to know."

"Alright, Mr. Muncie, thank you for coming over," my grandmother said.

"You're welcome, ma'am. You want me to throw him in the trash for you?"

"No, we'll take care of him."

"Good afternoon, ma'am. I sure am sorry."

"Thank you."

After Tom Muncie left, my grandmother got on the phone and called the chief of police and repeated Tom Muncie's story. The chief said he didn't know anything about Butchie attacking anyone or any police officer going to our house to shoot him. He said if a police officer had discharged his firearm, he certainly would have known about it. My grandmother thanked him and hung up.

"Go bury the dog out back, Edward," she told my grandfather.

The rain had stopped. I watched through the back door as my grandfather put Butchie's body in a wheelbarrow and pushed him out to the field behind the house, where he dug a hole and buried him.

I could see where Tom Muncie had been standing on our back porch in his bare feet. He had walked in Butchie's blood and tracked his bloody footprints all over the porch. When my grandfather returned, he hosed Butchie's blood and Tom Muncie's bloody footprints off the porch. Then he reported to my grandmother that he had buried Butchie in the field out back.

"I don't think a police officer shot Butchie at all," my grandmother told my grandfather. "I think one of the Muncies shot him. I can't prove it but if I could, I'd shoot the one that did it myself."

My grandfather said nothing. I didn't think the Muncies or a policeman shot Butchie. I was pretty sure it was old man Hudson. He had always hated Butchie ever since he nearly killed their dog. Anyway, her threat to shoot anyone was a hollow one since neither she nor my grandfather owned a gun.

I sighed and started to sit down on a chair at the supper table. Evidently my grandmother had not noticed that I had been standing in the backroom until I started to sit down.

"What are you doing out here?" she asked.

"Nothing," I answered.

"Go get yourself in bed. I'm sick of looking at you."

"Oh, Grandma, why do I have to go to bed? I haven't done anything?"

She said nothing but turned and went into the kitchen. She was back quickly with the stick. She hit me with two hard whacks across the back as I ran past her to my bedroom. They hurt like hell, and I let out a scream as I tried to keep from crying.

In my room, I lay on my bed sobbing from the pain – not just the pain from the stick, but the pain I felt for Butchie getting killed, the pain I felt from my sister yelling that I had pushed her down, and the pain of Tim leaving. Allyson knew she had lied. How could she lie like that? Why would she try to get me in trouble? I was angry, and I was growing angrier by the minute. However, my anger was soon interrupted by the sound of the screen door from the hall to the kitchen opening. Oh, no, I thought. She hasn't finished with me yet.

"You'll sleep in Tim's bed, now that he's gone," she said from the doorway. I thought she was talking to me, and I couldn't figure out why she wanted me to change beds.

"Why do I have to sleep in Tim's bed?" I asked.

"I'm talking to Allyson," she snapped.

"I don't want to sleep in here Grandma," my sister cried.

"I'm not interested in what you want, young lady. If I say you're going to sleep in here, this is where you're going to sleep, unless you want to go back to sleeping in the shed again."

There was a bright flash of lightning which lit up my grandmother as she grabbed my sister by the arm and jerked her off the floor. "Get yourself into Tim's bed," she said and then started to leave the room.

"But we haven't had supper yet," my sister reminded her.

"You don't need any supper. Maybe if you lie there and think about it, you'll learn how to behave yourself."

I heard the screen door slam, and then my grandmother hooking it so we couldn't get out.

My sister said nothing as she got ready for bed. When I heard her finally get into Tim's old bed, I called out to her. "Allyson," I whispered. There was no answer. "Allyson, answer me." Still nothing.

"Allyson, why won't you answer me?" I waited in silence, filling with anger. "Why did you tell Grandma I pushed you down in the water?" Still, she didn't answer me. "You're a dirty liar," I said.

"Now you know how it feels," she finally replied.

"What do you mean?" I asked, anger building up in me even more.

"You lie all the time, and you get me in trouble all the time. Now you know how it feels." Her voice was filled with hate.

"I ought to punch you in the nose," I said.

"Go ahead, I don't care anymore."

"You'll care if I break your nose."

"No, I won't."

"Why not," I asked with venom in my voice.

"Because," she said, "you can't hurt me anymore. Grandma can't hurt me anymore either." Her voice was calm and even.

"What are you talking about?"

"We're going to die here, and there is nothing we can do about it. I know that now, and I'm not afraid of anything you or Grandma can do to me."

"What do you mean we're going to die here?" I asked her, as if she didn't know what in the hell she was talking about.

"We're going to die here," she repeated.

I lay there unable to sleep for a long time thinking about what she had said. She's right, I thought. We are going to die here, and there is nothing we can do about it. My mother – our mother – was never going to come back for us. Somehow, I too knew that was true. I kept thinking about how we had become animals. We were living in a cage that we couldn't escape from, and we were going to continue to be beaten any time my grandmother felt like it. I thought about the change that had taken place in Allyson. I wondered whether she had given up or just decided she had nothing to lose by fighting back – the way a wounded animal would, trying to stay alive as long as possible and knowing that death was inevitable if it gave up.

Maybe that was why she had accused me when she ran into me and fell down in the puddle today. Maybe it was her survival instinct that drove her to accuse me. Or maybe she was just learning how to shift the spotlight off her and onto me, the way I had learned to shift it onto her a few years before. I suppose that since I had blamed everything on her, I shouldn't be surprised that she had learned to do the same to me. Recently she had shown more and more courage and demonstrated that she knew how to fight back.

I wondered how much longer I could live like this. Once I had thought about running away with Tim, but we had no place to go. I still had no place to go, or any way to get there. I was isolated. Tim was gone, Butchie was gone, my brother was gone, my mother was gone and Allyson didn't want to have anything to do with me. Hopelessness crept up on my chest and sat there, crushing my lungs, making it nearly impossible to breathe. I was twelve years old and I was being treated like a five year old. I still had to go to bed every night after dinner. I was still forbidden to drink anything before I went to bed. My sister was right: we were going to die here. I had to do something, but what? What could I possibly do?

The rain had started again, and I tried to concentrate on the sound it made bouncing off the leaves on the palms that lined the driveway. The millions of bullfrogs croaking together in chorus seemed louder than usual, and concentrating on anything was impossible. Thunder rolled in a long, low rumble across the sky. It was almost as if I could see it in my mind; it began on my right, slowly getting louder as it approached, then it passed directly over me and disappeared somewhere into the distance on my left. I tried to picture what thunder might look like. Was it like a cloud that rolled across the sky, gathering speed and bumping into other clouds, sending them crashing? I had heard my grandmother say that the thunder was God playing "ten pins", but I didn't know what that meant.

As I always did, I tried to picture what my mother looked like. It didn't surprise me that nothing had changed. I still couldn't picture her. I knew I ought to quit trying. I wondered where she was and what she was doing. I wondered where my brother was and what he was doing, and then I wondered where Tim was and what he was doing. And I wondered what I was going to do without Butchie. My mind raced with questions. What could I do to save my life? Could I save my sister's life, too? How could we get away from this place? Where would we go, even if I could figure out how to get away?

Sleep tried to wrap itself around me, but I fought it back. I didn't want to go to sleep until I had an answer to these questions. I was fighting, fighting, fighting it and just before it descended all around me, thunder crashed across the sky again. The rain slammed harder against the window, and as lightning lit up the room, my entire body shook with exhaustion. Sleep swept over me, but it was fretful and my dreams were frightening. I saw Butchie in the wheelbarrow, dripping blood as my grandfather pushed him toward a huge hole in the ground. Then I was lying beside Butchie in the hole as my grandmother shoveled dirt in on top of us. My sister was peering down at us, laughing. "You're going to die. I told you so," she laughed.

I began to panic and tried to climb out, but the rain made the sides of the hole too slippery and I kept sliding backwards, landing beside Butchie's face. I could see his eyes, wide open staring at me.

"Butchie, help me," I screamed. Then I remembered he was dead, and I began to cry. I looked up at the top of the hole in time to see my grandmother dump a wheelbarrow full of dirt over the side. Just as it landed on me, I jerked awake screaming, covered with sweat and shaking. At first I couldn't figure out why I didn't have any dirt on me. I looked around for Butchie and couldn't see him.

Then I realized that I was in my bed and not in a hole being buried alive. I was afraid my grandmother had heard me scream, but when I looked over at Allyson in the other bed, I saw that she was still asleep. I figured I probably hadn't screamed out loud, or I would have awakened her. I must have just dreamed it. Slowly, I lay down again, trying not to think about the nightmare that had awakened me. I didn't want to see Butchie's head with eyes wide open, staring at nothing, seeing nothing. Once again I tried to fight off sleep, and once again exhaustion won out. The pattern continued throughout the night: fall asleep, dream that I was trying to keep my grandmother from killing me, jerk awake, then fall asleep again.

By dawn I was even more exhausted than when I had gone to bed, but I was happy to see the sun coming up. I had lived through the night. I still didn't have a plan to get away, but I knew I had to try – and I had to stay out of my grandmother's way while I tried to figure something out. I wished Tim were here so I could talk to him about it. But he wasn't. I was the only one who could help me.

Seventy

THREE MONTHS AFTER AUNT JESSIE TOOK TIM TO LIVE with her and Butchie had been killed, I still worried about what was going to happen to me every day, and I was still trying to figure out a way to escape. My first priority was to avoid getting into any trouble with my grandmother. I did not want to take the chance of having her beat me to death in a fit of anger. I tried to talk to Allyson about it, but she still was having nothing to do with me. As the days and months passed and I continued to fail to come up with any kind of a plan, I became increasingly depressed. Then, just as I was about to give up, everything changed.

My grandparents had gone to a meeting of the Home Demonstration Club and left Allyson and me at home with Crystal. It was a gray afternoon with a constant drizzle. I was sitting in the backroom talking with Crystal as she did the ironing. Allyson was lying on her back on the floor, playing with the dirty one-armed doll she dragged everywhere with her. There was a lull in the conversation, and the air was filled with the incessant croaking of bullfrogs. I wondered how they could keep it up nonstop, day in and day out and all through the night. And I wondered why they only croaked when it was raining and never on a hot sunny day. I was sick of their noise and sick of the rain, too. It meant having to walk back and forth to school in it and then having to stay in the house when I got home. I would rather have been outside climbing in trees or throwing rocks at the Wilson kids.

"Go over der and switch on dat light, Billy. I's having a hard time seeing dis here ironing."

I slowly wandered over to the lamp near Crystal's ironing board and turned it on. Then I went back to where I had been sitting at the table. Just as I sat down, the phone rang. It sounded so loud we were all startled. Even my grandmother's stupid cat jumped.

It rang again, but Crystal just kept ironing.

"Aren't you going to answer it?" I asked.

"I will. I just needs to finish up da sleeve on dis here shirt. Hows come you can't answer it?"

"Grandma doesn't allow us to touch the phone," I answered.

The phone rang a third time, and Crystal put her iron down and walked over to the phone beside my grandmother's chair. "Christian residence," she said into the phone. "Who you say dis is? Oh, hello, Mr. Christian. Where is you callin' from? I can hardly hears ya. What? When? Oh, my good Lord, no!"

Crystal slowly sat down in my grandmother's chair, the phone in one hand and the other pressed to her breast over her heart. "Yes. Yes, of course, Mr. Christian, I can stay here 'til ya gets back. Yes, sir. Yes, sir. Okay, Mr. Christian. I'll be here. Yes, sir. Goodbye, sir. God bless ya, Mr. Christian."

Crystal hung up the phone. There were tears running down her face. Both Allyson and I stood in the middle of the floor, staring at her, trying to figure out what had happened.

"Come here, children," she said as she reached for us.

We moved closer to her and she put her arms around us and pulled us in close to her, hugging us so hard we could hardly breathe. Then she began rocking back and forth with us in her arms, sobbing louder and louder.

"What's wrong, Crystal?" I asked. "Why are you crying? Who was that on the phone?"

"That was yo grandpa. Sometin' terrible done happened," she said between sobs.

"What's happened to Grandpa?" Allyson asked.

"It ain't yo grandpa. It's yo grandma. She's dead," Crystal said, raising her head to look at us.

Both Allyson and I stepped backward, stunned.

"No, she's not," we both said together.

"Yes, she sho is," she said, pulling a handkerchief out of the front of her dress and blowing her nose. "Yo, grandpa just tol' me on da phone. He's at the hospital, and he done aksed me to stay here with you children 'til he comes home."

"When is Grandpa coming home?" Allyson asked.

"I don't rightly knows, child. He said he had some paperwork to fill out at da hospital, afore he can come home."

"How did Grandma die?" I asked.

"Yo grandpa say she just fell over dead while she was drivin'."

"Did the car wreck?" Allyson wanted to know.

"I don't know."

"Can we have something to eat?" I asked.

"I guess you is hungry, child. We ain't had no lunch, yet. I'll make us all a sandwich." Crystal said, rising up from the chair.

"Can we have peanut butter and jelly?" Allyson asked.

"If das what you want," Crystal replied, almost absentmindedly.

"Can I have two sandwiches" I asked. "And a glass of milk," I added.

Crystal slowly walked to the kitchen and started to make sandwiches.

"Okay, you children go sit at da table. I'll bring da sandwiches in a minute."

"Don't forget my milk," I reminded her.

Allyson and I sat at the table in silence, waiting for Crystal to bring the food. Neither of us could believe Grandma was dead. I wondered if her eyes were open like Butchie's had been.

"Allyson, do you think Grandpa will bury her out back in the field with Butchie?" I asked, but she didn't answer. She just sat there staring at her doll and poking her finger in the fabric where the arm had been torn off.

Crystal brought the sandwiches and sat down with us. I couldn't believe Allyson had her doll on the table. My grandmother would never have allowed that. But I couldn't believe I had two peanut butter sandwiches on a plate in front of me either. Usually, my grandmother would give me half a sandwich for lunch, with a half glass of milk. Crystal had filled our glasses to the top.

I drank half of mine down before I even took the first bite out of my first sandwich. Allyson finally picked up her sandwich and began to eat. I thought I saw the slightest trace of a smile on her face, but I wasn't sure.

After lunch, Crystal called her mother. "Momma, Miss Christian done passed away dis afternoon. I gots to stay here in Gulfport tonight. No, Momma, I'll be okay. No one gonna even knows I is here. I'll catch the streetcar tomorrow. I don't know when Mr. Christian gonna get back home. These children needs me to be here wid them."

Seventy-One

THE DRIZZLING RAIN CONTINUED NONSTOP FOR THE rest of the day. It was dark when my grandfather finally got home. A police car dropped him off in front of the house, and he walked down the driveway and around to the backdoor in the rain. Crystal had nearly every light in the house on, but my grandfather didn't seem to notice. I felt a surge of relief flow over me. No one cared that all the lights were on. And best of all, there was no reason for either Allyson or me to get spanked. The realization that there wasn't even anyone around who would want to spank us slowly began to sink in.

"Get yo self in here, Mr. Christian, and let me get you some dry clothes. Here's a towel. You go get yo self out of dem clothes, and I'll fix you some hot soup."

"Thank you, Crystal."

"Where's Grandma?" I asked. "Is she out back? Are you going to bury her with Butchie?"

"No, son," he answered as he moved toward my grandmother's bedroom. "She's at the funeral home. They'll keep her there until it's time for the funeral."

Allyson and I were sitting at the table, waiting for him to change his clothes and come back for the soup Crystal made for him. When he returned, I bombarded him with questions. I was not yet sure that my grandmother wasn't going to come in the house at any minute and beat the crap out of me for having two peanut butter and jelly sandwiches and a full glass of milk. I wasn't as brave as I had been when I asked Crystal to make me two sand-wiches. I needed to know that my grandmother was really dead and that she was never coming back.

"How did she die, Grandpa?"

"It was a heart attack. She died immediately, without any pain or suffering," he answered.

"Where was she when she died?"

"We were driving down Beach Boulevard, and she suddenly lurched forward and slumped over the steering wheel."

"Did the car wreck?" I asked.

"No, it just started to slow down, and I grabbed the steer-ing wheel and guided the car over to the side of the road until it stopped up against the curb. It was still drizzling rain, and luckily there were no other cars around."

"What did you do when the car stopped? Did you wait for someone to come and help?"

"I walked up to the house we had stopped in front of and asked the lady there if I could use her phone. I called the police, and they came, and then an ambulance came. They took your grandmother to the funeral home in the ambulance."

I knew my grandfather didn't know how to drive, so I won-dered what happened to the car. "Is the car still parked in front of that woman's house?" I asked.

"No, a policeman drove it over to the Gulfport Police Depart-ment."

"Are they going to keep it?"

"No, we'll get it back later."

"Now, you children leave yo grandpa alone," Crystal said. "You done been aksin' him questions ever since he got home. Let him be, now. Go play in yo bedroom."

Allyson and I slid off our chairs and slowly walked to our bedroom. I didn't want to go. I wanted to ask more questions, like what was going to happen to us now? I still hadn't gotten use to the idea that my grandmother was dead, but at the same time, I felt as if something very heavy was slowly lifting from my body. I wanted to be happy, but I was afraid to – I thought it could still all blow up in my face at any minute.

Seventy-Two

THE DAYS FOLLOWING MY GRANDMOTHER'S DEATH were chaotic. Two policemen returned my grandmother's car and parked it in the garage for my grandfather. It seemed like the house was full of people. Some of them had papers for my grandfather to sign, and others were friends of my grandmother who came by to pay their respects. Many of them brought food: there were cakes and pies and cookies, baskets of fried chicken, freshly baked bread and baskets of fruit. Everything was placed on the table in the backroom. For a while, I thought I was in heaven. No one even noticed if Allyson and I slipped a cookie or two off the table and into our pockets. We'd run to our bedroom and eat them in secret and then return to slip a couple more into our pockets. It wasn't long before we were sick of them and could actually pass the table without wanting anything. In fact, we didn't even want to see them anymore, and we avoided the table altogether until Crystal had put everything away in the kitchen.

I watched to see if she would count the cookies or the pieces of chicken, but she didn't. She didn't even count any of the apples or oranges. I knew I could have something to eat anytime I wanted it. And best of all I didn't have to ask or worry about getting caught. Instead of stealing something to eat and blaming it on Allyson, I found myself remembering to get her something as well. Although Allyson still didn't talk to me very much, she would bring me a cookie or an apple unexpectedly too. Clearly our lives had changed.

Crystal stayed for several days, only going home briefly to change clothes and take care of things she needed to do for her mother. My mother arrived by train two days before the funeral and had to take a taxi from St. Petersburg to my grandmother's house since there was no one who could meet her at the station. At first Allyson and I didn't know who she was. We thought she was just another neighbor, stopping by to leave a cake or a pie. We were curious as to why she had suitcases with her and just stared at her at first. We watched her hug my grandfather, and then she ran to us and hugged us both at the same time.

"My, my, how you two have grown, I hardly recognized you," she cried. Then she pulled us to her in a tight hug and began kissing us all over our faces.

We both squirmed and tried to get out of her grasp. Then, it hit me. I recognized the smell of her perfume. I remembered it from the bus station in San Diego, when she had hugged me years ago. Allyson and I began to cry, and soon all three of us were crying.

"Where have you been, Mommy?" Allyson asked through her sniffles and tears. "I needed you."

Then she broke down and cried uncontrollably. My mother put both arms around her and gently rocked back and forth with her. "Oh, baby, don't cry. I'm here now."

I tried to put my arms around both her and Allyson, but it was impossible, so I rested my head on my mother's shoulder while all three of us continued to cry. We probably would have just stayed like that if Crystal hadn't come over.

"Come on now, let yo' mama up. She just got here, and yo' gonna have plenty a time ta sees her," Crystal said as she gently unwound our arms from around my mother's neck. "Come on now, Miss Susan, I'll hep get you unpacked."

Alyson and I followed them into our bedroom.

"Billy," Crystal said, "you gets to sleep in da top bunk again so yo mama can sleep in da big bed. When Miss Jessica gets here, she can share da big bed with you, Miss Susan."

"That sounds like a plan," my mother answered.

My aunt Jessica was arriving from Chicago the following day, and my mother had to pick her up at the airport. My grandfather said he would stay at home and wait since he had some more paperwork to do. Allyson and I wanted to go to the airport with her, and Crystal asked if my mom could drop her off at her house on the way so she could check on her mother.

"Of course, I'll be happy to drop you off, Crystal," my mom said.

The next day, my mother backed my grandmother's car out of the garage and waited while the three of us piled into the back seat. "Crystal, I'll drop you off at your mother's house and then pick you up on my way back from the airport," my mother said as she backed down the driveway to the road in front of our house.

"Yes, ma'am, Miss Susan. I'll be ready."

"Bring a change of clothes back with you. I'm going to need you to stay with the kids while we go to the funeral."

"Yes, ma'am, Miss Susan. I'll sho 'nough do dat. Where ya'll gonna bury Miss Christian? Is yo' gonna bury her in Gulfport? I don't rightly knows where da cemetery is in Gulfport."

"No, she's going to be cremated."

"Oh Lordy, Miss Susan. I don't think ya'll should be crematin' Miss Christian. She needs a proper Christian burial."

"Well, her wish was to be cremated and have her ashes spread around the property at the house," my mother said. "She loved that property and she felt that if she were spread over the ground, she would always be a part of it."

"What does cremate mean?" Allyson asked.

Before my mother could answer, Crystal shouted: "Oh, child, that means they ain't gonna bury yo grandma in da ground. It means dey is gonna boin her up." Crystal never said burn; it always came out as "boin." Whenever I would get close to her while she was ironing, she would always say, "Now don't get too close. I don't want yo' to boin yo'self on dis here iron."

"After you burn Grandma up, can I throw her ashes on the ground?" Allyson asked.

"We'll see, honey. Crystal, you live down here off Tangerine, don't you?"

"Yes, ma'am Miss Susan, turn left at da next corner. Keep goin' 'til you done crossed Central, den turn right at da first street."

After my mother crossed Central Avenue, she turned right onto a dirt road that had weeds growing down the center and was lined with wooden houses on either side that were so close together it looked as if a person could not walk between them. The paint had come off almost all the houses. Some people walked down the middle of the road and were slow to move to the side as we approached. My mother had slowed down so much it seemed we were barely moving. People sat in groups on the steps and porches of the houses, smoking, talking and in some cases drinking from bottles they held concealed in brown paper bags. Wash tubs, along with washboards, were hanging on the front of many of the houses, and dogs were asleep in nearly every yard. There were no white people anywhere. Groups of two or three colored people stood on the side of the road and stared at us as we drove by.

"I've never seen so many colored people," Allyson said. "Everyone here is colored. Where are all the white people?"

"Das 'cause dis here's colored town, child. Don't no white people hardly comes down here," Crystal said gently. "My house is da next one on da right, Miss Susan."

Crystal's was like all the others, with the paint chipped off and a wash tub and washboard hanging on the front of the house. But there weren't any people sitting on the steps smoking or drinking. There was just a grey-haired old woman sitting in a rocking chair on the porch, slowly rocking back and forth. When my mother parked in front to let Crystal out, several dogs came running over to the car wagging their tails and trying to sniff us.

My mother said, "Please tell your mother I said hello, and thank her for me for letting you stay with us during our time of need. It is very kind of her."

"Yes, ma'am, Miss Susan. I'll sho do dat. I'll be ready when you gets back with Miss Jessica." She closed the car door and we watched as she walked up to the old lady in the rocking chair and kissed her before disappearing inside the house.

Seventy-Three

MY MOM DROVE DOWN ONE MORE BLOCK AND THEN made a couple of right turns until we were back on Central Avenue. We drove through St. Petersburg and headed for the road to Gandy Bridge, which would take us across the bay and into Tampa. The Tampa airport turned out to be an exciting place. There were airplanes parked everywhere. Some were beside the runway and some were in hangers. I watched one small plane with a single engine come in for a landing, and another small one waiting on the runway to take off. Then I saw the passenger terminal, where two large planes with twin engines were parked near the door that led out from the back of the terminal. We were early, so we got to see more passenger planes coming in and leaving. There was a steady stream of people getting on and off the airplanes. People laughed when they arrived and cried when they left.

We stood outside the terminal along a cyclone fence on the edge of the taxiway and watched the planes come and go. There were single engine airplanes, twin engine airplanes and a few with three engines. I was very excited and filled with anticipation at getting to see my Aunt Jessica and Tim. I was thinking about all the things Tim and I would do together when he got here. It would be fun to see my Aunt Jessica, too. Her breath always smelled good because she chewed Chiclets gum, and I knew she would give me a piece. Finally, their plane arrived. We watched as the Eastern Airlines plane taxied up to within a few feet of where we were standing. The engines were so loud that we had to cover our ears until the pilot shut them off.

"What kind of plane is that," I asked my mother.

"It's a DC3," she replied. "Look for your aunt. She should be getting off any minute."

I stood on my tiptoes and scanned all the passengers, looking for my Aunt Jessica and Tim. People walked past us from the plane, heading toward the terminal: men wearing suits and ties, holding their hats so the wind didn't blow them away; and women in dresses and white gloves. Then I saw her and started waving and yelling, "Over here, Aunt Jessica! We're over here."

She was wearing a green suit with a fox stole around her shoulders. I had seen that stole when she had come to take Tim back to Chicago with her. I remembered it because of the fox heads that hung down on one side. I liked stroking the soft fur. "Are those real foxes?" I had asked her.

"They sure are, and very expensive too. So make sure your hands are clean."

She saw me and waved back at us. I didn't see Tim. "Where's Tim?" I shouted, as she got closer to us. "Is Tim still on the airplane?"

"No, sweetheart, Tim didn't come with me this time."

"Why not?" I asked, filled with disappointment. I had counted on playing with him. "Why didn't he come?" I asked again.

"He has to go to school, honey. I couldn't bring him. And besides, it costs a lot of money to fly."

"How much does it cost?" I asked.

"That's enough, Billy," my mother said. "How many bags did you bring, Jessie?"

"I just have one suitcase. I'm traveling light," she answered with a big smile on her face as she hugged my mother. Then she looked at Allyson and me. "My, you kids are so big."

"Do people really look like ants from way up in the air?" Allyson asked.

"Well, I didn't see any people while we were in the air. So I don't really know, sweetheart."

We waited a few minutes until the baggage was brought over to the terminal, then we found my aunt's suitcase and headed for the car.

"Where's Dad? How's he holding up?" my aunt asked.

"He seems to be doing fine. Better than expected, actually," my mother answered.

We reached the car and my mother helped my aunt put her suitcase in the trunk. Then we all got in and headed out of the airport.

"How come Dad didn't come with you?" my aunt asked with a peculiar tone in her voice.

"He wanted to finish up some paperwork that the funeral home needs. So he stayed home to take care of that," my mother answered.

"When's the funeral?"

"Tomorrow at two o'clock. In her will, she asked to be cremated. Dad and I have made all the arrangements. Crystal is going to stay with the kids. We have to pick her up on the way back to the house."

"How's Crystal doing?"

"Fine. You know Crystal, just like a rock. She's been staying at the house to help me take care of Dad and the kids while I've been going through Mama's things. I've made arrangements to sell the house. I plan to take Dad back to Houston with me and the kids."

"You're going to sell the house?" my aunt asked, surprised.

"Yes, we won't get much for it, I don't think. But whatever we get will go to Dad. He can use it to supplement his retirement income."

"Well, you didn't ask me," my aunt said incredulously.

"I'm sorry. Dad and I talked it over and we thought that would be the best thing to do. I didn't think you would care if we sold the house. Neither you nor I plan to live in it, and we can't leave Dad here by himself. He doesn't drive and wouldn't have any way to get around. The logical thing to do seemed to be to just sell it and have Dad come live with us in Houston. We have a large apartment, and I know you only have a very small one in Chicago. I didn't think you would object."

"I'm not objecting, but you could have at least asked me what I thought." Aunt Jessica's voice rose. She was clearly upset. The car was suddenly filled with tension. My mother said nothing and for a while we rode in silence. Allyson slid back on the seat and began to pick at the hole in the material around the missing arm on her doll.

Aunt Jessica spoke again. "I just don't see why you didn't ask me what I thought."

"Jessie, we – Dad and I – just thought it made sense to sell the house. I have the room in Houston to take him in. You don't have the room with your little apartment in Chicago. I don't know why you're getting upset. What's the big deal?"

"Well, it sounds to me like you got it all figured out, Susan. So what are you and Frank going to do, supplement your income with Dad's retirement and the money from the sale of the house?"

My mother pulled the car over to the side of the road, slammed on the brakes and turned to Aunt Jessica. "Listen, if you have a problem with what Dad and I have decided, you take it up with Dad when we get to the house; but don't sit here and pick at me just because you weren't consulted."

"I'm not picking at you. I just think—"

"I don't give a good goddamn what you think. I'm the one who had to go through all of Mama's things, make the arrangement for the funeral, get things in order to sell the house and make sure Dad has a place to live. And quite frankly, I'm tired. I don't need you to sit there making innuendos that I am somehow trying to steal Dad's money or cheat you out of something."

"I'm sorry you feel like you've been put upon, Susan, just because you finally had to do something responsible for a change."

"What the hell is that supposed to mean?" my mother said through her teeth.

"You know damn well what it means. How many years have you left your kids with Mama? When was the last time you even came to see them? You knew Mama's health was bad, but you continued to stick her with your kids anyway, year after year – and now she's dead." Aunt Jessica's voice had risen to a loud shrill.

Allyson and I covered our ears and sat close together on the back seat.

"Jessica, you have no idea what you're talking about," my mother said in a much calmer voice.

"I just think you're avoiding the truth," my aunt replied. "How long do you think it will take Frank to drink up the money from the sale of Mama's house and Dad's pension?"

"Jessie, I've had enough of your hypocritical nonsense. I know you're upset, with Mama dying and all," my mother said in a very calm and quiet voice, "but I don't want you to say another word to me. I'm going to go pick up Crystal and drive us home. I just want you to sit there and be quiet."

"You don't need to—"

"Be quiet. If you say another word to me, so help me God I'll take you back to the airport and you can get on a plane and go straight back to Chicago. And if you think I'm not serious, just open your mouth again."

My mother pulled away from the curb, and we continued on in silence. No one spoke until we got to Crystal's house. I was afraid to say anything, because I didn't want them to start arguing again, and I didn't want Aunt Jessica to go straight back to Chicago. Allyson just kept picking at her doll and did not say anything either.

When we picked up Crystal, she sensed right away there was tension in the car, and after telling my aunt she was glad to see her, we continued to ride back to my grandmother's house without any speaking. I saw tears on Allyson's cheeks, but I said nothing. I was disappointed that Tim had not come, and I was sad over the argument my mother and my aunt had gotten into. I put my head on Crystal's shoulder, and she put her arms around both Allyson and me.

Seventy-Four

THE NEXT DAY WAS SATURDAY, AND EVERYONE WENT to the funeral except Allyson and me. We stayed home with Crystal. I was glad. I did not want to see my grandmother lying there in a coffin nor did I want to see her being cremated. When everyone returned to the house afterwards, we all met in the backyard to spread her ashes among the flowerbeds that she loved so much.

Even though Allyson had asked my mother if she could throw Grandma's ashes on the ground after she was "burned up," she declined when the time came. I also declined. I felt weird holding an urn full of ashes that once were my grandmother's living body.

The following day, my aunt Jessica flew back to Chicago. As far as I know, there were no further discussions about the sale of Grandma's house or my grandfather going to live with my mother. If anything had been said, it was not said around me anyway; and the tension between my mother and my aunt seemed to have disappeared. In fact, the mood around the house while my aunt was there was light and easy going. No one cared whether or not I ate everything on my plate or if I wanted seconds. I thought of Tim; I would like to have heard him ask for seconds and actually see someone pass a plate to him. When I had mentioned to my aunt that I was still sad he had not come, she said, "Maybe we'll be able to come and visit you in Houston, sometime. How would that be?"

"That would be great," I said. "Don't forget."

"I won't," she said stooping over to kiss me on the forehead.

When it was time for my mother to take my aunt back to the

airport in Tampa to catch her flight to Chicago, she took Crystal back to her house on the way. Allyson and I did not go with them. We did not want to, and there would not have been enough room for us in the car anyway because of the ton of stuff my mother gave to Crystal – things that had belonged to my grandmother. There were clothes, shoes, dishes, silverware and boxes of other odds and ends that my mother said she would just throw out if Crystal didn't want them.

"Thank you, Miss Susan. I sho 'nough do 'preciate yo kindness. My mama does, too. When is ya'll leavin' for good?"

"Wednesday morning," my mother answered. "It will take me until then to pack up the things we are taking with us. Anything we leave in the house, you are welcome to take for yourself, including the furniture. You just have to make arrangements to pick it up and move it."

"Thank you, Miss Susan. That sho is kind of you. I'll gets R.C. to hep me. But I's gonna need a letter sayin' it's okay for me to take dis stuff. I don't want no trouble with da poleese if somebody sees me and R.C. takin' stuff outta da house."

"I'll tell you what, you and R.C. get here early Wednesday morning, before we leave, and I will take care of the police in case there is any trouble."

"Thank you, Miss Susan. We be here real early Wednesday. I also is comin' back tomorrow and Tuesday to do da laundry and ironin' for you before ya'll leave."

"Thank you, Crystal. Let's get in the car, now. We don't want Jessie to miss her flight, do we?"

I watched as my mother backed the car down the driveway. Suddenly I was overcome with such an overpowering feeling of depression it almost made it impossible to breathe. I felt a pounding in my chest and my temples, and my legs buckled; I nearly dropped to my knees. What if she didn't come back?

Then, as quickly as it had hit me, it was gone. I knew she

would be back. She had to take us all to Houston. A brand new life was about to begin. No one was going to try and kill me anymore. My mother would take care of Allyson and me. I wanted to laugh out loud, I felt so good. I ran to the backyard and climbed to the very top of the tallest oak. Sitting there, gently swaying on a limb as high up as I could get, I felt the breeze blow my hair and I gazed out in all directions at the bright blue sky. It was as if everything was right with the world. Tears rolled down my face. I felt as though a huge weight had been lifted from around my neck. I wanted to shout at the top of my lungs, "I'm free!" But I couldn't, because I knew I wasn't really free. There was still another problem to face: Frank.

I wanted to go live with my mother more than anything else in the world, but Frank frightened me. I could not shake the image of him standing over me, cursing at me, after I had splashed the water out of the bathroom sink and onto the floor of the hotel room in San Diego. Nor could I forget the way he farted whenever he walked past me in a drunken stupor, or the way he cursed my mother if Bobby James or I made any noise louder than a whisper.

I could still hear my brother's voice telling me that Frank didn't want us around. "We won't be here very long," he had warned. "He wants Mom all to himself."

I shuddered and wondered how long it would take Frank to get rid of me after I got to Houston. Where would he send me? Would it be to Boys' Town, where he had sent my brother? Or would it be some other place I didn't even know about? Damn, I just didn't want to think about these things right now. Frank was definitely a problem I was going to have to face, I thought, but not right now. Right now Frank was a million miles away, my mother was here with me, and I was happy. I would worry about Frank later. For the moment, I *was* free; and I was going to enjoy it. No more dog biscuits for me.

Lightning Source UK Ltd.
Milton Keynes UK
UKHW012023020621
384816UK00002B/375